PRAISE FOR CHARI ̄

THE HANGI[

"Lyrical and striking, *The Hanging City* is an enchanting story of romance within a harsh world and an even more unforgiving society. Navigating class conflict, rigid social rules, and bitter hierarchies, *The Hanging City* explores the many types of love that people can find between one another, and is as unsparing in its depiction of the consequences of love as it is thrilling, rewarding, and heartfelt."

—Robert Jackson Bennett, author of *Foundryside* and *City of Stairs*

"Holmberg's latest is rife with forbidden romance, monsters, and unique worldbuilding. Not only will readers enjoy delving deep into the canyons the trolls call their home, but Lark's journey will also leave a mark deep on their hearts."

—Tricia Levenseller, *New York Times* bestselling author of *Blade of Secrets*

THE WHIMBREL HOUSE SERIES

"Filled with delightful period details and artfully shaded characters, this whimsical, thoughtful look at magic and its price is the perfect read for a cold fall night."

—*Publishers Weekly*

"Readers will be drawn in."

—*Booklist*

"This is Charlie at her best—intriguing mystery, creative magic systems, with plenty of romance to keep me turning the pages."

—Jeff Wheeler, *Wall Street Journal* bestselling author

"The quirky characters, period detail, and personal journeys . . . are well wrought."

—*Library Journal*

STAR MOTHER

"In this stunning example of amazing worldbuilding, Holmberg (*Spellbreaker*) features incredible creatures, a love story, and twists no one could see coming. This beautiful novel will be enjoyed by fantasy and romance readers alike."

—*Library Journal*

THE SPELLBREAKER SERIES

"Those who enjoy gentle romance, cozy mysteries, or Victorian fantasy will love this first half of a duology. The cliff-hanger ending will keep readers breathless waiting for the second half."

—*Library Journal* (starred review)

"Powerful magic, indulgent Victoriana, and a slow-burn romance make this genre-bending romp utterly delightful."

—*Kirkus Reviews*

THE NUMINA SERIES

"[An] enthralling fantasy . . . The story is gripping from the start, with a surprising plot and a lush, beautifully realized setting. Holmberg knows just how to please fantasy fans."

—*Publishers Weekly*

THE PAPER MAGICIAN SERIES

"Charlie is a vibrant writer with an excellent voice and great world building. I thoroughly enjoyed *The Paper Magician*."
—Brandon Sanderson, author of *Mistborn* and *The Way of Kings*

"Harry Potter fans will likely enjoy this story for its glimpses of another structured magical world, and fans of Erin Morgenstern's *The Night Circus* will enjoy the whimsical romance element . . . So if you're looking for a story with some unique magic, romantic gestures, and the inherent darkness that accompanies power all steeped in a yet to be fully explored magical world, then this could be your next read."
—Amanda Lowery, Thinking Out Loud

THE WILL AND THE WILDS

"Holmberg ably builds her latest fantasy world, and her brisk narrative and the romance at its heart will please fans of her previous magical tales."
—*Booklist*

THE FIFTH DOLL

Winner of the 2017 Whitney Award for Speculative Fiction
"*The Fifth Doll* is told in a charming, folklore-ish voice that's reminiscent of a good old-fashioned tale spun in front of the fireplace on a cold winter night. I particularly enjoyed the contrast of the small-town village atmosphere—full of simple townspeople with simple dreams and worries—set against the complex and eerie backdrop of the village that's not what it seems. The fact that there are motivations and forces shaping the lives of the villagers on a daily basis that they're completely unaware of adds layers and textures to the story and makes it a very interesting read."
—San Francisco Book Review

STILL

THE

SUN

ALSO BY CHARLIE N. HOLMBERG

The Whimbrel House Series

Keeper of Enchanted Rooms

Heir of Uncertain Magic

Boy of Chaotic Making

The Star Mother Series

Star Mother

Star Father

The Spellbreaker Series

Spellbreaker

Spellmaker

The Numina Series

Smoke and Summons

Myths and Mortals

Siege and Sacrifice

The Paper Magician Series

The Paper Magician

The Glass Magician

The Master Magician

The Plastic Magician

Other Novels

The Fifth Doll

Magic Bitter, Magic Sweet

Followed by Frost

Veins of Gold

The Will and the Wilds

The Hanging City

Writing as C. N. Holmberg

You're My IT

Two-Damage My Heart

STILL

THE

SUN

CHARLIE N. HOLMBERG

47N⬤RTH

Published by 47North, Seattle

www.apub.com

Amazon, the Amazon logo, and 47North are trademarks of Amazon.com, Inc., or its affiliates.

ISBN-13: 9781662525841 (hardcover)
ISBN-13: 9781662516801 (paperback)
ISBN-13: 9781662516795 (digital)

Cover design by Natalie C. Sousa

Map by Mapping Specialists, Ltd., from original art by Charlie N. Holmberg

Interior illustrations by Brooke Lynch

Printed in the United States of America

First edition

To Misha.
Never stop reaching for the stars.

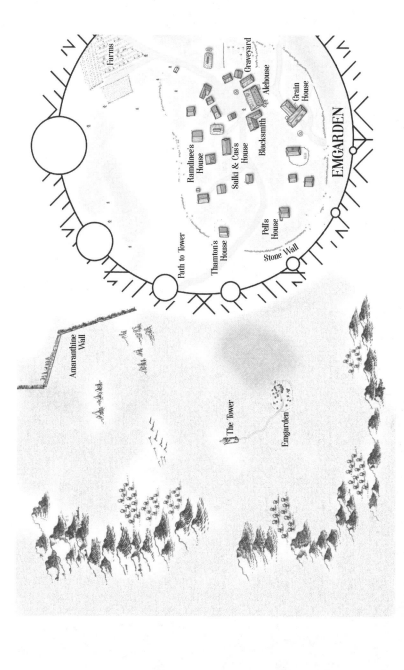

Farms

Ramdinee's House

Path to Tower

Thamton's House

Salki & Cass House

Blacksmith

Graveyard

Alehouse

Grain House

Pell's House

Stone Wall

EMGARDEN

Amaranthine Wall

The Tower

Emgarden

Chapter 1

Something is missing.

I turn the brass ball joint over in my hand, tracing the subtly raised edge with my fingernail. It attaches to a hollow metal cylinder with ridging, suggesting the cylinder once housed a pump. A lip on the cylinder looks like it connected to something else. If that something else is a track, then this might be the first evidence I've found that the Ancients utilized skidding systems. The style of metalwork alone denotes the artifact is of Ancient make, but without more pieces, I can't confirm my theory. My chest sinks at the thought that I likely never will.

Sighing, I set the damaged piece of machine on my little table. I didn't see anything else nearby when I dug up this gem. I suppose I can venture out again and search a little harder, but doubts keep me here. I found this artifact a year ago, and it was a four-cycle journey to the dig site. That's four cycles of food and water strapped to my back, and four cycles of camping on dust and dry earth. No way stations or people along the way. Just me. So I'm not exactly brimming with enthusiasm for a return trip.

Rolling my lips together and making a *pop* sound with my mouth, I push back from the table and stretch. I've been hunching over this thing for too long. I glance at the square clock on the far wall, one of two I constructed myself. The other hangs in the alehouse. The mist will settle in soon, but for my work, I prefer it. Keeps me from getting too warm. And if I wait for it to pass, I won't finish in time.

Nothing ruins a funeral like an unfinished grave.

I stomp into my shoes, wrap my hands, and tie the front of my hair into a knot on the top of my head—it isn't long enough for a proper tail—before stepping out of my single-room home. I built a little lean-to shed next to it, just large enough for a person to turn around in. From there I grab my tools—shovel, pick, rock bar—tie them up, and throw them over my shoulder before heading into town. The sun gleams brightly in my eyes, and I blink a few tears back as I cross the small village. A person could spit and reach the end of Emgarden, but it isn't like there's anything bigger around. There's *nothing* around, except for the amaranthine wall to the east and the abandoned fortress to the northwest, a giant tower brimming with broken Ancient tech, I'm sure, but even Arthen hasn't been able to get those doors open. We stopped trying years ago.

I skirt a random cluster of emilies in the road. The flowers are the fastest-growing things around and seem to be the only living thing that doesn't need water. *We* don't water them, anyway, but they thrive, sometimes in the strangest of places. One could pull up an entire patch of them at first sun and find them regrown a stone's throw away by late sun. Granted, the only good reason for pulling up emilies is for the roots. The flowers, though beautiful, are inedible, but the long, tough roots make good ropes and cording.

The flowers are the only pretty thing in this lonesome desert. The Serpent cast everything else in shades of brown and rust, save for the farmland, which we tirelessly water to keep green. The emilies, though, they bloom in pastel pinks, blues, and violets, with centers that glow as soft as the last breath of an ember. Random splotches of color on a dry and dusty slab. Only the amaranthine wall can compare, but that thing definitely didn't grow from the ground, and it's certainly never moved. We don't even know what it's made of, so we just named the strange, translucent material after its color.

By the time I pass the alehouse and reach the cemetery, just off the road to the farms, the first whispers of mist tickle the air. I already marked Entisa's grave with a few stakes. I brace myself as I look at them, breathing past the constriction in my throat. I hate crying, even with no one around to witness. Gritting my teeth, I focus on the technicalities. She'll be placed in the row right beside Ramdinee, who died a year ago. While Entisa's death was expected, Ramdinee's was not. The woman had been young and healthy, a baker and builder, but illness plagues the best of us, and she died quickly. I'd been close to her—I'm close to everyone, even those who'd rather I dedicate my entire existence to digging and cast my little machines into the fire. Ramdinee's grave had been a struggle to dig, like I'd been carving out the resting place for myself.

Ramdinee had believed in my machines, my theories. So had Entisa.

With Entisa gone, there are thirty-eight of us left. There have been no newcomers, no birth—

I lose my train of thought.

Shaking myself, I take the tip of my spade and trace the outline of the grave. It'll be roughly a meter and a half long and deep, and only a few decimeters wide, since Entisa was a small woman. A kind woman, though quiet. Patient, albeit less so in her final years. Still, I think of her lifeless body, lying on her cot, and *damnit I am not going to cry.*

Working is a good way to mourn. Makes me focus on the burn in my arms and back. Gives me purpose. While I'd love to spend the whole sun hunting for artifacts and trying to get them working again, or tinkering around with new builds to help Emgarden, I'm a digger. I dig graves, I dig furrows for crops, I dig wells. Bodies aren't going to bury themselves, and it's not as though water can grow on trees or fall from the sky.

The fog settles, slow and comfortable, and I dig.

Don't think about it.

I fall into the easy and familiar rhythm. After the first layer, my shoulders start to burn, but that fades after a few minutes. The key is to be careful with breaks; the more often I stop, the harder it is to get

3

started again. So I dig, that rhythm unrelenting, even when I hit clay. Clay clears the mind. Clay gives me arms even Arthen can admire.

I've toyed with sketches for an earth windlass, something to help pull soil up the way the other windlass I built brings water up from the well. But we don't have the supplies, and I'm the only one who would benefit from such a thing. Still, it comes to mind every time I pierce this shovel into the hardpan. Entisa had liked the idea, anyway.

By the time I'm halfway through, the fog has settled, like the weather is taking pity on me, crying on my behalf. The sunlight goes gray, mixing cool droplets with the perspiration beading on my temples and sliding down my spine. Here, I give myself a moment to drink and stretch. Here, I breathe in the mists and let them coat and cool my insides. Here, I listen to the hard thumps of my heart and ponder over Entisa's never beating again.

My heart aches for Salki. Entisa had been the oldest person in Emgarden, and while her daughter, Salki, is hardly young, she's my dearest friend, gracious and kind and hardworking. Knowing how much she loved her mother, and how much she will miss her, is my truest sorrow. And I hate that I can do little to help. But I can do this, and this is something.

So I keep digging.

The irony of my job is that I dig holes far deeper than I am tall. I'm strong, but I'm short, and so once I reach a meter down, since a stool would only get in my way, I start carving little footholds along the side of the grave. By the time I edge out the bottom, the packed dirt stands fifteen centimeters over my head. I climb out, tie my tools together, and wander to a clear spot not far from Amlynn's home. Lying down, I tuck my hands under my head and stare up into the fog-choked sky, watching little dots of light play within the mist. Close my eyes.

The mourning will wake me.

I clamp my hand on Salki's shoulder as four men prepare to lower her mother into the grave. Entisa looks peaceful, though the pallor and stillness of death warp her features, shaping her into a mere shade of who she was. She wears her favorite homespun dress. Her gray hair, which had always been pinned up, flows loosely around her shoulders. She wears a long necklace that I've never seen her without, a chain of tin with a poorly hammered pendant at the end of it. A stone ring speckled with pink flecks weighs down her middle finger.

The graveyard boasts the only section of Emgarden where our pitiful meter-high stone perimeter hasn't broken, eroded, or otherwise failed, as though even time itself wanted to show respect for the dead. It cradles our few fallen as though in midembrace. The sun casts dark shadows over the nearby alehouse and other homes, setting a mood of solemnity. Not that we need the help.

Arthen, the town blacksmith, pulls a shroud over Entisa's features, first on the left, then on the right, beginning the death wrap. The sun glints off his hairless scalp and catches in the uneven waves of his beard. Maglon, the alehouse owner, binds the shroud around Entisa's feet, while two of our farmers, Balfid and Gethnen, prepare the ropes to lower her down.

Salki's lip quivers when they finally lift the body toward my newly excavated grave. Otherwise, she's a picture of serenity. She'll cry later, in private. Like me, she hates making a public fuss, even when there's good reason to.

The men handle the body delicately; it makes no sound when it touches the bottom of the grave. Arthen and Balfid take turns covering it with dirt, one shovelful at a time. I want to help them. I want to do more, but my fingers still tremble faintly from my earlier exertion, and it would be selfish of me to take this service from these people. Instead, I sing the hymn of goodbye a little louder, knowing that Salki's throat is too choked to follow. Her mouth forms the words, and later I'll have to assure her it was enough, but she'll berate herself for not singing proudly in her mother's memory. Salki has a soul of amaranthine and a heart of glass.

When it's finished, I quietly hug Salki and step away so the other townsfolk can offer their condolences. Salki tearfully smiles at each person, absently thumbing a hammered metal brooch pinned to her shirt. One by one, the mourners make their way to the tavern, though a few return to their farm posts. It's already mid sun, and the plants need tending.

I gather my tools and start back, then notice Casnia kneeling down the road, unaware of the funeral. She's small, not any taller than myself, and round, thanks to Salki and Entisa's care. Short black hair warms her crown, and clean clothes stretch over her back and thighs. She squats, her narrow wood tablet against the ground, her little satchel of colored chalks open and half-spilled beside it. Her tongue peeks out from the corner of her lips.

I approach, making sure she'll hear my footsteps. "How are you, Cas?"

Though well into adulthood, Casnia has the mind of a child. She bobs her head to the right, then to the left, never taking her violet eyes off her art. She draws as a child would, often portraying the people of Emgarden. It always takes me a moment to sort out who she's trying to depict; despite many motherly lessons from Salki, Casnia never uses the right colors, merely whatever she fancies in the moment.

"Is that . . . Salki?"

She often draws Salki with red hair, or pink if there's no red, though Salki's hair is a pale gray with a few strands of blonde. Adjusting the tools on my shoulder, I ask Casnia, "Do you want to come to the alehouse with me to wait for her?"

Casnia continues drawing, seeming to not have heard me. She starts a new person beside Salki, sketching a lopsided head and rectangular body in brown. Yellow hair spikes out of the head. I know this one well—it's me. The brown is right, at least. I have tan skin, brown eyes, and usually brown clothes. My short hair is brown, too, though Casnia has always insisted it is not. After a few more passes of the chalk, she scoops up her things and clasps them tightly to her chest with one arm, then offers the other to me. I grasp her hand and help her up, then walk at her slow pace toward the alehouse. If nothing else, I can give Salki a little more time to mourn before she has to tend to her charge. Casnia is not hers by blood, but she might as well be. Then again, Entisa wasn't her mother by blood, either.

By the time I set my tools down and lead Casnia inside, Maglon has already resumed his post behind the modest counter, wiping glasses. Several people are inside drinking, discussing the funeral or taking their minds off it. Every death hits hard. Everyone knows everyone in Emgarden.

"You should be restin', Pell," Maglon says over the counter as I situate Casnia at my usual table, choosing a chair against the wall. Her balance isn't always steady.

"Rested enough." I tug absently at my breastband. The hot sun has made it especially uncomfortable. Serpent knows why I even bother wearing it; I don't have much to bind. "How are you holding up?"

Maglon shrugs. "Well as anyone, I suppose. Got a feelin' I'll be low in the barrels this sun."

The alehouse starts to vibrate; my hand finds a wall to steady myself. Maglon leans his weight on the counter, and Casnia pauses long enough for the quake to stop before continuing her work. Little tremors like this happen from time to time. Tampere, the name we've given this land, is often restless.

More people enter the alehouse, the ones I'd seen talking with Salki, though she's not among them. Good. She should go home. Take a mist or two.

I get an ale and a cup of water, the latter for Casnia. She ignores my offering and sets down her things, unbuttoning her pouch and spilling the chalk. Two sips of my drink go down before I lean my head against the wall and rest my eyes. They burn a little when I do. Guess I should get some water for myself, too.

". . . trowels aren't working," I hear when I open my eyes again. I wonder if I dozed off. The townsfolk fill the alehouse, leaving only a few chairs empty. Casnia has started a new picture, drawing me with yellow eyes.

Arthen rubs a hand over his bald head. "I can sharpen it again for you, but it's all I can do."

Frantess, another farmer, sighs. "The whole thing will snap in half if you do."

"Don't get on his case about it." Gethnen finishes off a glass. "He can't do nothing about it."

"I know that," Frantess snaps. "I'm just frustrated by it all."

"We're all frustrated," Balfid adds from another table. Amlynn, the town doctor, nods her agreement.

"Pell's got scrap metal," Frantess says. "Just take it from her."

"No thanks," I say. By the way her face reddens, I don't think she noticed me in the corner.

Skin flushed, Frantess leans into the argument. "And what good is the scrap to you? We need more tools!"

"What good is the windlass on the well?" I ask, picking at dirt beneath my nails. "Or the clock on the wall, or the flour mill you took from Ramdinee's?" All of which I constructed by studying and repurposing Ancient artifacts.

Maglon glances over. "Are you the one with the flour mill?"

Frantess's blush deepens. "*I'm* not the one who took it from her house! It's just been passed around. And it's not like Ramdinee's using it anymore. My point still stands."

"If you want artifacts"—I lower my hands and meet her eyes from across the room—"then go dig them up yourself."

"I'm too busy digging up your dinner," she snaps.

Maglon slams a cup down on the counter. "That's enough of that."

I force a deep breath into my lungs. Frantess has a point, but so do I. In truth, the idea of Frantess finding something new beneath the red-rock dust, melting it down without even letting me have a gander, makes me nauseous. I could do *so much* for this town if only I had more. More artifacts, more metal, more time. Unfortunately, not everyone shares my view.

In an attempt to keep the peace, I offer, "But if you need to melt down my rock bar, you can have it." It's the long steel lever I use for moving large stones when I dig. "I can use my shovel handle."

"We don't need it," Balfid says.

"It's not a bad idea," Arthen remarks.

The old argument about the Ancients and the pieces of civilization they left behind goes beyond me and Frantess. It comes down to tools. Emgarden sprouted up in the middle of nowhere, for reasons no one can remember, and its resources are minimal. Everything is minimal. We can't expand, we can't trade, and we can't mine. People need tools for mining, and we don't have the metal for tools, even if I sacrificed every artifact I have, which at the moment totals two: the incomplete piece I was just studying and a drafting compass. Any minute now, someone will bring it up. Again.

Gethnen doesn't disappoint. "We can try the mountains one more time."

No one responds. They don't need to. The mining of the mountains is a paradox; there are some ore deposits at their base, but we've no tools to access them.

"Keep the rock bar," Balfid says.

"I'd rather lose it than my scraps." I don't take offense at the term they use for my piecemeal artifacts. That's what they are, brass, steel, and other metal leftovers from an unknown history, and most in Emgarden see them as old toys from a time long passed. I've promised myself to forfeit all the scrap I have when our options run out, but the thought makes that gaping *nothing* in my core open wide and swallow.

Something is missing.

A familiar pang echoes in my chest. Rubbing my hand over my sternum, I take another sip of ale. Sleep and drink are the only things that keep that strange feeling at bay. The feeling that, like my broken artifacts, something about me, too, is incomplete. It's a sentiment I've never shared with anyone, even Salki. How could I put into words something so deeply visceral?

"Keep your rock bar." Frantess doesn't sound defeated. It's a promise of more arguments to come, perhaps without such an accommodating audience.

She wouldn't take the rock bar anyway. It's a necessary tool for digging the wells, and there's no water without the wells. Lore—some might call it scripture—claims that Tampere exists as one land among many, created by the World Serpent, whose discarded skin coils into entire planets, far beyond what our mortal eyes can see. But when the Serpent shed the skin we call home, Tampere kept all its water deep inside, so we have to dig for it. Only the hardiest plants with the longest roots—like the emilies—can survive without intervention. No wells, no food. The crops are planted where the wells are, which gives our farmland a somewhat eccentric shape, but who's around to judge us? There's only Emgarden. I've walked clear to the amaranthine wall and the Brume Mountains multiple times. If any living thing has built another village, town, or city, it's too far to reach. So it's just us and that old fortified tower. That's why no one ever bothered to repair, nor finish, the haphazard stone wall surrounding our little corner of Tampere. What do we have to keep out?

If I could get enough artifacts, figure out enough pieces, maybe I could find a way to collect water from the fog. By late mist, it leaves condensation on some things, especially glass and metal. But that just circles me back to the same problem as before: lack of metal. Lack of tools. Even Arthen couldn't spare anything for my experiments. The crops are too important, even if they're dug and harvested with brittle trowels.

I glance up at the clock above Maglon's head, the complement to the one in my home. It's a square box with two narrow platforms, the first marked with eight ticks, the second with five, to mark hours. There are small dots to mark minutes between them, but they're hard to see from where the clock hangs. Wider bands on the platforms mark first, mid, and late, for sun and mist, respectively. It has to be wound, but I timed the bands and springs in a way to align with the hours so the metal ball bearing that marks the numbers would be accurate. Once the ball reaches the bottom of the clock, a small plug kicks it back up to the top. Right now, the ball rolls past the fifth hour, into late sun.

Maybe I should get some food. And then some rest. But I'm not fond of the idea of trading Maglon for grain when I have some in my own cupboards. Standing, I stretch my back.

As if sensing my thoughts from the next table, Amlynn offers, "I'll watch her, if you'd like. Get her to Salki by first mist."

I glance to Casnia, who's finished her drawing and occupies herself by freeing a sliver of wood from the wall. "Thank you."

As I make my way through the crowd toward the exit, Arthen snags my wrist. "Where's my knife, Pelnophe?"

I roll my eyes and pull free. "For the last time, *Art*, I never borrowed it." I flick the side of his head and continue on my way. Next time that man asks me that same blasted question, I'm going to dump water on his forge.

Outside, I haul up my tools, feeling the soreness waking in my back, and head down the main road to my house. Mourners have crushed some of the emilies I passed earlier. I can't tell if their centers still glow; the sun shines too brightly. Skirting them, I continue on my way. Everyone but Salki has crowded into the alehouse, so the streets stretch quiet and empty. I'm nearly home when I hear a soft, distant tone winging through the air. One I might not have heard, were it not for the funeral pulling everyone from their homes.

I'm no musician. I couldn't pick the note from a scale or re-create it myself. But I hear it on the slightest stir of a breeze, as though it calls from the mountains themselves. A single high tone, softer than a new-born's breath. Then it's gone.

Biting my lower lip, I pick up my pace, stow my precious tools in their shed, and slip inside my little house. Kick off my shoes, soak some grain. Devour it when it's only half-softened, then drop into my bed before the ball on my clock can drop to the next platform.

I start at the knocking on my door. Stare at my ceiling a long moment while my mind shifts from dream to reality. I can't remember what I dreamed. A hand, a tree . . . but even as I try to recall it, it slips away, as intangible as the mists.

Mists. By the dimness of the room, I can tell it's high mist. I sit up, listening, wondering whether my tools fell over and clattered against the side of the house—

Knock knock knock knock knock. Firm, but not desperate.

Stifling a yawn, I slip out of bed, stretch my back, and rub my eyes. "I'm coming," I mutter, finger-combing my hair.

The knocking begins again. I wrench open the door, ready with a sharp word if it's Arthen, or a soft one if Salki has sought me out.

But as I stare up into the green eyes of an utter stranger, my breath catches.

One coherent thought worms through my mind: *He is not one of us.*

Chapter 2

I know every soul in Emgarden, every soul of this dry and lonely world, and none compares to the peculiar creature on my front step. He looks unlike any person I've ever seen. He stands tall and lean, with skin paler than the sun should ever allow. Deep green, like the leaves of a sorghum plant shrouded in fog, circles his pupils. His hair is even whiter than his skin, hanging long, just past his waist, and loose, in sharp contrast with his dark, robe-like clothing, fashioned differently than the simple tunics and trousers the rest of us wear.

"Pelnophe, let me in," he says, his voice crisp, confident, low. Accented in a way I can't define.

I don't react. My mind struggles to understand his presence, barely able to hear the demand past the hammering pulse in my ears. And, as he pushes past me, to understand how on earth he knows my name. Numbly, I close the door behind him, swirling tendrils of fog that seem just as curious as I am about this stranger's appearance. He doesn't acquaint himself with the small room. Indeed, he seems completely disinterested in it and merely turns to face me.

Are we not as alone as I thought? How far did this man travel to arrive here?

He's beautiful, in a bizarre way. The way a new artifact is beautiful. Striking and wholly *other*.

"I-It's just Pell," I try, finding my voice. I'm too shocked to be angry at the intrusion. "How do you know my name? Who are you?"

He studies me a moment, his face hard. "You're an engineer, and I'm in need of one."

I come to myself suddenly, as though I'm one of Casnia's drawings finally finished. "Excuse me? How do you know my name and what I do?" I glance at the table, the half-intact artifact there.

He doesn't follow my gaze.

"I have made it my business to know," he replies calmly.

"Who are you?"

"Are you capable or not?"

I turn his question over in my mind. "I'm a mere tinkerer."

He nods, as though expecting as much. "A mere tinkerer in a village of farmers will do. No one else understands the machines, and there is no one else, so I need you, *Pell*."

I look him up and down again, unabashed in my appraisal. Why shouldn't I be? This man barged into *my* home. I have every right to take a good look, though that robe hides most of him. He looks middle-aged, and yet somehow ageless.

It takes that long for a specific word of his to catch me. "What machines?" A hint of breathlessness dilutes the question. Any machine could only come from the Ancients.

"In the tower."

I lean back against the door. The *tower*. He could only mean the fortress to the northwest. "You . . . you're from there?"

"My companion and I, yes," he explains. "We've dwelled there a short time, and"—he takes a deep breath—"desperately need it operating again."

Operating? It's been a while since I last scouted out that tower, but it's impenetrable, with nothing of use on the outside. Five stories tall, composed of three diminutive, cylindrical tiers and a strange *something* jutting at a roughly twenty-degree angle from the top tier like a pruned tree branch.

Was it part of a *machine*? And that tower, it's so large, so strong. If the Ancients stored their tech inside, it must be in order. Far more whole than what I've been able to scavenge. The very thought of beholding such a thing, let alone touching it, springs shivers down my spine. My fingers twitch. It doesn't seem real. None of this seems real.

There's only Emgarden, and—

"Will you—" he begins.

"What is your name? Who are you?" I demand, desperate for clarity.

He exhales slowly. "My name is Moseus. I am one of two keepers of that tower. Will you assist me, Pell of Emgarden? The tower must be functional again."

The twitching intensifies. I want to scream *YES*, but I need more information. "Functional in what regard? What does it do?"

Moseus's lips press into a thin line. "That is not something I wish to discuss at this time."

"But if you want me to—"

"You have not yet agreed," he points out, the threatening sharpness in his tone betraying his thinning patience.

I'm aware that I'm stubborn, but our conversation has hardly broached the limits of what I'd consider tactful. Stepping away from the door, I ask, "How do you know what I do?" I gesture to the table. Everyone in Emgarden knows my fascination with the Ancients' tech, but Moseus is not of Emgarden.

He raises a white eyebrow. "Because I have eyes and a high vantage point. Your digs are hardly secret."

Oh, right.

"But you are," I point out.

Moseus runs the tip of his index finger along his chin, not at all disgruntled. "My companion and I, we are not . . . local. We are different. It is in our best interest not to make ourselves known, which is why I've come during the mists. Regardless, we need your help, and I would prefer to escort you to the tower while the fog holds."

Escort me to the tower. The tower. *What did Maglon put in that ale?* Gods and Serpent know how long I've wanted to crack open its doors and peek inside.

"You're unarmed?" I try.

Parting his arms, Moseus shows me the folds of his simple robe and turns out two simple pockets. He shakes his sleeves. "I've no motivation to hurt the only person on this side of the amaranthine wall who could possibly aid me."

Call it instinct, or perhaps my own desperation, but I believe him. His features are hard but not unkind. I lick my lips, playing like I'm still considering. When I can stand to pretend no longer, I cross to my table. "Let me gather my things."

"I have the necessary tools there," Moseus assures me, gesturing in an almost stately manner to the door. "Again, I beg your discretion. While the mists are high, if you would."

Glancing back at him, I pause, and in that moment of stillness, I think I hear another high, muted tone, echoing somewhere beyond the walls of the house. Another mystery from a world long forgotten. As though it bids me, *come.*

Disregarding his reassurances, I grab my bag of tools and collect those sitting beside my latest artifact, then sling the bag over my shoulder. "Lead on." Though I could pick my way to the tower with my eyes shut.

If this goes wrong, I remind myself as I step into the chill of high mist, *I can defend myself well enough.* I'm small but strong, and as we walk I keep my hand clenched around my biggest wrench, another tool that Frantess and others have suggested we melt down for farming tools. Eventually, we might have to. Only a fool values machines over food.

But for me, now, nothing is more important than *this.*

The tower—I know it by no other name—stands in stark contrast to everything else in this Serpent-shed world. It rises from the dusty, red-flecked earth in regal, tiered prominence, its white stone exterior bright and tall where everything else sits dull and meager. While our endless desert sports a number of natural rock protrusions—fins, chimneys, and the occasional arch—this monolith is entirely man-made, and in a fashion unlike anything to which Emgarden can aspire. From a distance its three cylindrical tiers look brilliant, nearly glowing, but nearer, the fortress takes on a more gray hue, powdered with dust and weathered by eons. It is the only thing left standing of Ancient make, unless the Ancients built the amaranthine wall, too. If they did, I cannot fathom how. It's translucent like glass but harder than any metal Arthen can forge. Slick and . . . radiating, for a lack of a better word. There's so much of it, horizons of it, and yet so little to see. Thus my interest has always been in the tower.

The tower has narrow windows with half-circle tops cut right into the stone. Only a few, and none easily accessible from the outside. Even if they were, they're too tight for a body to pass through. The flat ground surrounding the tower offers no vantage points.

The mists clear as we arrive. Gooseflesh rises in uneven lines up my back and down my limbs. For a moment I wonder if Moseus truly is a keeper of this stronghold. Why have I never seen him before? How long has he lived here? Where does he get food and water, for surely he and his companion can't sustain themselves within its walls? Do these promised machines harvest what they need from the ground, or do they only venture out when the mists are heaviest, forever hiding from the rest of us?

The questions roll around my tongue with a sharp flavor. Moseus approaches the tower's two south-facing doors—the only entrance to the fortress. With a heavy iron key, he unlocks the one on the right, and with his narrow shoulder, he shoves.

The heavy door loathes opening, creaking on what must be magnificent hinges, scraping the stone floor. Stepping beside him, I press my palms to the door and push, and it opens onto a dim chamber. Shifting inside, I blink rapidly, eager for my eyes to adjust. The only light streams from the second-story windows and trickles down a spiraling stone stairway just off-center, with no supporting walls or railing, as though it was built in a hurry. In front of that are two support pillars, equally spaced, and not ornate in any way. I glimpse the edge of another pillar behind the stairs as I enter, my careful footsteps echoing in the quiet room. The cool air stirs thickly, so heavy with dust, oil, and mildew that I can taste it in the back of my throat.

Like the exterior, off-white stone comprises the entirety of the interior, expertly cut but without decoration or polish. The stone gives it a cold feeling, both in aesthetic and temperature, and—

Thought evaporates. My body freezes and my lips part as a metallic glimmer to the left snags my attention.

It's . . . it's a *machine.* The largest I've ever seen.

An elongated mew escapes my mouth, but awe overpowers embarrassment as I run to it, echoes turning my quick footfalls into applause. "Serpent save me," I whisper as I touch the machine that stands easily twice my height and ten times my width. I instantly recognize the Ancients' handiwork in the intricate loops and coils that coat the exterior like lace. The metal appears to be primarily steel and . . . and some sort of alloy I can't name. Peering within, I see a few bronze pieces as well, and immediately I notice slipped bearings, as well as snapped fasteners and spines. Walking slowly around the behemoth, I spy sprockets and gears out of place and belts and chains come loose. There's a beam deep inside, or maybe an axle of some sort, and multiple wiring assemblies that will take me suns and suns to sort out. Like someone pieced it together for decoration only.

"It's broken," I murmur. *Very broken.* But I've yet to uncover anything from that era that isn't.

"Can you fix it?" Moseus's low voice hums behind me. "I've already done what I can, but as you can see, it isn't enough."

Backing away, I take in the whole machine once more. "I . . . I can try." I notice a set of screws, the metal of which doesn't match the rest. I run my hand over them. "It looks like you've done a good job. I'm not sure my expertise is any greater than yours."

"Guesswork only." He sighs. "I must implore you to try. Surely there is something we can compensate you with. Labor, knowledge, metal—"

I spin around. "Metal?"

He studies me for a few seconds before speaking. "There is surplus in this tower outside the machines we've found that is not necessary to the tower's operation. I saw your . . . *tinkering* . . . at your home. Would these scraps interest you?"

My mouth gapes. "How . . . how much do you have?"

He cocks a pale eyebrow. "Plenty."

I find myself nodding even as my brain warns me to barter a little more. For dignity's sake. "My town needs metal desperately. I'll take anything you can give me." A chance to learn Ancient tech *and* help Emgarden? I can hardly comprehend it.

"I will see it done. But only in return for your success."

I glance back to the machine. "Success*es*. This is a mess. Any improvement should be rewarded. And . . . you said there were other machines?"

"Three that we've found." Moseus tucks his hands into his robe and walks toward the stairs. "We've been unable to reach the others. The top two stories of the tower are inaccessible, as you will see."

I stare at a spot between his shoulder blades as we ascend. *Inaccessible?* Who builds a fortress and then makes almost half of it unusable? And wouldn't it be better to make the bottom more stalwart, to stand against an army? *But what army would wander out here to attack this citadel? It's defending nothing.* There's nothing to defend except, perhaps, the machines themselves. All of Emgarden couldn't penetrate this tower.

We reach the second floor, which has windows, which means light. A second machine sits to my left, almost exactly over Machine One. Whistling, I approach it. At first glance, it looks identical to the one on the first floor, but studying it closer, I see that's not the case. Machine One has a delicate feel to it, intricate like lace. This second machine looks intricate as well, but it seems . . . I don't know, *heavy*. Its casings and coils are thick and robust, and more of the machine takes on that familiar bronze color I've come to associate with the Ancients' tech, though this is another unfamiliar alloy. Already I can see where some plates should connect but don't, an easy fix. There's a notable pulley system here as well, though gods know how I'm going to access it.

"There's a third upstairs," Moseus says. I turn to glance at him, then notice part of the ceiling that's been cut away to access the third floor. "Cut away" is putting it kindly; it looks like it was hammered, chiseled, and clawed open. A ladder leans against the wall nearby. I walk toward the rough unevenness of the hole and peer upward. Above is well lit, but I can only see a ceiling.

"And you . . . can't do that for the other floors?" I gesture to the malformed hole.

The sharp lines of the stonework soften as the tower quivers in a gentle earthquake. I steady myself on the stout stone wall. The quake passes, leaving everything still and unscathed.

"No." Moseus glances out the nearest window. "We have tried."

I move to the ladder, but then I spot a large lantern beside it. Changing my mind, I grasp it, light it, and take it back downstairs. I approach Machine One again, holding the lantern high, peering between the expertly cast loops. When I hear Moseus's footsteps behind me, I say, "I'm going to need more light. And a stool."

"We have them."

"And those tools you promised." I walk around the machine, squeezing past where it nearly meets the wall, and press the lantern to the exterior, squinting at the gears within. "I can start now, if you'd like."

"Yes, thank you. The sooner these are functional, the better."

I turn to reply, but over Moseus's shoulder I spy a third person standing on the stairs. For a moment I think I'm seeing double, but no, these two are different. The newcomer radiates strangeness in precisely the way Moseus does—pale skin, long white hair, odd clothing—but his hair is loosely fastened in a braid, with another network of braids worked into it that reminds me of the machine at my side. His clothes are a mix of brown and deep green, mostly leather and a softer fabric similar to what Moseus wears. His face is broader than Moseus's, as are his shoulders, though his countenance is . . . hard. Stony as the tower itself.

He shifts, and light from the second floor hits his face. Like Moseus, he has green eyes, but they're bright, nearly acidic in both color and expression. He is bizarre and *other* and I can't take my eyes off him. The need to take a closer look, to prod at him like I have at this machine, overwhelms and confuses me. A sharp breath brings my thoughts back into focus.

I meet those eyes, and the ensuing tension drives back the chill of the room and kills my captivation. I can't really place it—that glare is the look of an enemy, a victim, and a skeptic all at once. It's both accusatory and . . . I want to say *hurt*, but he really isn't close enough for me to know. He might just have one of those faces. I certainly do. Still, the discomfort undulates, smelling like cool, moist clay.

Moseus cracks my mental poetry. "This is my companion, Heartwood. Heartwood, this is Pell."

Unsure what else to do, I tip my head in greeting. Heartwood merely turns and takes the stairs up, and I wonder how much of that four-second exchange was in my head. Unlike mine, Heartwood's footsteps don't echo. Like he's a ghost and nothing more.

"Charming," I mutter, resisting the urge to rub the lingering discomfort from my sternum. "Is he your brother?"

A sardonic half smile pulls on Moseus's mouth. "Only in purpose. The resemblance is happenstance. It's . . . common, among our people."

Our people. So there are others like them. It makes sense; I doubt the World Serpent just spat up two quasi clones after building this world. I try to imagine an entire village of Moseuses and Heartwoods, but my mind can't conjure it.

"Interesting name." I glance back to the machine, wondering where I should start.

"We are named for our animus," Moseus supplies. When I cock my head, he adds, "Our intendment. Our . . . initial purposes."

"Heartwood," I reply. His name weighs oddly heavy on my tongue. "That's like a tree thing, yes?" There aren't many trees around here, and the ones we have are short and bristly. *Just like you,* Arthen once said with a laugh, before I poured his ale into his stew.

Moseus nods.

"And what does yours mean?"

His lip ticks upward, a little more sincerely this time. "I am a peacekeeper."

"Okay, then." I set the lantern down, face the machine, and plant my hands on my hips. "Trees and peacekeeping. Got it."

No wonder they haven't been able to fix these things on their own.

Figuring out where to start proves my biggest challenge. Moseus fetches a small but impressive toolkit and watches me for a few minutes before blessedly retreating. I'm not used to being watched while I work. Not when I tinker, and not when I dig. Filling myself with a deep breath, I circle Machine One a few more times, turning sideways to push through where it nearly kisses the wall. Something tells me I don't want to go upstairs, where the bone-chilling Heartwood lingers. Not a fair assumption, maybe, but he wasn't exactly thrilled to see me.

Fix your own damned machines, then. But I don't mean it. I'm twitching again, desperate to get my hands on this mess, eager to understand how it works. There's just *so much of it.*

I decide to start on the southwest side. I prop open one of the heavy outer tower doors with a stone and find a convenient hook on the wall to hang one lantern. The other one that Moseus retrieved for me flickers on the floor. I notice some shieldings here—long, slightly curved bars of metal protecting the machine's guts—that have been loosened and pushed aside, likely by Moseus's hand. It's a good hunch; this area looks a little more accessible than the others.

I carefully turn hidden screws and loosen fasteners to move some of the shieldings and spines, then take an hour just familiarizing myself with the exquisite monstrosity of this machine. A gentle hum builds in my mind, luring me like a bewitching lullaby. I follow cables and test gears, marking on a slate which direction they turn, though most seem to twist both ways. Interesting. What did Moseus say this thing was supposed to do, again? Does he even know?

I pull the floor lantern closer, balancing it on a small beam, and run my index finger over a faint engraving on one of the bars. A simple symbol, but an intentional one. I've found them on about half the artifacts I've uncovered, though not this particular design. It's a half circle, flat side down, with a bottomless triangle cutting upward through its curve. At first I thought the markings labeled parts, but after seeing similar symbols on different pieces, I've determined it's some sort of Ancient signature. A way that the men and women of old said *This is mine.*

I'm halfway inside Machine One when footsteps approach. I peer back out, past the coils of a spring, to make out Moseus's robes. It's not until I shimmy free that I notice the dimming light outside. Have I been working so long already?

"You will return?" he asks.

Pulling a rag from my pocket, I wipe my hands. "Yeah, definitely." Then I remember. "The metal?"

"On your first success, as agreed. And I have a few requests before you go." Moseus frowns at the stone propping the tower door ajar.

"I'm listening."

"First"—he holds up a finger—"do not do that again." He points to the door.

Stifling a sigh, I nod.

"Second, do not take anything that isn't explicitly given to you."

Leaning my weight on one foot, I answer, "No stealing, got it."

"Third, do not discuss your work with anyone outside the tower."

I hold back a frown. "But—"

"Surely you see the value of these things." He makes a broad gesture to Machine One. "Please understand. It is my duty to keep this place, and my people, safe."

A whole two people, I think, but bite it back. "No one in Emgarden is a thief."

Moseus says nothing at all, only waits.

A sigh pushes past my teeth. "Fine. But I can't help if someone asks where I'm going."

"Which brings me to my fourth request," he replies. "Only come and go in the mists."

A sinking feeling, almost like hunger, lines my stomach, but I don't understand it. If he's worried about thieves or dangerous people, it makes sense to mask my comings and goings. It makes sense to avoid questions. And yet the request—more of a *rule*—sits uncomfortably. It's hard to see in the mists, yes, but not impossible. Not dangerous. Scorpions claim the spot as Tampere's biggest predator, and they're delicious. Yet something feels . . . off.

Then I remember that I haven't really slept for a few cycles.

"They'll ask where the metal comes from," I point out.

Moseus mulls over this, his lips rolling tightly together. "True. But try, and reflect on my third request."

Don't discuss the work. "You give in so easily?"

He tips his head. "I am a peacekeeper."

I blow hair out of my eyes. "Okay. Anything else?"

"Fifth," Moseus says, and I try not to roll my eyes. I won't squander this enormous opportunity. "Give me regular reports of your progress."

"Oh." I relax. "Can do. So far I've done mostly diagnostics."

"Thank you." Glancing at the door, he says, "You may go."

I retrieve my personal tools—I only used one of them—and reach into the machine to grab my smallest wrench, which measures just longer than my index finger. As I pull away, however, my head spins. I blink, and I see the machine in pieces at my feet, strewn across the stone floor, sprockets and gears and coils, bent and misshapen and—

And . . . then it's just as it was before. A broken but intact machine, standing twice my height before me, alloy pieces shimmering in the lantern light.

I . . .

I really need to sleep.

"First sun," I offer, pocketing the wrench and backing away from the machine, ignoring the uneasy squirming in my stomach.

"First sun," Moseus agrees.

And then I depart, into the mists.

Chapter 3

It's only by utter exhaustion that I sleep.

The walk back into Emgarden helped. The tower neighbors the town, but not comfortably so. During the first hour home, my mind obsesses over the machines. I sketch out everything I can remember of Machine One and promise to do the same for the others—surely I can learn something by drawing them. I've done this for every Ancient gadget I've come across, speculating on what their missing pieces might look like. If nothing else, my fluttering mind needs an outlet.

Eventually my thoughts are no longer new, merely recycled, driving me mad with thinking and rethinking. Some bitter mitemeal tea I traded Amlynn for helps settle me and grants my body several hours of rest.

I wake close to mid sun, eager to resume work but realizing it might not be best to break Moseus's mist rule on my first solo journey to the tower. So putting my own desires aside, I trek across town, slowing at Entisa's fresh grave, and out into the farmland that hugs the east wall of the village. The crops extend for about a hundred meters out, bending more or less to fit the shape of Emgarden and the locations of the wells. There are three wells in the farmlands, only one of which has the windlass I built to help pull up water. The farther the plants grow from a well, the harder they are to care for. The hardiest crops are planted farther out, with the more delicate close to the wells. I'd love to build something to make the endless process of watering easier, especially since farmers constitute more than half of Emgarden. Even I tend crops when things are slow for me. Something to pump water up through tubes and irrigate, or to carry heavy buckets of water to save us a few trips . . . I drew up plans for an irrigation rover once, but there are no resources with which to build it, and no guarantee it would work, so I abandoned them. Limited resources likewise mean no experimentation with other methods. Tampere's climate is livable, but it isn't always kind.

Hopefully this deal with Moseus changes things. A lot of things.

I find Salki out in the millet, kneeling and pinching hungry beetles in half with her fingers. Casnia lingers nearby, under a scraggly tree someone's thrown a blanket over for better shade. Balfid and a few others are there, too, eating lunch.

It takes everything in me not to screech, *There are other people here. I've met them. In the tower. We're not alone.* But Moseus's deal will make life so much better for us, so I can keep my mouth shut for a little while.

"You can take another few cycles," I say instead as my shadow falls over Salki. Time off to mourn, I mean, but she understands me.

Salki pushes up the brim of her hat. "Or I can be useful." She shrugs. "It was her time."

"Doesn't make it easy."

"Doesn't make it easy," she retorts, knocking a half-formed egg sac off a knee-high plant with a rusted trowel.

My tongue curls in my mouth, desperate to share my optimism about the tower, but I swallow that hope down. Maybe when things are more solidified, when I've earned a little more of Moseus's trust, I can let it slip. Salki wouldn't hurt a fly, and any secret I gave her would die with her, but I did agree to the keeper's terms, and I need those machines. We need that metal. So the story stays buzzing at the front of my mind, distracting and heady.

I crouch down and start pinching beetles myself. The adults are a shiny dark blue, and their guts spray a dark amber. They're too bitter to eat.

"Gross." Salki laughs. She's wearing gloves.

I reach over to wipe my hand on her trousers; she smacks me with the flat of her well-worn trowel.

Smiling, I pinch off a few more bugs. "I think I can get you some better tools."

Salki sighs. "There's no point sacrificing one trade's tools for another—"

A sharp pain stabs through my skull. A gasp catches halfway up my throat as my hands fly up to my forehead instinctually. *Gods' piss,* it hurts.

"Pell?"

Gritting my teeth, I push on the side of my head, beetle guts on my fingers, as though I could counterbalance the pain. The strange ache takes its sweet time abating, but gradually it crawls away, receding one stab at a time, like my brain is trying to square out its own grave's corners.

The trowel falls. Salki's hand rests on my shoulder.

"Without melting down what I have," I say, continuing the conversation. "I'm fine. Need some water."

She sighs. "I hope you know how ironic it is that you of all people fail to stay hydrated." Standing, Salki waves to a small woman a few furrows over. She brings a bucket and ladle. I deeply drink from it first, then Salki has her fill. Then me, again.

I wipe my mouth on my forearm. Salki thanks the water bearer before returning to work.

I don't trust myself to keep secrets while meeting Salki's eyes, so I focus on bugs. "I'm not guaranteeing anything, so I won't give any details, but I think in a dozen cycles or so, I might have something."

If I can fix the machines. Their make . . . it's above what I understand. And yet I *feel* I can do it, if given enough time. A gear can only turn so many ways.

"All right, then." Salki speaks as though I made a joke, but I don't mind.

We work down the row in comfortable silence, the sun heating the back of my hair. "How's Casnia taking it?"

"She says nothing," Salki murmurs, glancing toward Casnia in the shade of the tree. "But she slept in Entisa's bed last mist and refused to eat at first sun."

"We all mourn in our own ways." I clap my hand on Salki's shoulder. "Do you need anything? *Really*, Sal. Do you need anything?"

She glances at me, eyelids heavy. "Company, sometimes. Quiet, others. I'll let you know."

I squeeze her shoulder before heading back to get my own affairs in order, and to anxiously watch the ball bearing in my clock worm past the ticks and drop.

⁂

I find the right door unlocked when I return to the tower. The cool brush of mist kisses the skin of my hands and face, coaxing my cropped hair into uneven waves. I suppose I'd expected Moseus to be waiting for me, but only emptiness greets me. No one lingers outside the tower, nor in this first chamber. It's dark, save for the trickle of light shining down the spiraling stairway, and quiet. The sound of the door dragging shut feels like it should shatter the tower, but everything holds. Nothing could break this fortress.

Pulling away from the entrance, I notice two hooks for holding a bar across the doors, further barricading this place from the outside world. No wonder Arthen and I could never get in. I wonder for the millionth time what the Ancients used it for. I've wondered so much I've started to hate the questions. I merely want to get to work.

I take one slow lap around the first floor, perhaps expecting Moseus to pop out of the shadows. The room seems bigger than I remember. There are two other doors here, one behind the stairs, opposite the entrance, and one opposite Machine One, to the right of the entrance. I don't test my luck with either and return to Machine One. My lanterns are where I left them, so I light them and crawl back inside the machine, picking up precisely where I left off. I know the next ten steps. I've reworked them in my mind constantly, and each proceeds as it should, except for step eight, which requires a different entry angle for this thread feed than I had remembered. A lot of the pieces operate with cables and wires, some made of metal, others—like complex pulleys—made of gods-know-what. If this part connects to that part, they'll move together, or in sequence, depending on how the tendons, so to speak, are connected.

Another quake rolls beneath the tower, vibrating the delicate machinery. I wait for it to pass before refocusing.

These *wires*, though. I can see where several of them anchor, but the rest will be a headache. And yet I'm excited to follow and guess at their paths. I wonder if mothers feel this way with disobedient children, drowning in frustration while loving every moment of it.

I shift the light to figure out my next move. A smaller lantern would help *a lot*, but no one is around for me to ask, so I make do. Trace another carved symbol in what I *think* is a flywheel, or something that stores or adjusts power. The symbol is the same half circle and unfinished triangle as before. *Tell me your secrets,* I ask the symbol, pressing the pad of my thumb into it. *Tell me how you made this. Tell me how to fix it.*

The machine doesn't answer. Intuition whispers that the souls of the Ancients have long since abandoned this place, following the World Serpent through space and time to rebuild on some other world. If there's a godly being whose purpose is to create worlds, then surely there must be more worlds out there, however little I understand them. Maybe the great beast created one with more water and more metal. More *people*.

Yet, as I squirm away from the flywheel, I notice something I hadn't before. It's the angle, and the shadow, of a spine against the stone floor. Looping my foot through the lantern on the stone, I swing it closer, and the shadow doesn't move. Which means it's not a shadow, but a hole.

But why would part of this machine go through the floor? Its steady foundation balances it perfectly. But there it is.

After a minute of acrobatics, the lantern hangs off a strut and I am nearly upside-down, balanced halfway between a protective plate and a long metal support beam. There's a larger metal plate down here, secured with those fancy screws the Ancients were fond of using. It takes me longer than it should to loosen them with a ratchet, and I have to sit up and let the blood drain from my head before lifting the plate off.

It reveals a much bigger hole than I'd expected.

Several beams, shafts, and other Ancient nonsense pour through a hole nearly a meter wide and almost perfectly circular, but shallow. Definitely intentional. The machine disappears beneath concrete, and I'm positive it doesn't end there. Why take the time to cut a big hole in unyielding stone just to gain a few centimeters? Any smart engineer would just make the machine a few centimeters taller, or reconfigure it to function on its side, or *something*. Whatever that *something* is, it goes under the tower. Which means it's time to do what I do best.

Untangling myself from loops and bearings, I wipe black grease off my palms with the sides of my slacks and hold my hands to my mouth. "Moseus!" I call. "Mose—"

"Yes?"

I start and spin around. Moseus appears behind me from the first of those two shadowed doorways, which looks like it leads into an equally dark room. Taking a steadying breath, I say, "I need a shovel. And some bracing. I need to dig a really big hole on the other side of this wall. Part of Machine One"—I point to the machine in question—"goes beneath the tower. I want to see if I can reach it. It's close enough to the side that there shouldn't be an issue with—"

"You don't need to bother with that." Moseus observes the machine with an unreadable expression. "It would be a fruitless endeavor."

"But any endeavor that helps me understand the machine is fruit*ful*."

Moseus shakes his head. "I believe it will be a waste of your time."

"Well, it's my time, isn't it?" A little voice in the back of my head that sounds remarkably like Salki warns me to even my tone. I don't want to lose what I have when I've only just gotten my hands on it. Forcing my tight shoulders to relax, I amend, "Just let me look. I need to know."

Moseus frowns, and after several seconds, he acquiesces. "That room, there." He points to the second doorway, directly across from the exit on the other side of the stairs. "See if there's something you can use."

Quietly, he slips back into his chamber. I assume it's his chamber, anyway.

Venturing to what ends up being a small closet, I find an array of things, including broken bits of Ancient artifacts. They immediately catch my attention, and I pull some out into the dim light to see them better. They're not all machine parts. This looks like part of a sieve, that looks like . . . well, I don't know. But I want to know.

Let it go, Pell. With a long breath, I set the exciting toys aside. They're likely part of the scrap metal I'm to be paid with, so there's no point in getting worked up over them if they'll be melted down anyway. That, and I'd prefer to dig while the mist holds.

I find a shovel, a pick, and a broom. After grabbing the first two, I make my way through the front doors again, around to the west side of the tower, where the machine is. Thick mist coats my nose and throat. It's soothing after long, dry suns. Two emilies have sprouted nearby, both a pale blue that would blend with the mists if not for their softly glowing centers.

I stare at the hard ground beneath the tower and sigh. "Just like a well," I mutter.

And start digging.

My body moves into the rhythm easily, and I'm pleased to see that after a couple of layers, the earth loosens up. Maybe this was an emily bed recently, and the roots unknowingly lent me a hand before vanishing, as emilies tend to do. I dig down about five decimeters, then widen the hole. I'll know if I need shoring soon enough, but for now, I focus on digging.

I've made a sizable dent in the ground, about one-third of a proper grave, when I hear the swing of the pickaxe behind me. I turn, pause, blink.

Heartwood is here.

His presence radiates through me like I've taken a full swing at a boulder. Seeing him closer, even in the mist, jars me. Before, on the staircase, he'd seemed like an apparition, a figment of the imagination, but he really does look a lot like Moseus. Thicker, maybe taller, too. Like if Moseus ate more. I don't know how much of the peacekeeper exists beneath his baggy robes, but Heartwood is very . . . present.

He doesn't look at me, merely swings the pickaxe at the hard upper layer of the ground. His impressive mane of plaited white hair swings over his shoulder as he works. He's taken off his leathers and wears a simple shirt and fitted pants, still of a make unlike anything in Emgarden.

Pulling my eyes away, I force myself to refocus on the task at hand. "Thank you," I offer, adjusting my grip on the shovel. "I'm trying to get down beneath the foundation, toward—"

"I know."

They're the first words he's spoken to me, soft as the mist in volume yet hard as the sun in tone. I wonder at him a moment, long enough for him to pause and glance at me. Even in the mist, his green eyes are eerily striking. Where Moseus's gaze is alluring and calm, Heartwood's is invasive and alien, reminding me yet again of how different he and his companion are. No one in Emgarden has eyes like that, and Emgarden is all there is.

I'm not sure how to respond, so I merely nod. He returns to his work, and I haltingly return to mine.

Heartwood seems to know what he's doing, hastening our progress, though I silently congratulate myself when he has to take a break before I do. I try not to look at him; he's oddly distracting. That, and Heartwood doesn't seem pleased to be here, making me wonder if

Moseus coerced him into it. I dig until I hit concrete that matches what I saw beneath the tower floor, oddly smooth and slightly yellow in color.

"Is this . . . a chute?" I say more to myself than to Heartwood. I dig off to the side to find the end of it and manage to detect a slight curve before a chunk of dirt falls down and covers up my work. I'm going to need shoring soon, or I'll bury both of us alive. "It looks like it angles away from the tower . . ."

I turn in the direction the chute seems to be heading.

"Help me," I ask, climbing out of the hole. "I want to dig this way." I point away from the tower.

Heartwood says nothing, merely moves over to start breaking up more soil. The mist thins. I wonder if Moseus will ask me to stop soon. The tower blocks the view of the dig from Emgarden, but if someone decides to take a long walk, we could be discovered. I tentatively ask Heartwood, who quietly responds, "Then let us work quickly."

I dig with renewed vigor, moving aside what Heartwood loosens, filling in old hole to uncover new hole. I dig and dig and dig, until my back aches and my joints cry at me to stop. Until I'm huffing a windpipe of fire and sweat rivers down my torso. Past the protection of the mist and into the heat of the sun, but the concrete continues. Surely I'm nearly to the end of it. Breaking for a moment, I shuck off my sash and overshirt and chuck it out of the hole, then peel my sweat-drenched undershirt from my back and stomach. Stripping down makes me more susceptible to sunburn when I dig away from the shade of the tower, but the sides of the hole shadow me well enough. Wiping perspiration from my brow, I resume digging, my arms shaking from the effort. Then I hit rock.

"Heartwood, can you get the pick under this?" I gesture.

He pauses and glances at me, then averts his eyes like I'm the sun. Moving to give him space, I glance down at myself. What, is he allergic to shoulders? I check my breastband while he loosens the rock; all the bits are where they belong.

The stone in question comes free, and Heartwood resumes his previous work, refusing to look at me or even brush by me, despite the close quarters. Well, to each his own. At least I have the help.

It gets harder to dig the deeper we go, and I worry we'll draw the attention of Emgarden and tick off Moseus. But a dozen shovelfuls later, the concrete continues unabated. At this angle, it's going to get deeper and deeper, to a depth that surely only an Ancient could reach. Moseus was right. There's no way to uncover this, and no way to break through.

And so, with heavy limbs, I return to the tower, and Heartwood vanishes as easily as the fog.

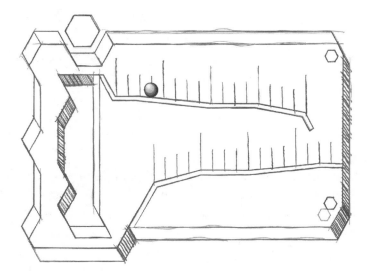

Chapter 4

Heartwood looms on the second floor of the tower when I return at first mist. I see him as I approach, even with the descending brume. I *feel* him, the way one feels the first curls of mist, a whisper of cold before the vapors settle. He stands half in front of a narrow window, his arms folded snugly across his chest, watching the path to Emgarden. Watching me.

I meet his eyes. Though the mists are still young, a shiver wriggles its way down my back. Heartwood turns back into the tower, a ghost once more.

I left at late mist last cycle and didn't give Moseus my update, so I knock softly with a single knuckle on the door of his room. If he isn't here, I'll wait for him to find me. I'd rather not explore the tower and run into Heartwood. The unease from his gaze still squirms beneath my skin, however much I try to disregard it.

"Come."

The door creaks open. I hesitate in the doorway.

It's so . . . *dark.*

Blackness engulfs the entire chamber. No windows, no candles, no lamps. Just . . . black. Impenetrable. I lift my hand in front of my face, and even with the dim light coming down the stairs, I can't see it. I've never seen darkness this absolute before.

"Do you have a report?"

I push the door open, guiding the dim light of the first floor inside. I should have brought a lantern. I'm able to just make out Moseus's pale skin and hair in the center of the small chamber. He's sitting upright, legs folded, palms on his knees.

"Merely meditating." He withdraws his hands and looks at me. I think.

Rubbing a sore spot on my shoulder, I give him my update: what I managed to repair last visit and what I intend to work on now. I'm sure he knows, but I add that the digging was unsuccessful. He doesn't chide me or point out that he was right, which I would have done, were our roles reversed. Merely nods. I think.

"I will not hold you up," he says. "Thank you, Pell."

I wave away the gratitude. "A smaller lantern would be useful." Candles aren't. They drip on everything, and the wax is hard to come by, anyway.

"I'll see what I can find."

I close the door and start toward my machine, pausing halfway when a three-second quake shudders and then sleeps again.

My machine. It doesn't feel wrong to think of it as such.

I start by running my hands up and down the metal loops and straps of its body. There isn't much space to climb *in* here, but these are definitely loose helical gears and more of that damn wiring. Pulling out a slate and chalk, I do some quick calculations to estimate the supposed angle on that axle, assuming it connects to that . . . hat-like thingy . . . on top. I set aside the slate, shove the tools into my pocket, and get to work.

I have to take apart a few pieces to get to others, which feels like regression, but it is what it is. I find a gear literally attached to nothing, just wedged between an axle and a beam. Great. I glance around, clueless, before tossing it out of the machine. Future Pell can worry about that. Sure enough, the axle goes right where I want it to go, if I adjust said hat-thing, which makes it align with what looks like a rotary unit, though rotary units are for moving fluids, and I don't see where any fluid would go. I bet the wiring over here goes up through—

I whip my hand back. Blood pools in my palm and trickles down my wrist. Damn it, I should have been more careful.

I blink, staring, a dull headache pulsing at my crown. The same wires. Glance at my hands. They're fine. Dirty, but fine.

What in Ruin's hell *was* that?

Leaning on one leg, I bring my right hand to my face and trace a pale scar. But this is an old scar. I got this at . . . was it Arthen's forge? Or digging Ramdinee's grave?

My pulse thuds behind my eyes, banishing the train of thought.

"Nophe."

Jolting, I jerk back and whack my head on that stupid hat-thing. Whirl around to see Heartwood there, his brows drawn together, a small, unlit lantern in his hand.

I'm breathing like I was digging. Rub the heels of my hands into my eyes.

"You weren't responding," he says softly. He's in his leathers again. The braiding on the seams looks more complex than anything in this machine.

Shaking myself, I pull my hands down. "Sorry. Thanks." I take the lantern, my index finger brushing his. The warm flash of his skin surprises me. In the back of my mind, I'd expected him to feel as cold as he sounds.

He regards me a moment before turning for the stairs.

Wait.

"What did you call me?" I ask.

Heartwood pauses.

I knead the handle of the lantern between my fingers. "You called me *Nophe*." It sounds similar to the end of my full name, but with an error in emphasis. A long O, instead of a half-forgotten, soft U.

Heartwood glances back at me, expressionless save for a raised vein in his forehead. And because he is aggravating, he doesn't respond.

My shoulders tense. Sharper than I mean to, I ask, "How do you know my full name? Moseus introduced me as *Pell*." No one calls me *Nophe*. I've never even heard my name shortened like that.

A beat passes, then another. "Moseus and I converse outside of your visits. This is our home."

Still. And now, to be obstinate, *I* don't respond.

He exhales. "I will adjust my address if you prefer." He walks away, taking the stairs up. I watch him go, just to make him uncomfortable. Because *I'm* uncomfortable.

After lighting the new lantern, I hold it up, inspecting my right hand and the scar there.

Then I slap myself across the face and get back to work.

※

As if this cycle couldn't get more annoying, I now find there's a power switch on this machine.

But it's in the middle of the machine. Hard to reach. Which is stupid.

And there's *nothing* here that could possibly power this hunk of metal. Nothing to wind, no engines for steam, nothing.

It doesn't make sense. Nothing makes sense.

"I hate you," I mumble to the machine as one of its bearings rolls oil across my forearm. I don't mean it. I love this gods-damned pile of garbage. That weird sentiment I get . . . that subtle incompleteness . . . it eases when I work on this monstrosity. Keeps my thoughts elsewhere.

But also, I hate it.

"Pell."

"One second." I tighten some cables before carefully pulling back, making sure not to cut myself on any loose parts. Moseus approaches. He's removed his dark robe and wears a simple gray shirt and pants, like what I've seen Heartwood wear. It makes him look long and lean. His unadorned white hair falls evenly down his back, just to where his spine dips at the base. The dark cloth of his shirt makes his pale skin look even paler, though the lantern light lends it some warmth.

He's not an unattractive man.

"There's a power switch in there, but nothing to power it," I report. "I don't understand. Maybe if I took the entire thing apart, but I can't promise I'll be able to put it together again."

That image from two cycles ago surfaces in my mind. Machine One in pieces on the floor. Not completely disassembled, but far less intact than presently accounted.

My head hurts.

"Are you well?"

Must have shown on my face. "I'm fine. Just tired. Thanks for—"

Moseus reaches forward and presses his palm flush to my forehead.

"—asking," I finish. He doesn't say anything, his deep green gaze unfocused. Tentatively, I reach up and grasp his hand, lowering it from my forehead. "Just overworked," I assure him. "By my own choice. But I appreciate the concern."

"You'll sort it out." Moseus retracts his hand and gestures to a gray sack near the door. "You may take that with you."

I rise to my feet. "Scrap metal?"

He nods.

I smile. All the backstepping and questions seem, for a moment, unimportant. The decent-sized bag looks full. Enough for plenty of tools. "Thank you."

"I appreciate your discretion. You need to leave now; the mist is lifting."

I hand him the small lantern. "I'll see what I can do."

The bag of scraps shakes Arthen's table when I drop it down. "Happy yearmark."

Arthen sits on a stool in the corner, straightening old nails, and he immediately puts down his pliers and approaches. "What on Tampere did you find?"

Strangers who opened the tower. Biting back the confession, I say, "Frantess is right." Though I'd practiced the excuse multiple times on my way here, saying it to another person feels like choking. I'm a terrible liar, so I had to practice this one. "I found these on my last dig." I pull pieces from the bag, one by one, and examine each, wondering at its use. Most have no distinct purpose—a sheet of that, an ingot of this, something that looks like a handle off a tankard—but a few things catch my eye: narrow tubes connected by a gear that certainly belonged to something complex, bits of metal the size of dining utensils forged like little arrows.

Oh Ancients, if only I could speak to just one of you for a single minute, I would learn so much.

I push the metal debris toward Arthen.

"Where on the Serpent's world were you digging?" he asks, his eyes wide. He picks up a piece of scrap and turns it over in his hands.

"Can you use it?"

"I can use all of it." He grasps those utensil things. "I'll need to get the forge *very* hot, but I can work this." He wipes his free hand down his face. "The backlog, Pell, I don't even know where to start."

I grin. "From the top, I guess."

He collects a few pieces that appear to be made of the same alloy and brings them to his forge.

"One request?"

Arthen pushes down on the bellows. "Anything."

"Do you still have those plans I made, for the rover?"

He pauses. Tips his head toward a set of drawers sitting as far from the furnace as a set of drawers can get. Starting at the top, I open the drawers one at a time. In the third one, I find parchment with my scrawl. It depicts a three-wheeled vehicle, the size of a deer, that would transport water buckets to and from the well, helping out the farmers. It was fun to design with Arthen, but we'd never had the materials to build it. I'm sure, with enough resources, I could build a motor to propel it. It could carry a dozen buckets of water or more.

I'd scrawled all of this in smudged charcoal, along with a little symbol in the bottom right corner, a rhombus with one line cutting through the top, and two smaller, parallel lines in the center. My own version of an Ancient symbol, were I ever to craft something of my own.

"That," Arthen grunts as he pushes on the bellows, "is at the *bottom* of the list."

"And I'm guessing darts are at the top?"

It's Arthen's favorite game. Used to have a board inside Maglon's alehouse, until Arthen melted down the darts last year to make Amlynn some needles for sutures and to repair her scissors. He snorts. "Only slightly."

I close the drawer. "I'll get the materials we need."

"Will you now?"

I wiggle my fingers at him in a show of facetious mystery and head back toward the road.

Before I reach it, though, Arthen calls out, "I want my knife!"

"Oh, for the Serpent"—I reel back at him—"I do not have your knife!"

He's focused on his fire. "Thirteen-centimeter blade, braided leather handle. It's got sorghum leaves etched onto one side of the blade."

Hand on hip, I reply, "It sounds beautiful, Arthen, but completely unfamiliar."

He clicks his tongue. "I could have sworn I lent it to you."

"So I could what? Stab the dead bodies I bury?" Rolling my eyes, I wave and leave. I'm not especially tired, so I consider heading to the farms to find Salki after I eat, but as I approach home, she finds me first.

"Pell!" She runs toward me from my front door. She's lively and grinning, a flash of her old self. The eagerness in her voice brings relief I didn't know I needed. Casnia lingers a few paces behind her, peering off toward the southern mountains. "Glad I found you! Look!"

She shoves something yellow into my hands. It takes me a beat to recognize it as Ancients' work, and it's covered in symbols.

My jaw drops. It's unlike anything I've uncovered, and nothing like the machines in the tower. "Where did you find this?" It's heavy, a flawlessly crafted circle about thirty centimeters across, with symbols carved on its face, close to its edge, framing about two-thirds of it. A right triangle protrudes from its center. Tarnish has given the metal a matte finish.

"We expanded a little last cycle, did some planting," Salki explains. "Gethnen dug it up. Wants to melt it down for tools, but I wanted you to see it first."

Before yet another argument about the use of my artifacts winds its way through town, she means. I turn it over in my hands. There are no signs of welding or breaks, no slots or rivets or holes to denote missing pieces. The artifact appears whole. And given how robust the thing is, and how close to the surface it must have been, I'm not surprised.

I rotate it in my hand. "I don't know what this is, Salki." There are O\ and /O symbols on either side of the protruding triangle in addition to the symbols—seventeen, to be precise—around the edge. That number is meaningless, but I do recognize some of the figures. They're digits. They stop and start at five in both directions, and—based on my count—if they're moving by ones, then the top number, across from the right triangle's perpendicular side, is a thirteen. Which correlates with the hours in a cycle, but . . .

"Your guess is better than mine," she offers. "Thamton thinks it's a fancy dinner plate for picky people. This"—she indicates the protruding triangle—"keeps the food from touching."

"Eat," Casnia says, kicking a pebble. "Eat."

I laugh. "Well, that's one theory." I glance toward the tower in the distance. "Do you mind if I hold on to it for a bit?"

Salki rolls her lips together. "Gethnen found it. You know how he feels about this stuff."

I consider this for a moment. "Tell him I gave it to Arthen to melt down. I already forked over some of my other finds, so it will balance out."

Salki's face falls. "Oh Pell, I'm sorry. I know you had plans for those—"

"Fair trade." I offer a smile and heft the new artifact, running my thumb along its edge. It's different from anything else I've seen . . . and something in my gut tells me it's important.

Chapter 5

When I return to the tower, Heartwood's presence in the dark first chamber startles me, and I nearly drop my things. His presence fills the room, thickening and overheating the air. I shake myself, determined to find my reason, but I notice something off about him. The lack of a scowl, yes—he's not actively glaring at me. But his face has taken on a gray pallor that camouflages it against the staircase he leans on. His back hunches as though he's fatigued or sore of stomach; he obviously isn't well. He barely seems to notice my arrival.

Chewing the inside of my lip, I pick up a lantern and cross over to him, leaving about four paces between us. Wild animals are always the most dangerous when they're injured. "Are you sick?"

He looks up at me as though it strains him. Still no scowl, just cool indifference. "I'm well enough."

He drags himself up the stairs to the second floor. The dragging would be easier with handrails, but however long these two strange men have occupied the tower, they must not have seen the need. Then again, what would they build them from? Wood is nearly as scarce as metal.

I wait until he's at the top, half expecting him to topple back down and wondering if I'd have a chance of catching him. I'm strong, but Heartwood is easily twice my size. Fortunately, he makes it upstairs, and I wonder at his poorly hidden ailment before forcing it from my mind and returning to Machine One.

I pick up where I left off: wires. It's remarkable how resilient these machines are. I can't guess their age, but they're old, and there's not a speck of rust on them. Even the most delicate parts are usable, if not in pristine condition. I wonder if Arthen could figure out the composition of these alloys. I wonder if Emgarden will progress enough with its metalworks to mine those mountains and create masterpieces such as these.

I work through the wiring from the back end, coming around toward the front of the machine, removing a plate to see what lies beneath—

I loop the chain over the wheel in the back. It isn't part of this gear system like I thought.

I blink, my hands still on the plate. Again. What *was* that? A reverie I have no control over? A mental lapse? It's the third time. Glancing up, I spy the wheel in question, and the chain. Set the plate aside and lift the chain. Scoff. It's too short to reach—

Wait.

Coming back to the side of the machine, I search through the fixed components until I find a silvery lever about fifteen centimeters long. I grunt as I pull it up, and the wheel, along with the box it's attached to, shifts forward.

"Ruin me," I whisper, returning to the front. Sure enough, the chain now reaches. I attach it. It's a pulley system of some kind.

Staring at the machine, I take a step back, then another. Rub my eyes and look again. I want to talk to someone. To tell Moseus or Salki what just happened, but if I can't even explain it to myself, how can I possibly explain it to them?

So I do the only thing I can. I work.

I screw the plate back in, covering the delicate pieces behind it. I venture to the back of the machine, cataloging what's needed there. It seems mostly intact, but I take a few things apart anyway, trying my best to understand how it works. Scrawl notes, take measurements. Grease some axles and test some ceramic inserts, which are essentially for turning or rotating. I might need to replace one of them. I write it down.

That's a Moseus problem. Another hour passes, and I use the stool to crawl up on top of the machine. From here, I can see that annoying power switch. I can also clearly see how the rotary unit works, even if there's no piping for fluid to access it. But I don't know what else to call it, so *rotary unit* it is.

An idea strikes me. I have no clue how this thing is supposed to get power, or how that switch can be for anything *but* power, but maybe I can rig it to take power. If only to see how it functions. If it functions, I'll understand it.

I stare at that unit a long time, ignoring a passing quake, turning ideas over in my head. Maybe if Arthen could weld a few things for me . . . and I could attach that there, have a bar come up and over . . . manpower would be the easiest source, but it couldn't be a rotational treadmill or any sort of rotary unit moving around the machine; there's not enough space between the machine and the wall. So something that can wind or pump . . .

This feels important.

Wiping greasy hands on the sash securing my shirt, I go to Moseus's room and knock softly. He doesn't answer. I rap louder. Receiving no reply, I push open the door.

"Moseus?" This time I brought a lantern with me and hold it high.

An empty room greets me. I start to close the door, but pause, taken aback again by how *dark* the room is. Why is it so dark?

Letting out a long breath, I leave his chamber and set the lantern at the base of the stairs. Climb up, blinking as my eyes adjust to new light. Mist swirls outside the cramped windows. Everything looks silver, except for Machine Two, which greets me in bronze splendor. I study it for a moment before tearing my gaze away. *One thing at a time.*

I don't see either tower keeper. Following the wall, I find a door identical to Moseus's. I knock firmly. No answer. So I let myself in.

The small room boasts only one slitted window, open to the mist.

This is definitely Heartwood's room. Its décor is sparse. The skin of a deer—a rare find—covers the center of the cold stone floor. A cairn sits in the back corner with no purpose other than to look pretty, and I can't help but think how pointless it is to carry stones up those stairs. A small table holds two little cups of succulents. There's a bundle of parchment on a pallet right under the window. A pack, some folded clothes, a knife with a leather-braided handle.

My hand loosens on the doorknob. *Leather-braided handle.*

Checking over my shoulder to ensure I'm alone, I slip into the room—closing the door to a crack behind me—and head straight for the knife. It's probably happenstance. Still, I grab it and pull it from its sheath—

A plain knife. It's the right length, but it's just a regular knife.

I turn it over, and my breath catches.

A design of sorghum leaves flows over one side of the blade.

"Where's my knife, Pelnophe?"

My mouth parts. Realizing where I am, I sheathe the blade, shove it into my pocket, and run for the door, but gentle footsteps outside the room freeze me in place. Cursing, I move behind the door, pressing myself to the wall, and hold my breath. I can't fit out the window, and there's nowhere else to hide—

The steps fade down the stairs.

Thanking the gods, I hurry from the room, closing the door behind me. I rush to the window closest to Machine Two and pull out the knife again. I'm not losing my mind. This is Arthen's knife. He's been pestering me about it for *months.* So why on the Serpent's abandoned world was it in Heartwood's room?

Speak of Ruin, and he shall appear.

Movement below catches my eye. I squint through the fog—it's Heartwood, still in his leathers. Leaving the tower. Where is he going? Probably to the latrine. But I bite my lip, trying to quell the uneasiness in my gut as my knuckles whiten around Arthen's blade.

I drop the knife onto Arthen's work table.

"Aha!" he shouts over his bowl of porridge. "I knew you had it!"

I hold my hands up in surrender. "You were right. I lost it. I'm sorry. I'll be more accountable moving forward."

He snorts, then winces like a kernel of something has lodged in his nasal cavity. He takes a long drink, runs a hand down his beard, and picks up the knife, unsheathing it. "Well, you kept it in excellent repair."

So it hasn't been used much. I make a mental note. Swallowing down my defense, I manage, "I always do."

He snorts again. "Tell that to the last shovel I had to sharpen." He flips the knife in the air, blade over handle, and catches it easily. Does it a second time, then tips his head to the far wall. "See that knot over there?"

I see a dark knot in an old wooden beam supporting the wall behind the set of drawers. "What of it?"

With a quick flick of Arthen's wrist, the knife goes flying, embedding itself dead center in the knot. He bows.

I mumble, "Show-off."

He returns to his work. "Where have you been lately? Not seeing you around much."

"Tinkering. Sleeping. For once." I shrug.

"Tinkering with what?"

I pause. That's right—Arthen thinks I gave him all my research. This is why I'm bad at lying. Fortunately, my brain comes around to an honest solution quickly. "Salki found something in the crops. Don't tell."

Arthen rolls his eyes. I wouldn't say he agrees with my insistence that artifacts should be saved for study, for future machinery, for the long-term benefit of Emgarden, but he's a decent person who believes in ownership, even if it keeps his forge cold. Arthen won't rat me out unless things get desperate. Well, *more* desperate.

He points to the hooks behind me. "See that?"

I turn. A weeding fork and the end of a hoe hang on the wall. My mouth tastes a grin. "Well, look at that."

"Don't suppose you have anything else you're willing to forfeit?"

I think of the incomplete tower machines looming over me. All the things I could build with them in Emgarden if Moseus and Heartwood gave up on the tower. "Soon."

"And is this related to where you've been wandering off to in the mists?"

Something sharp spikes up my torso. Feigning nonchalance, I ask, "Nosy much?"

Arthen smirks. "You know well as I do, there's not much to occupy a person's attention around here."

There are people in the tower. I got into the tower, Arthen. And it's incredible. "Consider a hike."

"To *where?*" he chuckles.

"Mountains. Wall." Each a journey.

Leaning back in his chair, Arthen says, "Knees aren't fit for the first, and the latter looks all the same, as far as it goes."

That's truth. As far as I've ever seen or explored, certainly. The amaranthine wall is smooth as glass and pink as a rose, extending forever north and south. The only variation comes at its uneven top, where it waves shorter and taller at random intervals, like Casnia drew it. I have always wondered why the Ancients built it like that, if they built it at all. Maybe all the Serpent's worlds have such a wall, denoting the path it took when it left its skin behind.

My gaze falls back to that knife. Crossing to the wall, I wrench it free. It's a good size, small enough to conceal but large enough to do damage. I barely have the thought before I ask, "Can I borrow this?"

Arthen's incredulous expression amuses me. "Really, Pell?"

"Can I?"

He frowns. "I suppose. 'Til I need it."

I sheath the blade and shove it in my pocket. "Thanks."

Heartwood is hale again, easy as the sun burns mist.

I see him while straddling the crest of Machine One, clambering about with a ratchet and a slot-head turnscrew. He comes down the stairs, I dare say with a spring in his step—an awfully fast recovery for a man too pained to stand straight one cycle ago. I purposefully focus on my work as he reaches the floor, feeling his eyes on me, his presence like the first shovelfuls of earth into a grave, and mine the body beneath. Writhing under my own paranoia. Regardless, he goes to Moseus's room, speaks with him in low tones with the door nearly shut for about five minutes, then returns to the stairs. The sensation of his watching me burns up my side, so I yank up my ratchet, rest my elbows on my knees, and stare right back at him.

His expression startles me. I'd been prepared for a contest of wills, a battle to see which of us can be more perturbed, but the sadness on his face strikes me so absolutely that I drop my tool, wincing as it clatters between shieldings. Our gazes lock for a moment only; he has no interest in staring me down. A flash of downturned eyes, loose lips, creased forehead, and he's up the stairs, swift and gone.

I watch those stairs a moment longer, wondering at his . . . do I dare call it despair? Almost like Salki's expression when she first told me of her mother's passing. My chest twinges, and I barely know the man. What on Tampere could Moseus have told him to hurt him so badly?

Why did it feel like it had something to do with these machines?

Because everything is about the machines, I tell myself as I pick my way down and snatch up my ratchet. *Because what else could it possibly be about?*

Moseus said that fixing this tower was important. Why? What is his connection to it?

I'm so enraptured by my own thoughts that I don't watch my step as I climb back up. My foot slips off a coil, and I lose my balance completely. My chin hits a beam as I fall back—

I brace for stone, but it's flesh that catches me. Flesh and the sound of rustling fabric. Clean scents of water and earth.

An arm rights me. "It won't help us to break our engineer as well," Moseus says calmly, but it almost sounds like a joke. He adjusts the wide, dark sleeve of his robe and folds his arms, and I'm struck by the thinness of his wrists, like a man starved. "It's looking better."

I clear my throat. Check my pocket for Arthen's dagger. "Thanks. And yeah, I have some ideas. I need some specific parts, though." Stepping toward the floor lantern, I pick up one of my slates—I have many now—and show him my design. "I think I can rig up power to this one. See if it'll move for me."

The glow of the lantern catches Moseus's face, and I realize how gaunt it has become. As though his health has been mystically traded to Heartwood, who now functions with renewed energy. Moseus looks like he hasn't slept for a dozen cycles. I consider offering the services of Amlynn, but he'll turn them down. Not a hunch, but a fact.

His brow twitches at the design. I debate whether or not to ask after his welfare and ultimately decide against it.

"That . . . work for you?" I try.

He nods, slowly. "You've worked quicker than I expected." Then, after mulling a moment, "Is this similar to what you've . . . 'tinkered' with at your home?"

I snort. "Hardly. But I strive to impress." I try to mask how much the comment bolsters me. I *can* do this. Take that, Ancients.

"I don't know how to make this for you," Moseus continues, handing back the slate. "Heartwood might be able to, out of wood, but the strength—"

"A blacksmith in town can build it for me, if I have the scrap, and if I can convince him it's more important than spades and rakes." I'll tell Arthen it's for the artifact Salki brought me and promise to return it right after, or distract him with other scrap metal from the tower. "It's simple enough. He won't know what it's for."

Moseus's deep-green eyes trail up the length of the machine. Something about his gaze feels deeply personal, almost intimate. Like he's not looking at my work, but at me. A sudden surge of insecurity flows over me, foreign and uncomfortable, and I find myself crossing my arms, which is awkward with the tablet.

"Have it done as soon as possible." Moseus's voice is distant, low, masculine. "I'll give you the materials you need."

Two cycles later, I return with my turning rod and affix it to the machine. It takes some ties and ratcheting, since I don't have equipment to weld like the Ancients did, but I secure it, hoping the angle and leverage will help me turn it and provide power to this mystery. Moseus watches from a couple of paces away. The shades of sickness have darkened on the planes of his face. Is he eating? Heartwood lingers near the stairs, appearing perfectly fed.

Hiding a frown, I focus on the machine. I push the end of the handle, which measures about two-thirds of a meter long. It doesn't budge. I lean my weight into it, but no luck. Heartwood starts to move forward, maybe to inspect my work or give me a hand, but then I abandon the rod and instead grab my longest wrench, lean into the machine, and nearly flay my arm reaching in to smack that switch in the middle of it. Returning to the rod, I push, push, *push* . . . and that gods-damned rotary unit starts to move. I grin, even as a few gears grind in protest, not quite aligned and certainly not oiled, but the machine moves. Quietly, briefly, I hear a tone, a note garbled amid the creaking and complaining. And then it all stops, the machine stuck on . . . I'm not sure.

"Functional *enough*," I say aloud, pushing the handle the opposite way and turning everything back to where it started. And that tone . . . I definitely did something right, if the metalworks are singing to me. I wonder whether Moseus or Heartwood heard it, but neither comments. "I'm still not sure what it does, but it's working."

"Excellent work, Pell." Moseus steps closer and puts a hand on the network of metal enveloping most of the machine. For the first time, I see him smile, and it lifts his entire countenance, shadows and all. I glance to Heartwood. That vein pops from his forehead again. His expression remains grim, his jaw tight. He tips his head to me. I suppose that's as much of a compliment as I can expect, from him.

Letting out a long breath, I tell Moseus, "That's an invitation, you know."

He pulls back his hand. "Pardon?"

"To disclose what these machines do," I specify, patting the turning rod. "Because if you want me to fix the others, you're going to have to tell me."

Chapter 6

Moseus frowns. "You are using the term *fixed* very loosely."

He has a point.

Heartwood moves closer, halfway between us and the stairs. Damn him, but I can't shake the heaviness of his company, which makes me feel like I'm underwater. I glance at him, but he looks away. His jaw remains tight. His countenance belongs at a funeral.

What in Ruin's hell is going on here?

I keep my tone light. "I'll know what I'm doing if I know what I'm doing. What is this tower for?"

Moseus and Heartwood exchange a look. A thousand unspoken words pass between them.

After a good twenty heartbeats, Moseus clears his throat. "We don't entirely understand it ourselves." He holds out a hand as though to stall protest. He knows me so well already. "But we believe it has something to do with the wall."

That takes me back. "The wall? The . . . amaranthine wall?" My pulse quickens. More answers. More questions. That hollow space in my core aches like hunger. *Something is missing.*

Moseus explains, "We believe that if we can unlock the Ancient magic in this tower, it will open a door in that wall. Our people are trapped behind it."

My lips part. "Your people?"

Moseus glances to Heartwood, who nods.

Then . . . there are more? We truly aren't alone? "How'd they get over there?" I ask. No one can scale that wall. Many of us have hiked all the way out there and tried. Too tall, too slick. Too . . . strange.

"We don't know." Hoarseness limns Heartwood's voice, and I can't help but feel another pang at the tone of it. "But they've been there a long time."

I mull over this. "I'm so sorry. You're . . . sure?"

They both nod.

"And they . . . look like you?" I gesture between them. "I'd recognize them, if I saw them?"

Heartwood frowns. Moseus answers, "More or less. You can understand the importance of the mission. And our frustration. Where we come from"—he touches Machine One, almost like it's a lover—"there's nothing like these. The Ancients weren't like us."

"They weren't like any of us," I agree. Despite all my study—my *attempts* to study—I don't know much about those who came before. They're legend, like the World Serpent and the gods. They were the first living creatures the gods made, strong and long-lived, and eventually they moved on. I can't say I blame them; surely other worlds shed by the Serpent have more resources and beauty than Tampere.

And that explains why none of us has ever seen people outside Emgarden. They must be behind that wall. To think we've been sharing this world for so long and never knew . . .

"But you're here," I offer.

Heartwood sighs. "We're here."

He looks and sounds so devastated that I don't dare interrogate him further. I wonder who lives behind that wall. A family. A wife, a mother, a brother. The thought of being parted even from Salki hurts; I can't imagine if I were separated from a child or other blood rel—

I lose my train of thought.

"One of these may open a door," Moseus says tentatively. "Another may be a means of communication. We're not yet sure. But, for now, the mist holds. Please see what else you can do." He crosses the chamber, his footsteps loud, and slips into his room. I wonder what shapes his thoughts take, that he's so comfortable sitting with them.

Turning back to the machine, I roll my lips. I'm not entirely sure what more to do. How could a machine here open a passageway in an impenetrable crystal wall kilometers away? But the Ancients crafted mysteries. Moseus was not off the mark when he called it magic.

"Is he okay?" I ask, not meeting Heartwood's eyes. "He seems . . . ill."

A long, slow breath stirs the air. For a moment I believe Heartwood will not reply, but after a beat he says, "He often is," sounding as hollow as Moseus's cheeks. I wonder whether that wall and the people behind it affect Moseus's health. Or, perhaps, if Heartwood does.

I press my hand against a silvery beam crossing Machine One's middle like a belt. I've come so far already. Proven myself. So why do I feel so far away? For a moment, it's as though the tower might crumble around me.

"Do you ever feel," I murmur, "like something's missing? I don't know. As though . . . your purpose is unfulfilled, your future is uncertain, or . . . like you're forgetting something?"

If the silence that settled during Moseus's departure was a snuffed candle, this one is a choked fire. A few seconds pass before Heartwood answers, "I wish I could."

Then he, too, leaves, abandoning me to the vexing mystery.

The following cycle, I'm near the end of my trek to the tower through the fog when I see a shadow moving away from it. I know immediately it's Heartwood. The more time I spend at the tower, the more easily I can tell Moseus and Heartwood apart, in more ways than one.

Moseus has slimmer features and a slimmer build. His eyes are a deeper green and endless in a way that makes him feel older than he is. An old soul, Salki would say. He's simple, unadorned in his appearance, behavior, and speech. He masks his emotions well. He sees a task that needs to be done and does what's required to fix it without complaint or fanfare. He thinks using facts, reason, logic. It's definitely something I can appreciate.

Heartwood has broader features, both in face and body. While he's far from gaudy, he likes embellishment. He wears more complex clothing than his counterpart, and his leathers are etched with an array of designs, most of which I've yet to identify. I've never seen him with his hair down or simply held back in a cord. There's always a braid, a knot, a loop, often all three. He tries to mask himself as Moseus does, to put on a face of serenity, but he isn't good at it. He's often frustrated, consternated, or simply sad. Sometimes I sympathize with him. Usually, I'm annoyed. When Heartwood looks at me, it makes me think of discovering a feral cat in a basement in the light of a flickering lamp. That eerie green sheen in the eyes, the hissing of self-defense, knowing it's too small to win a battle. Whether in the tower or the mists, something about Heartwood deeply unsettles me, like we're two magnetic north poles, repulsing each other with some unseen, unknown, and aggravating force.

But what really strains me is the knife. Why did Heartwood have Arthen's knife, especially when we're so desperate for metal? And why did Arthen think *I* took it?

Slowing my pace, I watch Heartwood leave as I approach. I've considered asking him about it directly, but while Moseus might be up front with me, Heartwood would not. He would have an excuse, dismiss the accusation, or simply not reply. Perhaps hide anything else that might give me answers to whatever happens in this bizarre fortress. I'm starving for answers. Can't risk it.

But I keep the knife on me, just in case, and wonder where Heartwood is going. There's nothing to see around here. There's a privy in the tower, and a well hidden in feathery, brown brush to the southwest. I enter the tower and light my smallest lantern. Sling two tool bags over my shoulders. Hang a couple of slates from my belt. I stare at Machine One, then trek upstairs.

I'm glad to be up here. Not just for something new to work on—something that might help me understand the remainder of Machine One—but because of the light. This floor has a friendlier feel and a slightly more open floor plan. The windows keep it from getting stuffy, whereas the air downstairs flows thick enough to chew, even when Heartwood's gone. I should stay here a sun sometime; I imagine it's downright pleasant.

And I suppose I'm more of a bronzy woman than I am silver, both in preference and appearance. Machine Two is just . . . prettier.

But it's also different, and again I get that sensation of taking two steps back for every step forward. As though I'm fighting against the Ancients themselves. They continually force me to retreat, but I won't be conquered.

"All right." I set down my equipment, save for a wrench and a hex turnscrew. "Let's see you naked."

I loosen plates, struts, and fasteners, cataloging each in small script on a slate, making a mental note to ask whether Moseus has parchment I can use. I don't know how he would, if he doesn't trade with Emgarden, but I saw some in Heartwood's room, so it's a possibility. Once I have a better look at Machine Two's guts, I carefully take off a cylindrical piece I don't recognize, surprised at how heavy it is. Put it back on, and do the same for . . . I want to call it a gear or a wheel because of its shape, but it doesn't have teeth or rivets, so I deem it a hell-if-I-know and move on.

Toward the center of the machine, spines and shafts bloom open like a flower. Doesn't take long to determine they shouldn't be doing that, yet I can't imagine what would make them fall apart in such a way. There's nothing to fasten them upward or apply pressure inward. They just . . . collapsed, as though weary of being part of something so large.

I'm reaching for one of the spines when I feel a hand on my shoulder and warm breath on my neck. Seizing, I whirl around, scraping myself on loose parts—

I'm alone.

Every millimeter of my skin prickles. Pulling away from the machine, dropping a screw and a washer, I turn around, scanning my surroundings. Touch my neck where I most *definitely* felt someone's mouth. "Moseus?" I croak, barely above a whisper. "Heartwood?"

No answer.

Pulse racing, I rush for the stairs. They're empty. Glare at the hole in the ceiling for the third floor, but it's too far for anyone to have hidden there so quickly. I throw open the door to Heartwood's room. Empty.

Returning to the machine, I grip a beam and lean into it, forcing slow, deep breaths. What is happening to me? That felt . . . It was so *real*. Someone touched me. Intimately. And I don't want to admit it, but it felt *familiar*.

I glance at Machine Two, wondering at Moseus's talk of magic. Are the Ancients *still* tied to these pieces of history? They're not here, not anymore, but what do I know of Ancients? They were less than gods, but more than mortals.

A shiver courses up my back. I notice, a hand's breadth from where I grip the beam, another Ancient symbol. This one is a circle with three lines dividing it, the center longer than the others. I press my thumb into it, hard, expecting the machine to react in some way, or for another . . . I don't know, vision, or mental lapse, or whatever keeps happening.

The machine doesn't react. I'm alone.

Something about that thought feels very poignant, and I'm not sure why.

⁂

"Thank you, Pell," Moseus says as I come down the stairs with my personal tools and slates. "Anything of note?"

Yeah, I'm slowly losing my mind. "No. Just trying to understand it all."

The door to his room stands open, a black maw. Lifting the lantern, I try to see him better. His voice sounded steady, and though it may be a trick of the light, he looks less sickly than before. His pale skin appears more even—unblemished—and its shadows have shrunken. The way the small light contrasts with the umbra makes him look silver, like Machine One. Long, straight, silver hair like an angel might wear, and eyes deeper than wells. His clothing blends in with the darkness of the room behind him, like it's a great hand holding on, unwilling to release.

Hesitating, I ask, "Why do you keep it like that? There's another room on the second floor with a window you could take." Then, to lighten the inquiry, "Heartwood surely can't be *that* insufferable."

The corners of his lips tick upward. He pauses, then gestures. "Come."

The mists will fade shortly, but if Moseus isn't concerned, I suppose I shouldn't be, either. I follow him, slowing as he passes into his room. The guy isn't going to murder me . . . not if he wants his machines fixed. Still, my fingertips find their way into my pocket and brush the hilt of Arthen's blade.

Moseus leaves the door open. After a moment, my eyes adjust. There isn't anything remarkable about the small enclosure. There's a bed, and I think that's a chest. A rug on the floor softens my footfalls.

Moseus sits, crossing his legs in front of him. "Please," he says and gestures to the space in front of him. If he'd worn gloves, I wouldn't have seen the motion.

I sit, facing him. Mirror his position.

"People misunderstand the dark," he explains, and I imagine he's closed his eyes, but I keep mine open. "Many fill their lives with anything they can grasp, and their minds with anything they can think. They disconnect from others, from the world, from the cosmos. The things they grasp, ultimately, hold no meaning. I seek the darkness to strip away meaninglessness. To remember myself and my mission." He takes a deep breath.

I mimic it. "You meditate?"

"Often."

Several seconds pass. Not uncomfortable ones . . . Moseus has never shared so much about himself, and I appreciate that. He has a point.

It's clear that nothing nefarious lives in this lightlessness, even if I prefer sunshine.

"How long has it been?" I lower my voice. It feels wrong to speak loudly. "Since you lost your people beyond the wall?"

"A very long time." His voice is a song. "I fear for them."

He doesn't expound, only reaches into that peace of his, his "animus" or whatever he called it. We sit like that for several minutes, long enough that my eyelids grow heavy. But I will not sleep here with a strange man I hardly know.

"The mist is fading," I whisper.

He turns his head as though there's a window in the wall, perfectly alert despite his stillness. "You may go."

I rise and turn toward the exit. I'm nearly to it when a pale hand pushes it nearly closed, thickening the darkness. Moseus, silent as a cat, presses against the door.

Pressed very close to *me*.

"Pelnophe." He says my name like it's made of eggshells. His breath brushes the tip of my nose. The room grows very small and very warm, and I try to remember the last time I was this close to a man.

"The machines," he murmurs. "It's direly important we repair them swiftly. It's been . . . a long time."

I nod, but unsure if he can see the gesture, I whisper, "I know, Moseus. I'm trying." I don't need to whisper. I'm not sure why I do. The odd intimacy of the situation just . . . calls for it.

"I—we—are asking a lot," he continues. "I am aware. But only you can do this. We will help you in any way possible, but we need you, Pelnophe."

Words fail me. Heat from his body radiates past the loose cloth of his robe.

"Stay, when you can." Perhaps noticing our positioning, he steps back, pulling the door open. "You are welcome to stay when you are able. The mists—"

"I'll follow the rules," I assure him, wishing there was more light so I could see his expression better.

He says nothing more, just pulls away, seeming to disappear into the shadows of his room. Off-kilter, I leave him behind almost guiltily and let the late mist swallow me whole.

I run home, shaking off the confusion that the tower delights in afflicting me with. I'm pushing it a little close. The sun burns against the side of my face as I reach Emgarden, as I've circled around so I approach from the west, not the northwest, but folk are used to seeing me come and go. Regardless, I savor the sun's warmth even as it makes me perspire. I should bathe. And sleep, though I prefer to rest in the mists. Get some work done. The farmers always need help transporting water. You'd think they'd be more supportive of me building another windlass, or that rover. I sigh. Might be time I start hunting for a good place to dig another well.

Salki and Casnia are walking my way when I arrive.

"Hi!" Salki carries a bowl covered in cloth. A worm of guilt burrows into my stomach. "Please don't tell me that's for me."

Salki rolls her eyes. "A *thank you* would suffice."

"Thank you," Casnia repeats, overenunciating the words. "Thank-thank you."

Grinning, I open my door and wave them in. Salki sets her gift on the table and pulls the cloth, revealing a loaf of bread. The scents of yeast and millet warm the room. I never make bread. I don't have the patience to grind grain into flour, let alone wait for the dough to rise and the oven to heat and all the other nonsense that goes with baking. But I do love bread. I bought it from Ramdinee once every dozen cycles or so, before she passed.

"Bless you." I rip the heel straight off the loaf.

"Gods help you." Salki clucks her tongue, takes a small serrated ceramic knife from my drawer, and cuts half the loaf into slices, handing one to Casnia. She squeals upon receiving it, then runs to the corner, sits on the floor, and munches away.

"How are things?" I ask, pulling out one of two chairs I own and plopping down. I kick out the other for Salki.

"Well, we had an entire row of sorghum fail." She sighs. "*My* row. I took one cycle's break, and the plants burned to nothing beneath the sun."

I frown. "Maybe it's disease." Hopefully not. That would be harder to cure.

"Maybe, but nothing else seems affected. And it happened so *suddenly*." She shrugs. "So at first sun Cas and I pulled them all up to start again."

"Same well water as the rest?"

"Unfortunately. But otherwise, I'm good. Getting back into the routine." She fingers her simple, misshapen brooch. "Without Mother, honestly, I have more free time, and I don't know what to do with it. I, uh"—she chuckles—"don't want to put in even more hours at the farm, even with the failure. I've been taking Casnia on walks, when she wants to come with me. Visiting the alehouse more often. Baking." She gestures to the bread.

"You could convince everyone to let you do this full time," I say around a mouthful. "No more farming. Sweating indoors instead of outdoors."

Salki laughs. "I don't know about that. I'm not as good as Ramdinee was." Her expression falls. I'd inadvertently reminded her how often death brushes shoulders with her.

Eager to change the subject, I tip my head toward Casnia. "How is she?"

A shrug. "Same as always. Oh"—she reaches into her satchel—"Casnia insisted I give this to you."

It's another childlike drawing of me, again with the wrong hair, even shorter than I wear it and yellow instead of brown. I'm wearing a long robe, or maybe a dress, in this one. Admittedly, the blue emilies around my feet look pretty good.

"She's getting better," I remark.

"She does enjoy it. I'll need to go gathering to get her some more art materials. She runs through them so quickly."

"I'll keep my eye out." There are some plants that make decent dyes around here. The emilies work for pastels. Wickwood burns wonderfully, but its bark can also be distilled into a red dye. Easier ones are charcoal for black and yellow sandstone for, obviously, yellow. That's what my hair has been scrawled in on this newest piece.

"Figure out the plate yet?" Salki asks.

The heavy, circular artifact sits on the far end of my table. "Honestly, no. I haven't put much thought into it."

"That surprises me." Salki takes a bite of bread. Unlike me, she takes her time to chew and swallow before speaking again. "You're usually all over this stuff."

You have no idea. "I'll be right on it."

We chat for another half hour before Salki glances at my clock. "We should get to the fields." She sighs. Casnia overhears and lets out a wailing protest, then grips the doorjamb with two hands as the ground quivers underfoot. It's a little stronger this time, but nothing my knees can't handle, and it passes within seconds.

"You're welcome to stay home," Salki says to Casnia as she rises and pushes her chair back in. "But you can't stay here."

Casnia pinches her lips and eyebrows together.

"I'm just going to nap, Cas," I insist. "It'll be boring."

Salki coaxes Casnia to her feet and, with a hand on her back, guides her out the door. "See you, Pell. Maglon says you should drop by sometime."

"Thanks, Sal." Visiting the alehouse would be a good idea, so people don't start wondering where I've run off to. I could use some friendly company, too.

She waves and slips into the brightness of the sun.

I wrap up the remaining half loaf and stow it in my cupboard, safe from pests. I bring down my clay bowl and cloth for a bath, then pause, my attention turning back to the artifact on my table.

Sighing, I pick it up and take it outside. Climb the rickety ladder at the back of my house to my roof. Moseus likes to think in the dark; I like to think up here. It feels like it's been too long.

I set the heavy plate with its funny triangular fin next to me and lie back against the sun-warmed shingles, staring up at a faded blue sky until my eyes hurt. I close them, and when I open them again, I know I drifted off. I don't drool when I'm awake.

Wiping my mouth, I sit up, then stretch and look over Emgarden. Most of our buildings are only one story, so I can see all the way out to the fields. A cluster of pink and green emilies has popped in the road leading out of the town, the same one I take to the tower. If only our crops could grow so fast.

I glance at the plate. "If you really are just for picky eaters, my opinion of your artisan is going to plummet." I pick the thing up; it weighs about a kilogram and a half. Set it on my knees. Turn it, following the numbers up to thirteen, then back down again to five. On the second turn, though, I notice something.

That right triangle jutting up between the fives. Or, rather, the shadow it casts.

Resituating myself, I balance the plate on my knees, turning it slower, keeping a steady grip. Watching as the shadow thickens and moves up the numbers. Like the magnetic ball bearing scrolling past the tick marks on my clock.

A clock? But why would the numbers one through four be excluded, with no markings to delineate the mists? There's those strange o\ and /o symbols, but they're not at the fives, eights, or thirteen. The sun shines for eight hours, and the mists settle for five. Always. But it does *seem* like a clock, especially with the high number being thirteen—the length of one cycle.

I flip the artifact over, expecting a hole of some sort for a connection to a rotational device, but there isn't one. Nothing to indicate moving parts.

Unless.

I stare at the sky until my eyes water, then climb up to the peak of my roof. Straddle it. Set the artifact right on top to keep it flat. Again, I turn it. The shadow falls up the numbers to thirteen, then back down again. There's not much of a shadow near the bottom in the curve between fives, but keep turning, and it starts again. Just how a clock might work.

I stare at those circular symbols with their lines. The first circle is to the left of the line. The second, to the right. Inverses of one another.

That's . . . not supposed to be the *sun*, is it?

Because that's the only thing that would work. This artifact isn't made to turn. But the *sun* could mark the numbers. But that would only be possible if the sun *moved*. The sun never moves. It stays right where it is, just off-center in the sky, slightly east. Steady, constant, unchanging.

I keep turning the dial in my hands, watching the shadow marker rise and fall.

But the sun doesn't move. The sun doesn't move. The sun doesn't move. But maybe, in the time of the Ancients, it did.

Chapter 7

I clench my teeth and hands and pull the pliers as hard as I can. My shoulders are ready to pull from their sockets when the stupid piece of debris finally comes loose, and I go flying toward the stairs, stumbling backward a few steps before falling on my butt. I curse Ruin and the World Serpent both before dropping the pliers and shaking out my fingers.

Grimacing, finding my feet, I glare at Machine Two. Snatch up my pliers and resume work. At least now I can move this beam, which hinges farther up on the machine's body and is made to move, and then pull up this plate at the base to see what's underneath. Machine Two bears only a few similarities to Machine One, so the guesswork has started all over again, though I think I'm getting accustomed to the Ancients' art of wiring.

It takes some effort, and some grease, to loosen the bronze alloy plate and lift it. Machine One had something similar, which was how I learned a piece of it went through the floor of the tower. This one's at a different angle, and when I move it—

I see the wall. A sigh blows sweaty hair off my forehead. "Whoever built this was drunk as a bard," I mumble, feeling in my pocket for the screws I'd pulled out. From the outside, it probably looks like the machine is eating me; I'm almost entirely horizontal in it, near the bottom, with a strut poking into my thigh. Screw in hand, I adjust the plate to push it back in, then pause.

And stare at the perfect, hair-thin crack running down the stone wall.

Biting my lip, I pocket the screw and set the plate aside, wriggling in a bit more to get a better look, tracing my finger down that line. It's not damage in the stonework. It's too straight and even for that. Noting that the usual pattern of unchippable mortar is gone from this section of the wall, which Machine Two sits tightly against, I follow the crack down, to where it meets another perpendicular to it.

"Is this . . . ?" I twist, though that strut and the tight confines do not want me to. I follow the seam a little more, until I can't reach any farther, but I can see it.

It almost looks like . . . a door. But if it were, there'd be no way to open it.

"Unless you move." I grunt in the narrow space, trying to get a better look at the floor. Machine Two doesn't respond. The beam supporting its base—does it join with the one at the front? If it's any kind of hinged arm, maybe Machine Two can move away from this wall.

Interesting. I start to crawl my way backward, only for my butt to get caught on that stupid strut. Grumbling, I wriggle left, then right, grabbing a support rod to angle myself free. Glancing up, I see something that both excites and irritates me at the same time.

There's a power switch. Right in the unreachable middle of the machine, with no apparent means for supplying power around it. Just like in Machine One.

"Drunk. As. A. Bard." A little more squirming, ignoring the rip I just put in my pants, and I slide free, new grease stains on my shirt and running up my arms. I'll be spending my time off making soap.

A headache forms behind my eyes. Sitting on the cold stone floor, I rub them. My brain refuses to contemplate another thought.

Blinking my vision clear, I glance at the hole in the ceiling across the room. That leads up to a third machine. And then two stories above that juts that extra mechanism, almost like an enormous peg hammered into the tower's northeast side, up at the top. As if the Ancients built the tower first and the machines second, without realizing how much capacity they'd need. At least, I assume it's a machine up there. Only one way to check. Just my luck: first sun pierces through lingering mist.

I hesitate. I'd be going out in the sun, but technically Moseus didn't say I couldn't scale the tower in the sun, and I'm not risking it in the mist.

I stand, stretch, and collect the tools. I need to know how I'm going to fix this place up, so investigating the protrusion is nonnegotiable. Or, rather I'm not going to negotiate, so the keepers can't tell me *no*.

Best way to climb to the protrusion would be through a window, to save myself some effort, but all the windows are cut the same—too narrow for even my body to fit through. A sigh slides through my nose. At least it's not too narrow for the ladder. A few heaves and a grunt later, and I shove the ladder through the window, letting it fall two stories below. I retrieve some rope from that closet on the first floor and head out into the brightness of first sun.

Finding some level ground that's not too sandy, close to the tower's protrusion but away from peering eyes, I set up the ladder. It's heavier than it looks. After ensuring it's secure, I climb up eighteen rungs and pull myself onto a second-story window.

I wedge my foot in, giving myself a moment to piece out the best way to do this. Manage to sidestep over a subtle lip to another window, which I cram my shoulder into for balance while I tie a wrench to the end of my rope. Takes four attempts to swing the thing up and into a third-story window, where the wrench catches. The tower's tiers get smaller as they go up, so there will be space to stand once I get up there. Purposefully not looking down, I haul myself up, and—

My lips part when I get an elbow up. "Ruin crush me," I whisper, pushing myself onto the floor. I'd been so intent on fixing Machines One and Two, I hadn't bothered to investigate the third floor. Through this slotted window, my eyes center on a third machine.

It's larger than the other two. Or it would be, if it weren't in pieces. Because this thing is in *pieces*.

Desperate for a better look, I slide down the rope to my ladder, and down again to the ground. The ladder bites into my bone when I balance it on my shoulder. Takes a second to get it through the front door, but the open floor plans allow me to make it up the spiral stairs all right. Reset the ladder and climb up.

The wreckage strikes me anew as I step foot into this new chamber, my lungs bellowing from the effort. I walk toward Machine Three cautiously, as though it might come alive and attack. Chunks composed of assemblies, shielding, and gods know what else spill across the floor. The foundation seems to be intact, but struts, coils, springs, shafts, and gears splay . . . everywhere. Hanging off cables and axles, forgotten against walls, or just haphazardly piled up. Like someone set off an explosion right at the machine's heart.

I crouch down on the balls of my feet, taking it all in. *At least I don't have to take it apart to see how it works.* But how will I ever know where everything goes?

Like Machine One, it's predominantly silver. Steel. I think it's meant to stretch the entire height of the room; I can see pieces attached to the ceiling, like some of it should connect up there. The fallen supports are certainly long enough to reach. It's like the Ancients got all the parts they needed, hauled them up here, then got into a fight using the mechanics as weapons. After, they sealed up this lone, scattered monolith and followed the Serpent to another world.

Leaning forward, I pick up a small sprocket.

"Don't—" a voice says.

Starting, I turn around. Heartwood stands on the ladder behind me, his pale features so severe they might have been carved from plaster. I ignore my speeding pulse; I'm surprised I didn't hear him, what with the shoddy make of that ladder and his weight on it. I stand straight, internally berating myself, and force my shoulders to relax. My heartbeat doesn't.

Rubbing the sprocket's teeth between my fingers, I say, "You're awfully quiet on your feet for someone your size." I turn the sprocket

71

over. Set it down right where I found it, in the hope that it will give me a clue to where it goes when I get around to assembling this mess. "Don't what?"

Heartwood's mouth works. His sharp gaze shifts from me to the machine, and I wonder if my presence somehow rankles him as much as his does me. He doesn't answer.

Suppressing a sigh, I cross the room and peer out the skinny window. I can see that jutting piece of machinery almost straight above me, sticking out of the tower's highest tier. "I know I'm supposed to be gone by now, but I'm going to go look at that thing." I don't have the mental space to start on this . . . mess.

"It would be pointless." Heartwood steps into the room. He seems . . . larger, somehow. I can't help but frown. I hate feeling small. "Moseus and I have already investigated it. There's nothing to be done."

"But *I* haven't investigated it." I move to the next window, grateful to put some distance between us and secure my wrench-grappling-hook. "I want to see for myself."

"It isn't safe."

I shrug. "Life isn't safe."

"Nophe—"

I glare at him. He sets his jaw.

"My name is Pell," I remind him. I skirt around him and climb down the ladder. Wait for him to stop me, but he doesn't, which is permission enough. Once he's down on the second floor, I shove the ladder out the window for a second time. When I exit the tower, I do so alone.

After shaking out my hands and any lingering, nonsensical jitters, I repeat the motions from before. Pulling myself up to the wide lip at the base of the third story, I tie my rope around my waist in a way I presume won't tear me in two should I fall. The tower isn't unscalable. There are enough projections to use as foot- and handholds, between windows, lips, and weathering. But it's not a walk in cropland, either.

I pull myself up to the fourth floor. There are masonry surrounds for windows, but flat, opaque surfaces block the openings. I poke at the edges of one first with my fingers, then with a turnscrew, but Moseus was right—there's no discernible way to enter the top of the tower, even if the windows were large enough to fit a body. Shifting sideways, I aim for a windowsill on the third tier, one story overhead.

My foot slips.

My heart lodges in my throat as I grab the edge of the window, barely keeping myself upright. *Maybe wait for the condensation to dry next time, millet brain.* Steadying myself, I climb a little higher, reaching the fifth-floor window, finding it closed off like the others. I also reach the base of the protrusion, and I rest easy once I can get a second loop of rope over a piece of it.

I . . . *think* this is a machine. It's entirely plated on this side, so it's hard to tell, and where it connects with the tower is mortared and caulked. No seams I can find. With a grunt, I heft myself up and over so I'm sitting on top of the protrusion. I'd say it's about five meters long and two meters wide—

Wow. The view from up here is . . . intense.

I've never been this high up before. I can see all of Emgarden, from the farm on one side to Thamton's home on the other. The rocky sienna juts of the Brume Mountains cup the south and west like a hand, while the amaranthine wall cuts sharply across the east, glinting like an enormous jewel in the sunlight. Rusty, dry earth stretches far to the north, interrupted by jutting natural chimneys, rocky fins, and the occasional shadow marking a dip or drop. Like the wall, it has no end. None that I can see. I have a feeling I could pack up all of Emgarden and still not have enough provisions to travel far enough to find it, if there is one.

Wrenching my attention back to the protrusion, I run my hands over its smooth covering. Plated up here, too. Peek over the side—yep. All plated. And no discernible seams or screws or anything to get the plates off.

I'm loath to let Heartwood be right, so I investigate anyway, carefully running my hands over the plates, looking for any divots, weathering, seams. From the corner of my eye, I spy movement down below. It's

Heartwood. He loiters down there, watching me, a contrast of pale hair and dark leathers. I ignore him and climb farther out onto the protrusion. He follows my movements. What, is he going to catch me if I fall?

I snort at the idea. More likely I'd crush him and kill us both.

Still, twenty minutes later, I concede. If there's anything inside this thing, I don't have the tools to get to it. I knock against thick metal, unable to detect any hollow spaces to drill my way in. Not that I have a drill that can pierce through this.

The looming question remains: Why is it even *here*?

Tired and defeated, I retrace my steps. As I lower myself to the fourth floor, I keep the rope looped on the protrusion and don't pull it free until both feet are securely on the third floor.

I'm sorry, a voice whispers. I lost my temper.

Spinning around, I'm greeted only by the pieces of Machine Three, though that voice sounded right next to me. Low, quiet, *present*.

It . . . sounded like Heartwood.

But Heartwood isn't here. *No one* is here. Dropping the rope, I rub my eyes, then massage my temples. Listen. A soft breeze comes through the window. A desert wren caws in the distance. Footsteps downstairs.

I open my eyes. *I need a break.*

I haul everything back inside and situate the ladder again.

Moseus approaches. "There's nothing to be done on that protrusion." He doesn't sound angry, just resigned.

"I'm aware." I stretch my back. "And Machine Three is a mess."

He nods, also aware. "Are you up to the task?"

"Yes," I say without thinking, but I am. However frustrating this tower is, it's given me a purpose I didn't realize I needed. When I'm pinched sideways inside Ancient technology, that little ache beneath my ribs fades. I feel more . . . whole. Of course, I relay none of that to Moseus. In the better light, I confirm that he does seem healthier, though hardly well. I wonder how he and Heartwood could be so physically similar and yet so notably different. Granted, Heartwood's health also seems to fail him often, yet he recovers quickly, whereas Moseus struggles to keep even a hint of color in his complexion. He's never complained of the situation, at least not to me.

"Good." He glances out a window. "Do you intend to leave?"

However much I love this place, I'm exhausted, and my brain feels like porridge. "I'll try to be discreet."

Moseus frowns. "That is not part of the deal. You must travel in the mists only."

"Yeah, I know, but if I'm not around, people will ask questions." I run a hand through my hair. "I'll loop around and come from another direction. People are used to me being about."

Moseus's frown persists. "Be careful. There is much at stake."

Grateful I don't have to sit around for seven hours until the mists settle, I continue, "And you're *sure* you can't punch your way into the rest of the tower? Like you did here?" I point to the hole above my head.

"I have tried." His voice sweeps like wind. "Many times."

"Are you . . . okay?"

The question startles him. "Okay?" He repeats it like it's a foreign word.

"You seem . . . tired." It's the kindest explanation I can give.

Moseus considers. "Such is my disposition. I am well enough."

"Peacekeeping taking its toll, I suppose." I wonder what happens at the tower when I'm away. How Moseus and Heartwood interact when there are no eyes to see. But I don't inquire, only make my exit.

Leaving my tools, I take the stairs down, meeting Heartwood at their base. Ignore the way my stomach tightens. Raising an eyebrow, I say, "I wasn't going to fall."

"No"—he looks away—"I don't suppose you would have."

He says nothing more, only passes me on the stairs, and I walk home with the unmoving sun in my hair.

My mind and body both need a break from the tower, so for the next two cycles, I stay in Emgarden.

I sleep for half a sun before treating myself to a visit to the alehouse. I catch up with several folk from town, including Maglon. He has always been easy to talk to. It's not the ale, which is often weak and sour, but his open demeanor and tight-lipped attitude. I could tell that man that I killed Entisa with my bare hands, and he wouldn't reveal it to a soul. Not that he wouldn't take retribution out on himself, in one way or another. Maglon is a vault, but he's just. When Frantess starts bragging about her "win" with my forfeited metal, he tells her to pipe down.

I pick up my grain rations, visit Salki and pull a sliver from Casnia's finger, then head home. I tuck away my artifacts, including the sundial, and then rest and watch the mist curl outside my window, without pattern or shape. I think I hear that distant tone when the mists arrive, but it might just be my imagination.

When the sun returns, I venture out toward the farms and test new areas for wells, marking two that might be promising. After that, I wander to Arthen's forge. He's not in, so I help myself to his drawers and pull out my rover plans, using a charcoal pencil to sketch in extra ideas and a few equations, things I've learned from working on the Ancients' enormous machines.

Arthen says nothing when he arrives, merely looks over my shoulder. Points with a thick pinky finger. "What does this mean?"

"It's an idea to use the energy of the wheels to keep them spinning," I say. "So the steam doesn't run out as quickly."

"Wheels powering themselves?" He snorts and grabs a bowl of new nails and a file to finish them.

"It could work."

"I suppose it could. Body should be easy enough, if I have the metal."

"I'll get it for you."

He studies me. Waits until I look up from the plans to speak. "Where're you getting it, Pell?"

I purposefully don't look up. "Digs."

"These digs are suddenly a lot more fruitful."

I glance through the nearest window, toward the amaranthine wall, though I'd have to climb onto the roof to see it. "I'm trying some new techniques."

Ugh, surely I could have come up with something better than that. Arthen must agree, as he tries to pry more information from me. I might be bad at lying, but I can be just as tight-lipped as Maglon. Or Heartwood.

New emilies have sprouted randomly throughout the road when I leave at late sun, one already crushed by a passing foot. Crouching, I pick a blue bloom at the base. The flowers are large, about the size of a man's cupped hands, and grow close to the ground. Its faint shimmer dulls as I carry it home, but its color stays true. Inside, I pour a little water from a jar onto a plate and set the emily in it. Something about the action itches the back of my mind, but I can't sort out why. It's not the first time I've saved one of Tampere's beauties, but it's been a while.

The tone of the mist reaches my ear through the window. When I turn and cock my head to listen, my elbow hits my little jar of water and knocks it off the table. Cursing inwardly, I grab the nearest cloth—a shirt I need to launder—and start wiping it up. That was the last of the water I had, and I'm not in the mood to trek out to the nearest well. Though I suppose it's my fault there isn't one closer.

As I soak up the water, I notice it dwindling—not into my shirt, but into a crack between the floorboards. Wood and stone, packed tightly against the hard earth beneath, make up my floor. The ground shouldn't absorb so much so quickly.

Setting the shirt aside, I crouch closer to the gap, which looks just a little wider than it should be. Curious, I knock against the wood, getting a dull thud in return. But when I knock on the panel on the other side of the crack, it sounds—

"Hollow." I dig my short nails into the side of the floorboard. Try to lift, with no luck. I run my hands over the boards. Ignore the bite of a sliver. Moving the table, I find where a cut has been made across a board, breaking the pattern.

I dig my nails in there, and it lifts. I gape as a panel about six decimeters wide and three decimeters long loosens from the ground, bringing soil and debris with it. Below rests a cool, neat hole with sharp corners, about three decimeters deep.

And within it lies an Ancient artifact I've never laid eyes on.

Chapter 8

The panel sits snug in the floor. The table in its place. The mist, rolling in.

I lean back in a chair, my arms folded, staring at the artifact on the table before me.

It's . . . I don't know what it is. It has a rectangular frame with filleted corners, made of *three* different metal alloys, artlessly hammered in some places to make the pieces fit. The frame supports a translucent spherical core in the center made of some kind of acrylic, with a weighted bottom that always faces down. Perfectly balanced. A few other doodads and coils connect to it. It's the most complete artifact I've ever seen of this size.

And I have no idea how it got into my house.

It's not like other Ancient work I've seen. The gyroscopic elements and the build of the frame don't resemble anything from the tower. And it's very piecemeal. Enough so that I don't think it *is* Ancient work, but Ancient scraps someone conglomerated into . . . whatever this is.

It makes absolutely no sense, but . . . *I'm* the only person who could have made this. No one else in Emgarden takes an interest in this sort of thing, and they certainly wouldn't have cut up my floor and dug out a cavity to hold it without my knowledge. Moseus might know, but I'm not sure how far his knowledge extends.

Machine One in pieces at my feet, strewn across the stone floor, sprockets and gears and coils, bent and misshapen and—

I close my eyes as a sharp pain lances through my skull. I'm in over my head. I have always prided myself on simplicity—simple work, simple life. These . . . *things* . . . I see are complicated. *This* is complicated. And nothing makes me more angry than needing answers to questions I don't understand.

Sighing, I push the artifact away and grab the edges of the table, shifting it off the panel in the floor. If it's supposed to be hidden, I might as well keep it hidden until—

The door snicks shut. His feet pad across the floor—

Every hair on my body stands on end as I whip my hands from the table and turn around, heart racing. But the house is empty. It's a one-room house; I can see every nook of it from where I stand. My lungs collapse on themselves with every strained exhale. No. *No.* I heard someone in this house. I *just heard it*, just now. Someone was here.

Mouth dry, I march to the door and rip it open. No one loiters in the street. Slam that shut and check the windows. No one. I can see every corner, but I physically walk to each one, listening to my footsteps on the floorboards for the sound of other hollow compartments. There are none.

Chills course over my arms. *I'm losing my mind.* A bird must have landed on the roof. Thamton must have closed his door across the way, and it's so quiet, it sounded like mine. That's the most plausible explanation.

Crouching down, I force more air into my chest. They've never followed me. All these weird lapses I'm having . . . they've only ever happened in the tower. Not here. I'm losing it.

No, it was just Thamton. My mind strains and my body tenses and Thamton lives too far—

No, he doesn't. He closed his door hard. That's all.

I shove the table aside, pull up the weird panel, and snatch the fake artifact, wanting it out of my sight, only to notice something that freezes me to the floor. There, engraved on its metal edge, small and precise, glints a rhombus with one line cutting through the top, and two smaller, parallel lines in the center. It's not an Ancient symbol. It's the same one I scrawled on the bottom of my plans for the water rover.

It's mine.

Heartwood is sick again.

I arrive at the tower a little early, eager to get my mind off the machine in my house. My attention latches on to him, desperate to focus on anything besides my discovery. Heartwood withdraws when I arrive, but the hunch in his shoulders and the straining of his breaths give him away. After he's gone, I ask Moseus, "What's wrong with him?"

"He's too long from home," the older man replies. I don't *know* that he's older; he just seems it. Though perhaps his illness ages him. "It happens from time to time. Nothing for you to concern yourself with."

"I didn't intend to." I wince at the defensiveness in my tone.

Moseus doesn't seem to notice. "Good."

He makes no comment about my absence the last two mists, so neither do I. "I'm looking more at Machines Two and Three this cycle," I offer. I haven't explained my numbering system to him, but it's not hard to figure out. Machine One is on floor one, Machine Two on floor two, Machine Three on floor three. By that pattern, there should be a machine each on floors four and five, but who knows what the Ancients might have crafted up there.

He sighs. "There is much to do. I can't . . . I don't understand enough to put the third back together."

After I get to work trying to unstick that arm beneath Machine Two, I realize I lied. I do concern myself with Heartwood. Namely after he leaves his room and descends the stairs, steps light, brow drawn, eyes focused. Extricating myself, I follow like a scorpion tracking a beetle, until he exits the tower. I stare at the door, debating with myself, but return upstairs and look out the window instead, his silhouette just discernible in the mist. Heading off the same direction as before, not to a privy or a well.

Arthen's knife feels heavy in my pocket. *Where are you going, Heartwood?*

I mull over it until I successfully pull a lever—more like a brake release—for the hinged arm, and as I suspected, Machine Two shifts away from the wall. Not by much, but enough for a person to get back there. I follow the seams, positive they outline a door in the wall. They're perfectly square, each a meter long. But *if* this is a door, its hinges are on the reverse side, and there's no handle or knob. The only other marking is a natural divot in the stone near the top seam, without real shape or meaning.

I push, knock, and attack it with an array of tools. The stone doesn't even chip. Did the Ancients make stone alloys, too? More uncertain questions with no feasible answers.

At least nothing in this tower assaults me with waking dreams.

Frustrated, I climb the ladder to the third floor and the mess of mechanics there, my thoughts insufferably pulling to Heartwood once more. Why did he try to stop me before?

Trying to shake my confusion, I organize what I can. Rivets here, gears there, bars that could be one of a dozen things over there, by size. By the time the mist nears its end, I haven't gotten very far, and Heartwood hasn't returned.

At least Moseus rewards me with another scrap bag.

The sun burns through the last of the fog as I get to Emgarden, but I pause on the way home, seeing several people out in the streets, shouting and milling about. I hop the broken stone wall around town and spy the doctor, Amlynn. I wave her down.

"What's going on?" I ask, lowering my bag of goodies to the earth.

"Casnia," she explains, and my spine immediately stiffens. "She's missing."

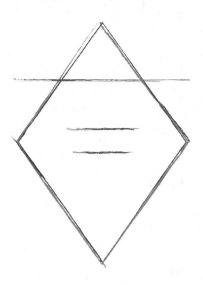

Chapter 9

Sometimes Casnia wanders. It's just something she does. She never gets farther than the fields, though. And it only takes a few people to find her.

Half of Emgarden floods the streets.

Trying to keep rising panic down, I ask, "When?"

Amlynn shakes her head. "Gone at least an hour. Salki said she was throwing a fit at first sun, so she went on a walk to give her space. When she got back, Casnia was gone."

"In the mists?" Casnia never ventures out in the mists.

Amlynn frowns. "Keep your eye out. It won't go well for Salki to lose another so soon."

And it won't go well for Casnia to get lost in the unforgiving dust.

Abandoning my bag, I run for Salki's home, passing several people calling Casnia's name. I know the house will have been searched, but I let myself in. Salki isn't home. The single-room house isn't much bigger than mine, but I search it anyway, looking for any clues. With so many people about, Casnia might have gotten frightened and hid. She's done it before.

I find only more of her drawings, as well as her art supplies. She didn't take them with her.

"Piss and Ruin," I mutter under my breath, hurrying back outside. The last time Casnia ran was when Ramdinee died. I can't fathom why she'd wander off now. I take the ladder up to Salki's roof and shield my eyes from the sun, scanning the town. For a moment I'm sure I've spotted Casnia, but it's only Balfid's wife, who also has dark hair. Hurrying down, I jog through the streets, calling Casnia's name, pausing at windows to see if she let herself into another home or tucked herself away in a shed. Casnia's either exploring or settling into a quiet, safe spot.

Safe spot. Turning on my heel, I dash back to my own house. Throw open the door, but Casnia isn't here. She wouldn't fit in the tiny cupboards, and though there's no lump on my bed, I throw back the covers anyway. I even look beneath the panel in the floor, though it's too small to hold anyone larger than a baby. Nothing.

Back outside, up my ladder, onto my roof. *"Cas!"* I shout, looking out. Folk mill outside the town limits, searching the dry, rusty expanse. Others retrace their steps. They'll have already combed through the alehouse. I try to get a better vantage point by standing on my toes. Determine where Casnia would have gone in the mist. But I can't even see Salki's house from here.

Frustrated, I curl my hands into fists, nails digging into my palms as I turn and scan.

In the distance, I see the tower.

And though the sun burns and the fog is hours away, I slide down the shingles, jump to the road, and take off for Moseus's home, sun be damned.

The somber first floor greets me without a sound. Moseus's closed door indicates he's likely sleeping or meditating. Taking the stairs two at a time, I huff up to the second floor, seize the ladder, and throw it out the window. Take up my rope and hurry down, out, and around the tower. Climb. My steps are a little surer this time, the stone a bit dryer, and I scale two and a half stories before looping my rope around the protrusion. I climb atop it, then a little higher. I have to jump four times before I can hook my hands over the top of the tower and pull myself up. Years of dust, sticky from years of fog, cling to the stone and to me. I stand and shield my eyes.

I can see all of Emgarden from here. It looks so small. There's an enormous cluster of emilies to the north, in between jutting rock formations that block my view. The amaranthine wall is a thin, straight ribbon of pink disappearing into either horizon. Dry earth in shades of red and brown extends for kilometers on kilometers on kilometers, interrupted only by the occasional rock formation, which would provide a shady sanctuary to hide in, but I don't think Casnia could have gotten that far already. She's slow.

I search for anything moving farther from Emgarden. I see something in the direction of the wall, but is that a tree, a searcher, or Casnia?

It's somewhere to start.

As I climb down, arms shaking with the effort, my sight blanks out for just a moment, **and suddenly I'm sitting on the rim of the protrusion, my feet dangling down, wind catching my hair.** I gasp, and it's gone. Just me pressed up against the tower.

Lowering myself to the protrusion, I stare out at it. *What?* I want to scream. *Do you want me to sit out there? Is that a sign for something?*

It seems stupid. I almost climb down. Then, with a grunt, I tighten the rope around my waist and sidestep to the end of the protrusion, cautious, careful. Sit the way I'd just seen. Inspect the view.

But there's nothing new to see, and there's no breeze. Nothing. Frustrated, I pick my way back down, forcing myself to move slowly so I don't plummet to my death.

When I push open the door to drop off the ladder, Moseus waits inside. Wait—no. That's Heartwood. The breadth of his jaw and shoulders give him away, but he's wearing a black cloak similar to Moseus's robe.

"Did you find something?" he asks.

"Nothing," I spit, ripping the rope from my body and tossing it to the ground. "I have to go. Casnia is missing."

I'm ready for a discourse about coming during the sun, but instead he asks, "Someone from Emgarden?"

I pause at the doors. "Yes. She's . . . she's different. Her mind doesn't work the way ours does. She can't make it on her own. I climbed up there to see if I could spot her."

He glances toward the open door. "That explains the town's activity."

I step out.

"What does she look like?"

Hand on the door handle, I pause. Study him. There's no malice or treachery in his countenance. He's fairly well masked, but a line of concern mars his forehead, and that sadness endures in his eyes. I realize, too, that he's hale again, standing straight, no shadows to his face. Odd.

"I thought you two didn't want to be seen," I counter, though we can use all the help we can get.

He considers this. "I will be discreet." Then, after a beat, "Do not tell Moseus."

My lungs push out a heavy, grateful breath. "She's short. Shorter than me, and more heavy-set. Round face, short black hair."

"Like yours?"

"Shorter. If . . . if you find her, bring her to the village. Or even back to the tower, just somewhere safe. If the mist settles . . . my house is just inside the northwest perimeter."

"I know it."

I pause at that, but of course he does, if Moseus knew where to find me. I nod to him once and hurry outside. Heartwood follows. He hesitates as I start east, before pulling the hood of his cloak over his telltale white hair and heading around the tower to search west.

I should have brought water with me, but I didn't. I'll deal. I pace myself, knowing I'll be no use to anyone if I burn out early and can't search anymore. It's critical we find Casnia before the turn of the fog, because we'll have to stop searching once it falls. It's one thing to navigate Emgarden in the mist; it's another to find your way out in the wilds, with no clear markers to guide you.

I'm able to jog for nearly half an hour before a stitch in my side and fire in my throat force me to slow. One minute to catch my breath, then I jam a knuckle into the pain under my rib and keep moving. "Casnia!" I call between pants. Far off, I hear an echo of the name. It sounds like Frantess, but I can't be sure. I have nothing on me to tell the time, but I imagine we're at mid sun, halfway through the light. Halfway to the mists.

Sweat drips from my temples, underarms, and back. I cup swelling hands around my mouth.

"Cas! Cas!"

The only response I get is shuddering of the earth under my feet. A few pebbles dance, then settle, leaving the red-rock world around me eerily quiet. I trudge on. A dry weed catches my foot, making me stumble. I skid down to one knee, hitting a lone emily, so the damage isn't too bad. Picking myself up, I turn slowly, scanning, searching for movement.

"Cas!"

A desert wren shoots off from a copse of wickwood trees. I head toward that, closer still to the amaranthine wall. Hope dies when I see nothing between the skinny, twisted trunks.

Wiping sweat from my eyes, I scream as loud as I can: "*Cas!*"

And hear, almost immediately, another cry: "Cas!"

Salki.

The voice echoes south of me. Pushing against the stitch, I run in that direction, over a swell in the dry earth, avoiding a snake hole. Minutes later I see movement in the distance, and as I close in, I see two women wrestling. The light-haired one is Salki, the dark-haired one . . . Casnia.

Thank the gods. I increase my speed, spying Maglon running out from the direction of Emgarden. I'm breathless when I arrive.

Casnia struggles against Salki's grip. She has *never* fought Salki, especially not physically. Salki cries, "Cas, stop! Please!" Tears stream from her eyes.

Strategically collapsing to my knees in front of Casnia, I put my hands on her shoulders. Her eyes meet mine. My lungs desperately suck in air. I shake my head.

"But!" Casnia cries, her tears matching Salki's. "Empty, empty!"

"Cas, please," Salki begs, and when Casnia tires, the older woman gathers her into her arms and holds her close. "It's not safe. Don't leave! You can't leave!" She sobs into Casnia's shoulder, and my heart cracks at the sight. Maglon reaches us, his tunic drenched. He stalls, unsure what to do.

"It's okay," I rasp, patting Casnia's back. "She's okay."

Maglon says, "I can carry her back."

"Empty," Casnia sobs, barely intelligible. "Empty, empty."

Tears leave uneven trails on her dust-strewn face, but she allows Salki to pull her to her feet and says nothing more when Maglon lifts her onto his back. We make the long walk back to Emgarden together.

Once Casnia and Salki are settled, I retreat to my house for a long drink, a quick scrub, and a change of clothes. I grab some jerky to take with me before retrieving my bag of scraps and tossing it in the shed.

The mist has descended by the time I reach the tower. Inside, I search for Heartwood, but he's not there, so I return to the doors to wait, chewing hard enough to make my jaw hurt.

About fifteen minutes later, I see him.

"Did you—" he begins, out of breath.

"We found her," I say over him, and a weariness settles into my bones. "She's okay. Thank you for helping us."

Heartwood's vivid eyes shift back and forth as they study my face. He stops two paces from me, like he's tethered to something and physically can move no closer. We stand there, an unnameable awkwardness between us, and I feel oddly exposed. I check my sash and belt to ensure

I'm not. Several seconds pass before I thank him again and turn inside. Pick up the ladder and drag it with me, forcing my eyes forward.

On the third floor, I pick out larger structural pieces and start guessing at where they fit. The pattern of joists in the foundation helps me. The larger beams would be much easier to maneuver with another person, and I consider asking Heartwood, but stubbornness keeps me going, and with some shouldering, I get things where they need to go, securing them loosely, in case I'm wrong and need to pull them apart again. After that, I climb down to Machine Two, shift it away from the wall, and work on the pieces in the back, taking a few things apart, wondering at the wheel near the power switch, and measuring parts to determine the feed rate of a spindle.

I still grip the ratchet as I lean my head against the cool door behind the machine. I don't recall closing my eyes, but mind and body give out all at once, and I'm soon fast asleep.

I wake to a sunlit room and an awful taste in my mouth, a crick in my neck, and a numb backside. Carefully I sit up, hissing as my body protests. Chill bumps cover my skin. The stone has zapped every trace of warmth from my body. Arching, my back pops twice. I hold my breath.

That's when I hear their voices. Moseus and Heartwood, on the first floor. Pulling myself up, I move toward the stairs, quiet on my feet. I realize Moseus, at least, does not know I'm here.

"—dangerous to involve yourself." Moseus's voice dips so low I can barely discern his words.

"I know," Heartwood replies.

"We cannot repeat mistakes. No matter the reason."

A long pause, and then, quiet as the mist, "I know."

They move away from the stairs, and I can no longer hear them. I pull away, back toward Machine Two. *Repeat mistakes.* What mistakes? And the involvement—did he mean with Casnia's search, or something else? My skin pebbles anew, sending a shiver across my shoulders and down my spine.

I want to ask. I've never shied from confrontation. And yet not knowing how either tower keeper will react to my eavesdropping concerns me. Emgarden needs the scrap metal. I'm not ready to leave these machines. Moseus made it sound like there was no one else who could help, and while I could lean on that . . . I determine it would be better to play it safe.

Still, it's not *my* fault they didn't keep tabs on me, so I resume my work on Machine Two as though nothing happened.

It's not until I've finished my calculations that I realize they'd been speaking in another tongue, and yet somehow, I understood every word.

Chapter 10

"I need a tool."

Moseus looks up from a *very* old and damaged book in his lap as I approach. I wonder where he got it. Books are rare. Expensive and hard to make. He sits in his room, the door propped open. A lamp gleams from the wall outside.

With a raised brow, he explains, "You're welcome to whatever you can find—"

"It's not a tool either of us has." Entering the dim room, I hand him my slate. Retreat for that lamp, but his eyes must be sharp because he reads my scrawl and diagram just fine. "I need something in this specific shape, with a head like this." I point. "It's the only way I'll be able to attach the flywheel on Machine Three." If it could telescope, that would be even better, but I'm not about to push my luck.

"I haven't seen anything like this in the tower." Moseus's words are measured, as always, but I detect a flare of annoyance. He passes the slate back, then rubs the space between his eyes. He must be feeling worse than usual.

"The blacksmith in Emgarden, he could make it within a cycle, I think—"

"I do not want to involve your blacksmith. Not again." Moseus closes his book and sets it aside. "Show me." A second passes. "Please."

I walk him up to the third floor, where I've gotten Machine Three looking like . . . well, a shape, whereas before it was . . . not as good a shape. Heartwood has come up in my absence and studies the machine, somehow looking paler than usual. He and Moseus exchange a tense glance, and I wonder if they've argued. I also wonder about the words I overheard before—*past mistakes*—but I try not to read too much into it. Speculating won't get me anywhere.

I show Moseus the flywheel and the frame I assembled for it, then gesture to the pieces of machine embedded in the ceiling. Explain as best I can the mechanics of it, and yes, I've already tried alternatives, and yes, I really do need a special tool, and no, I can't carve it out of wood.

"Perhaps she should spend her time elsewhere," Heartwood murmurs. He doesn't look my way.

"Perhaps she should fix the damn thing," I retort, earning myself an approving look from Moseus, and . . .

Why does Heartwood always look so . . . sad?

Soft feelings, I tell myself. Some people just have thicker skin than others. I probably offended Entisa every other sun. She was like that. Soft.

I inhale slowly, letting the air fill every crevice. "If you two don't have a way to make what I need, I can't fix it. Arthen is trustworthy. He didn't make a fuss about the handle for Machine One. I don't have to give him a lot of detail. Send me home with more scrap, and he won't complain."

"Arthen?" Moseus repeats.

Before I can reply, Heartwood answers, "The blacksmith."

I wonder when I told him about Arthen, then realize it was an easy deduction. I recall the knife still weighing down my pocket. I try to school my face as I study Heartwood, but I'm even worse at hiding my feelings than he is, and I look away before my stupefaction reveals me.

"Also, this." I move to a turbine two-thirds as tall as me. Grab one end and heave so its exposed center faces the men. "This needs to turn." I point to an axle I've managed to fortify with some fasteners. "But it's missing . . . something that goes here." I point to where a belt should be, or something like that, probably protected in a box or other casing. "I've dug through this mess twice and haven't found it."

"And you haven't taken it?" Moseus asks me, though he pointedly looks at Heartwood as the words leave his mouth. Heartwood's lips press into a thin line.

Straightening, I scowl. "Yes, Moseus. I decided to take some random pieces necessary for fixing the machine, and then to ask you for them. No, I didn't take them. The way you've kept this space, I wouldn't be surprised if one got knocked out the window."

Because really, it's a mess in here.

One of the aforementioned windows now fully occupies Heartwood's attention.

Moseus sighs. "See what you can do. Ask your smith for the tool. Be—"

"Discreet," I finish for him. "I will be, though no one in Emgarden is jumping at the chance to get their fingers in your machines." Except me, and my fingerprints cover every millimeter of them.

"Please do so." Moseus resumes his tranquility. "Before the mist lifts."

Slate under my arm, I nod, deciding to leave my tools here in the interim. Toes of my shoes on the edges of the ladder, I slide down, calculating the order of what I should fix.

I'm halfway to the stairs when the **explosion** hits.

My first reaction, for a shaving of a second, is that it's another earthquake. But the earsplitting noise, the shaking, emanates from above. Shrieking, I drop to my knees just as I reach the ladder, covering my head with my arms—

The piercing sound of silence drills into my ears, interrupted only by the thumping of my heart. I lift my head. No rubble around me. No damage. Lowering my arms, I twist back—

Just Machine Two and the ladder. No rubble, no smoke—just the garish hole carved into the ceiling.

Or . . . was it blasted into it?

"Pelnophe?" Moseus calls down from the hole in question.

My breaths are too fast. I'm light-headed. I force myself to drop my shoulders and suck in long gulps of air. "S-Spider," I manage. I'd wince at the awful lie, but I'm too distracted.

I . . . I *heard* an explosion. I felt it. I . . . I don't understand. My eyes water, and I don't understand.

Heartwood descends a few rungs of the ladder. "What happened?"

Swallowing, scrounging for my voice, I ask, "Did . . . did a quake pass, just now?"

His pale brows draw together. He shakes his head.

"Slipped," I chirp, sounding young. "Slipped. Spider. Bye."

I practically run down the stairs, grateful for the masking darkness of the first floor. Finding peace in it, like Moseus does. I stop at the doors, my palms pressed against them, without strength.

I never realized madness could be so loud.

I wait for Arthen to dunk a chest latch in his bucket of water before handing him my slate. My hands are still shaking, so I thrust it at him, hoping he won't notice. "I need this. Sooner than later. And no, I'm not waiting my turn. I'm the reason you can make latches."

"It's a hinge." He pulls his gloves off and takes my slate. I count one, two . . . ooh, even a *third* line furrows his brow. "What is this for?"

"Personal use."

He glances at me.

I shrug. The long walk from the tower only settled me so much; the rest I have to fake. "Ancients stuff. I'm piecing together something big. Come on, Arthen. You owe me."

"Do I?" He tips his head toward the back of the shop.

I scan in that direction, confused, until I see the frame of the rover. All my trepidation washes clear, like loam in the first strike of groundwater.

"Serpent save me, you didn't!" I rush over and crouch on the packed-dirt floor, running my hands over the beautiful rover. It's not refined or elegant like Ancient work, but it's solid. "It's not even the yearmark."

"Don't give me nonsense about debts." Setting the slate on his table, Arthen pulls his gloves back on. "I'll get on it before first mist. Just keep bringing me what I need."

"You've got it, you beautiful man, you." I rub his sweaty bald head. He elbows me in my side. Dancing away, I practically skip my way home.

But once there, alone again, thoughts of the tower drip in. That explosion . . . none of my lapses have ever been so . . . violent. And what does it mean? I swallow hard, twice. Right where the hole up to the third floor was. Didn't it seem to come from that?

I wish I hadn't asked Heartwood about the quake. If I hadn't asked, I could believe that's all it was. A quake.

I should visit Salki. See how she's doing after the scare with Casnia, and for my own sanity. But hunger tugs my stomach and drains my limbs, so it's only a thought in the back of my mind as my lunch grains soak. While I wait, I move the table, open the hidden panel in the floor, and pull out my mystery machine, studying it anew. Even after my meal is ready, I continue my examination, noting something at the base of the sphere in the center. Specifically, the angle at which the rod holds it up.

My lips part. I walk to the cupboard where I keep my other finds and pull out my newest one, not counting the thing under my floorboard, nor the sundial. It's a brass ball joint welded to a hollow metal cylinder with ridging, the same one I was studying the mist of Entisa's burial. The lip on the cylinder suggests it once connected to something else. I'm certain the piece holding up the sphere in equilibrium would fit perfectly there. Part of that strange device was harvested from this artifact.

I'd already determined this new machine was pieced together modernly. Either by me, followed by some mystical head injury no one talks about, or by someone who knows the symbol I invented for myself. A symbol I've only used on my rover plans, which have only been seen by Arthen, Salki, and, I suppose, Casnia.

Did someone leave this for me? But why make it so hard to find? Perhaps I wasn't meant to find it yet. But why? And . . . when?

Someone was here.

I set the artifact down and stare at my door. Sorry, Salki, I won't be visiting you. I'm heading back to the blacksmith.

Only this time, I'm asking him for a lock.

I need answers. I need to understand what's happening to me.

I want to know where Heartwood is going.

He's kept his distance the last seven cycles—all of which passed without any more lapses, two of which I spent starting a new well—but I've been watching. His energy started waning a couple of cycles ago, so I've been pulling long shifts, even working a full sun, which Moseus doesn't mind. Just means I'm fixing the tower faster.

I can tell when Heartwood plans to leave. He wears those leathers of his and carries a satchel. His cloak as well. When the mist settles, he leaves.

This time, I follow.

I'm fortunate that Moseus isn't present to witness. I give Heartwood enough of a lead that he won't hear the heavy tower door open, then I head northwest, the direction I've seen him go before. Away from the tower, away from the town. Everything quiets in the mist, so I walk on the balls of my feet, trying to mask my presence.

I find his shadow ahead of me. Wait for him to reroute to Emgarden. Maybe to slip into the forge and steal another knife. Yet Heartwood's path stays true, never circling back.

So much for that theory.

I've ventured all over this area looking for artifacts, though I've spent most of my time south of Emgarden, where I've had the most luck uncovering them, so this terrain eventually becomes unfamiliar. After nearly an hour, I pause at a copse of wickwood trees to gain my bearing. The moment I touch one, though, it crumbles to ash. Not just the branch beneath my fingers, but the entire plant, leaving only a few decimeters of narrow trunk standing. Pulling away, I rub fine umber dust between my fingers. Gently poke the next tree, only to have a sprig of it crumble the same way. I've never seen anything fall apart like this, especially not these hardy trees. Pressing my lips together, I don't test it more. I can't risk the sound of disintegrating trees giving me away, though the sight of piles of wickwood—crooked, thirsty things, but still a valuable resource—unsettles me. Perhaps I should turn back.

The veil of fog makes the journey all the more disconcerting, pierced only by the faint glow of the occasional emily. Doubling down, I leave the ashen corpse of the tree and hurry forward. I lose Heartwood twice as high mist rolls in, but the moisture helps to mark his footprints in the ground, and for a time, I follow those instead.

The mist lightens up. It's a mercy of the gods that I'm staring at the ground. If I hadn't been, I might have fallen.

There's a canyon here.

Not a large one. I can't determine how deep, but it's not wide, and it's shielded by rock formations. No more footprints. Did Heartwood climb down this?

I backtrack, squinting through the mist, but I can't fathom where else he might have gone. Taking a risk, I pull out the small lantern from the tower. Light it, which makes me a beacon in the fog. But it helps me see a little better.

There's a path. Uneven steps in the stone, some natural, some not.

A patient person would mark this, head back, and come again in the sun. Unfortunately, patience has never been my forte, so down I go.

But I'm not stupid. I move slowly, keeping one hand on the carmine rock wall. My luck holds; it's not terribly deep. Maybe seven meters.

I blow out the lantern. Down here, the mist lightens, and I can see better without the light. Following the narrow path, I realize I've entered a slot canyon. How it was formed, I don't know. But the ground proves level, so I walk until I reach a fork. Search for footprints, but there's only stone.

Something in my gut tells me to go right. A shiver courses down my spine.

I'm not stupid. I mark the wall with charcoal and move forward.

The path dips lower, perhaps ten meters below the surface, then up again. Another fork, but an easy one—the right path ends after ten paces. The left dips toward an arch. I duck down to fit under it.

The mist starts to lift. Have I been wandering so long? And there's no sign of Heartwood. But—

I nearly drop my lamp. *Serpent save me.*

It's . . . beautiful.

The stone walls open up to a small gorge surrounded by red rock. Brimming with plants. Not wickwood, or kettleleaf weeds, or even emilies, but green, vibrant *life*.

There are flowers, a deep pink, as vivid as the amaranthine wall. Succulent trees sprout up along a winding path. White-centered desert roses nest in carefully tended soil, alongside yellow-budding brush I have no name for. Round cacti pop up in patches, and a verdant vine curtains up one of the walls, reaching for the dispelling fog.

And there's *water*.

I walk to the spring and kneel beside it. Like the stairs leading down here, it looks half-natural, half-man-made. The rock has been chipped away to create a pool, shaded by a sandstone outcropping. But the water sits, bizarrely, at surface level. It's almost green, and when I reach down and brush it with my fingers, it's warm, with a faint sulfuric smell. The green shifts to a deeper and deeper blue the deeper it goes. One hand on the outcropping, I lean forward to peer into its strange depths. I've never seen a natural well like this. Never seen water I didn't have to dig for. Never seen this shade of turquoise. It's breathtaking.

"Pell."

Heartwood's crisp voice startles me. I twist to face him, but in doing so, I lose my footing, and there's nothing to grip. I glimpse a sliver of leather-clad shoulder before Tampere reaches up and swallows me. I fall headfirst, water rising up, sucking me into its warm depth—far deeper than I realized. I kick to right myself and reach up, only to strike my knuckles on rock. The spring dips below the crags. I can't find the surface, and I'm not a good swimmer. Wells are deep, but narrow. If I slip in one of those, I just have to stick my foot out to catch the side . . .

The first spike of panic shoots down my neck when a hand clamps around my arm, just above my elbow, and hauls me up. Turquoise depths give way to sunlit red rock as I fly upward nearly as swiftly as I'd fallen in. Heartwood deposits me, gasping and blinking, right next to the lip of the pool.

He crouches in front of me. "Are you all right?"

I nod, water dripping from my hair. I couldn't have been under for more than a few seconds.

Mechanically, Heartwood releases my elbow and sits back on his haunches.

I first rub my eyes, then slick my hair back from my face. Clear my throat. Piece together my pride. Glare from the walls of the gorge casts stark shadows on Heartwood's face, making it hard to read his expression. So much for staying clandestine.

I rise to my feet, my clothing heavy. He does as well, saying nothing as I wring out the front of my shirt. I steel myself, though I didn't technically do anything wrong. I glance at the exit, though if Heartwood wanted to off me, he could have just let me drown. Not that I would have. I could have felt my way out before I ran out of air. I'm fairly certain.

"I wanted to know where you were going," I say, squeezing water from fistfuls of my soggy slacks. I expect an outburst, or perhaps a cold demand that I leave. Maybe a sharp retort about my fall. But to my shock, Heartwood simply nods.

"You are welcome to stay, if you wish."

I'm momentarily dumbfounded. New drops of water drizzle down either side of my nose. "You . . . I can?"

Slowly, his gaze settles over the garden. "I ask only that you approach with care. It's difficult to cultivate these plants. I'd prefer you not share this location with your townsfolk, if only to protect them. And, perhaps, stay away from the spring."

Did he make a *joke*? I stare at him like I'm seeing him for the first time. "Of course. Thank you. I . . ." I take in the garden once more. It seems even more resplendent without the mists, like the sunlight has speckled everything with gold. "I've never seen anything like it."

Heartwood flinches. I glance at him, but he doesn't meet my eye. Then again, he hasn't been feeling well, though at the moment he appears hale.

"I'll leave you to it." He starts for the arch.

"You can stay," I blurt, awkwardness itching my skin. Or maybe that's the wet clothing. "I mean, it's *your* garden, and I came uninvited."

The slightest tick of his lip, and for the first time, a glimmer of warmth comes to his eyes. "Thank you, but I think I will hunt."

"There's not much to hunt."

"But there is something," he counters. Turns for the arch. Stops of his own volition. "Pell."

I can't help it. Maybe it's the swift rescue, the beauty of the gully, or his utter generosity when, if the situation were reversed, I would be raging at the invasion of privacy. In an offer of peace, I say, "You can call me *Nophe*, if you want."

Heartwood's expression shifts, warm and cool at the same time, like the first settling of the fog. Sad again, as though the weight of his own tombstone burdens his shoulders. His voice softens as he speaks. "I would ask . . . do not tell Moseus you came here."

That surprises me. "He doesn't know about it?"

"He does. But . . ."

And that's all the explanation I get. Heartwood disappears through the arch, leaving me to the splendor of his carefully cultivated piece of paradise.

Chapter 11

I spent a full sun in Heartwood's garden.

After he left, I walked the dirt path winding through it, ten paces to its western edge, thirteen back to the pool. I walk it several times, drying my clothes, discovering something new on each pass. I trace a sweet, earthy smell to a plant I don't recognize, with long spiky leaves and deep-violet flowers. There *are* wickwood trees here—two of them. I didn't recognize them before because I've never seen wickwoods this green. Judging by their size, they were here before Heartwood commandeered the gorge, but they, too, have been well tended. Everything is, for none of it would survive otherwise. Our crops alone require constant supervision and hand-watering. He must care for this oasis a great deal.

Comfortably damp, I find myself under one of the wickwoods, next to a budding sage bush that fills the air with scents of spice. Outside the shadows of the few stone outcroppings, it's the shadiest part of the garden. The sun shining through the branches casts patterns like lace on the ground. It makes me think of the sundial, but I put that aside and enjoy the beauty of it all, dozing off once, waking to the chirping of a desert wren.

I remember what Moseus had told me, about his people's names. They were called after their . . . what was it? Animus. Their purposes. Moseus had called himself a peacekeeper. He sought out peace, stillness, often meditating without distraction. Did that bolster him somehow? Heal him? If it did, perhaps Heartwood likewise needed something like this garden—something I've never seen elsewhere on Tampere—to find the same solace. That would explain why, whenever he returned, he seemed in good health.

What would my animus be? What recharges me? The earth? Water? The machines . . . I do have an affinity for them. And people. I like being around people. Perhaps I feel so outside myself lately because I'm not visiting Salki as often, or conversing with others at the alehouse, or waiting out the mists with Arthen or Maglon. Yet none of those ring true. I am not a machine, and I don't want to be named after one. Neither am I a person to be shaped by others. Which brings me back to earth and water. I suppose, in the end, I am a digger, carving holes into the ground to bring life or hide death. In that sense, I'm a shepherd of spirits, and I don't mind the lofty metaphor. Not here, where I'm surrounded by so much beauty.

Eventually I sit up, brushing an ant off my leg, and shake air into my sticky shirt, loosening the sash. I follow the garden path to its far end, where the slot canyon continues. Charcoal ready to mark my path, I follow it, sating my curiosity despite knowing it must be well into late sun by now. But I've never seen these sandstone channels, and everything around Emgarden is so stagnant, always the same. I want to explore.

At one point, the way gets so narrow I can barely squeeze through sideways. It forks again, and I choose right. Climb up a shallow rise and find myself off to the side of a small mesa. I'm circling it, wondering if I can climb up, when I hear the tone.

It's so loud, here. In Emgarden, when I catch it, I can excuse it as a ringing in my ears. No one else seems to notice the one-note song. Even out here, the desert wren's call has more weight to it, but I hear the note so crisply and clearly, I cannot deny it. It calls to me.

One hand on the mesa, I look out to the Brume Mountains, where they curve to cradle the country Emgarden rests upon. There must be something about the elevation, or the angle at which I watch, but I see the mist appear over the rough peaks. See it rise from one in particular, billowing upward in a column like steam from a kettle, measured and precise.

The thought forms so easily: the tone doesn't match the single note Machine One made when I got it moving, but it's similar. That sound, the formation of the mist itself, my mind names it *machine*, without any further evidence. Of course the mists come from machines. It makes sense, doesn't it? And yet I'm not startled by this revelation in the slightest.

And *that* scares me.

The next time the mist comes around, I return to Machine Three.

I sketch out what I think it may look like, drawing several iterations. Some of the loose pieces fit together, so I work on those, then sort out how they might fit into the machine itself. It's an enormous and frustrating puzzle, but I learn more about the Ancients' technology each cycle.

There's a coupling in this foundation, and after some searching, I'm confident I've found the shafts that connect to it. Those components all attached to a gear network that fits what I've already installed. With a grunt, I lift the thing into place, then reach to set the gears—

I whip my hand back. Blood pools in my palm and trickles down my wrist. Damn it, I should have been more careful.

I hold the hand up as I untangle myself from Machine One, trying not to get blood on it. Great, this will make the next few cycles real fun. I know I shouldn't press a dirty rag to it, but that's what I have, so that's what it gets.

I'm choking on curses in the back of my throat when two pale hands gently take my own injured one. Remove the rag, clean the wound, expertly wind dark bandages around my palm—

Air rushes out of me all at once.

It takes several seconds before I realize I'm on the floor, staring up at the ceiling. A small sprocket pokes my thigh. I don't remember falling. I stare, and stare a little longer, before pushing myself upright.

My hands shake.

"What is happening to me?" I whisper, pressing unscathed palms together. My fingers are colder than the stone floor. My blood pumps quick and hot. My pulse thrums beneath my skull.

Something is wrong with me. Something is wrong with these machines.

Then I'm on my feet, retreating from the half-formed behemoth, tripping over a steel coil. I'm not tired. This isn't lack of sleep. I was awake when I saw . . . whatever I saw. I'm always awake when I see it. And I've never seen *this much* before.

What is it? A mental lapse? A *vision*? Of what, the past? The future? It's not nothing. Once, it told me how to repair a piece of Machine One, and it worked. *It worked.*

"Ancients save me." No, not the Ancients. They're *doing* this to me. Somehow, their technology is messing with my head. Their *magic*, though I hesitate to believe in such a thing.

Reaching the window, I inhale deeply, letting curls of mist into my lungs. Stiff, I turn back to Machine Three. It's just as I left it. Unfinished, lifeless. A mystery.

The Ancients were powerful beings. The first created by the gods. Maybe only powerful people were meant to work on these artifacts. Am I testing the ghosts of those before, tinkering with the tower this way?

Don't be absurd, my mind snaps, but it's already absurd. These machines are doing something to me. Making me see things.

Has the same happened to Moseus? Is that why he can't work on them anymore? I could ask, but what if I'm wrong? What if I'm alone in this madness? He might dismiss me. Why does that thought make me feel sick inside? But I know the answer even before I finish the question.

Something is missing.

This tower fills a void in me, that empty space only ale could occupy before. There's something *here*, something important. I feel it in my bones. And what the machines have shown me . . . none of it is *bad*, necessarily. I saw an injury, yes, but hardly a lethal one. And I saw hands taking care of me.

Pale hands.

Closing my eyes, I rack the memory for details, but I can't recall anything definitive. Whose hands? No one in Emgarden has the same pallor as the keepers of the tower. So was it Moseus, or Heartwood? Or someone else entirely?

When, exactly, is this injury supposed to happen?

I trace my finger down my palm. I have many scars. It comes with the work. One on my right hand could match the injury in the vision. But it's—

I lose my train of thought.

Physically shaking, I storm back to Machine Three, imagining myself bigger and braver than I feel. I glare at the steel girding, the beams and gears.

"Tell me what you are," I whisper. Beg.

The machine does not answer.

I have to know. I *have* to know what these machines do. Why the tower was built. There's an answer here, somewhere. I just need to piece it together. If I can finish the work, these episodes will stop, and I'll know. Something. Anything.

So I climb up the machine and align the gears. They fit in place. This is right. I pick up the next hunk of mechanics and try to attach it, but it's wrong. Up there, maybe? But I'm not ready to work that high. I need to get the base done.

So I pick through a few more pieces. Walk around the machine. I bet these roller bearings go here. The only wheel small enough for this chain attaches over there. There's nowhere to hook the chain, so I just balance it on top. If I move this plate—yes, this three-meter strut could connect here with a few screws. Except it's bent . . . unless I put it in backward, it's going to interfere with those coils.

Frowning, I pick up the slender piece of metal and turn it over in my hands. It's light, despite its length, and shines a dark gray. It's an odd hook-shape, bending almost in the middle. But none of the other struts match that design, and Ancient tech tends to be symmetrical, more or less. I wonder if—

Pausing, I brush my fingers over the angle where the metal bends. Not smoothly, but in four little waves, each slightly smaller than the next. Honestly, it looks like a . . .

I pause. Form my hand into a fist and press it into the indentation. My knuckles are too small to fill it, but the shape matches.

Chills form in my fingers and course up my arms. What kind of creature could be strong enough to bend steel?

And more importantly, now I know that this machine wasn't unfinished. It was broken.

Deliberately.

Chapter 12

I don't return to the tower, nor to Heartwood's garden. I will, but I need time to think.

Because I know who did it.

I mull over this for the thousandth time as I sit, butt right on the dirt, in the corner of the forge, working on the rover as Arthen melts and shapes my latest scraps. He saves small, excess fragments and covertly sets them aside, and I know he's readying some for a new set of darts, but most are being diverted for my pet project. If we can get this rover working, it will help the farmers, which will help all of us.

The rover is a machine I understand. One that doesn't drill into my head and give me flashes of something *other*. In my hands are pure truth: tools, grit, sweat, metal. I made the ceramic pieces myself. They'll wear, but they're supposed to. Something I learned from the tower. A lot of what I'm doing I learned from the tower. I based the motor on a simplified version of the turbine system in Machine One.

I hate these pestering thoughts. They nag and bite like fire ants, and no matter how many times I sweep them away, they return, in numbers, relentless. The earth murmurs beneath me as another gentle quake rolls by, as if to agree with the sentiment.

Hands. I can't remember enough detail about the hands in that . . . vision. But the imprint in the strut is no flight of fancy. Moseus and Heartwood are similar in appearance, yes. But Moseus has a more slender build, more elegant. If that didn't exonerate him, his utter control of his emotions would.

Heartwood left that mark in the strut. His hands are the right size. The mathematician in me says I should measure to be sure, but I know. I *know*.

But I don't understand *why*. Which is one of the reasons I haven't returned to the tower. But that's fine. Emgarden needs me, too. I have other things to do besides tinkering around with millennia-old apparatus until the mist.

"Here." Arthen hands me the last piece I commissioned. The one I made him redo twice, because it didn't fit in the rover. It's cool and still damp from the quenching bucket as I accept it without looking up. I'm grateful. He knows I'm grateful. I'm just focused.

I remember the cycle when Moseus first came to my door, knocking at the height of the mist. Remember the stir of his cool breath as he leaned close to me in the dark of his room. How insistent he was that I help him. How important it was. The tower was the only means he had for getting past the amaranthine wall. For reuniting with his people.

And Heartwood had single-handedly destroyed it.

Had he done more? I dwell on the very first unwanted image the machines pressed into my thoughts: Machine One, in far more pieces than it had been when I first saw it. Was that something to come? Something from another lifetime? I hate trying to sort this out. I'd truly rather throw my head into the wall until my skull cracked.

"When was the last time you slept?" Arthen asks.

I merely hum in response, tightening the nut on the new piece. It's not until then that I realize the rover is, more or less, finished. I want a shell on it, to protect the mechanics from the elements and provide hooks for more pails, but . . . this is it. Just needs wheels.

I sit with the creation, numb, for a long moment.

"Pell?" Arthen prods me with the toe of his boot.

Coming to myself, I shove him away. "I just need wheels."

He helps me turn the thing over—it's heavier than it looks—and brings the wheels over, screwing in the one at the front while I do the two in the back. Then, with the tip of a nail, I carve my mark—a rhombus with three lines—on the underside of the frame.

With a grunt, we right it. I grab a banged-up kettle and pour water into the intake at the back. Wind the machine at the bottom, pull a cord to spark the simple engine. The rover shudders, barks, and rolls forward.

"Serpent bite me." Arthen puts his hands on his hips.

I cry. Almost. Moisture fills my eyes, my throat thickens, my head hurts. But no tears fall. Instead, as the rover picks up speed and exits the forge, I laugh. It hurts to laugh. Chasing after the thing, I stop it before it hits the shop across the road.

We did it. We built it. We made this.

I can do this.

"What in Ruin's hell is that?" Maglon's voice rings down the street. He steps out from the alehouse, wiping his hands on a towel. "Is that the . . . the thing?"

"The thing," I manage, clearing my throat and steadying myself. "This is the thing."

Arthen shows Maglon how to work it while I run to Salki's house. Casnia is sleeping. She hasn't left Salki's side since we brought her back home. She's not all there, but she's not irrational. Her disappearance was an emotional outburst that she didn't understand. Still, Salki moves quickly as I take her to the rover, not wanting to be away long.

Arthen has straightened out the machine and started it up again, so it heads straight down the road. It's as high as my hip and about a meter wide. Will measure wider, once I complete the shell.

"Wow." Salki gapes. Reaches out to touch it as it passes by, only to whip her hand away like it will sting her. "It's really . . . moving on its own?" She bends down, trying to see under the carriage.

"With some water and wires." I beam. I'm tired. Suddenly so very tired, but pride fills my chest, ballooning me up on heavy legs.

More people come out to see it, curious, unconvinced. In a show of bravery, Amlynn sits on the edge of the rover, then shrieks when it carries her off. I built it to hold a lot of weight. It can't move as fast as a man running, for now, but it can outlast one. Future adjustments and iterations will improve the design.

Mist settles in as we put the rover away, ready for its maiden voyage come first sun.

I accept praise and congratulations humbly, if only because I'm tired, and wend my way home, seeing Salki to hers first. I barely remember to lock the door before I drop on my bed and pass out like I've just dug a grave. Which is why, two hours later, I'm reluctant to peel my eyes open when someone knocks on my door.

I know it's Moseus. How I know, I'm not sure. I haven't memorized his knock, and he hates leaving the tower. Yet when I open the door, I'm unsurprised. Merely wave him inside.

"I was coming back next mist." I stifle a yawn with the back of my hand.

"I was concerned." Moseus looks me over. For injury, maybe. He looks hale, like the first mist we met. He stands straighter. His eyes are brighter, less sunken.

"I still have work here," I press. "I can't be at your every beck and call."

He lifts a fine white eyebrow. "I don't recall becking, nor calling."

I smirk, but the half-formed smile swiftly fades. Hugging myself, I peer out the window into the high mist, which obscures nearly everything. "I . . . do need to talk to you. Better here than there."

Moseus folds his arms, his hands disappearing into his black robe. "What is it?"

I gesture to a chair, my eyes straying to the hidden floor panel, then away. "Care to sit?"

"I don't mean to be away long. You understand."

Stepping away from door and window, I decide on straightforwardness as the best method. I don't want to hurt Moseus, but I value truth over his relationship with Heartwood, and I get the sense that he does, too. Still, to be sure, I extend my hand. "May I?"

Confusion limns his brow, but after a moment, he understands and reaches a hand toward mine. His remarkably pale skin contrasts starkly with mine; his walk in the mist has made his touch cold. I expected soft skin and a frail touch, but there's strength in these fingers, more than meets the eye. Still, I take measure of his knuckles, and I know I'm right.

Releasing his hand, I explain, "I thought Machine Three was forgotten by the Ancients, but it wasn't. It was broken. I've found damage." *The literal imprint of a fist, and what kind of a creature can cave steel with his knuckles?* Squaring my shoulders, I add, "Heartwood broke it."

I expect tension in his smooth features, a widening of the eyes, a step back at the news. But Moseus exudes only calmness. "I know."

Okay, *I'll* react that way, then. Louder than I intend, I counter, "What do you mean, *you know?*"

"I need you to fix it, Pell." He leans forward, determined, unruffled. "I will handle Heartwood."

I gape. "You *knew* he destroyed the machine you need to reunite with your people, and you didn't think it necessary to *tell me?*" Heat flares in my belly and licks out toward my limbs.

"Can you fix it?"

Grabbing a fistful of hair, I walk away from him. Release it and pace back. "I think? There is physical damage in the struts, and who knows where else. There's a lot to sift through!" One breath, two, three. "Why? Why would he do such a thing?"

A soft frown pulls at Moseus's lips. "Heartwood can be . . . volatile."

Volatile, great. I love the idea of working in a tower with a man who can just casually snap my femur if I look at him wrong. "He's dangerous?"

"I will worry about Heartwood," he reiterates. "He will not harm you."

Won't he? I almost say. I might have protested further, if I hadn't followed Heartwood into his garden. If he hadn't, oddly enough, welcomed my presence there.

Do not tell Moseus, he'd said. But why?

"Though, it may be in your best interest to give him a wide berth," Moseus adds.

I take a moment to settle myself. *Wide berth.* Why didn't I get this warning sooner? When I first came to the tower, for instance. Shouldn't one of the rules have been, *Stay away from that guy. He's volatile?* And yet Heartwood seemed anything but dangerous in the garden. He hadn't even left a bruise on my arm when he fished me out of that spring.

I work my jaw, my fingers. Ignore a headache blooming between my eyes. "Is there anything else I need to know?"

"Does knowing the reason for the machine's dilapidation alter the means you must take to repair it?"

I stew at that question and grind out, "Not particularly."

"I will handle Heartwood. I need you to fix the machines."

My neck a rusted joint, I nod, and Moseus sees himself to the door. "Next mist," he says, and vanishes into the fog.

As promised, I return to the tower during the next mist. I'm glad to have had a cycle to tamp down my anger, but it simmers around my bones, all the hotter when I get up to the third floor and pick up that bent strut. Moseus will have to concede and let me take it to Arthen, unless I can get the machine working without it. I don't know if Arthen will notice the imprint of a fist. I don't know if he'll have questions.

Always more questions, but never enough answers.

In a bout of fury, I chuck the thing across the room, the metal clamoring loudly against the stone floor. Guess Heartwood isn't the only volatile one in this tower. Repair, repair, repair, but my limitations continuously grow. My victory with the water rover feels paltry in comparison to the dismantled beast before me. How am I supposed to fix what I don't understand?

"If you want to start talking to me again and give me a hint, now's the time to do it," I mutter to the machine. I scoot piles of parts closer to its base, trying to map out their relationships. I'm thinking too far ahead. I know I am. I need to stay in the present. One little step at a time. But I'm overwhelmed. I'm looking at all of this, and I'm drowning in it.

Volatile. Strong enough to bend steel. Fantastic.

I work better when I'm angry. Faster. But I can't utilize that fuel because I'm lost, which only frustrates me more. I'm not gentle with the pieces, but they can handle it. The Ancients built these things strong. Just not strong enough for the people trapped on the other side of the wall.

Maybe they're supposed to stay over there.

I'm grumbling to myself as I shift the entry angle for a spindle feed, wondering if this hunk of machinery is supposed to run off of dreams and emilies, when I hear footsteps on the ladder. I push my socket wrench too hard and it snaps a screw, causing my hand to slam into a plate, and I curse loudly.

"Pell."

Heartwood's voice. Oh, buddy, you do *not* want to talk to me right now. Guess Moseus's suggestion to keep a wide berth wasn't shared with the other keeper.

Ignoring him, I shake out my hand, adjust the damn entry angle, and step back, grabbing a coil despite having no idea where it goes.

He pauses near the center of the room, halfway between the ladder and the machine. "You should not be gone so long without word," he says.

My blood boils hotter. "I'm not your slave," I bite back, setting the coil aside and grabbing a pile of gears. Maybe if I can fit these together on the floor, I'll figure out how they fit in the machine.

"I never said as much. I—we—were merely concerned."

"*Concerned?*" I drop a gear and stand up, glowering. "You're *concerned* for me?" So many venomous words rise in my throat, I almost choke on them. Forcing my attention back to the gears, I say, "Go away, Heartwood. I don't want you anywhere near me or this machine."

He doesn't retreat. "I don't understand."

Now I chuck one of the gears at the wall, feeling a little satisfaction when he starts. "Let me spell it out for you. I have to fix this garbage because *you* broke it. I know you did. I don't know what the hell you are, but I know."

His eyes widen, but he schools his features decently well, minus the eyes and the clenching of his jaw.

I try to turn back to my work, but I can't. Red curls around my vision like mist. Wielding an accusatory wrench, I advance on him. He starts heading back toward the ladder.

"Coward," I spit.

He flinches.

"I don't understand." I march toward him. "If you're so desperate to get these machines working again, why would you do something like this? What's your aim?"

His shoulders tense. He doesn't turn toward me. In the back of my mind, I know I'm walking a thin line, but my fury needs an outlet, and I want answers.

"Is this some kind of sick ploy against Moseus? He's trying so hard, Heartwood. He came and collected me himself. And he knows you're the reason the tower doesn't function. Even before I told him, he knew. I don't know how he has the patience and forgiving nature to keep you around, but I sure wouldn't."

I'm a pace away from him now. As usual, Heartwood remains silent, and the silence makes me rage. How *dare* he ignore me.

"Don't you care?" The thread of emotion leaking into my voice surprises me, and I grow louder to compensate for it. "If I miraculously find some way to put this back together, does it even *mean* anything, or will you just tear it apart again—"

I don't see it coming.

Heartwood lunges, a blur of white and brown. His hand grabs the front of my shirt and yanks me to the side, pressing me against the nearest wall and pinning me with inhuman strength. One fist against my collar, his opposite arm barring both of mine, one long leg pinning my thighs. I am helpless, and with his ghostly features looming over me, I realize how small I am, how stupid. Fear seizes my heart in cold, clamped fingers. Words die in my mouth.

"I broke it," he hisses, "because it took you away from me."

He releases me all at once, and I gasp in air like I've forgotten how to breathe.

Heartwood's sharp eyes peel away from me, and he vanishes down the hole in the floor, never once touching the ladder.

Chapter 13

I slide to the cool stone floor.

What . . . just happened?

I sit for a long time, not looking at anything, not thinking anything, because there is too much to think. The questions cluster and fight for dominance. My emotions swirl in a dark concoction. I still have the wrench in my fist. I let it topple to the floor.

Oddly, the first clear thought that wriggles to the front of my mind is, *He didn't hurt me.*

Overwhelmed me, certainly. Terrified me, yes. It's a wonder my trousers aren't soaked. But I'm unharmed. I can still feel the press of his hand against my collar, but it was never hard enough to bruise. I'm fine.

But I'm not fine.

Cold confusion blows out my anger like a candle. Shivers swirl circles between my shoulder blades. My breath slows. I say the words over and over, forming them soundlessly on my lips, but I don't comprehend them. *Took you away from me. Took you away from me. Took you away from me.*

What does it mean? All I have is an incomplete equation. The questions suffocate me.

Abandoning Machine Three, I take the ladder down, jumping past the last five rungs. I rush to Heartwood's room, uncertain what I'm going to say, only knowing I need more. I throw the door open.

He is not here.

That sensation of being very small returns. I hate it. I've fought against it my entire life, because it's something I can't change. No matter how strong I get, I will always, somehow, be small.

Machine Two watches with disinterest. I start for the stairs, intent on asking Moseus where his counterpart went, but I pause before I reach the first floor. *I will handle Heartwood,* he'd told me, very specifically. I definitely ignored that directive.

Instead, I grab a lantern and steal out into the mist, retracing my way to the slot canyon.

He isn't here.

The mist lifts, and I circle the garden twice. No Heartwood.

I don't have the fire left to chase him. And somehow, I know he won't give me the answers I seek. I don't know how many he even has. I don't *know.*

I kneel by the spring and splash my face with its warm, tangy water. Slick my short hair back, as though it will make it easier to breathe.

I wait.

Two desert wrens descend into the garden, providing me some entertainment. They flit between the wickwood trees, bickering. They fly away when I stand.

I follow the path once more, perching under one of the trees, looking out onto the garden. Breathe deeply the scents of sage and rose and earth. Notice a small pail tucked into the side of the rocky lip of the spring. So I return and fill it, watering the plants one by one, minus the cacti. I don't know if I'll hurt them with water. I don't know that much about plants.

The sun presses heat against my back as I finish. I return to my spot. Lie down in green ground cover of some sort. It's soft, comforting. Even though this garden is his, it's comforting.

I'm unable to unwind my thoughts, but gradually they dissipate, offering me a moment of respite. I should return before the mist settles in. And yet I can't bring myself to move.

The wrens return, deciding I'm not a threat. I watch them for an hour, at least. Flitting, grooming, eating. I absorb the quiet of the gully, imagining myself becoming one with it, growing roots as deep as the emilies', stretching my leaves toward the sun and drinking in its light. Such a simple life. I miss simplicity.

I study the lacework of the spindly trees, following the maze of their branches. Wren song chirps overhead. They've worked out their differences, at least. I wonder—

Turning my head, I blink sunlight from my eyes and stare harder at a knot in the tree. There's a growth there. Thorns? But wickwoods don't have thorns.

Curious, I prop myself up on my elbow and look harder. Then I stand, again spooking the birds. It's only me in the garden when I reach for the growth embedded in the bark and, with two jerks, pull it free.

It's not a growth. It's a gear.

It's a bevel gear, dark bronze and paper thin. Just smaller than the circumference of my hand. I marvel at it. Turn it over in my hand. Trace its teeth—

Breath escapes me. I know what this gear is. More important, I know where it goes.

How it got here is another question to add to the pile. But the gods have blessed me with direction, and I run the entire way back to the tower.

I crawl halfway into Machine Two and loosen three screws to remove a plate guarding the inner workings of its upper quarter. I've wondered about this section, because there's a base component and a shaft that would fit nicely together, but I have nothing to connect them. But this little gear fits in perfectly—it's made of the same alloy, too.

It takes me just a moment to adjust the parts I need and click the bevel gear in, and I'm grinning enough to hurt when it all fits into place. There's a lever just next to the components. Curious, I pull it. It resists. *Oh.* I pull it again, putting my weight into it. Then again, and again. It's powering something, functioning like a water pump.

After six pumps, I search and locate a depression just behind the gear, away from easy sight. I push it.

That upper quarter of Machine Two whirs, and to my shock, a knot of beams near its rear shifts. I watch that knobless door, waiting for it to open. It doesn't.

But the wall next to it does.

Chapter 14

It doesn't grind, quiver, or groan. The stone-faced panel merely slips downward, revealing a room behind it—more like a closet—just tall enough for a person to stand upright. Just wide enough to be comfortable.

I ogle it as I approach. The walls inside are smooth, but . . . there's nothing else. No artifacts, no writing, no knobs or levers. Just a closet, hidden away. But why?

"What is that?"

Moseus's voice startles me. "I don't know. It opened when I replaced a gear in the machine." I step inside, running my hands over the walls. Turn and see two things at once: Moseus marveling, far more expressive than I've ever beheld him, and a handle attached to a cord just inside the lip of the closet, within easy reach. I touch it, glance overhead to more cording, and laugh.

"What?" Moseus hurries over, pressing his hands to the smooth edges of the doorway.

"It's a lift." My words are all breath. I wave him inside, pressing myself hard to one wall to make room. We haven't been this close since meditating in his room. Stiff, I pull the handle, and the *capsule*, not a closet, shifts upward, taking us past the third floor of the tower to the fourth, and no farther.

Machine Four steals my breath away.

She's enormous, occupying two-thirds of the chamber and stretching diagonally from the floor just outside the lift to the opposite wall, nearly to the ceiling, long and lithe, like how I imagine Machine Three will be. She cuts through the room, a great cylinder of a million components, dark silver and slate gray. There are no broken pieces scattered across the ground, no hanging bits, no breaks that I can see.

Yet my gut tells me she's incomplete.

"Pell, this is astonishing." Moseus steps forward and rests a hand on the machine as I walk under it, suffocating on my own awe. Long pistons like organ pipes stretch across her center. She has cable assemblies, gearboxes, and flywheels similar to those on the other machines, but here they're bigger. Heavier. Peering between her support beams, I see the thickest chain I've ever beheld stretched taut in her center. I reach for it, but Machine Four is too dense, too tightly constructed.

Her togetherness will help me understand the others. I know it.

The lift recalls, but I doubt the Ancients meant to trap us up here.

"The windows." Moseus crosses to them, and it's only then that I realize the floor is well lit, though when I climbed the exterior of the tower, the windows were closed off. Pulling away from Machine Four, I approach the window next to Moseus. It's covered by a strange material. It's not metal, it's not stone, it's not wood, but something else entirely. Light but solid. So solid I don't know if I could break it. While I can't see through it, and from the exterior of the tower it's as opaque as stone, the sunlight filters through, offering much-needed illumination. I find no latches, hinges, or fittings that would otherwise facilitate motion. These panels are not meant to be moved.

"Another mystery," I murmur, and return to Machine Four just as the lift reappears, this time carrying Heartwood. That heaviness of his presence, the one I thought I'd gotten used to, washes over me, drowning me. I force air into my lungs just to prove to myself that I can.

He doesn't notice me at first. The moment he arrives, his face opens like a child's, taking in the room and the new leviathan it holds.

"It's . . . There's more." Heartwood fumbles over his words. "There's . . . more."

"We knew there had to be," Moseus responds.

Heartwood draws his gaze down the machine until it lands on me. He swiftly looks away.

It took you away from me, he said. That tangle of emotion and questions re-forms in my chest, bubbling up so abruptly I fear I'll puke. So I refocus on the machine. Climb onto her lowest end and carefully scale upward, not wanting to break her. But she's sturdy. She's stronger than the others, having been protected up here.

Pain pulses behind my forehead. Gripping a beam, I hold my breath as my vision blurs.

I whip my hand back. Blood pools in my palm and trickles down my wrist. Damn it, I should have been more careful.

I hold the hand up as I untangle myself from the machine, trying not to get blood on it. Great, this will make work the next few cycles real fun. I know I shouldn't press a dirty rag to it, but that's what I have, so that's what it gets.

I'm choking on curses in the back of my throat when two pale hands gently take my own injured one. Remove the rag, clean the wound, expertly wind dark bandages around my palm.

"I'm fine," I protest, though I can feel my pulse from wrist to fingertips.

"I believe you." Heartwood secures the bandages with a small knot, cheek twitching as he masks his amusement. "But we can't have you bleeding on the equipment, now can we?"

The present rushes at me like I've fallen down a well and plummeted into the water. Sweat forms on my temples. I'm too warm. My fingers hurt from gripping the beam; my skin's turned white at the knuckles. Acid churns up my esophagus, but I swallow it back down.

"Pelnophe?"

Heartwood notices me first. Of course he does. Shaking myself, I say, "I'm just eager to get started." I mechanically pick my way back down, not meeting either of the keepers' eyes as I pass to the lift. "I need my tools."

I wait for them to leave before throwing myself into the work.

There are answers in these machines.

That thought stirs over and over again as I examine every centimeter of Machine Four, taking note where anything appears crooked, broken, or missing.

If the machines pose the questions, then they must also have the answers. If I get this tower operating again, I'll understand what's happening to me.

To another, the logic might be unsound. To me, it's faultless. Fix the machines, fix myself.

I feel like Machine Four. Whole in appearance, yet internally broken.

I'm running. I know I'm running. I never knew myself as an evader. I suppose I've never experienced problems this deep. This . . . murky. I can't process them, so I don't even try. I want an empty mind, so I focus on Machine Four. Focus on my work. Focus on the parts I understand.

I'm beneath her belly near the lower end, sitting on my butt, when I pause. "Oh. You *are* female."

There's a large female piece in her middle. The thick chain links to its back end. But I don't see a corresponding male counterpart, which makes no sense. But perhaps I'm looking at it wrong—

Machine Three looms before me, wider in the center than at the ends.

A cry escapes me as I whip away from Machine Four, both hands going to my skull. "Stop it," I plead. Emotion burns the inside of my nose. "Stop it. Stop it."

That's not what Machine Three looks like. It's in pieces.

The vision imprints into my brain like a scar.

125

Squeezing my eyes shut, I suck in a long breath, release it slowly. In, out. In, out.

It's not right. It's imaginary. It's not right.

The lift takes me down to the second floor. From there, I use the ladder to reach Machine Three. It probably has a lift stop I can uncover, but it's not worth the effort. Half the machine still litters the stone floor. But I remember a few details. Only a few, and they're wrong.

Wrong, I tell myself as I pick up two beams and connect them with a bronze fastener. *Wrong,* I repeat as I snap it into place and connect wires, then an axle, then a bit shaped like a hollow trapezoid that I've never been able to categorize. *Wrong,* I say as I connect couplings the way I saw, and then step back, every part fitting where it belongs. The base begins to bow outward. The Ancients designed Machine Three thicker in the middle than at the ends.

It took you away from me.

My gut seizes, sending me to my knees.

Heartwood moves his hair over his shoulders. The mist-choked light casts shadows across the scars on his back. No, not scars. Not like the ones on my hands and knees. These are raised, branched, intricate, the skin no different from the rest. They branch out at his pale shoulders and taper at his waist, taking the shape of a tree.

I blink tears away to clear my vision. The tower room stands quiet around me. Again, stinging bile courses up my throat, but I swallow it down. Swallow, swallow, swallow, then remember to breathe.

I'm losing my sanity. I feel it. The machines are one thing; I'm learning more about them every time I come. I'm a tinkerer. Mechanics interest me. Of course my mind would make the jump to how to piece them together. Of course I'm learning their ways.

But Heartwood . . . I don't know how anything in reality or dream could conjure up something as strange as those scars on his back. I've never witnessed anything close. Even Arthen, with all his forge injuries, has nothing comparable.

Inhale, exhale. Long, slow.

"I'm losing it, Salki," I whisper, wishing she were here to reassure me. But she's not, and she wouldn't understand if she were. *I don't understand.*

I'm losing control.

"No. *No.*" I force myself to my feet and retreat to the window, sucking in mist-laced air. "I am here. I am whole. They're only machines." I refuse to cry over this. I'm not crazy. I . . . I'm not . . .

I have to know.

Does Heartwood have those strange markings on his back? If he doesn't, then I've lost my mind entirely. I'm too susceptible to these machines. I'll have to stop my work entirely and preserve what I have left. I can't sacrifice myself for these keepers. I'm sorry, but I can't.

But if he *does* . . . then the ravings of madness haven't descended upon me. It's something else. Something embedded within the Ancient tech I'm working on. Something connected to *them*. I don't know what it is, but it's not madness.

I have to know. I *need* to know.

Setting my tools aside, I plan.

I don't leave the tower during the next mist. I don't leave at all.

I should rest, but my mind and body are far too alert, so I walk through the tower, taking note of the keepers. I have a faint idea of their schedules, though Moseus's has proven more consistent than Heartwood's. Returning to Machine Two, I work on it until it's more or less functional, though I don't provide a means to power it by hand like I did with Machine One. I'm still clueless as to the machines' power sources, but I don't think they require separate sources to function. I can't believe the Ancients would build things that weren't self-contained, self-sufficient wholes. It's only time—and angry, confusing keepers—that tears them apart.

After that, I visit Moseus, who has returned to Machine Four, watching it as one might watch the mists descend.

"It's an excellent discovery," I say, trying to sound casual. "We're getting close."

"We are." His chest puffs out with a deep breath and a slight rattle. "Very close."

"I know it's important to you." I place a hand on one of the machine's spines, not daring to meet his eyes. "It's important to me, too. I think I could get more work done if I stay at the tower."

Several seconds pass. "You wish to stay here?"

"If I had accommodations." I tread carefully. "I wouldn't mind working longer shifts. I know you don't like me coming and going during the suns."

He considers this. It sounds more than reasonable to my ears, but Moseus has proven himself a very private person. We are allies, but I am still *other* to him, and a woman, too. Still, the idea of finishing the work quicker entices him. "I suppose it would speed things along," he says somewhat reluctantly. "This fortress wasn't made for comfort."

"I'm well aware."

"Would you stay here?" He gestures around the room. Because of Machine Four's angle, there's plenty of floor space for camping out.

"There's a room on the second floor." Easy, casual, nonchalant. I pull a small wrench from my belt and spin it around my finger. "Near the stairs." It's a small room, maybe twice the size of the closet on the first floor. But it's also straight across from Heartwood's chamber.

Though his lips pull into a frown, Moseus nods. "Very well. I don't have a lot to offer you for a pallet."

Heartwood might, I almost say, but I don't risk his name staining the conversation. I can bring my own blanket when the mists fall. My own food, too. These two live as bachelors. They don't have a well-stocked pantry.

"I'll be subtle," I say. Moseus can piece together the rest. Changing the subject, I report my other progress, which he seems only to half hear. Then I excuse myself and take the lift down to the second floor.

Now that I've been allowed to linger, I have to execute the second, and hardest, part of my plan. I have to catch Heartwood undressing.

Most people sleep during the mists.

Not every mist. At least, *I* don't sleep every mist. But the world cools down, and navigating becomes difficult, so folk retreat when the mists thicken. I don't know if Heartwood strips down to rest, but I figure it's my best shot.

I linger at Machine Two and pretend to fiddle with it as the sun grows late. I don't even look at Heartwood when he comes by, though his steps slow, and I feel him looking at me. My pulse quickens, but he says nothing and slips inside his humble quarters.

Gradually, the temperature drops as the fog collects. Taking my shoes off, I scan for Moseus. Clear. I toe my way to Heartwood's door. I may or may not have tightened up the knob's strike plate a bit earlier, while he was away. At the garden, most likely.

Gripping the knob, I turn it softly. So softly. Hold my breath. Push it just a crack. Realize I should have oiled the hinges, too. The bottom one creaks, giving me away. Heartwood, sitting on a stool beside the window, looks up at me. He's in a loose homespun shirt and breeches. So yes, he does change. But I misjudged my timing. I'm late.

He has a small book in his hands. Looks at me, then back at its pages. "I believe it's customary for your people to knock."

"What do you know of 'my people'?" I counter, realizing that I'm not helping my case.

His brow creases. I reset. There are other stones I need to throw.

"I want to know what you meant, before." I open the door a little wider now, listening to that hinge. "You said the machine took . . . um, me away from you."

He does not look up from the book. "I misspoke." His unhindered tone grates on me.

"You misspoke."

He doesn't reply, merely reads.

"All right." I can play his game. "Then why was that gear stuck in the wickwood tree?"

Now he looks up, his confusion genuine. "What gear?"

I hesitate, wondering whether or not to share. Heartwood seems fond of secrets. Perhaps I should guard some of my own. "Why did you have Arthen's knife?"

He blanches. *Caught you.* He pulls his eyes back to his book, but this time it seems forced. His shoulders stiffen. He clenches his jaw, but catches himself and releases it. Sighs.

"Well?" I press.

"Were you in here?" he asks quietly. Accusatory, yes, but not venomous.

"I came in when I saw my knife. You left the door open." I'm not the best liar, but I'd bet five cycles' rations that I'm better at it than Heartwood.

He turns the page. I wait. No answer.

"Are you fond of tense silences?"

Heartwood lowers the book. The pages dip under his hard grip. "I do not have an answer for you. No—Pelnophe."

"I said you could call me *Nophe*," I offer.

He shakes his head. Clenches, then unclenches, his jaw. "I do not have an answer for you," he repeats, too much air leaking into his voice.

"I think you do."

"Good night, Pell." The words are hard, final, but they give me pause.

"What does that mean?"

He glances at me, bright eyes hard. "What does what mean?"

"Good night," I repeat, letting go of the knob. "What's 'night'?"

His expression wipes clean, like a wet rag was swiped across a chalky slate. He turns to the window. "It's nothing. Please, leave."

Gritting my teeth, I start to pull the door closed, then stop. "You'll break the book, doing that."

Glancing down, Heartwood seems to notice for the first time that the pages are half folded over in his clenched hands. He releases it, letting it topple to the floor, and I give him his privacy.

For now.

The following mist, I bring a few things to the tower. Not everything; I don't intend to disappear from Emgarden completely. I'm still needed there, and my absence could raise more questions than I have easy answers for. But I bring enough. My moving in makes both keepers uncomfortable, but Heartwood especially. He won't meet my eyes and swiftly vacates any area I walk into.

Which helps when I need to oil his hinges. I do so, thoroughly.

He doesn't sleep the next mist, and he's gone the entire next sun. Garden or foraging, I assume. Or he ate something particularly foul and atones for it at the privy. I work on assembling Machine Three, worried that he's somehow caught on to me already, but he returns during the following mist. I'm quicker to follow this time. He sleeps, but in the window alcove, sitting upright against the stone, still dressed in his leathers, arms folded tightly across his chest. He snores, which is odd, because Heartwood doesn't snore.

I fumble the handle as I retreat. Bite my lip and close the door, relieved when I don't wake him, disturbed at my own thought. *Heartwood doesn't snore.* How would I know that? This is the first time I've ever seen him sleep.

Panic clutches my chest, because I'm so damn sure. *Heartwood doesn't snore.*

It took you away from me.

"I can't do this," I whisper, and take the lift up to Machine Four. No one can sneak up on me here. No one will hear my frantic pacing and self-assurances. No one will see me put my head between my knees and relearn how to breathe. My chest weighs me down like it, too, is a machine. There's not enough air in this room. *Not enough air.* I take the lift back down and climb to the third floor to press my head to the window, trying to empty my thoughts.

Madness has a feel to it. Smooth, subtle. Like the oil nestled in those hinges, but thinner. It doesn't leave a noticeable mark. No grease stains. When it first starts dripping, it feels wrong, the way I imagine a knife through the gut might feel. But I can see how one could become used to it. Even comfortable. Oiled up and slick and satiated, forgetting there was ever anything else.

And I wonder, staring out into the mist, if I've forgotten something. My theory of the Ancients speaking to me through their work has crumbled around the edges. The Ancients didn't know Heartwood. He isn't part of these machines.

Steeling myself, I return to the second floor. Heartwood's earlier position wasn't comfortable; perhaps he changed and now rests on his pallet on the floor. Maybe his leathers are dirty. That's two reasons to unclothe. And I am desperate. The oil is seeping in, and it terrifies me. I have to know.

Late mist. No clock, but it will dissipate soon. Quiet as an ant, I turn Heartwood's handle and open the door just a crack. Catch my breath before it can give me away.

He's awake. Facing away from me. Pulling off the leathers he wears over his clothes. He carefully folds a piece and sets it on the windowsill.

I pull back a moment. I'm ready. Whatever the answer is, I have to accept it. I will run, if I have to. Leave the tower and its machines—all

Ancient work—forever, to preserve myself. I'd rather have this missing piece nagging at me than lose who I am.

Ready, I peek through the crack again. But Heartwood isn't there. The door wrenches from my hand.

Heartwood's closeness exaggerates his size. Looking down, his eyes blaze like they did when he pinned me to the wall by Machine Three.

"What," he seethes, his voice low and callous, "are you doing?"

I stand my ground, wishing my knees didn't shake. "I want answers. I want to know—"

"Keep your voice down."

"Tell me what I don't know!" I hiss.

He lowers his face to mine. "There is nothing for you to know. There are no secrets with me or this room. Your only purpose is the machines. You must—"

He stops. I don't know why he stopped. Until I realize I'm crying. Ruin me. I hate crying.

Wiping angry hands over my eyes, I say, "I don't understand." I hate how my voice shakes, but all the bottled fear twists my stomach and pushes up my throat. "I'm seeing things, Heartwood. I see things in the machines. Hear things. Past, present, I don't know. I'm . . . I'm losing my mind." I try to suck in air, but it's a mere trickle. "Injuries I don't have, machines not . . . not as they are. And I see you."

He steps back like I've physically pushed him, insulted his person, his people, and his country while setting fire to his garden.

I wipe my face again—more like a slap—before any new tears can fall. "I see you, and I don't know why. I don't know what's real and what's not. I have to know if I'm going mad."

He says nothing. I wish he'd say something. I can't tolerate the quiet, so I keep talking.

"Y-You have these things, on your back," I add, and his expression slackens. "I don't know what they are. It was just a flash, really. Like scars, but not. And I know it sounds absolutely absurd, but I keep seeing strange things, and I don't know what they are, or what they mean, or if they even *exist*. I don't know what's happening!" I raise my voice despite his warning. Smack away a tear. "Please . . . just tell me if I'm sane or not. I need to know—"

"Stop," he whispers, like I'm hurting him. I'm not even touching him. "Stop, please."

I chew down a sob. Shake my head. A headache forms just beneath my skull, and I wince, ready for another vision, but none comes.

Heartwood's calloused hand grasps my forearm. He pulls me into his room, then shuts the door firmly. Pauses. "You did something."

"I oiled the hinges," I confess.

He sighs. Releases me. Undoes the single button at his collar, turns, and pulls off his shirt.

I gasp.

It's there. It's all there.

A dozen scars—two dozen—cross his broad shoulders, raised like someone filled them with water, though they don't look soft. Small, medium, large. They branch off his shoulders and join at the middle of his back, where they merge into one solid form that disappears beneath the waist of his trousers. It looks like a tree might, if we ever took the time to nurture one.

I reach forward, but Heartwood tugs the shirt back on, trapping his hair beneath it. "Go."

"I . . ." My feet have gone numb. My tongue, apparently, as well.

He pushes past me and opens the door. Peers out into the open area beyond before looking at me expectantly.

"But . . . what is it?" I ask, sounding like a child. "Why . . . how did I know?"

"You must be a seeress." His words are terse, and he doesn't meet my eyes. "Go, Nophe. Please."

Dumbfounded, I shuffle from the room. The moment I clear the door, he shuts it behind me, the latch clicking heavy and final.

Chapter 15

"Have I ever shown this to you?"

I stand in my house in Emgarden. Salki and Casnia are visiting with another loaf of bread, because Salki "hasn't seen" me lately and I've "seemed ill," which is an understatement. Moseus probably wonders why I left so suddenly. I didn't go back last cycle, and it's already the sun of the next.

I dug up the little machine from my floorboards right in front of Salki. I have nothing to hide from her, but as I show her the framework and equilibrated sphere with my self-proclaimed symbol carved into it, she slows her darning and shakes her head. "No, you haven't! You made that?" She touches it. "What does it do?"

Disappointment pulls at my shoulders. "Nothing." I toss it onto the table, then steady it when a five-second earthquake passes beneath the house. "Nothing."

"Yellow," Casnia demands, holding out her hands without looking up. She's drawing on the back of previous artwork. The process of pulping bark to make parchment is tedious, and Salki often doesn't have time. I usually help, but as Salki stated, I've been away, and yes, ill. Just not the kind of ill I can explain.

I see Heartwood's scars every time I close my eyes. I can feel them under my fingers, though he never let me touch him.

Salki sets aside her bundle of emily-root threads and searches through her satchel. She finds a nub of yellow chalk. Hands it over.

Casnia draws all three of us this time. I only recognize Salki and myself because I've seen Casnia's interpretations so many times. I only recognize Casnia because she's blended colors together into a semblance of her violet eyes. Her proportions are wildly off, but she's occupied.

"Are you eating?" Salki asks, poking my stomach. "You look a little thin."

I scoff at the insult. Salki doesn't mean it as one, but I've never liked the word to describe me. *Thin* and *strong* are not synonyms. "Yes, I'm eating." To make a point, I pinch off the corner of her perfectly executed bread loaf and shove it into my mouth. It tastes amazing, and I take a minute to savor it.

Okay, I haven't been eating *good* food, only quick food, but that's beside the point.

"Have you seen any strange people around here?" I ask suddenly.

Salki picks off thread where it's caught on her brooch. "Strange how?"

"Like pale. Tall. White hair."

She blinks. "Entisa had white hair."

Because she was old. "Never mind." I rub my temples. "I think I had a weird dream last mist."

Salki thumbs at her metallic, misshapen brooch, then changes the subject, interesting me in gossip. One of the farmhands was caught peeing in the well, so Maglon banned him from the alehouse for the next hundred cycles. Maglon, who Salki thinks is sweet on Frantess, which I find laughable.

"They're too different," I point out, and my chuckling fades. *Different.* Like me and Heartwood.

"You'd be surprised," Salki says. "At least he contaminated the far east well, so we'll only use it on the plants."

"Because the farmers never get thirsty on that end."

She sighs. "I think it'll be clean soon enough, with all the water we take. He regrets it, at least. Took my shift for me."

"That's something."

"Honestly, I'd be more upset if it weren't for that rover." She beams. "It's really so helpful, Pell! If we had a few more . . ." She retrieves her sewing. "I can't even imagine."

I'm happy the rover is helping. I'd love to make another, once I have the pieces. And to make the present one faster. Maybe give it a track to follow. I have a few ideas. But while the compliment was meant to bolster me, I don't feel it. Too much else takes up space in my chest.

They stay and chat a little longer, then excuse themselves when Casnia needs to use the privy. Alone, I turn back to my piecemeal machine, tracing my hands over it. I carefully dismantle a few pieces of it, just to peer inside. The frame seems just that—a frame. No special wires or wiring or hidden parts. I'd thought the translucent orb at the center couldn't pull apart without breaking, but I notice a seam on it that's similar to one on Machine Three. The right amount of pressure and a twist gets the two halves apart.

The acrylic halves are lined with glass inside, thin and carefully blown. One half sports hard wires jutting out of its bottom and branching out across the concave surface. Silver leaf lines the other half. I fit the halves together, watching those wires. Pull them apart again. The wires obviously need to connect to something. Nothing works with free wires. But connect to what?

As I piece the thing back together, I notice a hinge on the acrylic outer shell. It's made to peel away, like it's only there to protect the glass within. I return the orb to its weighted nest. Examine it a little closer.

"If I had to make a guess," I mutter, "I'd . . ." Well, it's stupid, but I'd think this was a light.

Why else would the orb be translucent, with that glass? And the frame resembles the frame of a lantern, though it's not freestanding. No chimney, but I can't guess what else the machine would be used for. There's no reasonable intake for oil, but I don't think it's meant to be lit. Not with a flame.

My stomach hurts, followed by my head. Another unanswered question. I still don't know why someone left it for me. Or why it's marked like I created it myself.

I'm aligning the pistons on Machine Four when another flash overtakes me.

"It's better that I—that we—don't involve ourselves with Emgarden," Heartwood says, glancing at the tower's door. "We are too . . . different."

I shrug. "Well, you're already involved with me, aren't you?"

Deep breaths steady me as the vision fades. I shoulder the piston into place. I had to bring a stool up here to do it, and eventually I'll need the ladder, too, though it won't fit in the lift. I might just set the keepers to building something new. No reason I should be doing all the work.

As I check the last piston, my eye catches on the tension cables behind, and the components holding them in place. "I know you." I point a finger at the trapezoidal frame. "And you," to a spine.

Abandoning my work, I move to floor three, find the parts, and assemble them on Machine Three as I saw them in Machine Four. The tasks go quickly, minus those involving the heavier bits, and by mid sun, the internal parts of the machine are all set for a trial run. It feels . . . off, to piece it together so swiftly, but the guts are so similar to Machine Four, which is intact.

To be sure, I bring up my turning rod and set it up as I did on Machine One. Machine Three stands easily three times the size of Machine One, so it takes some sweat, but I manage to crank it twice, and the parts turn, puffing out a gentle, dying tone.

I pause, listening to it. That tone . . . it harmonizes with Machine One. I'm not positive . . . I'd have to be able to hear both at the same time, and I only have one turning rod and an entire story between the two machines, but I think—

I catch movement from the corner of my eye. Heartwood approaches, wearing his leathers. He's either about to head out or he's just returned. His thick white braid falls over one shoulder, dusting his lowest rib.

My gut clenches. I see those markings in my mind's eye, branching like a tree over his broad shoulders. Feel his breath on my face as he says, *I broke it because it took you away from me.*

His eyes aren't sharp. The color, I mean. I thought them unnatural, even acidic, once. But now that I've seen his garden, I've reassessed. They're merely alive, whereas so much on Tampere is not.

I find myself suddenly self-conscious of my sweat- and grease-stained clothes. I wipe my palms on the sides of my trousers. "Yes?"

He glances at the machine. "It's nearly done."

I pat the turning rod. "It doesn't have all its outer structure, but it functions as well as the first does." Heartwood pauses two paces from me, studying my face. Searching for something. That self-consciousness grows. "What?"

He hesitates. "Do you know my name?"

What kind of a question is that? "Heartwood . . ."

"And the name of the other keeper?"

"Moseus. What is this about?"

He raises a hand, asking for patience. "How do you get to the fourth floor?"

I narrow my eyes but play along. "Through the lift. Which is attached to Machine Two, for some reason. Which also has a hidden door behind it."

He shifts. "There's a door?"

"Moseus didn't tell you?"

He shakes his head. "It must have slipped his mind." He examines the machine again. "Thank you, for your work. It means a lot to me. To us."

"You're wel—"

The sun hits Heartwood's eyes, shrinking his pupils, brightening the green. There's a deeper green, a star in the center of each, and I lean in, trying to better make out their edges. Yet as I do, they transform before my very eyes, forming the shapes of tall, needle-covered trees and thick boughs, of distant mountains capped in white. A glistening stream of water crinkles past lush grasses, where an animal—a deer?—grazes with her fawn.

I gasp. Blink the images away. I see Heartwood's chest. He's in front of me, his hands on my shoulders, his face close to mine. This time, though, he doesn't instill terror. My heart pounds anyway.

"What's wrong?" He searches my face.

"I . . ." I don't know how to answer. I told him I'd been seeing things. Does he understand now? *Seeress,* he called me. It sounded like an excuse.

I look into his eyes, wondering if they'll change for me again, if I'll see a far-off place too wonderful to recognize. He sees me searching, feels our closeness, and releases me, his countenance stricken.

"Forgive me," he says, more to the floor than to me, and leaves.

"I don't," I murmur at his back, but he doesn't hear me.

I halfheartedly piece together the exterior bits of Machine Three before slipping away to my room to nap. I manage to sleep, but it isn't restful. I change my clothing, throwing the soiled pieces into the corner to wash later, and pull my short hair into a flared tail at the crown of my head. I need to think, and I can't think the way I need to at the tower.

So I trek to Heartwood's garden, winding down the way I'd first uncovered in the mists. The rest of that disintegrating copse has crumbled. What portions of its umber dust that haven't caught on the breeze have mixed with the red-tinted soil, leaving a mark like a burn. I avoid crossing it, still unsettled by the trees' strange demise.

Salki hates feeling enclosed. She dislikes tight spaces. Said she'd rather be burned and join the sky when she dies than buried like her mother. But here, in the winding red passageways of the slot canyons, I feel safe. Protected. Private. The canyons project a natural calm that imbues my body with peace.

I smell the garden before I pass through the stone arch guarding it. I'm greeted by succulent trees and the buzz of insects. The desert wrens are out. I only make it a few steps before I see a shift of white against the green. Heartwood stands from a crouch, that water pail in his hand, and meets my eyes. My gut clenches again.

"S-Sorry," I offer.

He glances at the roses. "I was just finishing. You are welcome to stay." He comes up the path, giving me space as he passes, and returns the bucket to its place by the spring.

"Stay," I blurt. "I mean . . . you can stay. It's your garden."

"I understand if you want privacy."

"Just . . . stay, Heartwood." I'm not used to being embarrassed about much of anything, and I hate the heat climbing my cheeks. He studies me, then the arch, as if debating. I roll my eyes. "I'm not *that* bad of company. I promise I won't ask you to take your clothes off this time."

That catches him off guard, and I laugh at the chagrin enveloping his features. I'm grateful for it; it puts me at ease. I walk up the path a little way. Heartwood stays where he is, probably still debating whether to leave.

I point to a short bush with tiny yellow buds. "What is this? I don't recognize it."

"Retalia," he answers softly. "It grows natively in these canyons, in the more shaded parts."

"This big?"

"No. Tampere is too harsh for that."

He says it like there's another option.

I gesture to the deep pink flowers. "And these?"

"Soft hearts."

"I wouldn't say I have one, but thank you."

His lip quirks a little. He joins me on the path. "That is the name of the flower."

"I know."

"Do you?"

I eye him, unsure what he means. "And these are desert roses."

"Yes. My favorite. That is why there are so many."

"Mine, too."

He follows me up the path. "Do you know this?"

He refers to the cluster of spiky leaves with long tongues at their centers, upon which sprout small purple flowers. "No. Should I?"

"They're rare. Particular about soil and light." I feel his gaze on my face, but when I turn, he refocuses on the plant. "Chrystanus. Beautiful, but poisonous."

I blink at the seemingly harmless plant. It has no thorns, bark, or particularly bright coloring to warn creatures away. "Poisonous?"

"The root only, but yes, very much so. A dermal poison."

I study the garden with a renewed eye. The green vines are fairy wisps, and the succulent trees have a name too long to remember. I was right about the sage, in that it's a variety of sage.

"But not edible," Heartwood adds.

"And this"—I sweep my arms broadly around the garden—"is your animus thing?"

Heartwood lowers himself onto a large boulder. "Moseus told you about that." It's not a question.

"More or less. It's like what you're named after, or something."

He tips his head. "Mine is more for the forest, but this is the best I can make."

Forest. I know the word, but when I try to picture it, all I see are the images from Heartwood's eyes, and that wasn't real.

No, it *was* real. Because the scars are real. Right?

Lifting my right hand, I trace the scar across my palm. "I want to talk about Machine Three."

Heartwood immediately rises to his feet. "I should go. Moseus will be expecting me."

"You don't get to say things like that and then refuse to explain yourself." My voice is quiet, but my tone isn't.

Heartwood slows, stops. "I shouldn't have spoken." He looks away, his jaw tight again. He blinks a few times. "I'm sorry."

I walk up the path to meet him. To block him from the exit, though if he wanted to, he could easily displace me. He's slow to meet my gaze, but he does. He has a strong nose, broad cheeks, full lips. Trees and deer in his eyes, somehow.

"Give me your hand." I hold mine out expectantly.

Heartwood hesitates, then lifts his right hand and places it in mine. The little zip that rushes up my arm at the contact, like I've touched the steam chest on an engine, makes me uncomfortable, to say the least. Or rather, I want it to be.

I close his hand into a fist and press my palms against his knuckles. "That beam you wrecked. It's a good thing it's not critical to the function of the machine."

He doesn't reply, only watches our hands.

"What are you, Heartwood?" I release him gently, as though his hand is a bird learning to fly. When he presses his lips together, I add, "You have to tell me *something*. I deserve something."

He exhales slowly. I think he will refuse to answer again, but he grinds out, "I am not from here."

"Obviously."

"No, Pell. Nophe." He takes a step back and surveys his garden. "I am not from Tampere."

I wrinkle my nose. "And I thought *I* was the crazy one." Yet my heart quickens, as though warning me. My jest stalls him. Emboldened, I lift my hand and press it to his chest. He tenses, but doesn't move away. His heart beats nearly in time with my own. "Heartwood," I murmur, meeting his eyes. "What are you?"

He places his hand gingerly over mine. "Moseus and I both. We are gods."

Chapter 16

When I pull away from Heartwood, he lets me go.

"What?" A dry laugh escapes me. "That is—"

"Absurd, yes, I know," he finishes for me, the word half-formed on my tongue. He looks at me almost wryly, rubbing his chest where my hand just was, as though I've burned him. "And no, I can't demonstrate."

I was about to ask him to. To prove it. *Reasonable deduction on his part,* I think, but find myself shaking my head.

It takes me a beat to find my voice again. "I'd . . . I'd call blasphemy, but—"

"You've never been particularly religious." He looks out over his garden, again guessing my next words. Again striking me speechless. He can't read my mind . . . can he? "There are many gods," he continues, quieter. "I am not one necessitating worship."

I laugh again, because I don't know what else to do. I walk down the path a ways, then come back, albeit not as close as before. "Well, maybe I'm a goddess. And I also can't *demonstrate.*"

Heartwood sighs, like I'm a child, and it instantly puts me on edge.

"Okay, Heartwood"—I fold my arms—"from some other Serpent-made world, if we're to believe the lore. Why in the universe are you on Tampere?"

His answer softens me. "I'm searching for my sister." He meets my eyes. "What Moseus said about the tower, about the wall, was not false."

My shoulders are so rigid, they start to ache. I force them to relax. "And what, is she a god, too?"

He pauses. "I should not have burdened you with this." There's something else he wants to say; I can see it in the movement of his lips. But he adds nothing.

"Well, I'm burdened." I stride past him to the rock he perched upon earlier and sit. "Explain."

He rolls his lips together, debating.

"Tell me where you come from, Heartwood. Give me that."

He exhales long and slow. Without looking at me, he says, "We trace back—all of us—to the Well."

"The Well of Creation." I've heard of it. Amlynn is really into the legend.

He nods. "It was in the beginning. It made the fabric of the universe, the stars—"

"What are stars?"

He points to the sun. "The first life to extend from its depths was the World Serpent." He gestures to me, knowing I'm aware of the great snake. I swear on it often enough. "And after, it stemmed the gods."

Still skeptical, I ask, "And what number are you?"

A wistful cast envelops his face. "I do not know. After Ether."

"Ether?"

"My sister."

"They're . . . kind of all your siblings, aren't they?"

"In a sense." He kneels down on the path, then sits, folding his long legs before him. Pieces of hair have loosened from his braid and catch on the subtlest breeze that scoops into the gorge. For some reason, it . . . does make him look a little godlike. With the right lighting, he could have an etherealness about him. He's always been lovely, in that sense.

"So the Well just spit you all out, and you, what, followed the World Serpent around until you settled down?"

He shakes his head. "You are always so matter-of-fact."

"Am I?"

Heartwood's gaze turns inward. "The Well made the essence of our forebears, which the world formed. I am not a creation of the Well itself, but a child of it. My parents, if you will, formed me in the depths of a forest a long way from here. Thus my animus."

"And Moseus was formed somewhere . . . like this." I gesture widely.

He cocks an eyebrow.

"Somewhere peaceful," I specify.

I get a smile from that, and I push back against the fluttering it ignites in my stomach. "I'm glad you find it peaceful." He considers. "Moseus is very old. When he formed, it was very . . . quiet."

"And this sister, Ether, she just . . . formed in the air somewhere?" It was a joke, but Heartwood nods, which makes me feel stupid. Maybe he's right. Maybe I'm thinking about this too literally. I still only half believe him. And he gets that half because he *is* so other. So unlike anyone else in Emgarden. And because he bent steel to his hand, and not a bone on that hand looks like it's ever been broken.

I don't know the names of most of the gods—there are hundreds, at least. But I know the name of one. "I guess Ruin was real pissed when it came around."

The ground rumbles in agreement.

Heartwood is an interesting creature. An emotional one, yet severe. To save my life, I cannot imagine him at the counter of the alehouse. He sounds very sober when he explains, "Ruin was the last of the first. The Well gave everything it had. Life pulled every last drop from its recesses, until all it could do was *take*. That is what Ruin is. A consumer. Devourer."

"Balance to the universe."

He frowns. "Some have said."

Movement across the garden catches my eye. "Moseus," I say, less in greeting and more in warning. He stands at the entrance of the garden. He looks off—not just from the perturbance nesting itself on his brow, but the hollowness in his cheeks. In truth, I don't think I've ever seen him in good lighting. It's evident that while this garden renews

Heartwood, it does not have the same effect on Moseus, no matter how peaceful I find it.

Then I remember Heartwood asked me not to tell Moseus I'd come here, and that Moseus told me to give Heartwood a wide berth, and my stomach sinks to my knees. My tongue twists, trying to taste out a lie, but I'm not sure what I'm lying about.

Heartwood doesn't look overly worried. He stands.

"What are you telling her?" Moseus's usual serenity weaves through the question, but I can tell he's unhappy. Nervous.

"She asked," Heartwood replies.

Rising to my feet, I put out my hands in surrender. "I won't share it. I don't even really believe it." I'm not sure if that qualifies as a lie. I'm not sure of any of it.

Moseus holds Heartwood's gaze for nearly a minute. The garden air practically thickens with it. The sun burns too hot. I take in the shadows of Moseus's face and pin them to what Heartwood said earlier: that he cannot demonstrate his godhood.

He's too weak, I realize. *They both are.*

I want to ask why, but I also want to keep my head on my shoulders, so I excuse myself and venture back to the tower.

Moseus and Heartwood don't return for a long time.

I rest at home during the following mist, dreaming of gods.

It's the kind of dream that's hard to recount: more shapes and colors than anything else, but my mind finds a way to twist sense into it. I see a vast, endless universe of pale blue, and in it spins a great white ring, vomiting serpents and gods, until it turns inside out and becomes something else entirely. Something deep and hungry and dark. I'm eager to take my mind off the fading shapes and incomplete story. As soon as the next mist falls, its gentle, barely-there tone whispering on the breeze, I return to the tower.

Machine Four looks good. Most of its problems are at the top, which means climbing up its complex network of parts, but I enjoy it. Nearly drop my turnscrew, but I snatch it just in time.

"Kiss my mortal ass, Heartwood." I gesture crudely to him and storm toward the stairs.

"You don't know what it could do!" he barks behind me.

I whirl toward him. "You'd better walk before I show you what *I* can do."

He throws his hands in the air and storms away.

I blink, one hand holding tight to a beam as the vision dissipates. What are—were? will?—we even fighting over?

Chewing on my lower lip, I lean into Machine Four. Press my forehead to its cool metal and close my eyes, replaying the scene in my head. Heartwood so animated, so unlike the version of him I know now. I wonder why—

"I came to apologize."

I sit on the protrusion from the top tier of the tower, looking up at the sun. The mists have begun to gather across the Brume Mountains. I don't answer. It's childish of me, but I don't.

A full minute passes. He sighs. "I hate it when you sit out here."

Glad he can't see my smirk, I reply, "I know."

The vision evaporates. I wait, pressed against the machine, for another. Adjust my position. Roll up my sleeves, wondering if skin contact might trigger something new, but alas, the tower seems done with me, for now.

As I pull back, though, my hand brushes against . . . rubber? There's a short bar under this set of pistons, perpendicular to everything else. I think it's debris lodged in there, but when I twist and get a better grip on it, it pulls up like a lever.

Machine Four bucks.

I shriek as the whole mass twists suddenly to the left, and I yank my hand free while simultaneously getting a better grip with the other. It's falling, turning me under it. I'll be crushed. I'll—

The machine clicks loudly and stops, emitting a puff of air, leaving me dangling three meters above the floor. My tool bag, wedged between components, spills half its tools onto the floor. The lift buzzes, and as I'm trying to gauge how much it'll hurt to drop, Heartwood appears. I wonder if it's happenstance, or if he was lingering nearby and heard me shriek.

He rushes toward me. "Hold on, I'll catch you."

I adjust my sweat-slick grip. "I don't need to be caught."

"Stop being difficult."

"But you like it," I grunt. I'm losing my grip, so I let go, ready to bend my knees and roll to take off some of the shock of hitting stone, but Heartwood holds true to his word. His large hands grab my waist when I drop, slowing me down enough that I barely feel my heels touch the floor. My tool bag comes clattering down after me. Heartwood pulls me away from a toppling wrench, which results in my nose pressed up against his chest.

He smells earthy. Like his garden, but richer. Like plants I've never seen before.

My heart thumps hard. *Forest.*

Heartwood releases me first, obvious strain around his eyes. Picks up the wrench. I glance away, and—

"Holy . . ." I can't finish the exclamation. "Heartwood . . . look."

The machine's rotation has revealed a perfectly circular passageway in the ceiling, where it previously connected, and just past it, I see . . . light.

Rippling, silver light.

Chapter 17

Heartwood and I exchange a befuddled glance before we both dart for the low end of Machine Four. I reach it first and climb, clumsy in my efforts since the footholds I've grown used to are now on the underside of the behemoth. I slow down when I reach the circular passageway, brushing the ceiling, forgetting to breathe as I pass through.

Floor five measures one story tall, comprising the entire top tier of the tower, which is notably smaller than the floors beneath it, no more than three meters in diameter. The windows here are made of the same translucent material, but they're even smaller, narrower. And in the center of the room flows a wide column made of liquid mirror, cascading like water in a fountain. It ripples with unseen wind, casting silvery patterns across floor, walls, and ceiling.

I can't wrap my head around it.

Heartwood breathes audibly behind me. "It's . . . beautiful," he murmurs.

I step closer, reaching out my hand, but he grasps my shoulder, holding me back. "Is it . . . alive?" I ask.

"No." He releases me and steps forward, about a pace from the silvery wall. Its soft glow makes his pale complexion even paler. "No . . . I would know if it was."

"Because you're a god?"

He doesn't answer. I reach forward again. He tenses. "Nophe—"

"I'll be careful." I tap just the tip of my middle finger against the liquid that somehow defies gravity, then whip it back. Hesitate, unsure if I'd even touched it. I thought I did, but I feel . . . nothing. I try again, lingering a second longer. Nothing. Maybe a little coolness, but it doesn't even feel like liquid. The silvery substance barely sticks to me. The bit that does rolls off my skin like oil on water and doesn't mark my hand in any way.

I push my hand through it, then my forearm, then the rest of me— A fifth machine. I knew there had to be one, but it steals my breath away all the same.

It's slender and tall, reaching the full two stories of the tier. Its pale silver workings are made all the paler by the silver light. Its metal parts reflect the rippling silver, making me feel like I'm underwater. I walk around it, to where it forks and juts outward, through the wall of the tower itself, forming the protrusion outside. I whistle, running my hand over its shape, completely different from any of its companions. Like Machine Four, it appears whole. If anything is broken, it's within.

I wait for Heartwood to join me. When he doesn't, I pass back through the liquid mirror, oddly dry on the other side. Heartwood still marvels at the metallic fountain, cradling his hand to his chest.

"Are you hurt?" I grasp his hand and pull it back, shivering at the current his skin passes through mine. *It's a god thing,* I think.

I really am a bad liar.

Just as I see the blistering burns on the tips of his first two fingers, he curls them inward and tugs from my grasp. "I tried to follow." His gentle voice sounds reverent. "I could not."

Brow furrowed, I approach the column of silver again. Push my hand through. It's like water, but not wet. I circle around, the ripples following my movement, wondering if maybe I found the one secret entrance to the machine, but I can step through the material anywhere. And I do, coming face to face with Machine Five again.

That's when it strikes me. "They're fail-safes," I whisper, shivering. The fortress. The inaccessibility of floors three, four, and five. The hidden lift. The rotating puzzle of Machine Four. The . . . whatever this is, guarding Machine Five. They're fail-safes. They're *meant* to keep people out.

But why? What exactly is this tower trying to protect?

My mind spins, trying to piece it together, when I see something that steals my breath entirely. An engraving on a brilliant silver strut connecting the protrusion to the rest of the machine. A rhombus with three lines, the first cutting through the top, the other two nestled in its center, all parallel.

That's my symbol. The one I invented for myself, that I engraved on my rover. That I found on the little light machine in my home.

How . . . how could it possibly be here?

You're just not as clever as you think, my thoughts fill in. *It's coincidence.* But I know that can't be true. I've never seen this symbol on any of the artifacts I've dug up. I came up with it myself. Drew various versions on my slates until I came up with something I liked. This can't be happenstance. It *can't* be.

That subtle ache in my core, that sense of something missing, pulses within me. Gapes like a great maw. Consuming, hungry, empty. I have to fix this. I have to repair this tower. It's the only way I'll fill this hole. The only way I'll get the answers I seek.

Running my hands over the machine, I try to learn it, to memorize it. My tools are still below, but I need to find what's broken before I can fix it. I move around Machine Five slowly, gazing from bottom to top, top to bottom, though I'll need that ladder if I'm to reach the highest point, and the parts inside the protrusion are inaccessible. There are pistons similar to Machine Four's, an enormous plated cylinder that I'm guessing is another rotary unit, and a complex network of large gears. Closer to the center of the machine, there's a rod, easily six decimeters in diameter, angled above an equal-sized rubber grommet in the floor. A male piece that must—

—fit the female piece in Machine Four.

My jaw drops. I try to measure the trajectory of that male piece if it were extended without any tools, then dive back through the silvery shield. Heartwood hasn't left. He says something, but I don't hear it as I scramble back down Machine Four. Drop to the floor halfway down. Turn around and angle myself so . . .

Yes! They would line up, if I rotated Machine Four back to its original position! They'd fit together. They—

Wait.

Could they all . . . ?

"Nophe." Heartwood starts climbing down the machine.

"I have to see something," I call over my shoulder as I rush to the lift. "I'll be right back!"

I take it down to the second floor. Scramble down the stairs. Throw open the fortified door with renewed strength and run out into the sunlight. Turn, jogging backward, nearly tripping over newly sprouted emilies. The tower fills my view. More, more . . . here.

Lifting my right arm, I line it up with the protrusion jutting out from the third tier. Then lift my left, lining it up with where I *think* that deep piece of Machine One went, the part Heartwood and I attempted to dig out.

The same angle. One straight line.

Slowly I lower my arms. "It's all one machine," I whisper. "And the tower is its shell."

When Heartwood broke Machine Three, it broke all the rest, because they're *connected.*

My mind flashes to the first vision I had, of Machine One in pieces, strewn across the floor.

Because it took you away from me. And if it did, then there's a *before* I have no recollection of.

If . . . if these visions are *memories,* then Heartwood wasn't the first to break the machine. It was broken before. But who broke it the first time?

When was Machine One in pieces? When did Heartwood pull apart the third?

When . . . and what . . . did I forget?

Heartwood emerges from the tower, out of breath, more hair pulled loose from his braid. He slows when he sees me, turns and follows my gaze, but doesn't grasp the revelation.

When he catches his breath, he asks, "What's wrong?"

Nothing forms on my tongue, but it's not true. Everything is wrong. A few heartbeats tick by as I struggle not to drown in the torrent of my thoughts. "What were we fighting over?" I ask.

I feel his eyes on the side of my face. "I . . . didn't want you to hurt yourself, when you dropped—"

"No, not then." I turn toward him, studying his face like I should know it better. I should know it better, shouldn't I? "Before. On the first floor. I was shouting at you."

His eyebrows draw close. "I don't—"

"I told you to 'kiss my mortal ass.'" I lick my lips. "You apologized to me, there." I point to the protrusion. "But . . . I can't remember what we were fighting about."

His brows release like a bowstring snapped. He leans toward me, then takes a step back. "Nophe . . . what did you see?"

"I just told you what I saw."

His countenance crinkles in on itself, like he's going to scream, or cry, or . . .

My heart misses a beat. He is a man lost in the desert without water, a flower plucked of petals, a machine without a motor, dripping oil in a slow, rusting death.

Irritation forgotten, I reach for him. Touch his elbow. "Heartwood . . . what? What *happened* to me? To you?"

But he pulls away, as though I'm in a hangman's noose and he's the one who sentenced me.

"Heartwood!"

"Go, please." Gravel fills his voice. "Go home."

My chest hurts. It *hurts*, and I'm suffocating beneath hundreds of meters of sand. "But the sun—"

"It doesn't matter." He starts back for the tower. "Come back in another cycle, Pelnophe. But please, *please*, leave."

The despondency of his request makes it impossible to refuse. Answers are within reach, but I can't deny him. Not this time.

One of the wells has a collapsing wall, and I need to repair it. Yet for some reason, I find myself locked in my house, staring at my piecemeal light machine.

Is this something I'm supposed to remember? It doesn't speak to me the way the machines at the tower do, but . . .

But I have no ending for that thought. No direction.

This orb has a fuel compartment, unlike the tower machine. *Machine*, singular. But what in Ruin's hell am I supposed to power it with?

I rack my brain until my head's ready to burst. Abandoning my work, I get my digging equipment out of the shed and trek out to the farm. It's late mist, the fog thinning by the time I reach my destination. Before heading down, I set up a pulley system and a harness so I don't get stuck. I remove about half the fallen rubble before shoring up the sides of the well—a filthy job, but someone's got to do it. Then I dig out the rest of the rubble. At least it's not the well someone urinated in. The water's dirty, but it's water, and plants don't care about dirt. Good enough for now.

The next mist has fallen by the time I finish, my hands and knees scratched up. I begin marching home, tired and cranky. My new normal, apparently. But I'd rather be tired and cranky than desperate and weepy. I think of standing in Heartwood's doorway, tearing and scared. *Madness.* I'm still not entirely sure that's not what this is.

Gods. No mortal has markings like those. I wonder if Moseus has something similar, but the idea of asking makes me queasy. I don't know why—Moseus has always been the more reasonable of the pair. But . . .

He's never in the visions, I think, ignoring a chill creeping up my arm. *Why is it always Heartwood?*

Glimmers like small candles light the road ahead of me. Fresh emilies, glowing in clusters, unhindered by the mist. I watch them until I'm about to pass, then stop.

Glowing. Light. If that's not power . . .

Dropping my load, I pull out my shovel and stab it into the packed earth, right next to a pink emily. The roots are strong and deep. I dig down about two and a half decimeters before taking Arthen's knife and slicing through the thick taproot. The glimmer lingers in the center of the flower, but noticeably dimmer. I dig up two more, then carry the haul back to my house.

I carefully pull apart one of the flowers, trying to understand its components, but plants and machines are very different creatures. There's no pollen that I can detect, no residue left on my fingers. I grind a few broad petals in a bowl to make a paste, which I've done before for paint, but I don't discover anything new.

I turn to the roots. We usually shred them and spin them into thread, and they hold well. My shirt is made of emily fibers. But my mind, working overtime, now sees them in a new light. Not as threads, but as wires.

Opening up the sphere of my light machine, I try segmenting part of the root and attaching it to the wires. Nothing happens, even when I close the orb. Reopening it, I tinker with the pieces, noticing a *click* when I turn the base of the wires. Connect them, and—

The orb flickers and illuminates, a brilliant white pouring from the glass. I gasp, eyes watering as I stare directly into it.

Serpent save me, it works. But why? What is this for?

I twist the orb, shutting the power off. I need to show—

No one.

The thought comes unbidden, like it isn't my own. I need to show no one. Not yet. Rolling my lips together, I stash the machine below the floorboards. More questions, but I have one answer, at least.

It's time I get the rest.

Chapter 18

I don't wait for the next mist to trek to the tower.

I expect Moseus to be waiting for me when I arrive, to talk to me about what happened. He was frustrated about Heartwood's gods-talk in the garden, so I suspect he'll be disgruntled about these memories, visions, whatever they are. But when I find him, he's only pleased about the work. About the opening of the fifth floor and the final machine, which I learn he also can't touch. He's thrilled with my theory that it's all one machine, five parts working in harmony. He says nothing of visions or past arguments.

That's how I know Heartwood didn't tell him. And if they're truly like brothers, as Moseus once alluded, then why would Heartwood not tell him what I shared? What I remember?

Hopefully Moseus is happy enough about my progress that he'll excuse another absence. Because Heartwood isn't at the tower. Good.

It'll be easier to corner him in the garden, anyway.

He's there, sitting under the same wickwood tree I'm often drawn to, his back to the arch. I know he hears me—I don't approach with any semblance of stealth—but he doesn't move, doesn't speak, even when I sit beside him, legs folded in front of me, our knees touching.

"I have a lot of questions," I say after several minutes pass. "And you have answers."

He closes his eyes, jaw tight. All right, then. We'll start with something easy.

"Why are you here?"

His eyes open slowly, like he's stirring from a dream. He doesn't look at me.

Going out on a limb, I ask, "Is this the first or second time you've told me?"

A gentle breeze dips into the gorge, rustling my hair.

"A long time ago," he begins, low and quiet, "there was a war among the gods."

I say nothing. If he's talking, I need as many words as I can get before he shuts down again. I don't look at him, only wait.

"Ruin had devoured much, good and evil alike. Many took a stance against it, saying Ruin needed to be destroyed before the worlds as we knew them fell. Others insisted Ruin was a balance in the universe, as shadow is to light. The gods were split. Half went to war, and half refused. I was in the latter half." He swallows, but I hear the tightness of his voice, the shame lacing his words. "I clung to the argument of balance. Ether stood against the Devourer. The gods prevailed. They ended Ruin and returned to their domains. But Ether never did. I tracked her here, to Tampere." He raises his head. "But this world is not like the others. The moment I arrived, it trapped me."

"Trapped?" So much for staying quiet.

Heartwood nods. "It sapped me of my strength. I am only a fraction of what I was." Opening and closing his hands, he continues, "It did the same to Moseus during the war. He was never able to leave. He found me. And that rose ring around the planet, the 'amaranthine wall,' has trapped the casualties of the battle on the other side of the planet. We cannot pass it. No tool, weapon, or ladder can overcome it. Not as we are."

I take a few seconds to absorb this. "And your sister, Ether, lives on the other side?"

"I know she does." His hands ball into fists. "I can *feel* her there. I'm so close. I've been close for years, but never able to reach her."

I chew the inside of my cheek. "I've never been able to pass it, either, though I haven't tried very hard. Maybe if we get the people of Emgarden—"

"I do not wish to make myself known to them."

Pushing off the ground, I shift my seat to see him better. "Why?"

"We are outnumbered," he says, meeting my gaze, and I bite my tongue to stay silent. His brow weighs heavy with regret. Despair. A lump forms in my throat. "And we are weak," he finishes. "Should they deem us unfit or dangerous in any way . . ."

You are *dangerous,* I don't say. If Heartwood can bend steel with his fist in a *weakened* state . . . I can't imagine what his full glory must be like.

I guess I've accepted that he's a god.

"How do you know the tower will help?" I try.

"What else could it do?" he counters. "Moseus has been here cen-turies longer than I. He experienced the war firsthand, while I cowered worlds away. If he believes it connected, so do I."

"The Ancients built it."

"And they, too, have vanished," he affirms.

Coolness, like that of a deep well. Could the Ancients be on the other side of that wall, too? Gods were long lived, if not immortal. Were the Ancients the same?

All the more reason to fix the tower.

"The things I told you about before," I continue, "they feel like memories, but not all of them make sense."

Unclenching his hands, Heartwood knits them together and becomes incredibly interested in the dirt. "What have you seen?"

I recount everything in as much detail as I can. Machine One, in pieces across the floor. Machine Three, intact. Cutting my hand, and

Heartwood bandaging it. The half-formed argument between us. Breath on my neck, footsteps in my house. I think of the explosion I heard that wasn't real and worry it's too much to share. Like it might be the weight that tips the scale in diagnosing me as a madwoman.

He shakes his head. "That isn't much."

A zip of heat chases away the cool. "Then why did you react that way outside the tower? Why did you tell me to leave?"

Closing his eyes, he bows his head as if in prayer. "Because I have been away from home a long time, and I'm weary."

"Heartwood." I can't hold back the exasperation in my voice.

He rises to his feet.

So do I. "That's drivel and you know it."

He turns from me, as though I'm a ghost, unseen and unheard. He walks for the arch like he's on his way to a funeral.

"Damn it, Heartwood!" I chase him. Grab his hand, but he's strong and easily breaks my hold. "Tell me what I'm missing! Tell me what you know about those machines!"

But he continues on, insufferable and silent, past the spring and out of the gorge. Enraged, I scoop up a stone and chuck it after him, striking the archway.

"See if I'll fix your stupid machines!" I yell after him. He *needs* me, and I need answers. "Heartwood!"

He doesn't take the bait.

✺

I spend the next cycle piecing together the exterior of Machine Three, made all the more difficult by three brief, nearly consecutive earthquakes. Knowing the tower operates as one machine, I understand what to look for now. Machines One, Two, and Three align in the tower. After knocking around with a wrench, I discover a hollow internal beam in Machine Two. I ruin a hacksaw slicing into it and drop a screw inside, listening to it fall until it clanks off Machine One. With Machine Three,

I find a passage the width of my arm under a plate bolted at the base of its foundation. The top of Machine Three, the part already connected to the ceiling, pierced through to join with Machine Four, and Machine Four cuts across its chamber to join with Machine Five, once that male piece lowers. I sketch this all out on my slate and stare at it, wondering what it means.

I don't see Heartwood. He's avoiding me. Smart of him, since I'm ready to pin him to the wall myself and claw some answers from his skin.

Moseus yearns for the end of the work. So do I, but I can't ignore my duties in Emgarden. I bring the next batch of scrap metal straight to Arthen, saving a few pieces for personal study. I set them out on a table in the alehouse, sipping a drink. Not strong enough to fill the gap within me, just enough to calm my ever-growing nerves.

Casnia comes in with Amlynn. Salki must be working, and Casnia gets impatient in the fields. Amlynn sits Casnia down at a table and leaves to speak with Maglon. Almost immediately Casnia picks up her things and joins me, taking a long time to situate herself, never making eye contact. Sets up her art, but doesn't draw.

She picks up a bent metal plate, then sets it down, disinterested. "Hot," she says.

"Mid sun," I answer, studying a ball-joint hinge on one of the scraps. I don't understand how it can have such breadth of motion and still connect so firmly, but I'm afraid to take it apart.

"Hot," Casnia repeats. She draws wide scribbles across new parchment, and I wince, feeling the waste. "Hot, hot, hot."

Reaching over, I pick up the bent plate. It's room temperature.

Casnia attacks the parchment with her chalk, breaking off the end. "HOT!" she screams, alerting everyone in the alehouse. "HOT! HOT!"

"Cas!" Jumping from my chair, I grasp her shoulders. "Cas, calm down! Nothing's hot. Do you want hot food?" I wave to Amlynn, who looks concerned, letting her know I've got it under control.

Casnia shakes her head like bugs are crawling through her ears. Then I see her drawing.

She's drawn amidst the scribbles, messily made, a symbol. Three diagonal lines and a small circle at the end.

Reaching over, I turn the plate scrap around. It has the same imprint. Three diagonal lines, a circle at the end.

"Hot," she cries, slapping her parchment.

"Hot," I repeat. Guessing, I point to her symbol. "Hot."

Casnia says nothing.

I pick up the broken chalk and draw the same lines and circle on the corner of her parchment. "Hot," I repeat.

She looks up, sniffs.

I pause, pulse heavy. Pull my chair over so I can sit right next to her. "Cas . . . can you read this?"

She mews.

I grab the other remnant, turning it over. One piece has faint writing along one edge. "Casnia, what does this say?"

But she tilts her head all the way back and stares at the ceiling.

Sighing, I set it down. "Well, it was worth a shot."

"Beast," she murmurs.

"What?"

"*Beast!*" she screams, and starts attacking her parchment again, making harsh lines, but I can see a sloppy semblance of one of the symbols. "Beast! Core!"

"Beast core?" I repeat, just as Amlynn comes over. "Sorry," I apologize to her. "She's just . . . worked up." An idea crosses my mind. "Will you be here a minute?"

Amlynn nods, handing Casnia a cup of water. Casnia drinks it greedily.

I walk out of the alehouse calmly enough, but once I get to the road, I run all the way to my house. Grabbing the sundial, I hurry back. Casnia and Amlynn are just as I left them, though Casnia has relaxed some.

"Hey, Cas." I set the dial in front of her, keeping my back to Gethnen, who thinks I surrendered the sundial to Arthen. "Remember this? You and Salki gave it to me."

She spits a mouthful of water back into her cup.

"Cas? Can you read this?" I point to the numbers.

Amlynn looks at me like I'm crazy.

Casnia sets her water aside roughly, spilling the contents over the table. Amlynn curses and goes to Maglon for a rag. Casnia stabs her finger into the metal. "Six, seven, eight, nine." The rest devolves into grunts.

Lowering myself into Amlynn's chair, I breathe, "You *can* read this, can't you?"

Salki doesn't know any of the Ancients' language. I barely do myself. No one could have taught Casnia. No one I can fathom.

Casnia sobers suddenly, calm as death itself. She touches one of the symbols on the side of the sundial, the slanted line with the circle. "Morning."

"Mourning?" I repeat. "Mourning over who?"

But I've lost her. She hunkers over her art, coloring in earnest now, and no amount of cajoling grabs her attention.

"Give her a break, Pell," Amlynn pleads, cleaning up the water. "She's behaving."

Sighing, I gather my scraps.

Amlynn hands one to me. "Are these from the tower?"

I stiffen. Admittedly, I'm not *always* the most clandestine in my journeys, but . . . "No, why?"

Amlynn shrugs. "I guess you found a cache somewhere?"

"Why do you think they're from the tower?"

She hesitates at the sharpness in my tone.

I clear my throat. "Sorry."

"It's fine. You used to go there, is all."

I narrow my eyes. "Used to?"

Amlynn twists the rag in her hands. "I don't mean anything by it—"

"No, no," I force friendliness into my voice. "But what do you mean, *used to*?"

She glances at Maglon. "I saw you headed that way about a year ago. Place has always been shut up, so I wondered."

Blood drains from my face and pools in my chest. *A year ago.* Seven hundred fifty cycles. But I only met Moseus about forty cycles ago.

"You're mistaken," I mutter halfheartedly.

She shrugs. "Probably."

I'm making her uncomfortable. Without another word, I leave the alehouse, dump the scraps at the forge, and take the sundial back home. At least, I reassure myself as I lie in my bed and wait for the mist to fall, if I *am* crazy, I'm not the only one.

❧

I consider asking Moseus straight out, but he's meditating when I arrive. He's deep into it, too. Doesn't even budge when I open the door, and I never bothered to oil *his* hinges.

I don't search for Heartwood. I don't have the courage to. I need to think.

The tower machines don't have any notable compartments to put emilies in. I know that already, but I check again anyway, even investigating those hollow beams in Machines Two and Three. It would take a lot of the flowers to power this fortress, but if that's one of its secrets, I don't know how to utilize it. I could rig something up, maybe, the same way I could rig up steam power, but the machines weren't meant to be added to.

I notice something, however, as I move through the tower. The machines all line up . . . and so do their aggravating power switches. Discovering that, I sketch out more components and conclude that each machine has large wheels that align as well. After a few measurements, I confirm that it's an enormous pulley system, minus the cable. The tower's rope isn't long enough, so I make a note to bind extra wires and emily roots into a cord that will stretch clear from Machine Three to Machine One and back. The movement of Machine Three should power Machines Four and Five, if I've calculated it correctly.

I tighten a few nuts at the top of Machine Four, which I rolled back into place earlier, then realize I'm finished with it. All it needs now is the cord for the pulley system—

Breath on my neck.

I freeze, lungs seizing. I'm alone, but that . . . it feels just like before. Steeling myself, I slowly peer behind me—

I'm wiring Machine Two when Heartwood comes behind me, one arm around my waist, nuzzling my neck.

"You're back." I grin and lean into him, head against his shoulder. "Anything?"

"No." But he's not upset by it. "I had no expectations."

"Still."

The room returns to me, just as I'd left it. My hands, gone cold, shake. My lungs suck in air, protesting time without breath.

That . . . that was *real*. Denying it is pointless. I felt his arm around me, his lips against my throat. I *still feel it.* Even the leap of my heart at his return—he'd been gone a while. A leap, and then comfort. Contentment.

Reaching up, I touch the side of my neck. Then my cheek.

Why am I crying? I swipe the tears away and stare at the streaks they leave on my hands, as though I've never seen tears before.

A year ago, Amlynn said.

I can't do this anymore.

Leaving my tools, I pick my way down the machine, my grip tentative, my quivering limbs pebbling. I step into the lift and numbly pull the cord. Second floor.

My instinct is right. Heartwood's there, in his chamber, sitting at the window again. I don't bother knocking. I never did knock, did I?

He looks up, his body language soft and open for a split second, then closed and hard the next. "Pell—"

"Tell me," I interrupt. *Pell,* he said. Not *Nophe.*

He pushes off the windowsill. His unbound hair, slightly damp, waves around his shoulders and waist as he moves to push past me.

I shove both heels into the corners of the doorway, barring him.

"Tell me." I want to demand, to threaten, but rising emotion chokes and breaks my words. I step forward, and Heartwood retreats like I'm a viper, his hard façade melting until he's just as he was that first time, standing on the stairs, hurt and despairing and limned with regret.

I shut the door behind me, closing off his escape. "I remember," I whisper, blinking back a tear, "but I don't. It's all pieces and shards and fragments that don't fit together. But you know, don't you? Someone in Emgarden said she saw me coming to the tower a year ago. I wasn't here a year ago. Or was I?"

Through gritted teeth, Heartwood says, "I have nothing for you." And pushes past me for the door.

I grab his wrist, holding tight because I know his strength. "Heartwood, please." I swallow a sob. "Did I know you, before all this?" I tug, but he's unyielding. "Didn't you . . . love me?"

That's what does it. His arm goes limp in my grasp. He turns toward me, vibrant emerald eyes darting back and forth in short movements as he studies my face. I wonder what he sees there. Whatever it is, it's enough.

"Ether, forgive me," he whispers, breaking my grasp and seizing my wrist, pulling me to him, chest to chest, hand to hair, nose to nose.

And he kisses me.

Chapter 19

Heartwood's warm lips press, tilt, demand. The scents of earth and grass and *green* fill my senses, and I startle at the familiar shape of his mouth against mine. Nerves pop beneath my skin and bleed into my chest. When I respond, his touch turns hungry, his lips and tongue insistent. He releases my wrist and coils his arm behind my back, bending me to him, claiming me entirely. He is root and I am water. He is oil, and I am machine.

My lungs empty as I arch into him, desperate to be closer. My hands run down his bare shoulders and over the prints of his godhood, memorizing every dip and facet as he murmurs my name into my hair.

I jerk back, breaking the spell, though his arms are reluctant to release me. Another vision, another memory, and in the moment, it was every bit as visceral as the kiss that just transpired between us.

Heartwood steps back, the pink amor of our kiss evident across his lips. "Forgive me," he says. He'd said it before, but not to me.

I shake my head, bewildered even as my heart beats dizzying spirals beneath my ribs. I see him anew, *feel* him anew, the length of his torso, the brush of his hair. For a few shaky breaths, there is nothing but him. No window, no tower, no unmoving sun. "Why . . . why won't you tell me? Why *haven't* you told me?" When he looks away, I press, "You said Machine Three took me away. What happened at Machine Three?"

"This," he whispers without gesture. "You lost all of it."

My lips part, and I remember Heartwood approaching me after I used the turning rod on Machine Three, testing my memory. "But . . . but if we . . . why wouldn't you explain it to me sooner? How long has it been? Why would—"

"Because you betrayed us, Nophe."

My mouth shuts so swiftly that my teeth click.

Heartwood runs his hands up his forehead and down through his hair, the left one catching on a snag in the long, white locks. He tilts his head, and I realize he's listening. For what? Moseus?

"It was better this way." The coarseness in his voice makes my own throat tighten. "You forgot me—us—and the work, and we thought enough had been done to move on without you. We were wrong."

"B-But—" A headache blossoms across my skull as my mind desperately tries to loosen the knots of these revelations. "I wouldn't . . . I don't even know what I did, Heartwood, but I'm an honest person. Ask anyone in Emgarden—"

He casts me a withering, yet utterly despondent, look.

"But you won't, because of all your damn secrets," I snap.

He takes a deep breath. "Please keep your voice down."

I do. "Because of Moseus?"

"He . . ."—Heartwood struggles—"does not have the same bias I do."

Bias. The press of his body against mine certainly felt like more than a *bias.* My face flushes at the thought, but I ignore it.

Rubbing my eyes, I take a few seconds to orient myself. "Tell me what happened."

"I don't know."

"Tell me how I betrayed you," I specify, every muscle in my body tightening in self-defense. If so much as a pin drops, I'm going to burst into tears. *Too much, too much, too much.*

Heartwood brushes past me, but the room gives him nowhere to retreat. Folding his arms, he peers out the window. Sunlight pokes through fading mist, highlighting his features in a way that makes him look both young and old, both god and mortal. It is a breath-stealing

169

moment. I am completely intoxicated by his beauty and wonder how it didn't floor me the moment I first saw him on those stairs.

But that *wasn't* the first time I saw him. Why can't I remember the first?

"Theft," he answers simply. "You'd been stealing from the machines. And if they're incomplete—"

"The wall won't open," I finish. I shake my head. "Heartwood, I'm nearly finished here. I haven't found any missing parts, other than a cord I need to work the pulley system. And that thing would have been far too long and too heavy to steal with any sort of covertness."

His focus shifts to me, and for a moment I think he'll kiss me again. My stomach flips at the thought.

"Moseus has worked tirelessly to repair the machines," he says. "To document what needs to be replaced. But he doesn't understand them the way you do."

I try to find the best means of countering. "But why would I take pieces of them when I can study the machines here, whole?"

"Your people need the metal, do they not?"

I pause. "Was I not paid, the first time?"

He nods.

I work my mouth. Close the distance between us. Emgarden needs the metal. It's always needed the metal. But I would never have . . . there's no new machines in Emgarden! "Heartwood, you know me. Better than I know you, apparently. I would never—"

The hidden compartment beneath the kitchen table. The frame and the equilibrated orb.

The cog in the tree.

Serpent save me. It couldn't possibly be . . .

"We feared," Heartwood continues, mechanical now, trying to stuff his feelings back into whatever weathered chest he tries to keep them in, "that pressing the issue would hurt you further. Mortal minds are . . . delicate."

"Don't patronize me," I hiss.

He doesn't react. Maybe he's used to being snapped at. I can't remember.

Heartwood suddenly tenses. Grabs my hand and pulls me toward the door, which opens silently on its recently greased hinges. "He's alert. You need to go."

I stall in the doorway. "Heartwood, do you fear Moseus?"

That catches him by surprise. "No. But he is a passionate being, and you've betrayed him once already."

Moseus, *passionate*? I would laugh, were the situation not so dire. So confounding.

"I didn't, Heartwood," I insist, shocked by the twisting in my own chest. I don't want to leave. I don't remember him, but I don't want to leave him.

His brow buckles with agony, and my heart pumps a sharp pang into my core. "You merely don't remember it, Nophe."

"And that's not atonement enough?"

He presses his lips together.

I pull away on feet of iron. "What does it mean? *Nophe*. You don't say it right." I'd understood some of their language before, and yet this word eludes me completely. My memories are still too piecemeal.

A feather of warmth touches his lips. "*Nuffy* is a strange name." It's how the end of my name *should* be pronounced.

I wait.

He sighs. "*Nofe* is a word in my native tongue. It means *goddess*."

And he shuts the door, leaving me to my own echoing hollowness.

I loved him, I think, elbows on the table in my home, fingers turning mushy grain over with a spoon. The bowl of porridge sits full, oversoaked and underseasoned, waiting to be devoured. I hear others in Emgarden, about their tasks, socializing in the road, tending their animals, hollering to one another. The cacophony floats through my windows, providing an uneven ambiance to accompany my thoughts.

I force a bite of my meal down, but it does nothing to fill this gaping hole inside me. *Something is missing.* And I think I know what it is.

I've been looking at Heartwood differently the last few cycles. It would be childish to deny it. Foolish to think that, beyond the confusion and distress, I didn't enjoy his mouth on mine. But it was the vision, the *memory*, of so much more, that shook me. It lasted less than a second, but in that second I was another Pell, and that other Pell loved Heartwood with everything she was. Even cutting out the emotion of it, I know. I do not give myself freely, nor easily. I trust that she didn't, either.

You betrayed us.

My chest hurts enough for me to double over. I need to eat, but I'm not hungry. Maybe Salki or Amlynn can brew me a tincture to make me sleep. But you know who would probably be the best at that? Heartwood. He knows all kinds of things about plants.

Hey, would you mind drugging me? I could ask him. *I would like to not think about us for a while.*

He'd probably do it without complaint, too.

Groaning, I push the bowl away and stab my elbows into the table, cradling my head in my hands.

You betrayed us.

Pressing my lips together until they go numb, I stand, move the table, and pry up the floor, pulling out my hidden light machine. *Did I?* I've never stolen anything in my life—it's one of the reasons Arthen's accusations about his knife rankled me so much. Setting down the machine, I pull the knife from my pocket, examining the leather braiding on its hilt. Who's stealing what, Heartwood? I still don't know why he had this. Or why I did.

There's something else I'm not remembering. Something important. But . . .

Sighing, I stuff the blade in my pocket and hunt around for a piece of parchment. I don't have anything clean, so I rip a fresh piece from my old artifact notes. I scrawl, *Meet me in the garden.*

He'll know who it's from.

I make myself dig up emily roots for the rest of the sun and into the mist. Moseus helps me sort through his collected scrap for wires for the pulley cable. I've only just started twisting them together when the mist begins to lift.

I slip the note under Heartwood's door before grabbing my bag and heading to the canyon.

The mist has long dispersed by the time Heartwood comes. I sit in the shade beneath a drape of fairy wisps, my back to the red rock, not far from a poisonous chrystanus, my eyes closed, dozing but never truly sleeping. I open them when he approaches and reach for my bag.

Heartwood keeps his distance. "I do not think it's wise—"

"Here." I pull out the light machine and toss it to him. He almost drops it. "That's what I have. The only thing in my house I can't account for, that I might have taken from the tower. My blacksmith can confirm I never gave anything to him until the first load of scraps from Moseus, if you want to talk to him. I have a feeling I mentioned him before."

Heartwood studies me, then the machine. Turns it over in his hands.

"There was a cog, too, but I found it here. Could have been you who took it." I shrug. "I don't know, but it's in Machine Two now. It opened the lift."

Running his hand over the frame, Heartwood says, "I don't recognize any of this."

"Machines One through Four are working," I add, though he already knows. "Five was inaccessible, so it can't be from there."

Heartwood hands the device back to me. "What does it do?"

"Makes light."

His lip ticks. "I'm not surprised you would overcomplicate a lantern."

I slip it back into my bag. It has to go in diagonally, or it won't fit. I grab the strap of the satchel, but hesitate to stand. "What were we fighting about?"

He snorts. "Which time?"

I grin. I don't know why. "Often, huh?"

Mirth softens his expression, but he's tense. I see it in his body language, reading it the way Casnia read the Ancient scrawl on the scrap metal. Like I know part of it intrinsically, but my understanding lacks finesse.

I've hurt him, and I can't remember how. Can it really all tie to Machine Three? I make a mental note to watch myself around it.

Pushing off the rock, I get on my feet. Dust off my trousers. "I don't know what this changes," I offer, hefting my bag, "but I wanted to show you."

Mirth fades. "Thank you."

"I'll fix the tower machines," I promise. "I'm nearly there. Your tower will operate, and you'll see your kin again. I'll . . . go, after that. Leave you to your people, and your peace. I . . . I never meant to hurt you, Heartwood."

He looks away too quickly, teeth clenched, shoulders stiff. I'm doing it again, without any effort at all. Hurting him, and he's doing a pathetic job of masking it. Just like me. Sighing, I head through the arch. Heartwood doesn't follow. He needs his garden and his solace.

It's a long walk, but I stop at home to stow the machine before returning to the tower. The end is so close, but I have a lot of work ahead of me, and I intend to finish what I started.

The trip has exhausted me. I need to sleep. When I get to the second floor, I notice the lift has been called. Moseus has gone upstairs. Might as well fill him in. I need to dig up more emily roots. It's not easy, and it will not be happening until after a solid mist.

I summon the lift back and step in, letting it take me up to the fourth floor. No Moseus, and Machine Four has been rolled back to expose the passageway near the ceiling. I try to recall if I told him where the lever was. Curious, I climb up it, moving silently. I want to see what he's doing. If Heartwood is a riddle, Moseus is pure mystery.

I'm almost to the circular door, high enough to peer through it, when I nearly lose my grip on the machine. Moseus stands there, outside the liquid mirror. He's removed his heavy robe, and . . .

He's not complete.

I claw through mortification as I try to make sense of what I see. Moseus stands before Machine Five with his arms outstretched, like he's trying to commune with it. In his torso is an enormous, smoke-edged hole from the top of his shoulder blades to the base of his spine. I can see the mirror shield right through it.

Mouth dry, I quickly pick my way back down, desperate to stay as quiet as possible. Tiptoe to the lift and drop back down to floor two. By the time I reach my room, a cold sheen of sweat covers my skin.

Heartwood said Tampere took from him, that he's only a fraction of what he was. It took from Moseus, too. It took *a lot*.

If I didn't believe they were gods before, I definitely do now. And as I shut my door behind me, pressing to ensure the latch clicks, I decide to adopt Heartwood's methods.

And say absolutely nothing.

Chapter 20

For the next several cycles, I keep to myself.

Scrounging and digging for resources lets my body take over for my mind. Coiling and twisting roots, twine, and wires for a cable keeps me present. The Pell I was before never got this far. She didn't assemble a cable long enough to reach down five stories and back up again. She has no relevant memories here.

She was a different person, one whom I do not know.

It's the truth, and that truth grounds me. Keeps me focused on work and draws my thoughts from both Heartwood's kiss and Moseus's dark, gaping hole. Separates me from the literal gods I share this tower with.

I wonder what it will be like, when the others are free. I doubt they'll stay here. If I were a goddess, I wouldn't settle on Tampere.

Nofe *is a word in my native tongue. It means* goddess.

But I'm not Nophe. Those words become a mantra as my fingers blister and callus, assembling this never-ending cord, until finally, twenty cycles later, it's finished.

Once I replace the lever and fulcrum nestled in the heart of Machine Five, it's able to drop down to connect with Machine Four. I make a slow walk through the tower, inspecting each machine, all the way down to Machine One, where Moseus greets me.

"They should all function now." I press a hand to Machine One, to the part I earlier rigged up for a turning rod. "We just need to figure out how to fuel it. There's nothing I can find." I've gathered a lot of emilies, but it's not nearly enough. And I don't know how to connect a separate power source to this tower.

"Can you alter it?" Moseus asks, hands clenched beneath his long sleeves, voice eager. I try not to look at him. When I do, I see only that gaping hole. "Like you did when you wound it?"

I click my teeth together a few times. "I mean . . . maybe. To use manpower on each machine would have to involve Emgarden. A lot of Emgarden. But these machines weren't designed to function that way. I can't wrap my head around how the Ancients did it." I circle Machine One with my small lantern, as though the mechanism will finally reveal its last secret to me. It doesn't. "I think emilies could also be a power source, but . . . it would take a *lot* of emilies, and there's nowhere for them to go."

I haven't yet tested how long the energy of an emily can last. I think Nophe knew, but she hasn't deigned to tell me. The tower shivers as the earth moves below, but neither tower nor Tampere want to tell me, either, so I ignore them.

"Hmm." Moseus approaches Machine One until his nose nearly touches its outer coils. "I have meditated on this a great deal, trying to expand my mind. But"—he sighs—"I do not know, either."

I guess even gods aren't omniscient.

"I'll do the same," I offer. "Give my mind a rest and see if something comes to me." I've been in and out of all these machines. I know every millimeter of them, and *nothing* has given me a clue as to how to power them. I've speculated about everything, from the liquid mirror draining down into the tower and turning the mechanisms itself, to all this being a ruse by the Ancients to play with mortal minds. I genuinely don't know where else to turn.

"If Emgarden must," Moseus grinds out the words and punctuates them with a wearying breath, "then we will accept their help. But only if it must."

I turn around. "Where is Heartwood?"

"I am not his overseer. He is capable of tending to himself." Moseus rubs his forehead. "To be so close, and yet so far."

I hug myself, catch myself, and fold my arms instead. "We'll figure it out."

"See that you do."

I guess he missed the *we* in that sentiment, but I don't point it out. Moseus retires to his meditation. I stand there, waiting for something I cannot name, another vision or revelation, or for the tower to speak to me, but it answers with dark silence, punctuated only by the sound of my breathing.

I fixed the machines, didn't I?

So why do I feel as empty as when I first arrived?

I don't know what to do with myself.

When I get home, I eat and try to rest, but I can't. My mind spins. So I bring out a slate and attempt to work out the tower machines, but I don't know where to start, so there's nothing to write. I decide to work on something else, but the wells are fine and no one has died. I consider helping out on the farm, but by the time I get there, everyone has wrapped up. It's late sun, and the mists are near, and while it's not impossible to tend the crops in the mist, it's not the easiest, either. So I find my rover to see if it needs any maintenance—it doesn't—and wander home again.

I could visit the alehouse. But I feel like a wet rag wrung dry, and I don't have it in me to socialize. To pretend like everything is fine when it's not. There's no solution to this listlessness, plain and simple. I just have to endure until I . . . get better.

I rub a spot between my breasts nearly to bruising. *Something is missing,* it sings. *I know,* I counter, but what am I supposed to do? I can't power the machines on wishes and prayers. I can't pack in this gap with dirt or effort or anything in between.

I pace the length of my house, then the width, back and forth, crossing and recrossing my path. I've never thought of this humble abode as claustrophobic, but with the mist seeping through its open windows, it feels stifling. I want to cry and scream and sleep, but I settle for nearly ripping my hair out at the scalp, then throwing the door open and climbing the short ladder to the roof. Sprawling out on the shingles, I let the fog roll over me, claiming me as its own, merging me with the rest of Emgarden and our little corner of Tampere. I breathe it in, slow and deep, and let it out the same. Close my eyes and find no rest.

Several minutes pass before I sit up, a sigh on my lips, and plant my elbows on my knees. The solution for the tower will come to me eventually. It has to. If not me, then Moseus or Heartwood. Someone will sort it out. We're so close. We're all *so close,* and yet the task looms monumentally over us, murky and confusing and utterly unachievable.

I'm no engineer. I'm a *tinkerer.* A woman with too much time on her hands, who likes to wander the dry expanses around her town looking for artifacts of a people long past. I am nothing more, and I never will be.

Gritting my teeth, I rub the heels of my hands into my eyes. Blink away pink points of light and let the mist fill my vision once more. And—

My mind voids thought. Breath catches.

And . . . there's something familiar about this.

I can't pinpoint what. I've been up on my roof countless times. But something about it itches the back of my mind. Where I'm sitting? The fall of the mist? What? I want to ask the tendrils of fog, but I fear that speaking will somehow destroy this partially formed spell.

Leaning forward, I listen, search. Move up on the shingles, over, down—

179

Here. This is where I sat, before. With my toes against the eaves. And then . . .

Standing, I walk across the roof. Pause. Climb down the ladder. Yes, I did this. I've done it so many times, but I did this . . . then. I start back for my door, but no—that's wrong. I went this way.

Step by careful step, I wend my way west. Pause, consider, and continue. Not toward the main road. Not toward the tower or Salki or anyone else in Emgarden, but over this way, toward the eroded stone wall surrounding the town. It's more decorative than anything else. Not hard to step over it. I sit, then rotate on my butt and swing my legs over. Walk out a little farther into the mists, one hand out like I might run into something, though I know there's nothing of note over here. It's just . . . away. But that's what I was trying to do, wasn't it? Be *away.*

I pause, trying to gain my bearings. Trying to hold on to the slip of memory that's as intangible as the vapor around me. No, I didn't stop here. I went farther out. This way?

I walk a little quicker, turning more south. Yes, this is right. I went this way. And . . . quiet steps beside me. I wasn't alone. Who, then? Salki? Heartwood? Moseus? Arthen?

Here. I pause again. Spin slowly, but only see dull gray mist. But something happened here. Something important. Crouching, I drop my head into my hands. *Think, Pell.* What was it? What happened that's so important?

I suck in a deep breath. It's fading. I feel it fading, and if it leaves, I'll never get it back.

"Think, think," I whisper, pleading. "Come on, you know this." I swallow, palms moist. Lick my lips. Close my eyes. "Nophe, please," I murmur. "Help me."

Perched on the roof, I let my eyes unfocus. The subtle colors in an otherwise dreary mist come out when I do, showing pinks and blues and greens, not unlike the emilies sprouting across the road. I watch them for a long time, long enough for the mists to curl the ends of my hair. Long enough for my mind to empty.

I don't know how he saw me up on that roof. I would have missed him, had his foot not crunched in gravel. I think he wanted me to see him. Heartwood has always been light on his feet, when he wants to be.

Blinking the colors away, I look down. Scoot forward on the shingles so he can hear me without yelling. He's donned his black cloak; it makes him look foreboding.

"Not like you to wander town," I say. The mist is too high to see for sure, but I know he smiles at that.

"I wanted to see you," he confesses, and my skin pebbles. Not from the cool fog, but I blame the weather anyway, because it's easier. Safer.

I hold out my hands. "Here I am."

His head tilts to one side. That beautiful hair draped over one shoulder. "Can we talk?"

I don't answer, merely stand and climb down the ladder. He's there when my feet touch the ground, and I lead the way out of town; I know how he and Moseus feel about Emgarden. Best not to chat here. We're silent as we walk, me sliding over the stone wall, him simply stepping over it. Needing something to do with them, I shove my hands into the pockets of my trousers, which are thankfully clean. We walk a little ways before the silence makes me itch.

"I just need to adjust the framework," I say, "and the rest of Machine One should click in. There's this one gear that—"

"I don't want to talk about the tower."

I glance up at Heartwood, taking in the way the mist dances around him, like he's part of it. His hair loops in a conglomeration of plaits, and I wonder if he spent extra time on it, and why. Probably because he was bored. The tower seems unbelievably boring to anyone who isn't elbow-deep in grease and metal.

"Oh?" I ask. "What, then? Interested in starting your own crops?" I'm goading him, but goading him is one of my favorite pastimes, and it helps me ignore the racing of my heart. I silently thank the fog for keeping my skin cool. "You have to dig pretty deep for the richer soil; the stuff on top is almost entirely sand, so you have to turn it over—"

He pinches the bridge of his nose. "You are tireless."

I turn and face him. "You like it. I dare you to tell me you don't."

Those vivid green eyes study my face for a long moment. I'm sure he can hear my pounding heart. It shakes my thighs and fills my head. "I do," he replies, after eons have passed. "Unfortunately, I do."

"Unfortunately?"

He adjusts his cloak. He knows better than to offer it to me; I snapped at him pretty good last time. "Moseus—"

"Needs some booze and a very long walk," I offer.

He chuckles softly. "I have not been as subtle as I should be around him."

I swallow. "Subtle how?" But I know. I've caught his glances too many times. Accepted his assistance fixing the machines even when there's little to nothing he can help me with. I've lost sleep talking to him, only to be reminded by his counterpart of the criticalness of repairing the tower. Heartwood always sobers at the reminders—his sister is waiting for him, after all. I'm drawn to him, always, but root myself to the machines. He has nothing to root himself to.

He reaches forward and slides a knuckle beneath my chin, his warm touch a stark contrast with the fog's chill. "Subtle in the way I no longer wish to be. Nophe—"

"That's the second time you've called me that." My blood rushes through my veins swiftly enough to make me faint.

He rolls his lips together. "Do you want me to explain it to you?"

"No," I murmur, pushing his hand away and grabbing the front of his shirt. I'm too short to reach him, but he obliges me and meets me, his lips crashing into mine. The world around us slumbers, and yet a symphony sounds in my ears. His hands on my waist ignite me; I can't help the tiny moan that escapes me, the release of want I've been carrying cycle after cycle. My fingers entwine in that glorious mane as my mouth demands, demands, demands, but Heartwood gives, gives, gives, and I am undone by his tender passion, overjoyed that this desperation has not been mine alone. I kiss him with everything in me, content never to let him go.

I blink, and the mist cascades around me. He was here, before. I loved him, before. I—

I gasp so hard I nearly choke on it.

Serpent save me, I *remember*.

Chapter 21

I'm a little buzzed when I head home. We'd had a good game of dice going until Frantess opened her big mouth and ruined everything. Now everyone feels awkward, Gethnen especially. But it's probably for the best—I might have gotten carried away and had one or two glasses too many, and then I'd get lost in the mist and have a massive headache by late sun. I'm too old to drink more than a glass or two at a time, unless Maglon waters it down. Which he does, sometimes, especially when the harvest wasn't great. We all act like we don't notice.

I'm five paces from my door when I see a shadow in the mist. It nears, revealing too-white skin and too-white hair; a wraith clothed in black. When it moves toward me, I scream. Only a chirp of the sound makes it past my lips before the wraith's large hand covers my mouth and presses me against the house, barring both my arms with one of his. Not my legs, though, and I get in a swift kick on his upper thigh before he grapples me again and maneuvers out of harm's way.

"I'm not here to hurt you," he hisses, an unfamiliar accent clipping his words.

Ruin's hell he isn't there to hurt me! I kick again. Writhe, but the guy is strong. Incredibly strong.

"Are you the artifact collector?" he rushes.

That pacifies me for a moment. I blink away the fog, trying to get a better look at the stranger's face. He has abnormally long hair, whiter than Entisa's, pulled back in a braid. Several pieces have come loose and hang over his neck and face, making him look wild. His eyes . . . no one in Emgarden has eyes like that. Skin like that, strength like that. My mind can't wrap itself around his existence, let alone the predicament I've found myself in.

Where did he come from? There's no one else—

He repeats the question.

I nod as well as I can with his hand—it smells like *flowers*, of all things—pressed under my nose. How does he know about the artifacts?

He visibly relaxes. "Good." Then, "What's your name?"

"I can't say it with your hand on my mouth, half-wit," I mutter against his skin, completely unintelligible. He carefully removes his hand and lets up on my shoulders, but he stays in proximity, ready to strike if I try to run. I'm fast, but I don't think I can outrun those legs. So instead, I answer, "Pell."

He searches my face. "That doesn't linguistically match the people here—"

"Pelnophe. Who in Ruin's hell are you?"

He sets his jaw. "I am someone in need of your help. My comrade and I live in the tower, and—"

"Wait, what?" I push off the house. The stranger glances down the road, ensuring we're alone. "That tower?" I point in its direction. "No one lives in that tower."

"It's recent," he explains, sounding now more like a man dying than one about to abduct me. "We need it operating again, but we . . . we don't understand the mechanics of this world. You seem to."

I gape for a moment. "What mechanics could a tower possibly have?" My insides squirm at the possibility.

"The machines," he answers, and my stomach drops. "Machines built by creatures of old. They're in incredible disrepair."

185

"The . . . Ancients?"

He nods.

My mind can't picture it. All the artifacts I've been able to scavenge are small, and none are whole. What could an entire, *impenetrable* fortress hold? Far more than I've ever seen, surely. The very thought of beholding true Ancient tech, let alone touching it, sends shivers down my spine. My fingers twitch at my sides.

"I . . ." I try to find words, wishing I was just a smidgen more sober. "I . . . You want me to fix them?"

"Please. You can see them now, if possible. We . . . we don't want to be seen by the others."

"There's more of you?"

"One more," he states, and I recall him saying as much earlier.

I shake my head. "Who are you? What's your name?"

"My name is Heartwood." He steps back, giving me some breathing room. "Please, Pelnophe."

He says my name strangely, elongating the vowels. "PEL-nuh-fee," I correct. "Pell is fine. Preferred. And . . . how many machines?"

"Two." He again checks the road. "But we've nearly reached a third."

"Nearly reached?"

"I will show you, if you swear secrecy."

He has the wrong person. There's no way I'm capable of . . . but who else around here would be? And . . . I have to see for myself. Bring a kitchen knife and a hammer, in case things get ugly. I can fight myself out of a corner if I need to, especially if there are only two of them. Maybe.

"How do you know about me?" I ask.

"Not many venture out into the desert," he says. "We've seen you coming and going, with Ancient tech in your hands. You're our best hope at fixing the tower."

I digest this. "And . . . what do the machines do?"

He considers me for a long moment. "I will explain on the way."

Then, probably because I *am* a little drunk, I agree, and let this "Heartwood" escort me to a long-forgotten, impenetrable tower.

He doesn't touch me again.

The machines are . . . broken. Badly broken.

The first has most of a foundation, but the rest lies in pieces on the floor. The second is similar. The third . . . they're still burrowing through the ceiling to reach a third. They've made enough of a hole in the nearly impenetrable barrier to look through. A machine lingers there.

I wonder who attempted to build such an incredible network of technology, only to abandon it. And fear I can never possibly fix it.

"Heartwood is a strange name," I quip, hanging nearly upside-down in Machine One to attach some wires. "A deer made out of wood? Who names their kid that?"

He scoffs. "It's the center of a tree."

"Trees barely have centers." The wickwoods make up ninety percent of the trees around here, and they don't grow any thicker than my thigh. "Moseus has . . . well"—I grunt and turn a nut—"a *more* normal name. Can you hold that thing higher?"

Heartwood obliges, casting light over my work. Strands of hair stick to my eyelashes, and the blood rushing to my face makes it feel thick.

"Moseus's name is in a very old tongue," Heartwood replies. "It does not translate well."

"And yours does?"

I guess he nods, but I can't see it. A beat later, he says, "Yes."

"Well, what's your *actual* name then?"

He chuckles, more to himself than at me. "You would never be able to pronounce it."

"Try me."

He hesitates, suddenly sober. In soft tones, he confesses, "I have not heard my true name for a long time, even from my own lips."

Grabbing a beam, I right myself. Several uncomfortable seconds pass. "You don't have to . . . if you don't want to. I'm just goading you." Though I'm sincerely curious now.

The barest smile curves his mouth. "*Ytton'allanejrou.* That is my name in Thestean."

It's so elegantly lyrical on his lips, I don't dare try to repeat it.

I rest my shovel on the ground, wiping sweat before it streams into my eyes. We've dug a sizeable hole outside the tower, yet we're getting nowhere. The root of Machine One just keeps going, going, going.

"Why," I pant, "is Moseus . . . not helping?"

Heartwood swings the pickaxe once more before wiping sweat from his brow. He stripped off his leathers to his waist and coiled his thick braid atop his head. How he got it to stay there, I don't know. "He is of weak constitution."

"Well"—I stab my shovel down, moments from giving up—"if he dies, I have a great place to bury him."

Moseus has been working on something for a while, keeping to himself while he builds it, looking a little sicker every day. He doesn't give me any warning when he hammers something pink into cracks and dents that he and Heartwood chipped into the ceiling opposite Machine Two. I look away when he ignites it.

The *boom* deafens me. It reverberates through the tower and my entire body, shaking my bones and rattling my teeth, ten times stronger than any passing earthquake. Shock knocks me off my heels and onto my hip. Bits of pebble-sized debris fly past me, and I cover my head, afraid of more. Someone presses into my back, and I glance up to see Heartwood there, shielding me. He was helping me organize screws by size a moment ago. Now he's a wall between me and the other keeper's madness.

When the dust clears, he pulls away. "Moseus . . . ," he starts, but doesn't finish.

Lowering my arms, I stand and look at the wreckage. Stone and sand cover the floor. A slow-settling layer of dust coats everything, myself included. But before the hard words climbing up my throat reveal themselves, I notice what Moseus has done.

There's a hole in the ceiling. Blown right through the stone. Moseus sets a ladder against it and climbs up. For the first time, I see him grin.

"It's all here," he announces triumphantly. "I knew it."

Heartwood steps onto the second floor and pauses. "What is this?"

"It's a party." I sit on a blanket on the stone floor to protect myself from the cold. My trousers are never enough, and these sleeping shorts are certainly no better. Hefting the bottle, I shake it so the ale inside splashes.

Frowning, Heartwood glances down the stairs, but Moseus is resting. I've already checked. "I do not think this is a good idea," he says.

"Why?"

He has no answer for that. I pat a cushion next to me—stolen from his room—and pour him a cup.

Had I tried this, oh, thirty cycles ago, Heartwood would have shaken his head at me, retrieved the cushion, and retired to his room. But he's been spending a lot more time with me lately. I catch him watching me from the corner of my eye. He catches me watching him. I can't ignore the little spark in my chest when he accepts the invitation and sits beside me. It makes me feel a little guilty that I have an agenda.

I'm going to figure out, once and for all, what I find so *off* about him. Why he's so different. Why he speaks the way he does. Why he and Moseus keep so many . . . secrets.

It takes less ale than I'd planned.

"A god?" I reply, laughing. "That is absurd."

He cocks an eyebrow at me, which gives me the impression he isn't as inebriated as I've supposed. In fact, his expression looks entirely sober.

I reel back. "That's not funny."

"I wasn't jesting."

I study his face, waiting for him to break, but he merely holds my gaze. Almost to the point that his irises do that weird forest-thing again, and—

"Perhaps do not tell Moseus I mentioned it," he says offhandedly, glancing toward the stairs.

I curse inwardly, still unable to grasp the idea. "Can you . . . I don't know. Demonstrate?"

"Demonstrate how?"

"I . . ." I genuinely try to think of a suggestion, but two straight cycles of work have turned my mind to mush, and I'm not as well-versed in our lore as Amlynn is. "Like . . . smite someone?"

His lip ticks up, yet the expression is somehow equally sad. "I am not what I once was."

I look away. I have to. He gives me time to sort my thoughts. After a solid five minutes, all I can manage is "I'd say you were being blasphemous, but I've never been particularly religious."

"That surprises me."

I lift my gaze. His smile fuller, he mimics, "World Serpent this, gods that, Ruin this—"

I hit his leg. Not hard, just enough to protest. Is it bad to smack a god? Not that I believe he is . . .

Heartwood takes my hand. Holds it firmly in his own. "You need to rest. You can sleep in my room."

"But—"

"I don't mind." He leans forward, filling my nose with scents of earth and sage. "I will tell you more later." He rises to his feet and starts for the stairs. "And Pelnophe? You didn't have to intoxicate me. I would have told you, regardless." He must misread my face, because his expression darkens. "Do you fear me now?" His voice registers barely more than a slip of mist.

"No," I admit, both to him and myself. "I don't."

And *that* is what concerns me.

"I *had* to!" I bark at Heartwood, gesturing to the gutted corpse of Machine Two. "It was wrong! How many times do I have to say it?"

Moseus looms, silent as a shadow, across the room, but Heartwood looks ready to rip his braid out. "That is not a reason. It was functional!"

"But it wasn't!" I counter, kicking a wrench. "It *looked* functional, but it wasn't."

"You've failed to explain *how*."

"I just . . ." Anger boils so hot in me it's giving me indigestion. "It's just *wrong*. I feel it in my bones. I meditated like Moseus said, and it just . . . isn't right. I can fix it. I'm sure I can."

"But without a logical explanation—"

"And *if* it doesn't work, I'll put it back how it was."

Heartwood shakes his head, color rising in his pale cheeks. "That will set us back *days*."

"What the hell is a 'day'? Stop using that word!"

He flings his hands out. "It doesn't matter. Moseus and I are in agreement—"

"And *I'm* the engineer." I strike my chest hard enough to hurt. "It won't operate the way it's supposed to unless I reverse all this." I gesture to the bits and pieces strewn between us.

Heartwood seethes. "You are young, and you are foolish."

My anger burns white. "All right, omnipotent one, *you* can do whatever you want with it." I kick several springs out of my way.

He growls. "What are you doing?"

"Kiss my mortal ass, Heartwood." I gesture crudely to him and storm toward the stairs.

"You don't know what it could do!" he barks.

I whirl toward him. "You'd better walk before I show you what *I* can do."

Throwing his hands into the air, Heartwood storms off, but I reach the base of the stairs before he reaches his room. All the while Moseus "keeps the peace" in his own stupid, tranquil way.

✷

"I came to apologize," Heartwood says.

I sit on the protrusion from the top tier of the tower, looking up at the late sun. The mists have begun to gather across the Brume Mountains. I don't answer. It's childish of me, but I don't.

A full minute passes. He sighs. "I hate it when you sit out here."

Glad he can't see my smirk, I reply, "I know."

An oddly comfortable silence filters between us. After several minutes, Heartwood climbs out on the protrusion and sits behind me, letting his legs dangle over the curved edge as mine do. Unspoken apologies weave between us until we both breathe a little easier. I allow him to coax me inside when that gentle, one-note tone announces oncoming fog.

Seven cycles later, he kisses me in the height of the mists.

"Can I . . . touch it?"

Heartwood sits by Machine Three, his back to me, his shirt pulled down to his elbows, his hair pulled over one shoulder. First sun breaks through the mists outside, illuminating the raised scars on his back, forking out like the branches of the trees I've seen in his eyes.

The subtlest dip of his head grants me permission. Gingerly, with one finger, then two, I touch one of the slimmer branches near his shoulders. It doesn't *feel* like a scar, merely healthy, raised flesh. Like the Well of Creation simply made him this way, just as it made me with two arms and two legs and a dimple on my left cheek.

I trace the branch down to the tip of his shoulder blade, where it merges with others. I run my hand down the length of another, to the center of his back. He shudders.

Pulling back, I ask, "Does it . . . hurt?"

He shakes his head. So I follow another branch up to his opposite shoulder where, reaching back, he grasps my hand, knitting his fingers together with mine.

I tighten the belt, hoping that will help the rest of the mechanism turn a little better. I'm pulling back from Machine Three when I hear the ladder shift against the hole in the floor. I wait for a white head to pop up, but whether it will be Heartwood or Moseus—

Heartwood.

I ease myself down from the machine. He's gone hunting again, knowing I like meat (and Salki likes meat, though he's yet to meet her), and has been gone four full cycles. If he caught anything, he must have left it on the first floor.

He grins as I untangle myself from the machine and mutter chastisements at him. I told him it doesn't matter, and Moseus won't like it, but Heartwood is who he is, and I love him for it. I find my way into his arms and stay there a long moment, debating whether or not to apologize for the grease I'm undoubtedly smearing on his fancy-god leathers.

He's about to say something, but I hear Moseus approaching from below, so, interrupting as I do, I whisper, "Do you think you could come to Emgarden again? When the mists are high?"

His brow furrows. "Why?" He smooths a loose lock of hair from my face, only to have it fall right back. "What's wrong?"

"Nothing is wrong," I promise, splaying my hands over his chest. "I just need to see you. Away from here. Away from him."

He runs the pad of his thumb over my cheekbone, then kisses me chastely. "I will always come when you ask, Nophe. Always."

My lungs empty as I arch into him, desperate to be closer. My hands run down his bare shoulders and over the prints of his godhood, memorizing every dip and facet as he murmurs my name into my hair. Together we are everything, heaven and creation and hell, and I know in the deepest recesses of my mind, heart, and body that I will never be the same.

Chapter 22

Tears stream from my eyes like they are two broken wells. I lift dust-covered hands and press them to my mouth, stifling clipped breaths. My throat aches and swells. My fingers tremble.

Oh gods, Heartwood. I forgot him. I don't know how, or why, but I lost all of it. It's been . . . a year? Since that last memory. And all this time he stayed cooped up in that tower, while I went about business as though he never existed. As though *we* never existed.

I stand, dizzy from the blood pooling in my feet. *Why didn't you come to me?* Would I have accepted his explanation? *No.* I know I wouldn't have. But he could have tried! Why didn't he try?

You betrayed us.

"But I didn't," I croak, and the tears wash anew. I have no recollection of betrayal. If I stole something critical, I hid it somewhere even I cannot find. And if I stole something critical, how do the machines work?

But they don't work. Not yet. But I would remember dismantling the power sources for five behemoth machines and then patching up the work to make it look like they never had them. I'm no blacksmith, no welder. I couldn't have possibly—

The deep hollowness in my chest echoes so emphatically that I gasp and press both palms over it. *Heartwood.* I would have been so miserable, to be cut off so cleanly. Shattered. If he forgot me, us—

I have to see him. *Now.* I have to fix this.

I love him.

Surely it isn't too late, I think as I sprint through the mist to the tower. His coolness toward me, his aloofness, his *pain* makes so much sense now. Bearing my presence when I could not fathom his. Sucking it up, in part for Moseus's sake, no doubt. Our story closed half-unwritten, with Heartwood's part left to wander between the lines that once were.

Machine Three. Heartwood said it had something to do with Machine Three. But what did the Ancients hide there? What did Heartwood and Moseus awaken when they opened that hole through the floor to reach it? And why hasn't it affected them in a similar manner?

Because they're gods. My lungs start to sting. I force deeper breaths as I run, refusing to slow.

I remember it all. Heartwood and Moseus had been alone for some time before reaching out to me. Heartwood is a passionate creature by nature; he took an interest in me from the start, albeit not a romantic one. I sensed he was lonely. Made an effort to speak to him, though it was awkward at first. Heartwood conversed with me like a toddler learning to walk. I would have given up on him, if not for the work.

He became my sounding board. Every problem, every frustration, I took to Heartwood. We butted heads often. We were so very different. We *are* so very different. And yet his genuine nature and honesty drew me to him. His openness, his willingness to help—

The Heartwood I met the second time was a shadow of that man. Looking back, I can see glimmers of his true self shining through. Searching for Casnia, because he knew how important she was to me. Spotting me on the protrusion, worried I'd fall. Letting me into the garden we'd once shared. Gods, he even helped me dig that hole, knowing it wouldn't lead anywhere.

My legs ache as I near the tower. I imagine our roles reversed. Heartwood devoured by the machines instead of me. It would gut me.

I would hate him, and myself, and this damnable tower. I would never recover.

He's already lost his divinity. Already lost his sister.

I crash through the tower doors. "Heartwood?" The first floor greets me with its usual hush, so I rush up to the second and throw open his door. "Heartwood?"

The room is empty. I climb the ladder to the third floor. Seeing no one, I hurry to the lift and take it up. Moseus studies the machine there, trying to learn what I have not.

Breathless, I ask, "Is Heartwood here?"

Moseus looks at me, confused. "I don't believe so. Why? What has happened?"

But I don't take the time to convey it to him. Moseus was never a fan of our relationship, though I doubt he knew how deep it went. I shake my head, swallow against a dry throat, and make my way back downstairs and out of the tower.

Please don't be hunting, I plead, forcing my body to continue running toward the slot canyons. *Please be there.*

The mist dissipates as I sprint. I slow to a jog in the punishing heat of the sun. When I finally reach the hewn stairs of the slot canyon, I trip down them, then press my back against one of the tall red-rock walls, desperate for air. My chest heaves in protest. My legs buzz like they're full of flies. *Water,* my throat pleads, but there's water in the garden. I can make it to the garden.

Pushing off the wall, I can't convince my body to sprint, so I lumber through the narrow canyon, steadying myself against rock walls. I understand now how I found the garden the first time. I'd been here before. Heartwood showed me. I spent so much time here. Time with him. *Gods, let him forgive me. I didn't know.*

I stumble through the stone archway and find him, ten paces away, planting something in overturned soil. My heart lodges in my ribs. He glances at me, then stiffens and rises to his feet, his face knit with concern. "What's wrong?"

I can't take my eyes off him. How did I not see it before? How did I not recognize him the moment we reunited?

Despite my thirst, my eyes run again. I hate crying, but I haven't the strength to stop the tears. That alone has him marching forward to intercept me. "I remember," I blurt, my voice rough.

He freezes two paces away, rooted to the ground like the wickwoods. "Heartwood, I remember you." I sob. "I remember *us*. I'm so sorry. I'm so . . . so sorry." Weariness consuming me, I tilt to one side. He rushes forward to catch my elbow, the skin around his eyes tight, his brow furrowed. I grab the fabric of his sleeve in fists. "I don't . . . I didn't mean to. I don't understand how, but Heartwood, please forgive me. *Please.*"

His lips part. One hand cradles my jaw and turns it toward him. His eyes dart back and forth, searching for truths, for lies. His fingertips are cool against my hot skin, his breaths nearly as rapid as mine. Does he not believe me? Or is there hope behind that shimmer in his eyes?

"Nophe," he whispers, quiet as the fog. "Do you really . . ."

The question is too delicate to finish. Too broken to voice.

I grab the sides of his face. Stare until I see the trees in his eyes. "I love you, Heartwood," I whisper. Then, after a moment's hesitation, "And I was right about Machine Two."

The sudden openness of his expression shreds my insides to ribbons. He falters, as though his own strength has wavered. His hands clasp my wrists, but he does not pull me away. He whispers, "Nophe—"

But I'm done apologizing.

Pushing onto my toes, I kiss him, tasting sage and salt and *Heartwood*, reclaiming him for my own. It takes only a beat to convince him of my truth, a beat for him to respond, and I'm swept into his arms and off my feet, challenging him with lips and tongue and teeth, desperate to relearn every part of him. I drink his hurt, his loneliness, and his sorrow, choking when it mixes with my own. It is not so easily healed. Perhaps it never will be. But these are my scars, and I claim every last one of them, making a weld of remorse and renewed devotion, a poorly wired atonement and bereavement for all that we've lost.

Stone presses against my back. Our hands roam and pull and demand, but it's not enough. Our sorrow becomes need becomes heat, and it rages between us, devouring our flesh and searing our souls.

We are both entirely selfish, craving and taking, ravenous. No touch can allay the ache of our time apart, but there's a solace in it, a temperamental peace shattered and reforged as we remember together, until the garden and the tower and Tampere fall away, and there exists no world but ours.

After, I lie against him in a loose bed of fairy wisps, toying with a long lock of hair from his obliterated braid. Ear to his chest, I listen to his heartbeat and take comfort in the rhythm of his breaths. We stay long enough for the desert wrens to return, and only when they sing does Heartwood, drawing circles on my back, whisper, "Truly, Nophe?"

So I start from the beginning, detailing his somewhat violent manner of asking for my assistance at the tower. I detail the state the machines had been in, far worse than my second time around. My voice grows coarse, and I excuse myself for a drink before returning and stretching myself over him once more. Tracing his eyebrows and nose, I tell him of every stupid thing he ever said to me, and each rude retort I gave back, all the way to the dismantling of Machine Two, before he stills my hand with his own and pleads, "Enough."

I grin at him. "Then you finally believe me?"

He lifts his head and kisses me, wiping dried tears from my cheeks with his thumbs, marveling at me anew. "I do. But how?"

"You ask me this *after* partaking—"

"*Nophe.*"

Brushing hair from his face, I kiss his nose, then slide back to his side. "I don't know," I admit, quiet enough to be ignored by the wrens. "I've been remembering in fragments, but the pieces were so disjointed, I could never connect them. But whatever spell took my memories was breaking. I was on my roof in the mist when I felt the pull to know.

I followed it, and I remembered." A lump forms deep in my throat. I swallow, but it does little good. "I'm so sorry."

Heartwood runs a hand through my hair before guiding my mouth back to his. I kiss him slowly, lazily savoring him. When I pull back, he murmurs, "I've always wondered what you thought, seeing me again. The only memory you would have had of me was pulling that knife."

I blink. "Knife?"

"At the machine." Seeing the confusion in my face, he props himself up on his elbow. "After you forgot . . . I didn't understand. I *still* don't understand. And I kept asking you, and I scared you, and you pulled a knife on me."

I scan his face. Nothing but sincerity. Twisting around, I find my clothes—don the undershirt, just in case we have visitors—and pull Arthen's blade out of my trouser pocket. "This one?"

He doesn't need to examine it. He nods.

I turn the blade over in my hand. "No, I . . . I didn't know you at all. When I first saw you, that time, I just thought you looked like Moseus. I thought you were brothers. When Moseus came to ask me for help . . . I had no recollection of either of you."

Heartwood frowns. Tucks my hair behind my ear. "But now you remember the rest?"

"Yes." I recount more to prove it: work on the machines, stopping to repair a well, sleeping with him in my home. "But not that knife." I shake my head. "Arthen kept asking me where it was. I told him I didn't take it."

Heartwood frowns.

I lower the knife. "I didn't take anything else, either, Heartwood. I swear it. But . . ." *But something is missing.*

Heartwood said I pulled a knife on him *after* losing my memories. So I should remember pulling it. But I don't.

If Machine Three took my memories the first time, what took them the second?

"Perhaps time affects the Ancients' malediction," he assures me. "In time, you will recall."

I mumble an agreement, not because I believe it, but because there's no point in arguing. Not when I can't remember. I stare at the budding retalia, the poisonous chrystanus, and the verdant fairy wisps, as though they might reveal something to me. My relief to be with Heartwood again, to have his forgiveness, overwhelms my simmering frustration. I have *him*.

Putting the knife away, I ask, "How often does Moseus come here?"

He considers. "Perhaps three times since we first came to the tower. It is unlike him."

"Good." I push him back into the fairy wisps and climb atop him. "Because we have a lot to make up for."

My head pressed against Heartwood's chest, knees curled up, sleep comes easily.

I carefully align the sprocket with its track, balance the track on my shoulder, and twist the screw into place. It took me forever to figure out where these internal pieces on Machine Three go. My first guess seemed correct, but it would require me to bore new holes into the metal, which is not only difficult, but wrong. The Ancients made these machines a certain way for a reason. They functioned, long ago. I have to learn their patterns and follow them, even if it takes more time.

My clammy hand fumbles around the turnscrew. Heartwood should return any moment now. Over and over I've rehearsed what I'll say to him and how I'll say it. Prepared myself for a litany of reactions and a defense for each one. But he has to know.

Before I act, he has to know. He'll understand it better than I do. He's a god; he has to understand.

No, that wasn't it. I'm missing something.

Deep breath, focus. I check behind me, scanning the room before zeroing in on the hole in the floor. Listen, but it's silent. Too silent? I'm not sure. I never paid attention to the noises of the tower before. I've always been the loudest thing here.

I carefully align the sprocket with its track, balancing the track on my shoulder, and push the screw into place. I miss, the first few times. My nerves are getting the better of me. I wish Heartwood hadn't left. If he'd been here, it'd be different. I'd feel safer.

It took me forever to figure out where these internal pieces on Machine Three go. My first guess seemed correct, but it would require me to bore new holes into the metal, which is not only difficult, but wrong.

Holes. They make me think of him. Of the way her body crumpled. I'm trying not to. I have to wait for Heartwood. I fear that lingering in Emgarden will give me away.

Focus on the work, *I remind myself.*

The Ancients made these machines a certain way for a reason. They functioned, long ago. I have to learn their patterns and follow them, even if it takes more time.

My clammy hand nearly drops the turnscrew. Heartwood should return any moment now. Over and over I've rehearsed what I'll say to him and how I'll say it. Prepared myself for a litany of reactions and a defense for each one. But he has to know.

I hope I'm wrong. I pray to the World Serpent and the Well of Creation itself that I'm wrong. She's dead, either way, but there's a difference. An enormous, fundamental difference.

Before I act, he has to know. He'll understand it better than I do. He's a god; he has to understand.

Drawing in a deep breath, I steady myself. Step back and roll the sprocket forward, verifying its track is straight.

I don't hear Moseus behind me, but when his cold hands grab the sides of my head, I immediately know it's him. A scream bubbles from my chest and up my throat as I try to beat him away and—

And . . .

Where am I?

Chapter 23

I wake gulping moist air. Despite the settled mist, heat swarms my body.

Sitting up, I pant, trying to suck in enough air. Blink and orient myself. Push hair off my forehead. Garden, Heartwood. He's asleep beside me, curled in the fairy wisps with one arm bent under his head, the other across my lap. I haven't slept so heavily in a long time—

That dream. It felt very real. Almost like a vision. And if it was . . .

Moseus did it. Every hair on my body stands on end. *Moseus took my memories away.*

But . . . no. Wait. This was a *dream.* Every memory I've had since starting my work on the tower . . . the second time . . . I had while fully alert. I was definitely not fully alert this time. Yet my heart thunders in my chest, and my hands are just as cold and moist as they were before.

It's only the mist. But the thought offers little comfort. I swallow hard. Turn to Heartwood and lift a hand to stir him, then pause.

If I tell Heartwood what I "saw"—that Moseus somehow kindled up enough god-power to wipe my mind, and I'm *wrong*—what will that do to him? To Moseus, to the tower? To me?

You betrayed us.

Think, Nophe, I plead, rubbing fingers into my forehead. I'm shaking. Gods' damnation, I'm shaking, and I can't breathe. I'm in this beautiful haven with this beautiful man, and I'm utterly terrified.

What was I going to tell Heartwood? In that dream, I was waiting for him. I was going to tell him something. What?

Did I . . . did I really betray them?

A new thought chills me to my core. *What if I forget again?*

Very carefully, I lift Heartwood's arm and set it beside him. Find my feet. Pace, grateful I'd had the forethought to dress before passing out. I should just tell him. Maybe he would know something about it . . . but if he did, he wouldn't be so chummy with Moseus. And what if he told Moseus?

He won't if you ask him not to. But that reasoning does nothing to calm me. Something is missing. Serpent save me, I'm still *missing something.*

I can't forget again.

Crouching down, I think to rouse Heartwood, to explain I need to go, to record this, but I stop before touching him. What if it's real? What if Heartwood confronts Moseus, and Moseus does the exact same thing to *him*?

What if Heartwood forgets me?

Deep breath in, long breath out. I can't let that happen. I won't. I'll find out the truth one way or another, but I will not let Heartwood suffer for it.

"I love you," I whisper. "I'll be back, I promise."

Wiping mist from my eyes, I sneak from the garden, grateful for the cover of the fog, as though Moseus might jump out at me with his cold hands at any moment. *Just a dream just a dream just a dream.*

Not a dream?

The mist lifts by the time I get home. After locking the door behind me, I pull out my notes and every spare piece of parchment I can find. Grab a charcoal pencil and start, in very tight handwriting, from the beginning.

Pelnophe, you've been asked to work on the tower before. The first time Heartwood came for you, the second time, Moseus. Heartwood is your ally. He is your everything. If you're reading this, you've forgotten, but I (you) foresaw this, so I wrote everything down. Listen carefully.

I put my maker's mark—the rhombus with three lines—at the end of the sentence, then follow it with a few facts only I could possibly know. So future me will believe present me.

And then I write everything, every action and thought and theory, until my hand cramps and seizes, and I hide it away in that cubby in the floor, where no one but Salki could possibly find it. Or me.

⚡

I massage my hand as I stare out my window at the Brume Mountains, waiting for the mists to fall. Stress squeezes my stomach too hard for me to coax any food into it, and nothing on Tampere could possibly distract me from the issue at hand. The earth shakes once, then twice, while I wait, as though my nerves have found a way deep into the soil, disrupting the entire desert.

I've walked to the tower in the sun a couple of times before, but Moseus prefers the mist. I don't want to draw his ire, just in case. *Please be wrong,* I think as I push on my thumb to stretch out my cramped writing muscles. I need to be wrong. But I also need to see Heartwood and explain. He'll wonder where I went. Perhaps I should have woken him with a sort of explanation, but my mind wasn't in a good space. It still isn't. I'm clueless as to what words could bridge this uncertainty, but I have to bridge something. I have to learn the truth, one way or another.

I feel the slightest chill on the breeze before the mists foam over the peaks like the head on a drink. I dance restlessly, waiting for the fog to stretch its hand over Emgarden. The moment the air gets the slightest fuzzy edge, I'm off to the tower, too nervous to walk, too afraid to run. If my dream held any meaning, I can't let Moseus suspect anything is wrong. Not one word, movement, or hair can be out of place.

It's the same mindset I had in the dream, and it didn't help me then.

The shadow of the tower pierces the mist, growing in clarity with every step. I still have no idea how to power the machines, but I've got to work it out, or at least put on the air of working it out. My goal is Heartwood. I pray he hasn't said anything to Moseus about the state of my mental retentiveness.

The first floor, shadowed save for where blue-tinged light slips down the stairs in its center, stretches quiet as a grave. The silence makes me nervous. I push the door shut behind me, loud and steady, as I always do. I glance toward Moseus's room. The door is ajar.

I take the stairs up. The tower's tool bag sits at the top of it; I grab it and carry it with me, scanning the floor. The hairs on the back of my neck rise. Heartwood's door is shut. I head straight for it, grateful again for its oiled hinges—

He's not here.

My nerves double over and twist in complex knots. He wouldn't still be in the garden, would he? Perhaps higher in the tower?

I see the room anew. I've sat in the alcove of that window. I brought the pink quartz on the top of the cairn in the corner. I found it while turning new land for the crops. Heartwood doesn't sleep well in here; the bed is nearly as hard as the stone floor. He prefers being outdoors.

"Are you looking for something?"

Moseus's voice behind me screams like a giant bell, with me hanging from the clapper as it rings. I turn around, forcing myself to relax. He looks better than usual. Less tired, and that sets me on edge.

I need to get good at lying *right now*.

"I was hoping Heartwood could help me out with the machines." I mentally scramble for details, because I know Moseus will ask.

He stands at the top of the stairs, his narrow face tilted slightly to the right, his arms folded. The pale fingers of one long hand rest atop his sleeve.

Cold hands grab the sides of my head—

"For what, precisely?" he asks.

I turn toward Machine Two, taking half a second to glance over it, quietly rejoicing when something valid comes to mind. "To move the door," I say. I'd nearly forgotten about the seams in the wall; I'd been so distracted at the discovery of the lift, and subsequently the fourth and fifth floors, that I hadn't revisited it. I realize it probably masks the mechanics for the lift itself, but it's something I haven't fully explored. "I want to know what's behind there, and I thought he might be strong enough to move it." I search my memories, careful not to recall anything I shouldn't know. "No offense; you don't really strike me as one who enjoys physical labor."

Moseus cocks an eyebrow at me but doesn't dispute it. His dark green eyes shift toward Machine Two. "I've tried. We both have. It's immovable."

Grateful for a reason to move away, I approach Machine Two, set down the tools, and trigger the mechanism to shift it away from the wall. "Maybe if I study it a little longer I can figure it out." I clear my throat; my voice pitches too high. *Go away, go away.* "It's got to be this or Machine Five—"

I hear steps on the stairs, and Heartwood emerges. Moseus shifts aside to give him room. Heartwood's gaze immediately locks on me, and a mix of confusion and relief pulls at his features. "Nophe, where—"

"Here," I interrupt, gesturing to the hidden door behind the machine. "This is where I need you, but Moseus said you already tried." *Need a reason, a good reason . . .* "I want to see if I can wedge a turnscrew in here, and if not, maybe file one down to get between the slabs of stone. Look, I'll show you."

I emphasize the last words as subtly as I can, jerking my head in the direction of the door. *Play along, Heartwood, please.*

I don't wait for him to follow, just crouch down like I'm getting to work, praying to any gods outside this tower that Moseus will leave. He doesn't. But Heartwood approaches and crouches down beside me just as I pull my narrowest turnscrew from the tool bag.

I don't look at him. "Say nothing while he's here," I whisper. Plead. I hand him the turnscrew and point out the seams. "Hmm," I say a little louder, "They really are tight. We can't break through like you did with the ceiling?"

"We were able to find a weak spot in that floor's integrity," Moseus answers. "There are no others. I've spent years searching."

Exactly how long have you been here? I want to ask, but I can't figure out if that's something memory-wiped Pell would say or not. I'm over-thinking this, I know I am.

"Well." I stand. Refuse to look at either of them and plant my fists on my hips. "Give it a good push anyway."

Heartwood, bless him, pulls his concerned gaze from me and gives it a valiant effort. I direct him to try pushing against different corners of the wall, then pushing more up, more down, and so on. Thank the Serpent, Moseus gets bored and leaves, stepping into the lift and letting it suck him up toward the top of the tower.

My strength leaves me in one great breath. I drop to the floor.

Heartwood crouches with one hand on the door. "What happened? Why did you leave?"

"Where were you?" I press my palms to my eyes. "I came back here to find you, and—"

"I went to Emgarden. To find you."

I drop my hands. Of course he did. And he had to wait for the mist. He probably took a roundabout way to stay off the road. We passed right by each other.

I search for words. "I'm sorry. I . . . I had a disturbing dream, and I had to leave and document everything."

Brow furrowed, Heartwood pushes off the wall and shifts closer to me. "Dream? About me?"

"No, about Moseus." I pause. "You said I lost my memories at Machine Three, right? What happened, exactly?"

He shakes his head. "I don't know. I wasn't there. You . . ." He pauses to swallow, to mask the emotion. He masks emotion about as well as I lie, though that last one seemed to fool Moseus. "You started screaming. I came as quickly as I could."

I roll my lips together. "Tell me everything you remember."

He frowns but situates himself more comfortably, leaning close. "I came up the ladder; you were backed into the machine, and Moseus was trying to calm you. Trying to explain where you were. You didn't know. You remembered your name, your work in Emgarden, but not the tower, the machines, nor . . . us."

"He got there before you?"

"He was handing you tools as you worked on the machine's core. I rushed to your side, trying to comprehend what was happening . . . I admit, it took me longer than it should have to understand. I kept asking what was wrong, and why you didn't know my name." The softest flush crosses his nose. "I panicked. Got a little physical with you."

"Physical?"

"I grabbed your arm. I didn't hurt you," he rushes to add. Swallows. "And you pulled that knife on me." He gestures to my pocket. "Moseus stepped between us, managed to settle you. At your request, he took you back to Emgarden."

"And you didn't?"

He glances up at me through pale eyelashes. "I wanted to. Desperately. But you were so frightened. I've . . . never seen you like that, Nophe. Not then, and not now. Moseus thought it best that he take you. And when he returned . . . he withheld information about you on my behalf, not wanting to . . . disappoint me."

"Information," I repeat, "of my so-called betrayal."

He presses his lips together.

"I showed you everything I have, Heartwood—"

"You haven't remembered everything yet, Nophe," he counters, and the truth of it deflates me. "You don't remember pulling the knife. You said we were strangers to you, when we called upon you again."

"Heartwood." Pushing myself onto my knees, I touch the side of his face. "You said you and Moseus . . . your power has dwindled, being on Tampere. You do . . . plant stuff. You're still strong. Does Moseus . . . have any special abilities?"

"He calms," Heartwood explains. "He is a peacemaker."

I frown. "Calming someone doesn't feel like a godly gift."

"I think we've established that your idea of gods is slightly amiss."

Worrying my lip, I stand up, eyeing the lift, and pace a moment. Heartwood follows. "Nophe—"

"Don't tell him." I'm whispering again, though the thick stone of these walls should mask anything I say. "Don't tell him I remember, Heartwood. Or have you already?"

"I haven't had the chance." His eyes narrow, but he takes my hand. I squeeze his in return. "Nophe, what's wrong?"

"My dream . . . I dreamed that Moseus was there, at Machine Three, when I forgot. Like . . . he was the one who did it." The way his countenance falls, I immediately regret the words. "But that's the thing, Heartwood. It was a dream. Every memory I've reclaimed . . . I've had them fully awake. They press into my mind like I'm reliving them all over again. I've never had any come to me while I was sleeping. So I don't know if it's a dream, or—"

"Or not," he finishes for me. Jaw set, he contemplates. "I have known Moseus a while. Several years. He doesn't possess anything that—"

The lift hums. I release Heartwood and return to the door, crouching before it just as Moseus steps out. *Cool and solid as the marble. I am this wall.*

"Nothing I do will allow us to pass the shield," Moseus says to Heartwood, referring to the mirrorlike substance surrounding Machine Five. "It must be up there, perhaps in the enclosed piece projecting from the tower. Pell, I need you to construct something to allow us passage past the silver. Perhaps I will understand something you do not."

I nod, running my hands over the door seams so I won't have to turn around. So my face won't give me away, the way Heartwood's does him. In truth, all I want to do is bury myself in Heartwood's arms and hide my face from the world, but this fear ties me down like the jaws of an animal trap, and—

My hand runs over that divot in the stone near the top of the door. It's shallow and looks like a natural formation of the stone. And yet now, as I stare at it, it seems familiar to me. I've looked at it before, in the time I'm not supposed to remember. I trace it now as I did then.

I look at it from a few different angles, then stand and take a step back. Gasp.

I know this shape. It's not random—I've seen it before. It's the exact same cut, the exact same size, as the brooch Salki wears.

"Pell?" Heartwood asks, and behind my excitement, I thank him for withholding his preferred nickname for me.

Straightening, I turn toward the tower keepers. "I think I know how to open this door."

Chapter 24

Thamton calls out to me as I race by in the mist, but I can't make out his words, and I don't stop to ask. I race to Salki's home, thinking that with all this running, I'm going to need to up my food rations. I pound heavily when I reach the door. "Salki! Wake up! It's Pell!"

Another round of rapping, and Casnia opens the door with a frown. Her short black hair is plastered to one side of her head.

"Pell," she says simply, and doesn't resist when I push my way in.

Salki sits up on her cot, rubbing her eyes. "Has something happened?"

"I need your brooch." She isn't wearing it.

She blinks at me. "My brooch? Why?"

"I . . ." I try to think of a good reason, but my ability to lie can only stretch so far. "This is going to sound insane, but there's a door inside the old tower with a notch shaped exactly like that brooch."

Salki stares at me. "Wh-What? You . . . you got into the old tower?"

I sit on the cot beside her. "Don't tell anyone, okay? I have good reasons, and I can explain them later, but I'd love to get back there and test my theory before the mist lifts." I have no idea what connection Salki's brooch has to the tower, but that's a mystery I can figure out later. She most likely discovered it while tending crops, like the sundial. Like I have with all my Ancient artifacts, pre-tower.

Casnia starts moaning, either because I woke her up or because she's hungry. Likely both.

Salki grabs my arm. "What's in there? Can I see?"

"Uh, maybe. Listen, I can't promise anything, but I need that brooch. I'll bring it right back."

Salki glances over to the little table between her cot and Casnia's. "That's where all the scraps are coming from."

"Yes. You'll keep it a secret, right?"

She nods absently. "What door?"

"Salki." I grasp her shoulders. "I will spill my guts to you later. But the mists. I have to return before they lift."

Rising, she moves to the table and pulls out its little drawer, picking the tin brooch from it. Holds it tightly in her hand. "You're not going to bend it or melt it down, right?"

I leap to my feet. "I promise."

Somewhat reluctantly, she hands it to me. Its shape really is peculiar: one edge of it licks up then drops into a right triangle. The body is mostly square, with a tuck at the base like the stomach of a dog. The other "corners" are rounded, with a cutout between them like half a keyhole. The whole thing measures about two-thirds the size of my palm.

"Where did you get this?" I ask.

"Entisa had it made for me." A hint of sorrow tilts the words, but she shakes it off. "I hate waiting for stories," she mourns, ignoring Casnia's muted whining.

"Oh, I have a story for you. An insane story." Even before, I never told her what I was doing. I wasn't able to.

Cold hands on the sides of my head—

Stifling a shudder, I embrace Salki briefly and head for the door. "I'll be back, I promise. See ya, Cas."

Casnia doesn't respond, and I zip back into the mists.

≫⫛⩺

Both tower keepers are waiting for me when I return. At first I think to avoid Moseus's gaze, but then I fear that's too obvious, so I meet it with what I hope is a look of triumph. And it is. The sooner I get this tower working, the sooner I'll be done with him.

What will become of me and Heartwood, once his people are free? That concern hadn't surfaced before. I didn't get this close to finishing, before.

The intense expression of hope on Heartwood's face hurts. I want to reach for him, but I stop myself and approach the door, spinning the brooch in my hand so it will fit in the divot.

And it does. Perfectly.

Yet nothing happens.

I hold it there a moment longer, then, chewing my lip, pull it away and brush it off. Try again. Reverse it so the pin side lays against the stone, even though the edges won't align, but that likewise does nothing. "I don't understand. It's a perfect fit. Heartwood?"

He crouches beside me. I press the brooch into its matching imprint, hard, and he shoves into the wall as he did before. The stone doesn't budge. There are no whistles or tones, no shifting, no reveals.

My gut sinks into my hips. I was so sure. This brooch and this impression can't be a coincidence!

"Let me see it." Moseus holds out his hand.

I pass it to him, purposefully avoiding any contact with his skin.

Lips downturned, he turns the brooch over in his long fingers. Taps his fingernail against it, even bites it. Hums deep in his throat before pressing it to the indentation, just as I had. Heartwood and I both push, but the door doesn't yield.

Defeated, I sink to my backside. "I was so sure."

"I will trace this and create another," Moseus says. "Perhaps the alloy is wrong."

He walks off with the brooch. Heartwood slumps, defeated. I take his hand in mine and squeeze, trying to reassure him. Then I follow after Moseus; I promised I'd return that brooch, and I don't want the "peacekeeper" to insist on keeping it.

Fortunately, he doesn't. He traces it with a graphite pencil, right onto the stone on the far wall, multiple times and at various angles, before handing it back to me. "Don't lose that."

"I won't." The mist starts to clear. "I'm going to try something else. I'll be back."

I have nothing else to try, but I don't want to stay in the tower if my presence isn't necessary, even if Heartwood is here. Especially if Heartwood is here. I'll slip, somehow.

I'm still so afraid.

Pocketing the brooch, I head down the stairs and through the dim first floor. Out the door I didn't close behind me. I've only taken a few steps across the dry soil outside when Heartwood's voice sounds quietly behind me.

"Nophe."

My chest constricts as I turn around. He pushes the tower door shut. Between that and the lightening mist, we have a semblance of privacy. So I encircle his waist with my arms and press my forehead into his chest.

"I'm sorry. I know you miss her. I thought this would work."

"We'll figure it out." He tilts my head up, forcing me to look at him. "Are you all right?"

I press my lips together. Release him, but don't step back. In as hushed a whisper as I can manage, I say, "Don't leave me alone with him."

He glances to the tower. "Moseus isn't—"

"I know," I interrupt. "I have no real reason. He's been your companion for so long. He's probably comforted you during—"

"Moseus is no comfort to me." He speaks without animosity.

I pause, waiting for an explanation.

He exhales slowly. "His abilities have no effect on me. Either because of this planet or because of my making"—his godhood, he means—"he is no comfort."

He might as well have reached down my throat and seized my heart. This whole time, alone without Ether and without me, and he had no balm?

"Comfort doesn't have to be magic," I protest.

Heartwood's lip ticks. "I wouldn't call it magic." The smile vanishes. "But yes, you are right."

"Let me be right a little longer," I plead, clutching his shirt in my hands. "Don't leave me alone with him. Not yet."

Somber, he nods.

"I wrote it all down," I continue. Heartwood leans forward to catch the words. "After I left the garden. I wrote down every single thing I can remember, in case it happens again. I won't forget you twice, I swear it."

Something is missing. I wince at that spot of emptiness in my soul. But what else is left? What am I not seeing?

Heartwood cups the side of my face. Runs a thumb over my brow. The mist fades.

Standing on my toes, I kiss him, relishing his scent and his warmth for as long as I dare. "I'll be back." Regretfully, I pull away. Turn toward Emgarden with the sinking feeling that I will always be here.

But Heartwood will not.

I turn the brooch over and over in my hands as I walk, barely noticing the kilometers go by, as though I might discover something new about it. But it remains only a worthless piece of artistic tin.

When I enter Emgarden, I steel myself with a deep breath, trying to keep my helplessness at bay. That dream still limns my thoughts. It doesn't fade, like dreams do. I wish it would.

To my relief, Salki hasn't left her home, though she's dressed for farmwork. Casnia holds a small parasol, ready to accompany her.

My expression must give me away. "Didn't work?" Salki asks as she accepts the brooch from my outstretched hand. She pins it to her shirt.

I shake my head. Lean against the doorway. "I was so sure. I don't know what else to do."

She glances at Casnia, then motions me inside. Shuts the door behind us.

I fold my arms and press my back into the wall. "You'll be late."

"They can wait a few minutes," she insists. "Tell me more about this tower. Is that where you were, before?"

I meet her eyes, remembering Amlynn's claim of my comings and goings. "Before?"

"A little over a year ago, you were busy with something. Said you were working on your tinkering. Didn't see you very much. Like now."

"Yeah, that's where I was." It's such a long story, and there's so little time. Still so few answers. "And I figured out some things. I'm fixing that tower, Salki. But there's a piece missing. And there's this door, nearly invisible, in the stone. No hinges or latches, only seams and what looks like a natural indentation that just *happens* to match *that* exactly." I gesture to the brooch. "It fits perfectly. Same size, same shape. I thought it was a key. But the door won't move. I can't be doing it *wrong* . . . there's only so many ways a door can open." I throw up my hands. There's so much more I need to tell her. I stretch my hand to relieve the soreness from all the writing I did. "You should go."

"There is . . . ," Salki begins, thumbing her brooch, "my mother's necklace."

A shiver shoots down my spine. "What?"

"Don't you remember?" She studies my face intently. Casnia sits on her cot, twirling her parasol, seemingly unaware of us. "Arthen made this for me. He modeled it after my mother's necklace."

I move toward her. How could I have forgotten? "She wore one just like this," I murmur. The same shape and everything, on a long chain around her neck. She never took it off.

Salki wrings her hands. "She never told me where she got it. I don't think she knew, honestly. Family heirloom? But . . . maybe that would work."

"It has to!" I grab her shoulders. "Salki, it's a *perfect fit*. I knew it couldn't be a coincidence! Where is it?" My enthusiasm falters as Salki's face crumples. Slow, careful, I repeat, "Salki . . . where is it?"

She sighs. Pats one of my hands. "Pell, you buried her with it."

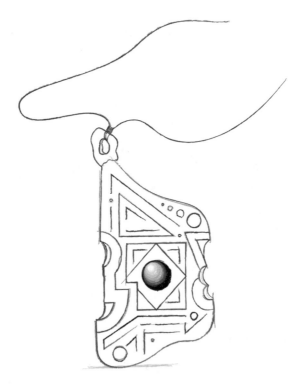

Chapter 25

I am the worst friend.

We wait until the mist falls again. Fewer witnesses, fewer questions. Salki comes with me, because she claimed Entisa as her mother and Entisa claimed her in return, and if anyone does stumble upon us, she'll be able to turn them away. I won't. Salki left Casnia and her artwork with Maglon at the alehouse and followed me, wordless, out here.

It feels wrong, that first shovelful of dirt. I apologize to Salki again, but she just clicks her tongue, annoyed at the repetition of my regret. It's easier to be annoyed than hurt. I'm hurting her. I'm hurting everyone. And yet they let me, again and again and again.

But I have to know. *Something is missing,* and I have to find it. This necklace is a literal key to that.

"Why didn't you keep it?" I asked.

"Because it was hers," Salki replies. "She never took it off, even when she bathed. It felt wrong to separate them."

And yet here we are.

I'm a few decimeters down when the guilt suffocates me. I pause. "We don't have to do this. There has to be another way."

"Just do it, Pell. Quickly. You can make it up to me by explaining it all."

Not while I dig. At the pace I'm setting, I'm too breathless to talk much. "Do you remember where I pulled out that machine?"

She hesitates. "The floor in your kitchen?"

I nod, and dig.

It's not a pretty job. I don't measure out my perimeter or shore up the sides. I just dig, straight down to where Entisa's head should be, my fingers cold vises around the shovel handle. I know I'm getting close by the smell. I grit my teeth and bear it, but Salki moves away, facing the road, her back to me.

I'm so sorry, I'm so sorry.

I dig carefully, not wanting to skewer the decomposing body beneath its white wrap, which the earth has turned sepia. The moment I uncover the burial shroud, I pull out Arthen's knife and cut into it. It takes me a long moment to figure out which part of the rotted corpse I've found—the shoulder. Turning as far away as I can, I get a few cleaner breaths of air before digging further, revealing more of the burial cloth. I cut it away, nicking one of my fingers and then uncovering a cluster of maggots.

My stomach seizes. Swallowing bile, I rip the cloth back, finding more beneath it . . . her dress . . . and—

A silvery chain.

I grab it. I'm not gentle. I'm bathed in the stench of death, and if I don't pass out, I'll surely be sick. So I yank and twist the chain up. The pendant gets stuck under the burial cloth. I hack away at it, desperate to finish, and the tin medallion comes loose, just like Salki's but with a green edging like rust.

Pulling a turnscrew from my belt, I shove its narrow end into a link and twist, breaking the chain and freeing the pendant. Then I rebury Entisa as quickly as possible. I'm a third done before I have to scrabble out of the grave and vomit behind the headstone. Salki, ever generous, steps over and pats my back, then crouches and starts filling the hole with her hands. Wiping my mouth, I grab the shovel and help her, glad I was at least able to hide the body before Salki had to see it.

It's a filthy job, but we finish before the mist lifts. Anyone bothering to look will see that the soil has been disturbed. We retreat to Salki's home and scrub filth from our hands—me from my entire body—then set out rosemary and dill to purge the scent of decay from our noses. There are emilies blooming right outside Salki's door, but they don't carry a scent. Only that soft, eerie light.

"I'll tell you everything," I promise once I'm dressed, Entisa's pendant biting into my closed fist. "I promise."

"Okay," she whispers sadly, but without judgment. And I leave her there alone, without her mother or Casnia, hoping to make it back to the tower before the mists lift, knowing I'll have so much to make up for when they do.

The mist has cleared by the time I arrive at the tower, Entisa's pendant pressing red lines into my fingers and palm. Heartwood watches from one of the windows, and in a flash he's downstairs, pulling open the doors. I half collide with him when I arrive.

"I have it." I heave for breath and blow sweat-stuck hair from my forehead. It hurts to open my hand, but I show him the flat tin piece, with its square body and curious corners.

Three fine lines form between his drawn eyebrows. "I thought you were returning it."

"Not this." I squeeze his arm before pushing past him, grabbing the hem of his shirt to pull him with me. "This is different. The other was a copy."

My legs protest every step of that winding staircase, but my heart pumps hard, enticing them forward. Machine Two remains pulled away from the wall. I wipe perspiration from my eyes and race to it, crouching again before that door. A new set of hurried footsteps sounds on the stairs; Moseus has overheard the commotion and come to see. I'm so focused I hardly think twice about him. This is it. I feel it in my bones, in that hollow chasm punched through my core.

With the tower keepers looking on, I press Entisa's pendant into the subtle indentation of the wall.

A sudden hiss of air from the hairline cracks startles me. I whip my hands back, but the pendant sticks to the stone like it's been suctioned there. The stone door pushes outward. A mechanism behind it groans as it slides the heavy stone to the right, revealing a doorway one meter tall and one meter wide. Soft pink light radiates from within.

A laugh escapes me. Heartwood whispers my name like a prayer, and Moseus exclaims something in a language I don't recognize. I crawl through. The revealed chamber is small, just large enough for two adults to stand side by side. A tall, rose-colored crystal takes up the rest.

I gape at it. It's as tall as I am, narrow at the base and flowering out at the top, cut in clean, symmetrical lines. Translucent, dull, quiet. I press a hand to its surface. Room temperature.

Heartwood remembers my request not to leave me alone with Moseus and enters before the older man. His eyes and mouth are round, his movements reverent. "Is that . . . ?"

Swallowing against a dry throat, I pull my hand away. "It . . . it looks like the wall."

Just like the wall. The great amaranthine wall that spans as far as the eye can see, an insurmountable construct without beginning or purpose, other than to separate two peoples who never knew one another.

"It is." Heartwood's breath stirs my hair. "This is amaranthine." He, too, presses a hand to it, closes his eyes, and says something in his godly tongue—words far more lyrical than whatever vernacular Moseus had uttered. I recognize a word that means an expression of relief or wonder, but I don't catch the rest.

When had Heartwood taught me that word?

Moseus elbows his way in, and I press back toward the door, not wanting to touch him. He stares at the crystal, cheeks sucked tight to his teeth.

"But how did they get amaranthine for power?" Heartwood asks.

"Maybe it was mined?" I squat. "Look."

There are raised conduits stemming from the base of the crystal, matching the stone of the walls and floor around it, jutting off in straight lines and right angles into the surrounding walls, disappearing where we can't reach. But they go to the other machines. I'm sure of it.

Keeping a wary eye on Moseus's stiff back, I say, "I'll have to study it. Understand how it works. It might react to emilies."

Heartwood turns to me. "Emilies?"

"The flowers that grow here. I haven't had the opportunity to investigate them, but they function in a circuit. They provide power, for machines built to take it." I raise empty hands. "Perhaps this will react to them. It's worth a shot. I have some here, from the cording I made, but they're old, and . . . I don't think they'll be enough."

Heartwood says, "I don't think—"

"Yes." Moseus's response is breathy but firm. "Yes, that might work. Can you get more now, Pell?"

Heartwood shifts between the crystal and me. "If we could—"

"No, it's incomplete." Sweat beads on Moseus's brow. "It needs to be repaired. The emilies are a good idea."

Heartwood's uncertain eyes flick between Moseus and me. "Then let me. Pell needs to rest."

"I can do it." I touch his hip reassuringly where Moseus can't see, though Moseus's attention remains locked on the crystal. I could strip naked and sing, and he wouldn't notice. Still, I lower my voice so only Heartwood can hear me. "I couldn't sleep now if I tried." I chew on the inside of my lip. "Heartwood, Ether is so close. We're *so close*."

His countenance warms. The pad of his thumb brushes my jaw, but he lowers it, glancing at Moseus. "I'll help you."

"We'll both help." Moseus finally steps back from the crystal—my cue to slide out the door to avoid being crushed by bodies. "We don't know how many emilies it will take. But first, Heartwood, I need your assistance upstairs."

"I passed a few clusters of them on my way," I offer as Heartwood, followed by Moseus, climbs out of the hidden room. "One had over a dozen."

Moseus nods, his dark eyes distracted. "We may need hundreds. Fresh, not the corpses you left here."

"We can get hundreds," I assure him. And then the door will open, and Moseus will leave, and my dream will be just a dream and nothing more. And Heartwood—

I can't think about Heartwood yet. I can't let myself crack when we're so close.

Knitting my ring and pinky finger with his, I say, "I'll start. I'll pick them in Emgarden, and you can harvest them farther out."

Hope dances in the whites of his eyes and across his full lips. It's only a brief goodbye, but I want to kiss him. I want to hold him for as long as I can, to make up for our time apart, and to steel myself against our unknown future. But this discovery trumps everything else.

Something is missing.

I push the sensation down. "I'll be back," I promise, and hurry down the stairs, through the shadowed first floor and out into the stark sunlight. I passed the first cluster of emilies about two hundred meters back, not far from the road. I really should rest, or at least get some food into me, but I coax enough energy from my limbs to move at a light jog. Eagerness and anxiety provide my fuel.

I find a bed of ten flowers, their glow only evident when my shadow falls across them. I kneel and, using a turnscrew to loosen the soil, dig down several decimeters before cutting through the tough root and lifting the flower whole from its bed. I set it aside and cut a second, a third, a fourth. When all ten are free, I loop their stems together and hang them off my belt, then hurry toward Emgarden, to the other cluster I passed earlier.

I've nearly reached them when the ground shakes so hard it sweeps my feet from under me. I fall hard onto my right knee, skinning it. A curse tangles on my tongue as I wait for the quake to abate, but it doesn't. It grows stronger, bucking the earth beneath me, throwing dust into my face. Spitting, I squeeze my eyes shut, my pulse racing through my veins as my body shakes back and forth in uneven intervals. It's *never* been this bad before.

When the quake slows to a rumble, I pick myself up and look ahead. People are milling about in the streets of Emgarden. Alarmed shouts pock the air. Then, glancing over my shoulder, I nearly lose my balance a second time.

Steam rises from the tower windows, and the giant protrusion at the top *turns*.

Chapter 26

It's working. The machine is *working*.

Yet blood drains from my face, neck, arms, dragging me toward the now-still earth, leaving me feeling empty and small and scared. Why? Why does my heart beat so hard, and so shallowly?

Abandoning the emilies, I race back for the tower. The space between my lungs burns and my thighs ache, but I hurry until I reach its doors, knotted emilies hanging from my hip. Leaning against the right door, I push—

It doesn't give. I lean into it again. Dig in my heels and push with both hands, but the door stands resolute. I switch to the left door and heave with all my might, but the doors are locked. Barred. Impenetrable, as they were before Moseus first came to my door. Before Heartwood did.

I stumble away from the tower. *Wrong, wrong, wrong.* Something is wrong. Why is it locked? Why is the tower moving? Moseus knew how to use that crystal. He recognized it, didn't he? But then what are the emilies for?

Pounding a fist on the door, I yell, "Moseus! Open up! Heartwood!"

No answer.

Holding my breath, I press my ear to the door, listening. The protrusion stops turning, and the ensuing silence pierces.

I back away and cup my hands around my mouth. "Heartwood!" I call, then scream. *"Heartwood!"*

No answer. No movement. Nothing.

I retreat a little more, checking the windows. The second- and third-floor windows have no covering, but I see nothing. The fortress is impenetrable. I tried so many times before its keepers opened its doors. If I could get another rope, tie it to a wrench like before, *maybe* I could get it through a window and pull myself up, but I won't be able to get in—

Fingers trembling with panic, I return to the doors and bang on them again. "Moseus! Let me—"

Be quiet. Don't let them hear you.

I choke on my own voice, chest heaving for air. That . . . I know that thought. I've had it before. Here? In a doorway—

And yet the more I try to pin it down, the more ethereal it becomes, until I lose it completely. I'm forgetting something. Something important. I crouch down, pressing my hands to either side of my head. *Think, Pell. What is it?*

That dream comes up again. The dream that's haunted me since I reunited with Heartwood. *His cold hands on me.* I was waiting for Heartwood. I needed to tell him something important. What was it?

She's dead, either way.

Lowering my hands, I stand, vertebra by vertebra. That sinking sensation in my gut sours and tightens.

Someone was hurt. Someone was—is?—in danger.

Swallowing, I retreat from the tower, desperately searching its windows one more time. Heartwood wouldn't leave me. He is stubborn and frustrating but entirely loyal. Perhaps to a fault. This isn't his doing. *Oh gods, please don't let Moseus hurt him. I only just got him back.*

Heartwood said Moseus has no power over him. But how true was that? Moseus was supposed to be a peacekeeper. There isn't a shred of peace alive in me. But I can't help Heartwood. I can't get into the tower. Not yet.

Skin pebbling with an internal chill, I turn from the tower and bolt back for Emgarden, fear my only fuel. *She's dead, either way.*

I sprint for Salki's home.

People are still in the streets, looking at the tower, murmuring to one another. "I'm sure it was turning," one says. Another, "It's never shaken that hard. Look how it broke my shutter!"

"Pell, do you know?" Frantess asks as I pass.

I shake my head and keep running, searching faces, sidestepping Amlynn and nearly colliding with Maglon. No Salki. My shirt sticks to my back by the time I reach her home. I don't bother knocking.

"Salki?" I push the door open.

She's not here, but Casnia is, sitting at their little table, drawing furiously. I step in, as though Salki might suddenly appear from behind a cot or within a cupboard, but there's no trace of her.

"Cas." I put a hand on her shoulder. "Where's Salki? Is she in the fields?" I used to know her schedule to the minute.

Cas shakes her head back and forth, scribbling so hard that her chalk breaks. She's drawing me and Salki again, the colors off as usual, as are our proportions. I'm nearly a head taller in this rendition.

"Okay, I'm going to find her." Releasing Casnia, I head to the door. "Stay here."

Casnia ignores me and continues coloring with a nub of yellow.

I shut the door, turn for the road—

Be quiet. Don't let him hear you.

I freeze, my hand on the door handle. This. Something before . . . It was like this. No . . . like *this*, and I lean into the doorjamb. Bend my knees, trying to trace the memory the way I did with Heartwood's. Like . . . this. I didn't want to be seen.

It's slipping away again. I feel it slipping. This wasn't right. This—

Lifting my eyes, I notice the corner of Ramdinee's house across the street—not directly, but askew, set back from the road. It's still empty; Emgarden is so small, and no one's needed the building. But in the moment my eyes glimpse the edge of the roof, my skin tingles with electricity.

There.

I don't blink. Barely dare to breathe. Cross the street, nearly running into Balfid. He says something to me, but I ignore him. *Concentrate.* It was there. I know it was.

Reaching the small house, I press my hand to its stonework. Mist. I was here during the mist. The high mist. Came around to the only door.

Entisa's been so sick and so demanding. Salki's wearing herself thin. It's the least I can do.

Cakes. I came here for cakes, for Salki. Ramdinee made the softest, sweetest cakes—

I approach the front door. Touch the handle. Lean back against the doorjamb. This is right. I was hoping she wasn't asleep, because it was dark inside. But I heard a shuffle. I didn't knock, did I? I thought she'd fallen.

Depressing the latch, I push the door open a few millimeters.

It's so dark, I can barely see. Darker than the mist could ever make it. Blacker than any shadows the closed shutters could afford. If not for the shock of white hair, I would have missed him. I would have walked right in—

Ramdinee's feet don't touch the ground. Her knees curl in, her hands clasped around his wrists, her eyes wide, her mouth open in a silent scream. There's a pit in his torso, a dark and empty vacuity, spiraling, growing larger as Ramdinee's skin turns ashen. As her grip weakens.

Whatever Moseus is doing to her, I can't stop it. I can't fight him. I release the handle and tiptoe away on shaky legs. Rush back to the tower. This proves my fears in the worst of ways.

He is no peacekeeper. He is a sucking pit of darkness.

I'm wrong. I have to be. But all of Heartwood's stories make me think of it, until I can't shake the idea from my mind.

I whip my hand back from the door and press it to my mouth. Bile burns my gut. I slide down the jamb until I sit on my backside, staring into nothing, shaking as though struck with fever. Sick, like Ramdinee had been a year ago. So suddenly, and then she was gone, just like that. Sick, because I couldn't remember otherwise.

I'd gone right to the tower, but Heartwood wasn't there. I thought Moseus hadn't followed me, hadn't heard me, but I was wrong. He'd suspected me, just as I'd suspected him. For so many cycles I'd suspected him. The obsession with the tower, the craving for darkness, little comments he'd make that tickled at lore. But I never shared it. Thought I was losing my mind then, too.

A shudder courses up my spine. He took my memories, just like he took Ramdinee's soul. Sucked them into himself like some kind of inhuman vacuum. Like some kind of *void*.

I don't dare say the name out loud, though I've cursed by it more times than I can count. Heartwood came to Tampere in search of his sister, who had joined the war against Ruin. The god created by the inversion of the Well of Creation. A creature that could only *take*.

Moseus is Ruin. I knew it then, and I know it now. He made me forget. I can't be wrong, because why would he take false knowledge from me? He took it all from me, discarded me, until realizing he needed me for his tower.

Leaning heavily against Ramdinee's empty house, I manage to put my legs under me. But . . . what on Tampere does the tower *do*?

I blink. *I* hid that cog. The one missing from Machine Two, the one I found in Heartwood's garden. I remember it like it just happened. I'd been skeptical of Moseus's motivations. Off things he said, his sickness, his behavior. I'd seen through the windows the *first* time I climbed to the protrusion. Seen that dark pit in his center. I'd feared, but I had no proof, and I had to be careful, for Heartwood's sake—

I had just discovered the lift. Then I found Moseus with Ramdinee . . . I went to the garden to tell Heartwood, but he wasn't there. He was hunting the scarce deer again. For me. I couldn't let Moseus access the rest of the machine. I still didn't understand it, but I felt in my bones I couldn't let him use it. I hid the cog in that tree. Came back to Emgarden and borrowed Arthen's knife. Thought I could defend myself, if needed. I took it, and I lost it, and Heartwood kept it after Moseus pulled us apart—

"Serpent save me," I whisper, pushing hair out of my face with quivering fingers. "I know why I made that machine."

And I know why I hid it under my floorboards, too. I never voiced my fears about Moseus, but *if* I was right . . .

I built the machine and hid it under my floorboards so even Heartwood wouldn't see it. So Moseus could never know. Just in case. A few cycles later . . . Ramdinee, and then Moseus took it all from me. But I got it back. I remember, now. How?

Because he's sick, I think, and shudder. *Diminished. They both are. His magic isn't holding.*

I sit on Ramdinee's porch for a long time, trying to sort my thoughts, trying to breathe beneath the weight of them. When I finally stumble away, I barely see the street in front of me. Run into Arthen. Mutter an apology and distantly wonder why people are still in the street. The earthquake passed. The tower sits inert.

"Look at it, Pell." Arthen squints skyward, one hand shadowing his eyes. "What does that mean?"

Numb, I follow his gaze. Shield my face from the sunlight—

Wait.

Cycle after cycle, the sun has beaten down on Emgarden. I know the sun like I know my own hands. Even in the mist, one can make out its distant orb. Never has it *moved.*

But now it's moved. Only by a fraction, but it's moved, beaming from straight overhead. And if that sundial Salki found is any indication, it will continue to move. My gut clenches and my eyes water, forcing me to look away and blink spots from my vision. I see the edge of the tower over the squat homes of Emgarden.

Heartwood is in that tower.

One thing at a time. Find Salki.

I push past the crowd and slip into her home. Casnia throws a piece of chalk and marches over to me, her latest piece of art, colored edge to edge, wrinkled in her tight hand.

"I'm going to the fields to find Salki." Salki never goes to work without Casnia. At the very least, she leaves her in the care of another. "Stay here."

"Member!" Casnia shouts at me.

"Stay *here*," I repeat, and turn for the door.

Casnia's feet pound on the floorboards. She grabs my shirt and huffs, jerking me back. "No! You! You!" She shoves the drawing into my chest.

Gritting my teeth and begging the gods for patience, I inspect the drawing. It's supposed to be me and Salki, but I'm tall and lithe with choppy yellow hair, and Salki boasts locks of flowing red and a white dress. I've never seen Salki wear a dress in my life. Around us are scribbles of green, and above, long lines of black with random blue dots in it.

"It's very nice, Cas."

"Sal!" She stabs her finger at the page, screeches from deep in her throat, and grabs fistfuls of her hair.

Sighing, I set the artwork aside and gently cup her elbows. "Calm down, Cas. Big breaths."

"No!" she shouts at me, so loud I freeze. She snatches back the picture and shoves it at me. "Member, Pell!"

"Member?" I ask. "*Re*member?"

Casnia slaps her hand against the picture, each thud reverberating through my chest.

"I already have," I whisper, though Casnia knows nothing of the tower. "I've already remembered. I need to find Salki."

I start to turn, but Casnia grips my wrist and yanks me back. Her bright violet eyes lock with mine. She *snarls* at me.

"No. *Remember*," she snaps, jerking me off balance. As I topple forward, she presses her palm to my forehead. Heat like the moving sun shoots through skin, muscles, and bone.

And I remember.

Chapter 27

I duck under the bough of a tree, into the little grove that Cas'ra-neah indicated. Twilight deepens the colors of the sparse wood, highlighting the cluster of green and pink emilies growing nearby. She's already here; Cas isn't one to be late. Gauzy fabric hangs off her shoulders, and her long, messily plaited hair cascades over one shoulder. She comes to life when she sees me, crossing the way so swiftly she barely gives me space to enter the small clearing.

"What?" I ask. "What now?"

She looks up at me with her vibrant purple eyes. "We're going to lead it here." She speaks in Thestean, one of the languages of the gods.

"It? Ruin?" I sputter in the same tongue, and she hisses for my silence. "You want it to come to Tampere?" I grab a tree branch as the Serpent moves, rumbling the ground beneath our feet. The glowing emilies recede back into the earth as it does.

She nods. "It's a newer world. Less known, and safer. Unpopulated."

"*We* populate it, Cas." Our city has grown since the goddess's last visit. We have mills and forges and an apothecary. A second cistern, even a small courthouse. Our people aren't as numerous here as in other places, but we're thriving, building, growing, learning. That's what she and the greater gods *asked* us to do. It's why they created us.

But Cas'raneah shakes her head. "It has to be here. Ruin doesn't know this place, not yet. It's small and new; your Serpent hasn't even shed it yet."

I gawk at her. "What?" Step back and look at the ground I'd just been standing on, as though it might open a window into the planet's core. "It's still here?"

She gestures to the emilies. "Where the flowers grow, the Serpent spins. I will—"

"You moved us to a gods-damned *unshed planet*?" So many more words fight to climb up my throat, but only a few nonsensical syllables make it past my tongue.

Holding up radiant fingers, she stalls me. "It's perfectly safe—"

"No wonder we get so many tremors." I knit both hands into my hair. "Our whole city could fall when it sheds—"

"The Serpent does not destroy what it so laboriously creates." The edge to Cas'raneah's voice warns me of her thinning patience, though in truth, she should be more concerned about mine. "I will rehome—"

"*This* is our home." I switch to the Ancetti language without meaning to. The language my people formed for ourselves.

She frowns. "And Elet'avar was your home before this."

"That's not fair."

"You complain about the Serpent and then refuse to leave it?" She clasps her fingers under her chin, pleading, and steps closer. The top of her head only comes to my sternum. "None of this is *fair*, Pelnophe. There will be no Tampere, no Elet'avar, if we don't stop Ruin. We can't destroy it—we haven't figured out how. But we can imprison it. Far away from the other worlds. Here. I know I'm asking you to leave your city—we will imprison it far away. Preserve your city, if we can."

I scoff. I don't want to share a world with the Devourer, no matter how they build its prison.

"Ruin is old and powerful," she continues. "We need your magic to seal it."

I gawk at her, waiting for the punch line, but none comes. A cool breeze blows gold hair into my face; I swipe it back. Time to hack more off, I guess. "It isn't magic," I explain. Again.

But the goddess merely smiles. "To Ruin, it will be."

Cas'raneah hesitantly peeks into the small vat. I've set it up in the camp that our war party—for lack of a better term—has established in the middle of nowhere, halfway between our evacuated city and the location the gods selected for Ruin's prison. But simple bars and stone will not hold the Devourer.

She, Arthen, and I crouch around the steel pot on its little burner, watching large bubbles form in the thin, liquid silver below. It casts a soft glow, almost like that of the emilies, against the sides of the vat. "It's that brine silver I discovered when we moved out here," I explain. Cas'raneah splits her time between Tampere and the battlefront itself; I haven't seen her in almost fifty of Tampere's days. "That shiny stuff at the bottom of those salt pots?"

"You went in there?" she asks. "Are you hurt?"

"I used *magic*." I wiggle my fingers, which earns me an eye roll. The salt pots are filled with variations of blue and green boiling liquid. I don't know what the World Serpent did or ate that created such a phenomenon in its skin, but it's unsafe to touch bare handed. Nothing a drainage system and excavator can't handle.

"There isn't much of it," I add. "It's a rare substance. I was studying it, doing some experimental metallurgy with heat and aluminum chromate. Look."

I stick my hand right into the silver.

"Pell!" Cas'raneah grabs my wrist and pulls it out. Arthen laughs.

"It's only warm," I assure her, watching the bright, silvery liquid drip off my hand and back into the pot. And it's only warm because of the burner. Otherwise, I can't even tell my hand was wet, that's how low its density is. "Look how thin it is, and you can't see through it. It's reflective. I wonder if we can't utilize this somehow. Privacy, camouflage—"

Cas'raneah pokes a bead of silver as it runs down my forearm, then gasps and whips her hand away. For a moment, I think she's joking—trying to get back at me for scaring her with the pot. But she cradles her hand. Burns swell over her radiant, godly skin. A blister starts to form on her fingertip.

Arthen and I both stare. I've never seen a wounded god before. I don't think he has, either.

"C-Cas." I check my hand for silver residue before reaching out. "I'm sorry, I didn't know—"

"What is this made of, again?" she asks, a wince still pinching the corners of her eyes as she studies the wound.

"A handful of things. I can get you a list."

"How much can you make?"

I hesitate.

Arthen draws a hand down his golden beard, which is even longer than Cas'raneah's hair. "You want it as a weapon."

She nods. "If it can hurt me, it can hurt it."

Ruin, she means.

"Not a lot." I hate dampening her budding hope, but I have to be honest. "The brine silver is rare, hard to find."

"How much?" Cas presses.

I glance at Arthen. "If we dig out *all* the salt pots . . . seven, maybe eight thousand liters."

Cas'raneah curls her finger into her fist, hiding it from us. "The amaranthine won't be enough."

I catch where she's leading. Amaranthine is a strange substance the gods alone can create. It's pale pink in color, almost like glass in its smoothness, but harder than tempered steel. Unbreakable, as far as I know. And incredibly difficult to make. It takes a lot out of the immortals, taxes them like little else does, but it also replicates their power, their essence. It would make a fantastic battery, if I can ever convince any of them to give me some.

They're building Ruin's prison out of it.

"You want to flood the prison with this . . . silver." I'm going to need a better name for it.

She claps her hands. "Flood it, line it, whatever you can give me. Another line of defense."

"It won't be enough," Arthen comments, eyes unfocused. "We'll need more."

Cas'raneah peers into the vat. "We'll need more. But this is a start."

"I know how to do it."

My eagerness to get to the stump-table in Arthen's forge alerts the others—Maglon, Salki, and Cas'raneah. With chalk and a slate, I draw a giant circle, then a smaller one within, scribbling in a diagram I'm sure only I can read.

"Cas had a point. This world is new. Tampere's Serpent hasn't moved on yet." I stab chalk into the smaller circle. The first World Serpent was made by the Well of Creation, but its children continue to populate the heavens, expanding the universe and life within. One of those children is adding its last touches to Tampere. I sketch a great fork cutting through the first circle to the second. "So what if we trapped it here?"

Salki pushes long red hair from her face. "Come again?"

"I don't understand," Cas'raneah says. She hovers a foot off the ground to better see my diagram.

"Because *this*." I draw a sun symbol to the left of the diagram and circle it three times. "The planet turns with the motions of the Serpent. Ruin is, above all else, a void god. A creature created from lack, the inversion of the Well. It draws its powers *from* lack." I turn to the goddess. "You said the prison wouldn't be enough, even with the amaranthine and the acetic silver. This would be enough."

"It draws strength from darkness," Cas'raneah murmurs, fixed on the slate. "From coldness. Emptiness."

"From night," I agree, marking the right side of the diagram with an *X*. "If there is no night, then Ruin has no fuel."

"Interesting." Arthen rubs the roots of his long beard. It hangs nearly to his knees. Used to be to his ankles, before it caught at the forge and ignited. Again.

"It can still feed, though." Salki turns to Cas'raneah. "Can't it?"

The goddess meets my gaze. "It would limit Ruin, yes, but not destroy it. Should it escape by some chance, it would need only reach the dark side of the planet to regain its strength."

"That's the gods' problem," I spit, ruffled by even the slightest push against my genius. "Your army captures it, and we'll imprison it. Weaken it."

Cas'raneah purses her lips. "You won't survive. We'll ruin this planet."

"Pun not intended." Maglon winks.

His humor dies before reaching anyone else. "We were going to leave, regardless," I say, still chaffing at the idea.

"No." Salki knits her hands together as though in prayer. "We should stay. If this works, we *must* stay. We can't leave such a prisoner to its own devices."

Silent agreement spreads through us. "We'll need help." I fold my arms tightly across my chest. "The sun will burn out the land. We'll need something to cool it."

"We'll figure that out," Maglon assures me.

"What if it escapes?" Cas'raneah flexes her long fingers. "What if it finds this machine?"

"Through the amaranthine and the acetic silver? Through perpetual daylight?" I counter, but Cas'raneah only frowns. The longer the war stretches, the more she doubts . . . everything. "We build the machine far away," I offer. "As far from its prison as we can get."

"Without touching the night?" she counters.

"As far as we can get," I repeat, because it's the only answer I have. "And we'll guard it. Plus the amaranthine. Plus the acetic silver."

The goddess rubs her arms.

"We'll do what we can," I offer. "We can house the machine in a fortress and physically guard it ourselves. We just need something to power it."

After a long hesitation, she nods. "Do it, then. I'll sort out the rest."

The work is merciless. Constantly pumping the bellows at the forge, tinkering, assembling, planning. Little to eat and even less sleep, but the war is nearing its peak, and the universe shudders with it. Ruin will destroy everything, if given the chance.

The machine is enormous. It has to be, to trap a creature one can call a god in its own right. The Serpent cannot leave; its turning, its feeding, keeps the planet rotating. When it leaves, the power of its exit, along with the laws of the universe, will continue Tampere's rotation. Set it, leaving us no mode to stop it. Which means the Serpent has to stay. We have to imprison it, along with the Devourer. We can fathom no other way. Not in such limited time.

And so we erect the machine. Build it in five pieces, with redundancies, for a single failure could shatter everything. War affords no mistakes.

"And this will do it?" Cas'raneah asks, looking at the half-built monstrosity beneath the light of stars.

Raising a forearm to simulate the planet's crust, I thrust my opposite hand behind it and clench my fist, mimicking the machine's underground claw. "Just like this," I promise. "The drill will do most of the digging. It will be quick, if we can feed it enough power."

"The planet will stop, and we'll cage Ruin in the sun." She sounds unsure, but Cas'raneah seldom thinks in absolutes.

"We need a power source." Amaranthine is our best bet.

"I know." The irritation in her voice isn't directed toward me. We're all exhausted. "I'll deliver it soon. A few of the others will help me."

My hackles rise. "I thought you weren't telling others about this." We can't risk word getting out to Ruin. We have *one chance*.

"They're trustworthy." She looks heavenward, sudden nostalgia softening her features. "I can't do it alone. I am not the Well."

I sigh and nod, though she doesn't see it. But if a goddess herself is this concerned, I don't know what chance the rest of us have.

✺

We've nearly finished the tower; its walls and floors align snug and tight. Hagthor and Amlynn are fantastic architects; no one will be able to get through the fortress by the time she's done with it, though I worry that the speed at which we erected it will create problems, so I put in extra fail-safes. Arthen thinks they're a waste of time, but Cas'raneah's fear pushes me to be thorough. Hide the amaranthine crystal behind a door and entrust its only key to our most discreet citizen. Block off the top three sections of the machine, with a hidden lift for maintenance, and a trapdoor in the shaft for floor three. I make it so all five parts of the machine can disconnect, and we have enough acetic silver to coat the topmost piece.

Now I have plans on a giant piece of parchment stretched out between our group. Again Cas'raneah hovers to see over our shoulders; for whatever reason, our gods made us taller than themselves. At least, taller than the ones I've met. "We'll snatch the Serpent at the last possible moment." I point to the outline of the machine and the great folded claw attached to the drill. "We can't tip off Ruin or any of its spies."

"How will you know where it is?" Cas'raneah chimes in. "When to do it?"

"The emilies." I lift my head to point them out, but none are growing here. "That's how the Serpent feeds." The powerful buds suck sunlight down through their deep roots and into the Serpent itself, which feeds almost like a plant would. "There's a pattern; the Serpent makes a complete rotation every twenty-six hours. The flowers follow its path. When the flowers return here"—I point toward the tower—"we act."

The heavens thunder, the ground groans, the stars fall. The gods have brought their war to Tampere.

I know when Ruin arrives. Unholy darkness swallows the night of his coming. Our lanterns and motor-powered lights barely pierce it. The darkness is a physical thing, like dust or breath.

Maglon turns on the fog emitters early, thinking they'll mask our work. They don't quite align with the movements of the sun, but if this works, that won't matter.

When the sun dawns, I ready myself at the tower. We complete the machine. It's massive and functional and the most beautiful thing I've ever constructed. Would be even more so, if we'd had the time. I wait, poised at the top of the tower, but the signal doesn't come. Ruin is too powerful.

It devours. A scout reports an enormous crater, kilometers from Emgarden, but whether the earth was eaten or merely crushed by the power of gods, we can't be sure. The forests begin to decay. Animals sense the wrongness of the void god's presence and flee as the vegetation curls and withers. We stay, waiting, ready.

The wait hurts. I can't sleep. My muscles are in a constant state of winding, ready to spring at a moment's notice. Fear sours my belly. What if it doesn't work? What if Ruin catches on and flees? What if the gods can't pin it down? What if it *wins*?

"Then we'll all be dead, and it won't matter," I tell Salki callously over thin soup. I'm terrible at comforting, and she knows it. She shouldn't have asked. It's an unfair thought, but I have to be unfair. If I dwell on our demise when our people have only just begun, I will unravel. I need to keep myself together. I need this machine to work.

The planet rocks the day they seize the Devourer.

Our small shelters collapse. Dying trees topple, canyons open, mountains jut, and a shrill whistle sings out across a pale sky—the gods' call.

They have it, and the emilies thrust up through the soil, drinking in sunlight, marking the path of the Serpent.

Almost as soon as the signal sounds, the darkness spreads. It rushes from the land far to the west, spreading out in patterns like broken glass, black and sinking and sucking. Entire rock formations crumble atop it as it passes. Brush turns brittle and collapses beneath its own weight, and the darkness pours into Emgarden.

My people panic and run, some not quickly enough. I watch Hagthor fall to it. Watch his body gray in an instant, his eyes dissolve in their sockets, his hair fall from his head. He never screams, only shrivels and wanes until there's nothing left of him.

We are not gods. We retreat.

I desperately seek out Salki, Arthen, but there's no time to search, only to sprint for our lives. I don't know how long it will take for the gods to strip Ruin enough to imprison it; I only know that it will consume everything within its reach while they try. Maybe even the Serpent itself.

The tower.

My lungs burn. The garage has fallen; there's no time to free the off-world transports. I have only the legs the gods gave me, and if they're not enough, then we all fail.

I bolt for the tower, sprinting on my toes, pumping my arms with the silent plea to move faster, faster, *faster*. The heavens thunder and darken as I reach the heavy doors and haul them open, slipping into the darkness of the tower.

My long legs take the stairs three at a time. To the open door of the power source. I trace the hidden runes at its base, and the rose-colored crystal burns to life. Backtracking, I push the door seamlessly flush with the wall, then cover it with the second part of the machine. Only Entisa will be able to open it now, if the universe wills that she survives.

Up, up, up to the top of the tower, to the master engine I created with my own hands. Through the acetic silver that harmlessly cascades over me. I drop the turbine into position and throw my weight into the lever. The tower rumbles and spits, venting hissing steam through its windows. My body vibrates as the drill surges through the crust, and I grip the machine with golden knuckles blanched white to keep my balance. When the claw hits, the machine bucks me off, throwing me back through the acetic silver and into the wall. My vision blackens for a moment, but my mind stays alert, and I push onto my feet as the tower jerks north, then east, as the Serpent tries to free itself.

We did it. The movements still. The claw struck true.

The machine settles, steam dissipating. With the clamp released, the Serpent within the planet will be unable to turn. We've locked Ruin's prison in perpetual day.

But I have to guarantee it.

Pinching my lips together, for it pains me to destroy what I've created, I drop to the fourth floor and start pulling parts free, dislodging gears, cutting wires. Down through the tower, I destroy the mechanisms that brought us hope, each a little more than the last. I crush, dislodge, tear, scatter. Cut and tear out the cording that links its parts. The machine will hold, but it will never again *release.*

I stumble out of the tower, the sun frozen two hours from its zenith, but a brighter light bursts beneath it, a star exploding outward with the power only a goddess can possess, and I know instantly that it's Cas'raneah, come to initiate the machine herself if she has to. But I'm still here. We're still here.

Should it escape by some chance, it would need only reach the dark side to regain its strength.

Realizing what she's doing, I stumble at the blaze of light, my strength gone. "Oh, Cas." Not this. Not you, too.

Her power bursts from her in a cascade of amaranthine. It sweeps the land, growing and burning and hardening into a wall that seems to stretch on forever, that surely encircles the continent in its entirety, an impenetrable guard to keep any from climbing it and reaching to the cold abandon on the planet's other side.

And then she falls, lifeless, toward the earth.

"Cas!" I shout. I try to run, but my weary body falters. I fall to palms and knees, scraping them on the rough soil. Pushing up, I limp forward, desperate to reach her—

Ruin's black tendrils fade to little more than a shadow of gray. I'm so desperate to reach Cas that I don't even notice when I cross one. But I feel it. Immediately, I feel it.

It doesn't devour me, as it did Hagthor. Ruin is too weak. But even as it sinks into its prison, the Devourer consumes. My dwindling strength leaches out through the soles of my feet. The golden glow seeps from my hair and skin. My bones shrink. As the sun-bright sky blots to darkness in my vision, I collapse.

And I forget.

245

Lids scrape over my dry eyes, and mist-strewn sunlight fills my vision. With a groan, I push myself up. My blood feels made of grit, and my skin, cracked leather. I take a moment to gain my bearings. Where am I? Why do I feel like this? Ugh . . . my head feels like the clapper of a giant bell.

Someone is crying.

Picking myself up—it takes a few tries—I teeter toward the sound. I think it's a child at first, but when I find the source in the hazy fog, it's a small woman, curled up on herself, her dark hair falling over naked back and shoulders.

I crouch in front of her. "Are you okay?"

She blubbers a little longer. "No," she wails. "No, no, no . . ."

"What's your name?"

She doesn't seem to understand me. She squirms from my touch, sobbing and muttering choppy nonsense. I stay with her a long while. I have so little energy. But eventually I hear other voices, more clear and precise, more intelligible, elsewhere in the fog. Voices I know, somehow, but can't quite place. I try, and . . . lose my train of thought.

"Here." Standing, I offer my hand. "Let's find you some clothes." My own hang off my frame; my trousers barely stay up. "Better to cry where it's safe than out here." Wherever *here* is.

It takes some goading, but I convince the naked woman to take my hand. Her body spasms a few times, then allows me to lead her toward the others. She drags her feet and mumbles under her breath, but I catch part of it.

"Cas . . . neeee." She shudders and tries again. "Casss . . . neeee!"

"Is that your name?" I ask, but she doesn't reply. Doesn't seem like she's able to, like her mind is elsewhere, connected to her body by only a thin string. After a few more attempts, she says, "Nia!"

"Casnia," I supply for her, and she doesn't object. "I'm . . ." It takes a moment for me, too. "Pell. Pelnophe. I'll help you, okay?"

She stumbles then, dropping into the dirt as though her strength has left her entirely. I have a little left, so I carry her the rest of the way.

Chapter 28

My forward momentum sends me colliding with the old planks of Salki's floor. I catch myself with my free hand and fall onto my hip. Casnia releases my other and falls into a heap beside me.

Just like before.

"Cas!" I cry, rivers streaming from my eyes. *Rivers.* I remember rivers. Oh gods, I remember rivers and trees and night and stars and *Cas'raneah.* I roll her onto her back and smooth hair from her face. I barely recognize her like this. She's so changed, so . . . mortal.

She gave everything to create that wall. She pulled the power for it right from her mind, right from her soul. Left her like this, but it didn't kill her. Thank the Well it didn't kill her.

But she couldn't tell me. She lost herself to the confines of her own prison.

"Cas. Cas." Hovering over her, I pat her round cheeks. "Cas'raneah, can you hear me?" I pull back one of her eyelids; her iris rolls back. I check her pulse. Heart beating. Still breathing. But she doesn't wake, no matter how hard I shake her. "Cas!" Tears hit her collar and my knees. "Cas, I'm so sorry, I'm so—"

Serpent save me, I *fixed the damn machine.* Tampere's World Serpent is free and turning. We're heading into night, and it will only take about six hours for Moseus—for Ruin—to reclaim his true power.

How did it escape? How did it obtain a physical form and reach the tower?

Arthen pushes open the door just then. "What—" Seeing us, he rushes to Cas'raneah's side. "What happened? Is she okay?"

Oh, Arthen. He's so different from how he used to be. So much smaller, weaker. Aged. We used to be so much more. Strong, tall, golden. Halfway to gods. All of us, and Ruin took it from all of us. Devoured our shadows of divinity as it was sucked down into its terrestrial prison.

"She fell." I wipe my eyes. I remember, but Arthen doesn't. Casnia gave the last of herself to make me *remember*, and she had nothing left to give. "I don't know if she'll wake up this time, Arthen."

"This time?" he lifts his eyes, then pauses. Blinks. "P-Pell?"

Lifting the collar of my shirt, I catch stray tears. Arthen's never seen me cry before—

"What happened to your hair?" he asks instead. "Your . . . eyes?"

"What do you mean?" Panic leaks in with my renewed understanding. I rise to my feet, turning, spying a metal spoon on Salki's table. Rushing to it, I pick it up and peer into the convex side. My lips part.

I expect to see my old self, to see eyes and hair turned gold. But no—my brown hair has darkened to jet black, and my eyes . . . my eyes are a brilliant violet, *just like Cas'raneah's.*

In that moment, staring at my warped reflection, I understand how Ruin did it. Why Moseus and Heartwood look so similar. The paleness, the green eyes, the hair—they're not features of his people. Of gods or otherwise. They're all features of *Heartwood.*

Cas'raneah gave her power to me and subsequently changed my appearance. When Heartwood came here looking for his sister, Ruin must have *stolen his.* It had nothing to do with the planet. The only curse upon Tampere is that bastard locked inside *my tower.*

Moseus needed Heartwood. The forest god was his damned battery, but he wasn't enough—thus Moseus's sickliness. The dried-out copse of wickwoods, the ruined row of crops . . . Moseus must have been siphoning life from them in attempts to hold on to his stolen form. He needed Heartwood to remain physical, and he needed me to fix the machines. But in six hours, he won't need either of us anymore.

I can't do this alone. I never could.

"Get her to the bed," I shout, storming toward the door. "And get everyone to the alehouse, *now*—"

I run right into Salki, nearly knocking her over. But she steadies herself, her eyes round as ball bearings. She, too, is a sliver of her old self. Her short hair grayed, her body wrinkled, her stature small—

She's holding a stack of papers. *My* papers. The ones I hid under my floor. The ones with my hundreds of paragraphs of what happened to me, should I forget a second time.

I'm relieved. It will make the rest that much easier.

"Salki, I'm ready to explain *everything*. To everyone," I promise. "And I need you to help me do it."

The table I stand on in Maglon's alehouse creaks with my movement as I address the crowd. Everyone is here but Casnia, who still lies unconscious but has been deemed stable by Amlynn. People fill the pub, and they've left the doors open to accommodate more bodies. Farmers and craftsmen alike sit hip to hip on the bar. Every chair is taken, every disbelieving eye on me. Had they not seen the tower and the sun move, had Casnia not overlaid her colors on me, they never would have believed my story. But these are three witnesses that something has changed, and so the crowd listens, albeit with a thick air of skepticism.

When I'm done explaining, Frantess says, "So you want us to believe that *we* are Ancients, and we forgot because Ruin itself lives on the planet? But you remember because *Casnia* of all people cast some sort of spell on you?"

"Casnia was changed by the war. We all were," I repeat, struggling to keep a hold on my temper. I could call salt salty and she would disagree with me. "I don't have time to debate it with you. Salki?"

Salki, in the doorway, turns away from the crowd. She's checking the sundial, which she had lain in the street. "Five and a half hours," she reads.

"That's how much time we have before Ruin returns to his full power. *Its* full power." It's hard for me to think of the Devourer as anything but *him*—Moseus. "I need help. We have to get into that tower."

"We've never been able to get into that tower, Pell." Arthen works his hands.

"We've never gotten the whole of Emgarden to try," I retort. "Do you not understand? Ruin will destroy *everything*, and it won't stop with Tampere. I can't give your memories back to you, I can only tell you what I know, both before and after this happened!" I gesture to my changed self. "Don't you wonder why we don't have blood parents, or children? Why none of us can remember a place before Emgarden?" I stop to rub a throbbing spot on my brow. "If nothing else, there's an enormous amount of metal in there. Enough to supply us for a long time. Let greed entice you, I don't care. But I *need help*."

The crowd grows silent. My gut knots.

"Arthen, you had the longest, most annoying beard." The table creaks as I lean toward him. "You would never cut it. You accidentally lit it on fire all the time. And Balfid"—I twist toward the farmer—"you were the size of an ox. You thought the gods liked you the most because of it, but you were lazy as a rock."

"Hey!" he protests.

"Amlynn"—I find her in the crowd—"you were an architect, and a healer. You always have been. But you were also a brewer, and you'd come up with all sorts of weird potions in what I considered a very obvious attempt to impress Maglon."

Amlynn's face brightens to a ripe shade of red.

I turn again. "Maglon, that scar on your back isn't from a fall, it's from a horse. We used to have *horses*. Gethnen used to sing late into the nigh . . . the mists. He could make up a song on a whim and never lose his meter. Frantess, you were so young, so new, so intrigued by the world around you. So gods-damned annoying, too."

A few chuckles echo across the room.

"Thamton." I scan the room and find him in the corner. Oddly enough, emotion chokes my words. "You were the oldest of us. The first. You helped us find ourselves, our purpose, especially once the war started and called away our makers." I swallow, trying to regain my composure as I search the doorway. "And Salki, you have been and always will be my best friend and greatest supporter. Ruin took so much from you, and yet somehow you still find it in yourself to forgive, even when I'm narrow-minded and selfish. I'll make it up to you, somehow."

I don't have time to single out each one of them, but I do make eye contact with every person who allows me.

"I'm going to the tower. I know more—remember more—than I did before. We built that tower; we can tear it apart again." Fists clenched, I continue, "I would like to believe I've never done anything that would lead any of you astray. I want to believe I've earned your trust. This is a lot. I wouldn't believe me, either. But help me for the next six hours, and I'll be in your service for the rest of my life."

"Can't we just," Balfid treads carefully, "turn off the machine?"

"No, we'd have to re-employ it, and the Serpent won't return for twenty-three hours. It'll be too late." I take a deep breath. "Everyone needs to bring a lamp. I'll answer any other questions on the way. Now move."

The folk closest to the table scoot back to allow me to jump down. I start toward the door, then turn back and, standing on a chair, pull the clock from the tavern wall. With it under my arm, I push my way to the door. I will do this by myself, if I have to. I'll fail, but I'll try.

The sun has passed its zenith, warning me of my dwindling time. I need to run. I must hurry. Too many lives are at stake.

Salki, bless her, falls into step beside me. She says nothing. She doesn't have to. But I do.

"I need you to run back to my house and get the machine in that nook." I hand her the emilies looped through my belt. "Then I'll tell you my plan."

She nods and runs ahead.

We pass a house, then another. I'm about to break into a sprint when footsteps behind me signal the arrival of Maglon, followed by Balfid and Gethnen. Behind them, Arthen runs from the alehouse. A few more follow him, and then a few more.

I grin at the blossom of hope opening in my chest. I might not have won over all of Emgarden, but I will have enough.

I see it before we reach it. Hope it's a trick of the moving sun. Memories aside, it's been a *long* time since I saw the natural rise and fall of daylight. I need that empty spot at the base of the tower to be a shadow and nothing more.

Arthen slows first. "What . . . is it?"

"A hole?" Maglon guesses.

Even before, I was never part of the war. I'm not a soldier. Even if I were, I couldn't fight amidst gods. Mortality binds my life to physical form, to gravity. I never saw Ruin with my own eyes, before it took the shape of a wayward forest god and settled into this tower.

Heartwood, I'm coming. I take solace in the fact that Moseus still needs his battery alive. For the next five hours, anyway.

I approach the dark spot where the doors used to be, stopping ten paces back. It hurts my eyes to look at it—a two-dimensional rift in a three-dimensional world. It has no true color, just endlessness, darkness, eternity, a void, a gap in reality where nothing is nor can be. Just large enough to engulf the heavy double doors into the tower.

Ruin siphoned Heartwood's strength to take the form it has now, but to create something like this should have drained Moseus immensely. But Moseus is smart. So long as nothing disturbs him or this tower, all he has to do is sit around meditating for five hours and he'll have everything he wants.

Meditating. He never drew his strength from peace, but from lack. That sheltered room was an artificial night, but never enough to truly heal him.

"Can we climb it?" Salki asks, my little machine in her hands. She wrings the frame.

Arthen responds, "I've tried before."

"Ladder?" Balfid suggests.

"Windows are too narrow," Maglon says.

Crouching, I close my eyes and work my brain. I can do this. I helped *build* the damn thing. Does it have another weak spot, outside that apparent gap between floors two and three?

I would reprimand whoever constructed that floor, if I could recall who it was. Then again, they wouldn't remember, either.

Frantess throws a rock into the void. It makes no landing, no sound. Amlynn grabs her elbow and pulls her away.

"Your tools won't work, Arthen?" Salki asks.

He must have shaken his head. I hear no other answer.

"There's no back entrance?" Maglon shuffles, like he's going to walk around the tower to see. As if in all these years, we'd never bothered to check.

"Maybe if we throw in enough," Thamton calls from the back, "that blankness will fill in?"

"And then what?" asks another. "Can we dig under it?"

"No," Salki answers. She'd know. She read it in my book.

"I say we still build a ladder," Balfid says.

"Or . . . a hook? To open a door?" Frantess suggests.

"What door?" Frustration leaks into Arthen's voice. "There is no door!"

Build, I think as sweat drips from my temple. The mist should be coming any time now. Except—

I shoot to my feet so quickly it makes me light-headed. "I've got it. But we need to go back to Emgarden *now*. Arthen, can you run?"

His eyes widen, but he nods.

"Good." And I take off for the town.

※

Back at Arthen's forge, half the water I chug spills over the front of my shirt, but I don't care. I toss the bladder aside and finish my slapdash sketch. "Like this. I need you to make this as fast as you can. It needs to be thin and light."

He stares at the crescent-shaped sketch. "It'll be brittle—"

"I only need to use it once. Go! Balfid, help him."

Frantess, Maglon, and Salki come huffing through the falling mist, carrying my rover between them.

"Right here!" I bark, pointing to the opposite end of the forge. They oblige. Amlynn comes with my tools. I pull her over to help. If she had her memories back, this would go so much swifter, but we have what we have, and only four and a half hours to get this done.

"Hex turnscrew." I hold out my hand. Amlynn shuffles and hands it to me. Salki returns a moment later with a lantern. "Wrench. Thamton, see that gear over there? It's a flywheel. Bring it to me. With the—yes, that. Just bring it all."

With a heave I turn the rover over and pull apart its belly, wiping sweat from my eyes. Frantess hands me a bladder. I drink half of it, then dump the rest over my head, desperate to cool off. "Make sure the others are drinking," I insist without looking up from my work.

"Sprocket," I say, and Amlynn hands me one. A few minutes later, Frantess hands me a strip of dried meat and a bar of grain. I thank her and chew while I work. "Hold this."

Amlynn puts her hands on the slide head. I tighten the prongs holding it, then use screws to make a crude shaft for steering, though I'll have to depend on the distribution of weight for tighter turns.

"I need water," I say to no one in particular. "A lot of water."

Footsteps vanish from the forge as Arthen fills the room with blistering heat and the pealing of his hammer.

I connect a makeshift piston and seal up the rover's belly. It won't last long, but I only need a couple of hours. More than that and we'll be doomed, anyway.

Amlynn helps me right the thing, and I make my final adjustments. Water arrives, and I fill the cylinder with as much as it can hold, then fasten another bladder atop it. I'll cut it loose if it weighs down the machine too much. I wedge the clock and my tool bag between the two.

"Mag, help Amlynn carry this to the road. Salki—" I gesture to the back entrance of the forge, and Salki follows me out into the mist.

"It's so dark," she says.

It's not even sunset yet, but the mist does seem darker. I worry the onset of night will scare my help away, but there's nothing to be done. If this next step doesn't work, we fail. If Salki can't accept this final request, we fail.

I plant my hands on her shoulders and look her in the eyes. She stares in wonderment, seeing Casnia in mine.

"I need you to listen very carefully, because I can't do this part," I say in low tones. "I'm going to show you how it works, and then what to do with it, and we only have time to go over it once. Do you understand?"

She nods, and I begin.

※

Arthen finishes the crescent-shaped piece. I look over the hastily crafted part—it's still warm—and hand it back to him. "Get on."

His eyes bug at me. "What?"

"I can't lift what I need by myself." There's *barely* enough room for the two of us. "If we slow down at the mountains, you'll need to get off, but we'll see what happens."

Charlie N. Holmberg

Balfid gapes. "You're going to *ride* that thing?"

I ignore him. "Arthen, get on."

He holds out the crescent-shaped piece he made, the new chamber plate. "Don't you need to attach this?"

"It's not for the rover. Get on." To the others, I say, "I want you to wait halfway down the road to the tower. With ladders. *Do not* approach the tower, do you understand me?"

"I'll make sure," Salki assures me.

I pass her a grateful look as Arthen gingerly straddles the water rover. I shove his shoulder to seat him, wind the motor, pull a cord, and jump on just as the vehicle pops and bolts forward. I nearly collide into a barrel as we take off down the road at an alarming but intensely satisfying rate. Hopefully my slapdash work holds up long enough.

Arthen yelps as we take a sharp turn out of Emgarden, grabbing my shoulder for balance, his other arm wrapped around the chamber plate. The ground between Tampere's random rock protrusions is mostly flat, so the rover holds steady, kicking up a monumental dust cloud in our wake. Without the mist, the thing would be visible for kilometers. Regardless, I don't care if Moseus is watching. There's nothing he can do to stop me. Not until nightfall, and I intend to beat him to it.

My pulse counts down the seconds. *Gods let this work. Let this work.* I pray my memory of the machines proves correct. It's been a long time, but with so much of my past having been safely stored away, maybe it didn't have the opportunity to decay like everything else.

The earth inclines as we reach the mountains. I know the path, and it's barely wide enough for the rover, but not entirely smooth, and the machine bucks over rocks and dips. Arthen yelps; I hold my breath. The incline builds, and the machine slows.

"Come on, come on," I murmur, stroking its hot sides like I would a horse. "You can do it."

"How much farther?" Arthen yells.

I look up the path as the rover climbs and shakes. "Not . . . too far." *Come on!*

256

"I'm going to jump off."

I whip around and look at him, only to force my attention forward and lean hard to avoid a rock. "What?"

"You said it'll go faster, right? I can run. It's just up this path, right?" He swallows, and his nerves carry on his breath, tangling in my hair. "I can follow the tracks."

I nod. "Yes, thank you. Quickly."

The rover whines up a turn, and Arthen jumps. With roughly two-thirds of its load gone, the vehicle lurches forward with renewed life. I glance back to ensure that Arthen hasn't injured himself before the rover zips behind a natural stone wall, ever climbing.

The path forks. A twist of my steering stick and a lean to the right takes me up to a ridge. The rover slows again, struggling in loose dirt. When the machine moves slower than I can run, I reach down and shut it off. Grab my tools and hike up the rest of the way, pausing for a few seconds atop the ridge, giving my lungs a chance to catch up with me.

It's here, behind a short outcropping, settled in a depression in the rock. This is the fourth of six fog machines—the one I saw near Heartwood's garden is six of six. It consists of a brassy set of pipes connected to a giant metal belly. There's a pump system under all of it, pulling water from underground, pressurizing it, and spitting it out over our chunk of land. The mist thins here, standing beneath the pipes.

I slide down to it, quickly refamiliarizing myself. I shut off the timer first thing. The pump halts, though the air will take a while to clear.

Next, I gauge the pipes, select the one I'll have to redirect the least, and close off the others. The farthest one's stopper is stuck open, so I slam a hammer into it until the aperture pinches shut.

Three hours, nine minutes. I check the clock too often; my own circadian rhythm has been askew for . . . I don't even know how long. And I don't have time to dwell on it.

Loosening the fixture holding my selected pipe in place, I twist the thing northward, then leave it there, waiting for the mist to clear. Heavy huffing comes over the ridge.

"Perfect." I run up to meet Arthen.

Sweat marks the front of his shirt and underarms. He holds the chamber plate to his chest like a newborn, uttering no complaint when I relieve him of it.

"Follow me," I direct, and he does, panting and wordless. I set the plate aside. After climbing the body of the machine, I loosen the upper half of the pipe. This piece alone measures two meters long. "Can you reach this from where you are?"

Arthen wearily stretches up his hands. To my relief, he can.

"Hold it," I instruct. "I'm going to lift it up and out. Don't dent it."

On the count of three, we both heave, though the angle drops the bulk of the pipe's weight onto Arthen. Exhausted as he is, he has the arms of a blacksmith, and with a stifled grunt he manages to pull the thing loose and set it ungracefully on the ground. Scaling the remaining portion of the pipe, I grab a ruler and peer in, sighing as I confirm my measurements.

"Hand me that plate."

He does, then wipes sweat from his brow as I shift, trying to get as much light from the waning mist and setting sun as I can. "What is it?" he asks, hands on his hips, back hunched.

"Plate for an ignition chamber." Tying a thin rope to it, I carefully lower it in, then slide down the exterior of the pipe to adjust the flange bolts and secure it.

"No . . . what is *this*?" He gestures to the machine as a whole.

"This is where the mist comes from."

"The . . . what?" He steps back, taking in the enormity of the machine. "*This?*"

"I'll explain later."

He pauses. "What do you mean, *ignition chamber*?"

I work swiftly, my tools slick in my hands. "I'm going to blow a hole in the tower."

He says nothing for several seconds. Only when I jump down and run to the back of the machine to harvest parts does he speak. "You're making a cannon."

I'm glad he remembers what cannons are. "The tanks are already pressurized." I pull free parts that will obliterate the fog machine, but we won't need the fog after this. "I'm going to direct all of it to one pipe and aim it at the tower." But I chose Arthen to assist me for more than his big arms. "We did archery, once upon a time. You were rather good at it."

He merely stares.

"Find me good stones that will fit in that." I point to the top half of the pipe. "Go!"

Urgency restored, Arthen rushes past me. Gods bless him.

By the time he piles up his last stones, I'm more or less set up. *Two hours, forty-two minutes.*

"Give me your shirt."

He doesn't question me. With the way he's sweating, he's likely glad to be rid of it. He pulls it over his head and hands it to me. Honestly, the perspiration will probably help with the wadding. I shove it into the pipe, using a fallen branch from a wickwood tree to tamp it down as hard as I can.

"Okay, help me with this." I wipe sweat from my eyes and loosen the base of the pipe a little more. With sore muscles, I grab the pipe and squint over the rise of the mountain. I can see the top of the tower from where I am. "Arthen, your aim is good. Tell me where to point it."

He stands on his tiptoes, shading his eyes from the lowering sun. "It's far. How hard a punch will this thing have?"

"Hard enough." Or so I hope.

"We'll need to aim high," he suggests, grabbing the pipe and shifting it up, to the left, and up some more. "I think that will do it."

"Run ahead and make sure."

He does. Takes his time—and he should—scanning the tower and the pipe. I secure the thing where he indicates. *Two hours, twenty-nine minutes . . .*

"Okay." I take a breath, steadying myself. "Can you hold this down?" I point to the upper half of the pipe. He does as I ask, and with a hammer, I smash the smaller end of it, turning it every few whacks to get a point. Arthen then holds the pipe vertically, pointed end down, while I fill it with rocks, estimating the total weight in my head. Hesitate toward the end and take the last one out. It will have to do. I hammer the broader end shut as well, trying to keep the makeshift closure as flat as possible.

"Help me load it." Together we heave and groan to get my enormous, elongated projectile into the bottom half of the pipe. My limbs feel like oversoaked grain by the time it's in there, but I can't slow down. I'll rest when I'm dead.

Arthen huffs. "What now?"

"Get behind the machine and plug your ears."

With renewed energy, he does so. I engage the fog machine's engine and hunker back with him, knees digging into the red soil, fingers pressed into my ears. After a few seconds, the machine starts to rattle.

Please, please, I beseech the universe. *Please let this work. Please let it miss Heartwood and skewer that bastard instead. Please help me save them all.*

The earth rumbles. Through my plugged ears I hear the machine bubble and hiss and groan, and then a thunderous *boom* ruptures from the unblocked pipe, spitting an immense column of water vapor with it, blinding us with a thick vomit of mist. The body of the cannon has cracked.

Rushing to my feet, I feel along the hot metal to the pipe. It's split open. The projectile launched. But did it—

A second, distant rip of thunder echoes through the mountains, followed by a handful of faint screams from the Emgardians.

I'm too scared to hope. I wave the mists away. The machine can no longer produce them. Will not produce them ever again without extensive repairs. I climb higher up the peak as the fog-propellant clears, trying to see over the mist. The mountain soon gets too steep to climb without equipment. Steadying myself, I peer into the valley. The fog settles there like a blanket, but a line of it has thinned, since this machine no longer contributes. I can just make out the top of the tower. It hasn't fallen. My bones go limp within me.

I stand there, staring, exhaustion leaking into my limbs. Rack my brain for another option. Arthen calls up to me, but I barely register his words. Machine five of six . . . I could try again, there. It's close enough to do some damage. I just don't know if we'll have enough time.

Serpent save me, I have to try. I don't have another crescent piece, but . . . I have to try.

Stumbling back down to the ruined machine, I snatch my tool bag and bark at Arthen to get back on the rover. "We missed. We have to make it to another machine." *Please let the rover's power last,* I pray to no one, yet in the back of my mind, I see Cas's face.

Arthen doesn't question me. He helps me turn the rover and hops on as we take the mountain path down, moving much more quickly with the help of gravity. There should be a narrow trail heading north up ahead. The fifth fog machine doesn't have the same elevation, but—

"Pell."

"What?" I snap over the roar of the rover.

"Pell, *stop.*"

Gritting my teeth, I pull the brake. "*What,* Art?"

He points into the valley.

I squint. The mist from this peak has dissipated even more. I can see the west edge of Emgarden. Just make out the tower . . . and the great pile of rubble at its base, to the left of Moseus's door-eating void.

"We . . . ," I start, shivers coursing up my spine. "We hit it."

The projectile struck right where the tower meets the ground. There's rubble, red rock and white alike. And where there's rubble, there's a hole.

"We hit it!" I cry, suddenly full of air and energy and need. "Hurry, we have to hurry!"

We race back to the rover. Gravity propels the tired rover down, down, down the mountain, toward the cluster of people waiting to strike.

One hour, fifty-eight minutes . . .

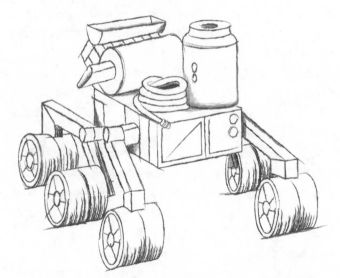

Chapter 29

The dust from the impact has cleared by the time Arthen and I return, leaving us with about two hours to find Moseus and stop him. The people of Emgarden have forgotten their pasts, but they aren't stupid. In addition to having lamps and lanterns to pierce the mist, they've armed themselves with shovels, hoes, knives, and other tools, many of which, ironically, Moseus supplied the metal for. While the Ancients—us— had been trained in knife work, archery, and the like, none of us are soldiers. We never realized we'd need to be. To think how much more prepared we might have been, had Ruin not reached out its claws with its last free breath before the gods locked it in a prison kilometers away. One I've never had the opportunity to behold, but one the dwindled demon managed to escape.

I take my hammer and a wrench from my tool bag and hand them to Arthen. Pull his knife from my pocket and squeeze the hilt. "They look very similar," I explain to everyone as we near, adding to the tale Salki has already shared in my absence, gleaned from my pages of notes. "Do *not* hurt Heartwood. He's our ally." I detail the differences between the two gods, which seem so obvious to me now. "Do not hurt Heartwood," I repeat, though only those closest to me hear it. *If I haven't hurt him already,* I think, and my blood runs cold. I should have taken him with me. I'd been firm that Heartwood not leave me alone with Moseus. I hadn't considered that I shouldn't leave Moseus alone with him.

The projectile blew a great hole in the ground at the base of the tower, some seven meters across and, at its deepest, three meters down. Several of the farmers hurry forward to move away stone, giving the rippling void a wide berth. I hang back, sitting on my haunches, gathering my strength. Offering a silent thanks when Salki brings me a grain bar and water, with a whisper to stay calm. She's right, but moving the stones is slow work, and we've so little time. She and the others marvel at the sky's changing colors as the sun nears the mountain-edged horizon, looking larger and darker. It makes the amaranthine wall—Cas'raneah's wall—glow. Beyond the wall, the heavens adopt a shade of periwinkle that no one else has ever seen. Or can remember seeing, at least.

"Pell," Salki whispers.

I look up to see that the farmers have uncovered a hole, roughly two-thirds of a meter in diameter, blasted into the tower. "Let me go first." I run to it, careful not to fall into the sandy gap in the earth where my cannon's projectile sits half-buried. Accepting a lantern from Frantess, I peer inside, listen, then wriggle through.

This is not my tower.

It is, but the cause of this darkness is more than the setting of the sun, more than the absence of first-floor windows. It's deep and thick like at the bottom of a well, tangible as the high mist. Across the way, Moseus's door hangs open. I've blown a hole right beside Machine One, but I needn't worry about damage. Moseus has already seen to that. My hard work lies, for the second time, strewn across the floor. I wonder if he tore into it before or after sucking the tower's entrance into a pit of nonbeing. Before, I hope. If he had enough strength to do this much damage *after* exerting his limited magic, then we're in more trouble than I feared.

And yet, I'm glad. We can't utilize the machine anyway. Not before nightfall. *Waste your strength, you corrupted putrescence. I'm coming for you.*

I squeeze my hands into fists to hide their trembling.

Maglon crawls through behind me, grunting as he struggles to fit through the hole. Barely above a whisper, I warn, "Be quiet. Bring in only a few, and leave the others outside. Leave Arthen. He's tired." I don't think he'll fit through the hole, besides.

Amlynn comes in next, followed by Frantess, Gethnen, and Balfid. Salki hovers nearby; Maglon puts out his hand to stay her, but I motion him aside and squat down, taking my little framed lantern from her, then grasping her hand to pull her through. To Gethnen, I whisper, "Stay at the bottom of the stairs. Send in others if we call for help."

He nods. I give back my framed lantern to Salki and approach the stairs, shielding Frantess's lantern with my hand. It seems impossibly bright in the gloom, but my eyes are not what they used to be. I listen, hearing only my own heartbeat and the hushed, quick breaths of the brave souls with me.

I gesture them forward, shielding the lantern so closely that I burn my hand as we ascend the stairs. As I peek over the second floor, I see my reflection in Machine Two's discarded beryllium copper shielding. I quickly peer around the rest of the floor—empty. Despite the windows, it has the same thick shadow as the first floor, like the ghost of death has chosen this tower in which to lay his head.

Passing the lantern back to Amlynn, I remove my shoes and tip-toe to Heartwood's room, pressing my ear to the door before pushing it open on its oiled hinges. The empty room mocks me, its window warning of every minute lost. Stepping away, I squint at the lift. I'm not positive, but I think it's raised. Moseus must be in the tower above us.

Amlynn bites down on a squeak as Maglon brushes by her. I pass them and move to my room. The open door reveals the few belongings I left here. I motion Amlynn toward the ladder. She hesitates, so Balfid takes the lantern and, removing his shoes as well, slinks toward me, the light glinting off the whites of his eyes.

Light in hand, I climb, wincing when the fourth rung creaks under my weight. I've never tried to be quiet in this place, so I never noted its sounds. Still, I peer into the third floor, greeted by the same black mist. It's loath to dissipate, even when I hold my lamp high.

"Heartwood?" I whisper, searching.

Machine Three glimmers in response. If Moseus damaged it as well, I can't make it out from where I am, and I'm too frightened to step off the ladder.

Returning to the second floor, I gather the others around me. "Balfid, stay at the stairs. Be ready to relay a distress signal to Gethnen if we need it." To the others, I quickly explain the lift and how it works. "It can take two at a time. I'll go first. Salki, come with me."

"I can come," Maglon offers. I deeply appreciate his bravery, but I need Salki. "Come with Amlynn right after," I tell him.

He nods. Salki shivers, so I take her hand, squeezing it tightly to reassure both of us. I approach the lift, the drum of my heart beating louder with each step. *I'll die either way,* I tell myself, and it's somehow comforting. *I just have to save as many as I can before I do.*

It's a risk, but I can't get to the fourth and fifth floors without the lift. I built it that way on purpose. So I call back the lift, knowing the motion and sound will alert Moseus. I lift Arthen's knife as I step in, bending my knees, ready to spring. Salki, ever the good student, pulls the cord to direct the lift upward.

It moves too fast. My stomach flips inside out and lodges in my throat. The door opens onto Machine Four—

Intact. Dark. Empty, unless Moseus is hiding.

Swallowing, I direct Salki into the shadows, then wait and scan until the lift returns with Amlynn and Maglon. I snuff out my lantern. Blink a few times before slinking forward, skirting the walls, searching, listening. I walk under Machine Four, peering into its heart as though Moseus might be embedded within it, ready to drop on me like a spider. I reach the other side, pressing the knife into the darkened corners. No Moseus.

I curse deep in my throat and look up. Fifth floor, then.

I come around the machine. Amlynn holds the extinguished lantern. Maglon brandishes a long cooking knife in one hand and a pickaxe in the other. I gesture toward the tilted body of Machine Four and wait until I know he's seen me. He murmurs something to Amlynn, perhaps telling her to be ready to pass along a distress call.

Throat tight and fingers slick, I climb Machine Four. I can't see my handholds, but I've worked on the thing enough—I *built* it—that I find my way in the dark easily. It will be harder for the others. Hopefully they're watching closely.

The silver curtain around Machine Five emits a soft, unbroken light. Good, it's intact. I crouch, knife ready, listening. Someone climbs onto the base of Machine Four. I don't pull my eyes away from the liquid mirror in front of me.

I climb off and creep into the third tier of the tower. Holding my breath, I move around the silver cascade, keeping my back to the wall. There's little wiggle room around Machine Five, so it's unlikely that Moseus has crouched back here, unless he's run out of places to hide and is licking his—

White hair on the floor, strewn with braids.

"Heartwood!" I gasp, rushing toward him, throwing my tool bag to the side.

Serpent save me, he's lying *in* the acetic silver, half in, half out, the liquid wall spilling across him diagonally from his chest to hip. Thinking of the way it burned him when he touched it—thinking of Cas'raneah's blister—my mind floods with white-hot panic. I grab him under the shoulders and heave. He moves a couple of centimeters. He's so damnably big—

Footsteps. "Maglon!" I hiss as tears blur my vision. "Help me move him!" Maglon comes around the other side of Machine Five, wary of the silver.

"Quickly," I beg. "It won't hurt you. Neither will he."

Dropping to his knees, Maglon grabs one of Heartwood's arms, and I take the other, pulling him toward the wall. Heartwood jerks to a stop, the silver seeping into the fabric around his calves.

"Chain," Maglon says, pointing to something on his side. "He's chained down."

"Come here. Stand over him like this." I get on my hands and toes and arch over Heartwood so the silver washes over me instead. Seeing that it doesn't hurt me, Maglon takes a similar pose. Crawling under him, I drop my ear to Heartwood's lips, feeling the lightest wisp of hindered breath. Relief chokes me, but he's not safe yet. None of us is. Reaching the chain, I follow it to where it's clasped above Heartwood's knee. His pants are torn, and the iron cuff makes direct contact with his skin.

I don't understand. Even dwindled as he is, even with his divinity leached, Heartwood is stronger than Moseus. He ripped apart Machine Three with his bare hands. How—

Then I smell it. Something earthy, slightly floral—

Oh gods. Chrystanus. It grows in the garden. Heartwood told me the roots were poisonous, even to his kind.

Moseus took no chances.

"Give me the pickaxe!" I shout.

Awkwardly positioned, Maglon lifts it. I grab the thing, heft it with both hands, and aim for the center of the chain. My aim is true, and the old chain snaps under the force. It's loud, but I don't care. *Heartwood, wake up. Please.*

I grab him under his shoulders and pull. Maglon grabs his legs and pushes, still blocking the silvery waterfall. When we free Heartwood, Maglon hurries around the machine and hisses for Amlynn to come up.

Grabbing fistfuls of fabric, I tear Heartwood's trousers at the seam, from upper thigh to ankle. The cuff fits snugly. Locked. Does Moseus have a key, or does he even need one? I doubt he had plans to free the god who unwittingly gave him a second chance at power.

"I'm sorry," I murmur, and wedge the tip of the pickaxe between the ends of the cuff, where a link of chain connects them. "This is going to hurt."

I try to break it, but Heartwood's body moves with the force, and I can't get good leverage, though he's definitely taking deep bruises. Maglon, Amlynn, and Salki appear, Amlynn quickly rushing to the patient. "Heartwood?" she asks me.

I nod. "I need you guys to hold his leg. And the cuff, but not with bare skin. It's poisoned."

Salki pales, but she comes over and sits on Heartwood's shin. Maglon straddles his thighs. He pulls his sleeves over his hands and grasps the bottom of the cuff. Amlynn cups her hands over Maglon's, steadying them.

With all the strength Ruin left me, I heave once, twice—

Maglon curses as I pinch his fingers, but the chain link snaps. I knock it loose with the pickaxe, sending it under the silver fountain.

"Water." Amlynn's voice takes on a commanding tone. Salki fumbles with a bladder on her belt and hands it over. Amlynn cleans the poisoned skin with a handkerchief, as well as the puckering wound from the pickaxe. I hand the tool to Maglon, who stands guard.

"Heartwood." I kneel by his head and take his face in my hands. "Heartwood, can you hear me?"

A lantern comes to life behind me, illuminating Heartwood's injuries, and I gasp.

His clothes are torn. Burns mar the pale skin on his exposed leg. I pull up his shirt. The parts of him that Moseus left under the acetic silver are raw and red, meaty, running from just under his left pectoral muscle down to his right hip. Amlynn grits her teeth.

"I didn't bring enough supplies for this," she grumbles, but gets to work anyway.

"He's a god. He'll make it," I say, assuring myself more than anyone else. I turn back to him, smoothing hair from his face. "Heartwood?

Can you hear me?" Though I can now hear his strained breathing, I press a hand to his neck to check for a pulse. It's slow, but it's there.

Salki brings me back to the task at hand. "Where is Moseus?"

My gut sinks to my hips. Where is he? We've searched everywhere . . . was he hiding behind Machine Three?

"Pell." Maglon takes a few steps forward.

Getting to my feet, I follow his gaze. I'd missed it, in the rush to get to Heartwood. There, camouflaged within the clinging dark, bubbles a hole like the one consuming the tower doors, but this one glimmers a violet so deep it borders on black.

It's right over Machine Five's protrusion.

"He's outside." My tongue sticks to the roof of my dry mouth. The windows are too narrow to fit him, and screened with that translucent material, so that hole must be a portal. He must know we're here. We've only minutes left.

"Nophe."

My thoughts crumble at Heartwood's voice. Whirling around, I drop to his side. His eyes are open to hair-fine slits. His breath rattles up his throat.

"Heartwood, you're going to be okay," I promise, cradling his jaw. "Will your godhood pull you through? You'll be okay, right?"

"Ru . . . in," he whispers, then coughs.

"I know. Will you be able to heal, with what it took?"

He coughs.

"Where is Moseus?"

Weakly, Heartwood lifts a single finger and points toward the portal.

I place a soft kiss on his lips. "Amlynn is a doctor. She's going to help you." I glance back at her as she gingerly dabs something over the worst of Heartwood's burns. Hopefully gods respond to mortal medicine.

Heartwood blinks. For a moment I fear his consciousness is slipping, but his lids lift a little more, his pupils narrowing on mine.

"Heartwood?" I grasp his hand.

In a voice rough as sand, he says, "You have my sister's eyes."

Dizziness strikes me like a blow to the head. "Your sister?" I squeeze his fingers. "Heartwood. Ether. What was her real name? Her name in Thestean?" He grunts from Amlynn's ministrations. I pat his cheeks to keep his attention. "Heartwood. What was her name?"

He swallows. Seems to fall asleep for a moment, but his lips murmur, "Cas'raneah."

Tears fill my vision. This whole time. Ether is Casnia. She's been in Emgarden since the war, and he didn't know. None of us knew. Moseus used him. He used all of us.

"I'll take you to her," I promise, "if you live." It's half promise, half threat.

He doesn't answer. Regretfully, I pull away from him and turn toward the purple emptiness on the wall.

"Maglon, with me."

He nods.

I meet Salki's gaze. Neither of us speaks.

I got us into this mess, so it's only fair that I pass through the portal first. Grabbing both of my weapons, I let it suck me in. It feels cold, which I suppose I should expect.

Ruin waits for me on the other side.

Chapter 30

Moseus—Ruin—stands on the top of the tower, his gaunt face peering west to the nearly sunken sun. He is clothed only in black shadows and smoke, and that gaping hole in his torso spews darkness like the fog machines spew mist. It rolls off him in a bubbling dress, cascading off the sides of the tower like the acetic silver wall. His eyes, the same noncolor as the void at the tower door, sit atop sunken sockets. His cheeks and throat are hollow. The whiteness of his skin has rotted to a splotchy, ashen gray, as has his hair. A cool breeze stirs it, tossing tangled locks over his sharp shoulders. Whether overexertion or the nearness of night caused his transformation, I'm not sure. The fog lifts, revealing the bold colors of sunset.

As Maglon steps through the portal, Moseus says, "I'm impressed, Pelnophe." His voice sounds like the scratching of a dozen hands down a slate, folding over one another in broken harmony. "But it's too late."

I lift two fingers at my side as I stand on the protrusion, the encased branch of Machine Five. Maglon pauses before moving into Moseus's sight. His jaw tenses at the rolling darkness. Finding a handhold, he climbs up and southward. Moseus faces west.

I need to keep Moseus talking, but I don't want to show my hand. Guess it's time to see if I learned anything about lying. "I don't understand, Moseus. What's happened to you? I . . . Let me help you. You're hurt."

He turns and grins. He actually holds my gaze and grins. A shiver courses down from my neck to the backs of my knees at those empty, lifeless eyes. "Watch, and you will see."

He raises his arms as orange rays of sun dim against the sky—I'd have to move to the end of the protrusion to see the setting star myself, but I don't dare move. *Twenty minutes* . . . Hues of periwinkle and indigo swirl through the sky. That slip of sun is a mere candle against Ruin's power.

A shadow shifts to Moseus's left. *Maglon.*

"Where is Heartwood?" My voice shakes. I hope he reads it as worry or awe.

A dark cacophony with the semblance of a chuckle emanates from that gaping hole in his torso. "You are an empty fool, Pelnophe of Emgarden."

I grit my teeth. "Moseus, come down. Let me help—"

A sound like a snuffed fire issues from the void god's mouth as Maglon's hands connect with his shoulders, shoving him toward the lip of the tower. Toward the five-story drop.

It happens in a blink.

Moseus teeters. The darkness at his center pulses, gushes. He grabs Maglon by the throat as he falls and twists, landing on the protrusion between me and the portal. The god's rotation continues, and as he releases Maglon, the barkeeper's skin turns to ashen dust, just like those wickwood trees. Just like Hagthor's.

"No!" I scream, reaching for Maglon, but his body falls into the stretching shadows, puffing into ash when it hits the ground.

A commotion rises; the others are still down there, waiting for our signal. Waiting to help. Will they flood the tower in an angry rampage, or cower at the death of one of our own?

"He is nothing to you!" I scream, wiping my eyes. I need to see. I have to be able to see. The portal ripples. I watch Moseus's dead eyes as I reach behind me, where I folded over my shirt inside my waistband. My hands form tight fists. I desperately try to breathe through the shaking of my shoulders.

"It is *all* nothing to me," Moseus hisses, his skin growing more hale. Tone lower, echoing, hateful. He steps toward me. I raise my chin and ignore my trembling knees. "I will enjoy devouring you, Pelnophe." That sneer returns, and he looks past my shoulder at the falling night. "My time has come."

A tear slides down my cheek as I nod. To Moseus, it would look like capitulation. To Salki, it's a signal.

She charges forward, my lantern in her hands, its frame perfectly matching the dimensions of the hole composing Moseus's middle. She shoves it into him, spilling more darkness over the protrusion.

Moseus grunts and spins, and I'm ready. I pull the iron cuff from the folds of my shirt and leap onto him, clamping it around his neck. I've no lock to bind it, but when the poison touches his skin, he hisses and whips toward me, throwing me off with a great sweep of his arm. I roll across the protrusion, clambering for a hold—

Salki twists the middle of the lantern.

The machine burns a brilliant white, powered by as many emilies as she could shove into it while Arthen and I raced for the mountains.

The angle of the protrusion protects me from toppling off its end; I grab its welded lip to steady myself. Moseus screams, scraping at his middle as his stolen form disintegrates around the light. The emptiness of his eyes spreads into his brow, cheeks, chin. Salki hurries back, falling once before catching herself just outside the portal.

Moseus screams something in a thousand clashing voices. Something in a tongue older than Cas's. He collapses to his knees and claws toward me with the stubs of his fingers.

I pull myself up. "I remember everything, you ripe bastard," I sneer. "This is for Cas."

A violent shriek like thunder tears from his throat as he reaches for me, bubbling and twisting, spewing darkness against the dimming light of the setting sun. Then, with one barely corporeal hand, he grabs the frame of the lantern and rips it out.

Cold blood retreats from my skin. *No.* Oh gods, no. I didn't think he'd be able to—

The poisoned cuff, loosened from the tussle, falls to the protrusion. Standing, teetering, Moseus crushes the lantern in his malformed hand. He's still humanoid, still *something*, but there is so little of Moseus left in him. He—it—is a leaning, bleeding monster, a swirl of black and violet and colorless *emptiness* that my mind cannot piece together. My skull throbs with the effort to understand.

Foul words in a tongue I don't recognize drip from his lips as he moves for me, slow and uneven, reaching that hideous, murderous hand toward my neck, just as he did with Maglon. I don't even try to hold my ground this time; I saw what it did to my dear friend. I retreat, my steps unsure, nearly sliding off the side of the protrusion.

"Run," I croak to Salki, never taking my eyes off Moseus. I don't know what good it will do. Stupid of me, to think a flower-powered lantern would quell the Devourer when it required the stilling of an entire planet to manage it before. In his weakened state, I thought—

Twilight climbs up the eastern sky.

Moseus says nothing. Nothing about how he should have killed me the first time, or how weak I am. No gloating about my failure or his restoration. He merely stumbles forward, his hand reaching, reaching—

I pull away. Run out of machine to stand on.

The void god's lips crack as my balance breaks. My hands fly out, but there's nothing to catch me. I fall backward, gut lurching with the sudden weightlessness. Cool air whistling by my ears fills in the gaps between heartbeats as I plummet. My eyes take in the growing tendrils of violet in the sky, and in the back of my mind, I'm relieved. Relieved that I'll die like this, beside Maglon, but with my soul intact.

The tower floors whip by. I notice their slowing before I feel the pressure around my waist, like a serpent coiling. My neck pops as my head whips back at the sudden deceleration. I can't see what's beneath me, but I haven't hit.

Suddenly the serpent pushes me upward with a sound like clicking and stretching and digging. It twists, setting me upright, and only then do I see the green of the coil—not a snake at all, but an enormous verdant vine. A massive fairy wisp, of all things.

My heart drops into my pelvis and springs back as the plant releases me onto the crest of the tower, right beside . . . not Moseus, nor Salki, but a being who hovers a hand's breadth above the stone.

I recognize Heartwood, yet I don't. It might be the adrenaline, which courses like hot oil through my limbs. My pulse thunders in my ears. His back hunches with the pain of his burns, but his vivid eyes are resolute, his skin radiant, his presence . . . intense. He is not himself, no, but he is more than he was.

I realize the moment he speaks that the lantern wasn't a complete failure. It hurt Moseus, forcing him to release part of what he stole.

Moseus, alone on the protrusion, looks at us with dead eyes.

And laughs.

The laughter echoes in that gaping hole. More heavy darkness spills from it. "You're too late," he says simply, his voice so *other* I can barely understand it.

Only the tip of the sun's crown remains above the horizon.

"An army of gods couldn't stop me." Moseus staggers forward. "And neither will you. You're only a fraction of what you were."

Heartwood's brows draw together. "So are you, my friend."

Moseus hisses. Darkness curls out of him, growing, growing—

Heartwood turns to me. Grabs my shoulders. "Hide, Nophe."

Words jumble up in my throat. "But—"

"There is no time."

Heartwood leaps, and immediately the colorless, dark streak of Moseus collides with him, knocking him off the tower. A scream rips up my throat, but they don't fall. Even broken, they are not bound by the world the way mortals are.

But Moseus is about to become far more than Heartwood can manage. The Devourer will swallow him, and us, and all of Tampere, and that will only be the beginning.

I have to do something. I can't let Cas and the others' sacrifices be for *nothing*. My skin tingles at the thought. *Nothing*. That's my only chance, if I can move quickly enough.

Running for the protrusion, I jump down, then throw myself through the portal into the fifth floor. I collide with Salki.

"You're still here?" I grab her and push her toward Machine Four. "Go, Salki! *Go!*"

She doesn't question me. With the speed of a far younger woman, she climbs onto the head of Machine Four and starts scaling her way down, breathing hard. The entire tower shakes; not from the movement of the freed Serpent, but from the battle of gods overhead.

I turn back to the acetic silver. It's the only weapon I have. It hurt Cas'raneah and Heartwood; it'll hurt Moseus, too. I shove my hands into it, trying to cup the airy-feeling liquid, but it slips through my fingers like my hands are sieves. No matter how tightly I press them together, I can only get a coin's worth in my palms. I need a bucket, a syringe, *something*—

The tower screeches as something slams into it, knocking me forward. I catch my hands on Machine Five but can't stop my momentum. My forehead smacks against a truss. Pain bursts between my brows.

Had my hands not been gripping the machine, I would have been whipped away with the top of the tower when it blew off.

I can't hear my own shriek over the sound of the breaking and the torrent that follows. Sky dark as a bruise—nearly dark enough—swirls overhead, highlighting the bodies of the two weakened gods hurling themselves at one another again and again. Orienting myself, I take in my surroundings and the seconds I have left. I need a bucket. I need—

A bucket.

The tower walls curve around me, the floor firm beneath my feet. A bucket.

Blinking sweat and blood from my eyes, I bolt halfway down Machine Four. Press my body against it and reach between its beams, fumbling for the lever that rotates its body. I pull it. Jump to my feet and run up its length as the behemoth turns. I stumble, barely catching my balance, and dive into Machine Five's chamber just before Machine Four seals it off.

Grabbing my tools, I duck beneath the acetic silver and drop to my knees. Memories restored, my hands work with the practiced efficiency of decades as they remove bolts and nuts and plating. I know exactly where the fountain is, how it works, how to dismantle it. A wrench, a turnscrew, a *twist*, and I break the thing myself.

The fall of silver recedes and seeps out from the base of the machine, pooling on the floor. I shift a lever to close off the intake in the floor, and the silver begins to climb my legs. Grabbing the machine, I heave myself up and climb to its top, blinking blood from my vision. Heartwood has Moseus pinned to the broken lip of the tower but struggles to hold him. The creature's corporeality fades with the light. Any second now, he will be the Devourer in full.

I race along the top of Machine Five, over the protrusion. Heartwood looks up.

And I realize there's only one way to do this. But we've all sacrificed something, haven't we? I suppose it might as well be my turn.

Let him go, I mouth.

Heartwood does.

Moseus shoves the forest god away, reaching both hands for the night sky—

And I embrace him from behind, holding on to everything left, digging my hands into his empty middle to chain us together. Wrenching us both backward, we fall back into floor five, where the machine has dribbled out the last of its acetic silver into a pool a meter deep.

I hold my breath on instinct, but the floor knocks half of it from my lungs. The silver swallows us, muffling Moseus's screams as it eats away at him. He writhes and claws, and I lock my legs around him and *pull*, forcing him against me. Holding him under the surface of the god-searing silver.

I feel his body burn. Feel the way it liquefies and seeps into my nose and mouth, strangling me from the inside. Slides under the cut in my forehead and tears. Slickness dives into my ears and shouts into my brain, burying every thought but *hold him, hold him, hold him*. Moseus squeezes my lungs, ripping away my last traces of air, ravaging every part of me he can find, fighting me, hurting me, violating me.

But I am the Devourer's prison now, and even in death, I will not let go.

His efforts begin to lose strength, but I do not relent. My body spasms, mind darkens, chest blazes, soul hurts. I have just enough of myself left to realize the faint sweetness amidst the bitter—that there is still something of Heartwood in the evil I hold.

At least I'll die embracing him.

Chapter 31

I open my eyes to light. So many lights . . .

Candles and lanterns around and above me, filling the room as though the sun has come down for a closer look. It's too close, too hot. Burning, aching, a sharp contrast to the cold, swirling darkness in my core.

When I vomit, it comes up silver.

"Don't touch her," snaps a voice that sounds remarkably like Amlynn's. It hurts. Her voice, the sound of footsteps, the rustling of clothes. Like they move inside my brain. A hand thumps against my back, and agony blasts shock waves through my ribs. I cough hard enough to vomit again. Less silver, this time.

"It will not kill me," Heartwood protests, and some of the lights dim as he moves in front of them. His shadow mitigates the brightness and gives me a moment to orient myself. The tower, Ruin, sunset, silver. It hurt me, in those depths. I'm not sure how long we fought, but Ruin didn't steal my memories this time. They emerge sluggishly, piecing themselves together like Ancient artifacts. My artifacts.

"After that? Are you so sure?"

I blink silver from my eyes. Cough again. Try to ask what's happening, but when I try to speak, I choke on silver.

"Let her purge," Amlynn insists.

Farther away, Salki asks, "Is she all right?"

I don't hear a response, only a sigh of relief. And suddenly warm hands on my face, tilting it up, smoothing wet hair back.

"I said don't touch!" Amlynn barks. "You want to lose a finger? Damn it, I need more water!"

"Nophe," Heartwood whispers.

I blink, his features coming into focus before me. Shadowed from the lanterns. So much fire is making the room unbearably warm, but I feel a little more myself with each shaky breath. A little more present.

Cold water gushes over my head. I start, gasp, shake. "What—"

Droplets splash off the amaranthine beneath me.

I freeze, staring at the smooth, pink, translucent floor, and the silvery pool beneath it. Run my hand over it, smearing water and silver droplets. It hugs the west side of Machine Five, spanning from the machine to the wall before curving down to meet with the floor. The other half of the space has only a few inches of acetic silver in it; Machine Four's been rolled back, spilling the precious liquid into floor four. Pulling my gaze back, I notice Heartwood's hand beside me, red and angry and blistered. Burns from acetic silver.

He pulled me out.

The lights, they're from the others. From Emgarden. The pool. I was holding Moseus in the pool—

I look up, meeting Heartwood's gaze. His luminescence has faded entirely. He looks like himself again. At least, the self I know. The self that has been away from the garden too long and grows sick with it.

My gaze crawls upward, past the lights, past the machine, to the indigo night above. Serpent save me . . . did we succeed?

"It will not hold forever," he says, quiet, tired. "I cannot reach help as I am now. We will have to make a beacon to summon the others."

"Gods?" Amlynn asks.

He nods.

Gods. I examine the pink crystal beneath me. Trapping Ruin as his first prison did.

"You gave up your godhood," I croak, still coughing. "You made this."

Heartwood touches my face. Hushed enough that only I can hear, he whispers, "It was an easy choice. Thank you, Nophe. For this, and for the chance to try again."

I swallow. Amlynn offers me a nearly empty water bladder, but I ignore it. "Try again?"

He kisses the side of my forehead, avoiding the injury at its center. "To finish what my sister started."

Understanding dawns on me slowly. A coward, he'd called himself. No longer.

"The light won't hold forever," he says to me, Amlynn. Through the doorway half-blocked by amaranthine, I see Salki standing on Machine Four. Others congregate below her. "We must keep the room lit at all times, even during the day."

"Day?" Salki repeats, more to herself than anyone else.

After ensuring I'm mostly silver-free, Heartwood gets me down to the lift on the fourth floor. He's injured, too, and without his godhood, he'll heal slowly. How slowly, only time will tell.

The earth quakes as we step out of the tower; Heartwood grabs the door hard enough to splinter it. The tremor passes quickly. When I step out of the tower, I catch a writhing shadow against the night sky, winding away from our world. The Serpent, finally free.

I sob. Body-shaking, throat-wrenching sobs. It isn't over—those lights, this prison, will hold for a month at best. But it's finished for now. For now.

I drop to the cooling earth, mourning everything lost and celebrating everything saved, watering the feet of my creations, my tower, with tears. Heartwood stands sentinel, allowing me to grieve. Salki drops beside me, a steady and reassuring presence.

A minute passes before she asks, "Pell, what are they?"

Lifting my head and wiping my nose, I find her raised eyes and peer upward. A laugh wheedles its way past my lips.

"Oh, Salki. Those are stars."

The gods had been many.

The Well of Creation brewed deity of all kinds, and they, in turn, created. Sometimes they formed other gods, like Heartwood and Cas'raneah, sometimes telluric creatures, like us. Many of these beings partook in the war to imprison Ruin. Several survived. And so, were we to call out to them, they should answer, or so Heartwood believes. He cannot do it himself. The divinity that once flowed through his veins, the strength stolen by Moseus—Ruin—was destroyed imprisoning it. Heartwood will never again be who he was. None of us will.

He accepts the sad fact too easily as we sit outside the tower, watching the first sunrise in many years. I never counted the years. Never thought to, thanks to the stupor that Ruin trapped us in. But Heartwood says it's been nearly thirty since the first imprisonment. I was eighty-six when Cas'raneah brought the war to Tampere. It's strange to think I passed my centennial mark and never realized it.

I am tired. We are all tired. The recapture of Ruin resulted in only one death, but it's a death felt heavily by all of us. Heavier, I dare say, than Ramdinee's, Entisa's, and Hagthor's, though only I remain to remember the last. Maglon was a gatherer, a friend of all, a connector of neighbors and balm to the mourning. Ruin consumed him so completely . . . we have nothing left to bury except a gray streak on the red-tinted earth, but I will dig a grave for him regardless. It's the very least I can do to honor him, for without his efforts, I don't think Salki or I would have reached Moseus in time.

Heartwood is a casualty, but he will live. He is burnt and sick and bandaged, but he's alive, and he will heal. We watch the stars crawl across the heavens, and the rebirth of the sun chases them away with blue, pink, and orange light.

I drift off at some point, leaning back against the tower. When I open my eyes again, the sun beams full and yellow, the sky an easy cerulean. "A beacon, then. To call them."

Heartwood picks up the threads of our previous conversation. "It will have to be large. Powerful. Tampere resides on the outskirts of our universe."

It will have to be built quickly, too. We cannot risk Ruin freeing himself. But we built great machines before, with little time to spare. We can do it again. I wonder if any of the gods remember us.

I reach for Heartwood's hand and knit my fingers with his. A bandage pokes out from his sleeve. He squeezes, then murmurs, "Nophe."

"Hm?"

"Take me to my sister."

Rising, I pull him up. Our height difference makes me an awkward crutch. We shuffle our way into Emgarden, but we make it, and once within its unassuming, incomplete walls, others step up to help me.

Salki should be resting, but when we arrive at her door, she sits beside Cas'raneah's cot, caressing her hair like a mother over a child. I will tell her stories of the goddess who saved us. I will share everything I know. I will remember what others cannot.

Cas'raneah has yet to awaken. I don't know if she will. She diminished herself so much already, making the amaranthine wall that still stands, locking us away from the rest of the world. She, too, lost much that she will never be able to reclaim, and I realize our casualties are far higher than I originally counted. Our war never truly ended.

Salki vacates her chair, and we help Heartwood into it, the others excusing themselves in a gift of privacy. Salki moves to the far side of the room, busying herself, her movements awkward and weary.

Bracing himself against the cot with one arm, Heartwood leans forward and traces a thumb across his sister's brow. "It is her," he says, "but it is not."

"She tied her spirit to Tampere. To the amaranthine wall." I grasp his shoulder, offering what little comfort I can give. "She is here, Heartwood. She is wired through every millimeter of this world. She is everywhere."

He sits silently, watching Cas'raneah's still face. Her breaths are deep and even, but weak. I don't speak. After a minute, Salki finds a reason to leave and does so without a sound.

"I didn't realize," he says at last, "how much destruction I had caused."

"Heartwood—"

"Perhaps, had I heeded her call and joined the war, she would not have had to do this," he adds. "Perhaps, had I investigated more carefully, I would not have fallen into Ruin's clutches. If I had searched more diligently and feared less, I would have found her before it was too late."

"Tell me your name again."

He glances up, shadows forming half moons beneath his eyes, confusion weighing his brow. *"Ytton'allanejrou."*

I carefully repeat it, syllable by syllable. The word tastes like power on my lips. "You have strived for peace. You journeyed between the stars in search of her. You suffered a mortal world, a mortal life, in pursuit of her. You let your heart break, to choose her." My voice drifts as my throat squeezes. "You hurt yourself, and lost your divinity, to end the war she fought. You could blame yourself. You could blame the gods for not doing more, or my people for not fulfilling our part. You can blame Ruin, or the Well of Creation itself. And yet none of it will change our sacrifices and our truths. We can only move forward and find joy in what's left. And there is so much left, Heartwood."

I run a knuckle over his ear. He leans into my touch, letting out a long, hollow breath. "You are right. But it will take some time for me to believe it."

"We have time." Outside, the sun climbs steadily higher, marking the hours on our behalf. "A little time, at least. I might suggest you spend it recovering."

I brace his arm. Taking the cue, he allows me to help him stand. "The alehouse is near." An empty pang hits my chest at the thought. "As is Ramdinee's home, if you want a private place to convalesce. Or we can drag your sorry body back to my bed."

He groans, one hand pressed to his raw abdomen. "You know which I'd prefer."

I smirk at him and secure his arm around my shoulder, though my own legs are drained of strength. I want to lie down and sleep for ten cycles . . . then again, we don't tell time that way anymore. I'll settle for five *days*. How utterly bizarre a thought.

But alas, Ruin has not left us with a plethora of time. My work is far from over.

"We'll build the beacon," I say as I pull open the door. "And then we'll climb that wall and return to our city."

"City?" he asks.

"Where we started. What we left." On the other side of the planet sprawls a city that has sat in the frigid dark for thirty years. A metropolis cut off, sentenced to die before it could truly live.

"You can't pass the amaranthine wall," Heartwood says. "I've tried."

I allow myself to smile. "There's nothing yet that a god has built that our technology can't demolish. I'll find a way."

Heartwood grunts his agreement. As we pass through the door, into a bright and east-leaning sun, I glance one more time at Cas'raneah's resting form. Perhaps it's an illusion of the slowly moving shadows, but I swear on the Serpent I see her finger twitch.

Acknowledgments

I always start and end with the same people, and this will be no different. Thank you, Jordan, for all your support. For helping me through stress, for listening to me rant, for sharing and swapping ideas, and for being there. Thank you for always believing in me. This book was a left-fielder and a quick turnaround, and you held my hand through all of it.

Thank you, Leah, for being the most dependable and swiftest alpha reader, and to Alethea, for doing the same *and* lending me your mechanical-engineering brain. It was enormously helpful. (They're sisters. Must run in the family.)

Many thanks to speed-reader extraordinaire Amanda "Misha" Burnett, to whom this book is dedicated. You ignored a party to dissect the first half of this book and take notes for me. It meant a lot. (Also, I never realized how fast you can read, and it sort of freaks me out.)

Much appreciation to my assistant Kayley, both for the assisting and for yet another quick reading turnaround to boost my morale when I was STRUGGLING. Please never leave me.

All the gratitude to my sister Andy and my bestie Caitlyn, for helping me comb through this story's snags at the last minute.

Thank you to Adrienne, who took a chance on me with this book and who consistently trusts me to regurgitate something comprehensible; to Jason Kirk, for buttoning it up and dusting off its shoulders; and to the 47North team of editors, designers, typesetters, and others who make my books both readable and pretty. I want to specifically thank Michael S., because your thoroughness gave me confidence in this novel.

Finally, thank you to the Big Man Upstairs, especially for that intense dream I had about four years back, in which a woman had to fix a tower full of machines for two strange, pale men in black, one of whom later confessed, *I broke it because it took you away from me.* I wrote it down, and then I *wrote it down.* The inspiration continues to be of great help to me, and I really appreciate it.

Cheers. 💜

About the Author

Charlie N. Holmberg is a *Wall Street Journal* and Amazon Charts bestselling author of fantasy and romance fiction, including *The Hanging City*, *Star Mother*, the Paper Magician series, the Spellbreaker series, the Whimbrel House series, and the Numina trilogy. Charlie also writes contemporary romance under C. N. Holmberg. She is published in twenty-one languages and has been a finalist for a RITA Award, as well as the Goodreads Choice Awards for *The Hanging City*. Born in Salt Lake City, Charlie was raised a Trekkie alongside three sisters who also have boy names. She is a BYU alumna, plays the ukulele, and owns too many pairs of glasses. She currently lives with her family in Utah. Visit her at charlienholmberg.com.